On a Knife's Edge

Lynda Bailey

She was once his sweet salvation...
Lynch Callan has been a dead man walking most of his life – nothing out of the ordinary for a member of the 5th Street biker gang. There was a brief period, though, when *she* made him believe he could be more. That he could be worthy of her, and her love. To protect her, he went to prison. Except now the Streeters are in danger. But in order to save his crew, he must first betray them. If caught, he'll end up dead for sure. It'll be the mother of all balancing acts, especially with *her* in the picture. But Lynch will do whatever is necessary to protect the people he loves.

He was once her deepest desire...
Shasta Albright doesn't break the rules. Not anymore. As an unruly teenager, she defied her family at every turn...even secretly befriending, then dating, *then* falling in love with a bad boy Streeter. Finally, her recklessness caught up with her – with lasting and even dire consequences. Now she leads a pristine existence, always staying within the lines and keeping her secrets hidden. That is until *he* gets released from prison. Can Shasta hold her perfect world together, or will everything get hurled into chaos?

With young girls going missing, the sleepy town of Stardust, Nevada becomes an unlikely epicenter for an illicit slave trade, with Shasta and Lynch caught in the middle. Amidst the rising body count, they fight to keep their loved ones – and each other – safe. A single slipup could have deadly repercussions. It's an untenable and treacherous position. Much like walking *On a Knife's Edge...*

ON A KNIFE'S EDGE

Contact Information: Lynda.r.bailey@gmail.com
Visit us at www.authorlyndabailey.com

Book Design by The Killion Group/Hot Damn Designs

IBSN-13: 978-1720036456

Publishing History
First Edition, 2016

DEDICATION:
To my husband, Pat...I couldn't do any of this without your rock-solid support. I love you.

ACKNOWLEDGEMENTS:
To Suzanne, the best CP a gal can have!
To Kim, Erin and Charlie, the best betas a gal can have!
To JJ, thanks for the tips about the Nevada State prison system!
To the folks at Scotland Yard Spy Shop, thanks for your help with nanny cams and more!

OTHER WORKS BY LYNDA BAILEY:

Alyce – Through the Lycan Glass

Battle-Born Love

Battle-Tested Love

Erotic Escapades of a Married Couple

Mended Trust

Naughty Neighborhood

On the Corner of Heartache and Hopeful – MIC

On the Corner of Heartache and Hopeful – KIRA

On the Corner of Heartache and Hopeful – GRACE

Shattered Trust

Wildflower

On a Knife's Edge

Chapter One
(Prologue)

May, seven years ago...

HUNKERING BEHIND A clump of lilac bushes, seventeen-year-old Shasta Albright observed her brother climb from his massive, crew cab truck then tramp up the sidewalk toward the courthouse. Once Sheriff Dell Albright crossed the threshold, she counted to fifty to ensure her dear brother was safely established in his basement office then pulled her sweatshirt hood over her ponytail and moved into the open.

Head down and hands in her jacket pockets, she strolled toward the truck, the spare key clasped tightly in her grip. She shivered as the early morning breeze raised goosebumps on her bare legs. Under her cut-off jean shorts and sweatshirt, she wore only her bikini. Today was Ditch Day – when juniors and seniors ditched school for a party trip to Lake Tahoe.

She cast stealth gazes to her left and right. At six forty-five in the morning, Main Street in the miniscule rural town of Stardust, Nevada stood all but deserted. The only people dumb enough to be out this early were commuters heading to Reno or Carson City. And of course her stupid, controlling brother.

Anger seethed her blood. He had no right to take away *her* truck when she hadn't done anything wrong. At least not this time.

"It's for your own good," Dell had told her while confiscating her keys. *"You're not cutting class to go drinking at the lake. It's not safe. You're my responsibility now."*

His responsibility? God...she hated her brother. A smug smile touched her lips. She'd show him.

Behind the F350, she pressed the door open button and the lights blinked along with a single horn toot. She peered around the truck bed to make sure brother dearest didn't come charging from the courthouse. When the only movement remained the tree branches swaying in the slight wind, she hustled around to the driver's side and hoisted herself inside.

Jesus...this thing was big. Way bigger than the Ford Ranger her dad bought for her sixteenth birthday. Though she'd ridden as a passenger in Dell's gargantuan truck plenty of times, sitting behind the wheel gave her an entirely different perspective. She could hardly see over the dashboard while her feet were nowhere near the pedals.

Fumbling for the seat control, she managed to heave the bucket seat forward enough so the front of the hood came into view and the tip of her right sneaker reached the gas. She jammed the key into the ignition and turned it.

She ducked down at the thundering roar of the engine. All she needed was to be caught in the act of taking Dell's truck. If that happened, she'd be grounded until forever.

She peeked up. No one in sight. After buckling her seatbelt, she wrenched the gearshift into reverse and gently pressed on the gas.

The behemoth vehicle lurched backwards. A startled yelp escaped her lips. She slammed on the brakes and closed her eyes. She inhaled a slow, deep breath. Then another one.

Calmer, she put the truck into drive and rumbled out onto Main Street only to realize she hadn't adjusted the rearview mirrors. Oh well. No other cars were on the street at this time of morning anyway.

A block and a half away, she felt sufficiently confident, and more than a little cocky, to pull out her cell. She flipped it opened and hit the speed dial for her best friend, Cassie.

"What up, bitch?" she shouted into the phone at Cassie's groggy hello. "Still in bed? Slacker."

Cassie groaned. "Yeah I'm in bed cuz it's like the middle of the night." She yawned loudly.

"No it's not. It's Ditch Day, remember?"

"I remember." Another yawn. "I also remember neither one of us has wheels."

Shasta couldn't contain her giggle. "Not anymore, girlfriend."

"What? Your brother gave you back your truck? When?"

"He didn't *give* me anything. I took it."

"How? Thought he put all the keys to your Ranger on his ring."

"He did, but forgot about *his* truck's spare key."

Silence met her statement.

"What the hell..." Cassie's voice dropped to a whisper. "You...*stole*...Dell's truck?"

"How is it stealing if he's my brother?"

"Girl...that's one baaaaaad idea. He will fucking *murder* you."

Shasta brushed off Cassie's concern. "Don't be such a killjoy. I'm on my way to your house so get ready."

"Nah, uh. No way, sister."

Irritation peppered Shasta's nerves. "Oh, c'*mon*, Cass. You can't punk out on me."

"Sorry, Shay...you've really gone off the rails this time."

A long pause echoed in Shasta's ear.

"Look, Shay," Cassie said, "I know things have been rough since your dad died, but–"

"Don't." Shasta infused as much fury as possible into her voice. "Don't talk about my dad."

"But honey–"

Rather than continue the conversation, Shasta snapped the phone shut. She barely resisted the urge to fling her cell at the windshield. How *dare* Cassie bring up her dad. It'd been just seven months since he'd shot himself in that freak hunting accident. Seven months since she'd talked to him or seen his smile or heard his laugh. Seven months of hell....

Scrubbing an angry hand at the tears in her eyes, Shasta stiffened her spine. She didn't need Cassie, loser that she was. She didn't need *anybody* – not anymore. In less than sixty miles she'd be basking on a sandy, warm Tahoe beach. That's all she needed.

She turned right onto Road 314 and headed for the Grab-n-Go just this side of the Grant County line to get beer and snacks. It was a badly kept secret that the minimart owner, Felix, had no problem selling alcohol to high school kids.

Ten minutes later, she maneuvered her brother's monstrosity of a truck into the tiny parking lot, past the two gas islands and up to the front door. Thankfully no one else was around as she took up almost three spaces. She killed the engine then hopped out of the cab. Retrieving her debit card from her jean pocket, she strode inside. An auto beep announced her arrival.

"Morning, Felix."

The forty-something owner looked up from his newspaper. "Shasta? Shouldn't you be in school?"

"Not today." She headed toward the refrigerated section. "It's Ditch Day." She pulled out a twelve-pack of St. Pauli Girl, juggled it under one arm and snatched two huge bags of tortilla chips along with a handful of power bars on her way to the register.

Felix stood with his arms crossed, frowning. "You know I can't sell you beer."

She placed her items on the counter. "Why not? You sell it to everyone else at school."

"Not everyone else is the sheriff's sister." He shook his head. "Sorry. No can do. If I get caught again, I'm gonna lose my liquor license and probably go to jail."

She tapped her debit card against her opposite palm and squinted. "I'll make you a deal. Sell me this and I promise to tell you if I hear anything about Dell setting up another underage sting."

Felix twisted his lips.

"Please," she entreated with a small side-to-side sway. The slight movement gave her a certain innocence. Older men were suckers for that. "C'mon, Felix. It's *Ditch Day*. Pretty, pretty, pretty please." She batted her eyelashes with her finest beseeching look.

She knew the second his resolve collapsed. His face crumpled like he smelled rotten fish. "Fine, but not the imported stuff."

She turned, the German beer in her hands. "No problem."

"And make it light beer – and only a six-pack."

Rolling her eyes, she walked down the aisle as the entrance beeped again, announcing another customer.

She'd just grabbed two sixers of a high-end domestic light beer, no way was she leaving with a single six-pack, when a man opened the glass door on her right.

Shasta immediately recognized the guy's jacket. And him. Lynch Callan of the 5th Streeters.

Holy shit.

Her stomach did a flip-flop. Everyone in Stardust knew about the 5th Street "motorcycle club," as they called themselves. Motorcycle club sounded less disreputable, less infamous than biker gang. But they were hoodlums. Criminals. A blight on society, or so her father used to say. Did this guy have a gun? Was he planning to rob Felix?

Her insecurity dissolved. No way would he try anything like that, not with *her* in the store. After all, she was the sheriff's sister. Sometimes that fact came in handy.

Out the corner of her eye, she watched Lynch reach for a carton of milk. What kind of a badass bad guy drinks milk? He shut the refrigerator door with a thump and walked behind her to the far aisle. She closed her own door and stared at his reflection in the glass.

Disheveled dark blond hair stuck out from under his half-helmet while a scruffy beard covered his cheeks and chin. With his sunglasses on he looked hard and menacing. And sexy as hell...

She slowly headed back to the register, her gaze fixed on Lynch. He now stood in front of the shelf of cereals. Milk and cereal? That seemed so...normal for a thug. Wouldn't cold pizza be his typical breakfast? And where was the hard liquor, or at least the beer? Lost in thought, she placed the beer on the counter.

"I told you *a* six-pack." Felix's statement whipped her around. He situated one sixer off to the side, a stern scowl on his face.

She opened her mouth, but her protest died when a container of two percent, a box of honey bran cereal and a package chocolate chip cookies appeared next to her alcohol. Heat infused her body at the Streeter's close proximity.

"Gimme five bucks on pump three, when you get the chance."

Lynch's low, rolling voice percolated shivers up her arms. He didn't shop like a notorious gang member...and he didn't sound like one either.

Felix nodded while ringing up her purchases. She handed over her debit card, trying her damnedest to act cool. She glanced over.

Still wearing his sunglasses, Lynch rubbed a hand across his neck, his head bowed. He looked tired. Exhausted even.

Late night breaking the law?

Shasta bit her tongue to keep the snarky comment locked in her mouth. She might be the sheriff's sister, but she wasn't a total imbecile.

She punched in her pin number as Felix bagged her chips and power bags. Purchases in hand, she moved toward the entrance, putting an extra swing in her hips in case Lynch checked out her ass.

Outside, she tossed the items onto the truck's back seat then clambered behind the wheel. She clicked her seatbelt, started the truck and put it in reverse. She turned the wheel, but still hadn't fixed the mirrors. The horrible crunch of metal reverberated. She slammed on the brakes, rocking the truck to an abrupt halt. Several moments of deafening quiet surrounded her before...

"What the fuck...*my bike...*"

Her door swung open, and she stared at an infuriated Lynch Callan. With arms akimbo, wide stance and his mouth bowed into a vicious frown, she'd never seen anyone look so angry – not even her brother.

"Get out," he commanded.

She recovered enough to scoff. "What? No freakin' way."

If anything, he looked more furious. He stepped onto the truck's running board, reached over the steering column and twisted the key from the ignition. In one smooth move, he unfastened her belt and jumped to the ground. "I said out."

"And I said no."

He wrapped his large hand around her arm and none too gently dragged her from the cab.

She yanked away. "Let me go."

He tightened his hold and lugged her to the ass end of the truck.

She stumbled behind him. "Do you have any idea who I am?"

"Yup." He didn't even slow down. "You're the idiot who just backed into my bike."

He whirled her around. Her sandal caught on his boot and the asphalt quickly rose up. Only his grip on her arm kept it from meeting her face. She swiped flyaway strands of hair from her eyes, ready to set him on fire with her best scathing glare.

But his sunglasses were now tucked into his t-shirt's neckline. And he glowered at her with the most enthralling blue eyes. They were a pristine, crystal blue, like the water at Lake Tahoe. If Shasta thought him sexy and ominous before, he positively oozed sensuality, and danger, now. Any attempt at being scornful died.

He pointed to a giant Harley lying on its side next to his bag from Felix's store. "Look."

She gave the scene a cursory glimpse and hitched her shoulder.

"Sorry."

His eyebrows lifted as his jaw dropped. "You're *sorry*?" He crossed his arms. "You're paying any damages."

"What damages? I barely tapped it."

Now he scoffed. "Barely tapped it...you *toppled it over*." He waved his hand at the downed bike. "The left mirror's busted and the paint's scraped. And that's just what I can see. You're paying for that and anything else you wrecked."

She faced him square, her fists on her hips. "How do I know those things didn't happen before today? You could just be trying to extort money. That's what people like you do, isn't it?"

His eyes became shards of ice. "People like me?" An unspoken warning clear in his tone.

"Uh, excuse me."

Felix's hesitant voice turned both their heads. "What?" they demanded in unison.

The store owner's gaze rifled between Shasta and Lynch. He held up a police scanner radio. "Just heard there's a BOLO out for the sheriff's truck. They say it's been stolen."

Air thickened in Shasta's throat. She'd hoped to be on a beach before Dell realized his precious ride was missing. And she never expected him to put out an all-points bulletin. Maybe Cassie had been right about this being a bad idea.

Shit.

She stared at the ground, thinking. Maybe she could put the F350 back without Dell knowing she took it. That was a mother-fucking-big maybe. Still...she should at least try.

"I gotta call it in, Shasta."

Her head snapped up. "What? Why?"

"This isn't selling beer to minors. I could get charged as an accessory to grand theft."

"That's ridiculous. Dell would never–"

"Yes he would and you know it. In any case, I can't take that chance." Felix turned to go back into the store. "I'm sorry."

"But, Fe-lix," she whined. "You can't do that to me."

Lynch stepped forward. "Hang on, man," he said to Felix. He looked at her. "You stole the sheriff's truck?"

She threw her hands in the air. "It's not *stealing* if he's my *brother*."

Lynch blinked, his eyebrows squished together like he didn't quite understand her words. Then his face split into an enormous grin that showed off perfectly straight and blindingly white teeth. She thought only lifeguards and male models had such flawless teeth.

He laughed. A huge laugh. A-throw-your-head-back-and-howl-at-the-moon kind of laugh. Just like his teeth and voice and shopping choices, Shasta didn't think criminals laughed like that. She and Felix exchanged confused looks.

After what seemed like a full minute of chortling, Lynch's hilarity finally faded. "Whooo." He wiped his fingers over his eyes, still chuckling. "Goddamn...that's funny shit." He cleared his throat, but his grin remained. "Tell you what, I'll take care of this."

"You?" Shasta said. "What are you gonna do?"

"I'll take the truck someplace where the cops can find it."

"But I gotta call it in, Lynch," Felix said.

"I know. Just gimme fifteen minutes to get to the other side of Stardust." He picked up his groceries. "I'll gas up when I get back and keep my milk cold, will ya?"

Felix's mouth flattened as he reluctantly took the bag. "All right. But fifteen minutes, Lynch. No more." The owner stalked back into his store.

Shasta stared at Lynch. "Why—"

He bent over his Harley. Seeing his faded jeans stretched tight across his butt stole her ability to speak. He hefted the machine upright like it was a bicycle instead of a motorcycle.

He looked at her. "Why what?"

She frowned with a head shake. "What?"

A furrow appeared between his eyes. "You said why. I simply asked why what."

"Oh, right. Why help me after I supposedly busted up your bike?"

"There's no supposedly, you did bust up my bike."

"Then why?"

"Because I'd have given anything to see your brother's face when he realized his truck was missing. Since I can't do that, I can at least make sure he doesn't know who took it."

"But why do that?"

"Cuz it'll eat the shit outta him." He squatted down for a closer inspection of his Harley.

"I still don't understand."

His shoulders stooped on a heavy sigh. He shoved to his feet. "Look, I'm beyond tired. If you don't want my help, just say so." He dug the truck fob from his pocket and held it out.

She shifted her weight, torn between wanting to go to the lake and needing Lynch's help. "If you take the truck, how will I get back?"

"I'll drop you off at school."

"School? I'm not going to school today. I'm meeting friends at Tahoe." She pulled back her shoulders. "Today is Ditch Day."

However, the appeal of Ditch Day had lost its luster. It sounded so...juvenile now. So childish. Maybe the combined drama of Cassie bailing on her, being reminded of her dad and Dell knowing his truck was gone before she managed to get out of town had soured her on the time-honored tradition. Or maybe it was the man standing before her who made her rethink her plans. She didn't want Lynch Callan to think her juvenile...

"Okay then." He tossed the fob at her and pushed his bike off to the side. "Go."

Shasta barely managed to catch the key because the way his jeans rippled as he manhandled his bike distracted her. A funny zing, like electricity, hit her low in the belly, making her feel achy and restless.

She'd experienced a similar feeling a few times with some of the guys she'd dated, but nothing this strong. She had chills while sweat beaded on her forehead. She licked her suddenly dry lips.

Lynch set the kickstand and turned. "So what's it gonna be?"

She bit the inside of her cheek. With her father, and then her brother being the sheriff, none of her boyfriends ever had the stones to do more than kiss her. No serious petting. Definitely no sex. Nothing passed a little light necking. But maybe a biker – an *outlaw* biker – would have the stones to do more.

She graced Lynch with her most beguiling smile and cocked her hip. She wished she wasn't wearing this dumb sweatshirt. While her boobs weren't all that impressive, her bikini top made them appear bigger. "On second thought, going to the lake doesn't seem like such a good idea anymore." She pitched the fob back at him.

He held her gaze for a long heartbeat then shrugged. He stuffed the key in his pocket and retrieved a large wrench and screwdriver from the pack behind his seat. "Okay." He walked to the driver's side. And promptly smashed the window.

Ice water splashed through her belly. "What the fuck, dude? Why the hell did you do that? *You have the key.*"

Lynch opened the door. "Yeah, but how would a thief have gotten it?" He climbed inside and took the screwdriver to the steering column, splintering it open. "It has to look like the truck was broken into and stolen, right?"

She blew out a breath. Damn, she never thought of that.

He pulled out some wires and tapped them together. The engine roared to life. "C'mon. If you're not going to school, I'll take you home."

She hoisted herself into the passenger seat. "Oh...I think we can come up with a better plan than that." She placed her palm on his forearm. Her chest fluttered at the sinewy feel of his muscles. "Don't you?"

He stared at her hand like it was an alien creature before lifting his gaze to hers. The blue of his eyes seemed brighter. More intense. He grasped her hand, bringing it to his mouth where he brushed a chaste kiss to her knuckles. The whiskery sensation of his stubble erupted a geyser in her belly. He squeezed her fingers and released her. Wordlessly, he put the gearshift into drive and maneuver the truck back onto the road.

Shasta settled into the seat, her hands clasped together to hide their shaking. She fought to calm her unsettled stomach.

Oh God...was this really going to happen? Was she really prepared to *let* it happen?

Her unsettled stomach turned riotous as excitement warred with caution. What would it feel like to be kissed by Lynch Callan? Bet he was a great kisser. Not like her wimpy boyfriends who were too afraid to even French her.

And how would Lynch's callused palms feel on her skin? A shiver danced along her spine. Then cold fingers closed around her heart.

What if she changed her mind? Would he allow that or would he...she swallowed hard...make her?

She inhaled a breath and looked out her window. There was only one way to find out...

~*~

Lynch drove the dirt roads which skirted the perimeter of Stardust. He kept his gaze straight ahead, but remained acutely aware of every move the sheriff's sister made beside him.

Shit. He did not need this right now. He was too worn out to think clearly. Having just finished a grueling thirty-six hour run, escorting three separate shipments of primo weed for distribution to the Bay Area, he'd gone into the Grab-n-Go for something easy to eat before crashing. That's all. He never expected to play savior, especially to such a damn fine damsel.

He knew who Shasta was before she dropped the bomb about Albright being her brother. But the Shasta he remembered had been all gangly legs and lanky arms. Not the curvaceous creature with burnished brunette hair and root beer eyes who seemed to suck the oxygen out of the cab interior.

Despite the bulky sweatshirt, which covered a good portion of her body, his imagination worked overtime imagining how pert her breasts would be and how her sleek, sexy legs would feel wrapped around his waist...

He wrestled his thoughts away from that temptation. Fucking with a man's truck was one thing. Fucking his sister – *his underage, kid sister* – was a whole different kettle of fish, as his mom would say. And having that sister be related to the sheriff...

He sighed. As much as he reveled in being a rebel, that didn't make him suicidal.

Still, the way Shasta kept rubbing her thighs together made his cock twitch. There was little doubt she been flirting with him earlier. But no way could she be truly aware of who she was messing with. She probably thought it was just harmless teasing. Right. Harmless. Until the rubber was forced to meet the road.

But nothing was going to happen. Lynch prided himself on not being a complete hound dog. He wouldn't take advantage of an innocent girl.

He knew the instant Shasta realized where he was taking her. She sat upright, her head swiveling around to stare at him. He eased the truck to a stop behind a small stand of elm trees on the backside of

Albright property.

"Why are we here? I don't need anything from my house."

Without putting the F350 into park, he reached across her lap and opened the passenger door. "But I need to sleep."

She undid her seatbelt and curled toward him, her fingers tripping down his arm to where his hand gripped the steering wheel. Tightly.

"Sounds perfect," she purred.

"Sleep alone."

She straightened, her eyebrows furrowing. "Alone?"

"Yup. Like I said, I'm tired."

"I'm sure we can think of...something that'll keep you awake."

He squinted out the windshield. "Sorry. Not interested."

She snatched her hand away. "Why?"

"Guess you're not my type."

"Bullshit. It's because my brother's the sheriff, isn't it?" She sniffed. "I woulda thought a biker would have bigger balls than that."

Her churlish tone clenched his jaw. He turned and drilled her with his glare, holding her gaze, allowing the silence to grow. Expand. A blush made a slow creep up her neck to her face.

Leaning over, he seized her chin between his finger and thumb in a firm, but not painful grip. "Do you honestly think you're ready for something like this?" He dropped his voice to a sinister whisper. "Ready for *me*?"

Her pupils dilated as her delicate throat muscles labored to swallow. To her credit she didn't avert her eyes. In fact, she narrowed them slightly. "I'll never know unless I try."

A humorless chuckle gusted past his lips. Damn, talk about balls. This girl had a pair.

His hand fell away. He didn't have the mental strength to tangle with her. Hell...tangle with anyone. He rubbed his neck and sighed. "Why are you doing this? Does it have anything to do with me being a 5th Streeter? What am I to you? A thrill ride? Just another way to poke at your brother, like taking his truck?"

The rosy stain on her cheeks turned crimson and she lowered her gaze. "None of the guys I've dated ever did more than kiss me." She hitched her shoulder. "It's kinda sad being the only seventeen-year-old in town who's still a virgin."

He again captured her chin, but this time his hold was gentle. The angst in her caramel brown eyes pinched his heart. When was the last time he cared about something so simple as teenaged peer pressure? "Don't be in such a hurry to grow up. It ain't all it's cracked up to be." He released her. "And you're too young to start gathering regrets."

"Do you have regrets?"

He quirked a grin. "Only a million or two."

Her expression became one of amazement. "Really?"

"Why is that so hard to believe?"

"I guess because you're a..." Her shoulder did another hitch as she stared at her hands.

"Gang member?"

She looked up. "Yeah. Is being in a gang something you regret?"

He shook his head. "Nah." But that was a lie. If it weren't for his mom being old lady of the Streeters VP, he doubted he'd be in the MC at all. Doubted he would've dropped out of school when he was a year younger than Shasta. Doubted he would've been the youngest member to be patched into the Streeters. Doubted a lot of things...

"What *do* you regret?"

Her quiet voice brought him back. She looked so earnest, as though she truly wanted to know, he had a hard time ignoring her question. He draped his hand over the steering wheel and sighed. "For one, not staying in school."

Her face scrunched up like one of them just cut the cheese.

He laughed. Her reaction was so typical of a teenager. Funny...he wasn't really that much older than her, maybe eight years. It felt like eighty. "Hey – you asked."

"You sound like Dell."

"As much as I hate agreeing with your brother, in this case, he's right. School's important. I know you think it's lame, but if I could have one do-over, it'd be to take school more seriously and not drop out." He sighed again, switching his gaze out the windshield. "I sometimes wonder what my life would've been like..."

The tips of his ears heated and he cleared his throat. "Anyway, I'm sure you're gonna do whatever you want." He glanced over. "Right?"

A shy smile touched her lips, "Probably."

Lynch felt sucker-punched in the gut. He'd always thought her pretty, but right now she looked way more than simply pretty. She was beautiful. No. Not just beautiful either. Exquisite. Perfect. Like a rare gem.

Something shifted in his chest. Tightened, then released. His head swam with sudden dizziness. When he realized he was staring, he looked away with a rough cough.

She turned to exit the cab, then pivoted back onto the seat. "You like cookies, don't you?"

He tilted his head. "'Scuse me?"

"Cookies. I saw you buy some at Felix's."

"Yeah...so?"

"I bake a mean chocolate chip. I have a secret ingredient my mom showed me when I was a kid. It's cinnamon. It gives the cookies an extra little zip."

"And?"

"And would you like me to bake you some? Cookies," she added when he didn't answer.

"Why would you do that?"

"As a thank you for...you know...helping me with the truck."

"You don't have to–"

"But I want to. You really saved my ass. And I appreciate you didn't lecture me...you know...about school and stuff."

He shrugged. "I never found lectures to be very useful."

"Tell that to my brother. All he does is lecture."

"Yeah, well, he's just looking out for you."

"Maybe." She swiped her hand over the seat cover. "So what about the cookies?"

"I won't turn down homemade cookies."

She beamed a huge smile. "Great! I'll make them this Friday after school." She lowered her gaze, but her smile remained. "I don't suppose you'd let me bring them to your place on Saturday." She peeked up at him. "Will you?"

He smothered his grin. "No."

Her nose wrinkled slightly. "That's kinda what I figured. Okay if I drop them off at your mom's salon?"

"Sure."

After opening the door, she jumped to the ground.

"Hey..." He pulled the truck fob from his pocket. "Here."

"Oh...right." She stepped onto the running board and took the offering, gracing him with another smile. "Thanks."

"And what about your stuff in back?"

"Keep it. I wouldn't be able to explain the beer anyway." She hopped down again then paused. She shifted and licked her lips. "Guess I'll see you around."

He stared at her mouth for a moment then met her gaze. "Yeah. See ya."

She heaved the door shut and headed for the underbrush surrounding the elms. He tracked her movement. Fuck she had fine legs. Probably a fine ass too. But he couldn't be sorry he'd turned her down. She was just a kid, and a confused kid at that. She needed to be protected from making some very bad decisions.

She looked over her shoulder with a small wave. His lips kicked up as he lifted his hand from the steering wheel in farewell. Then she disappeared...

Chapter Two

Present day...

LYNCH CALLAN SPLASHED cold water on his face and chest, welcoming the biting slap in the hope it would clear his mind.

He dreamed of her last night.

Fuck.

He gripped the sink's stainless-steel edge and braced his arms, his head bowed. He allowed the memory of brown eyes that sparkled like a freshly opened bottle of root beer and apple-cheeked innocence to wash over him. Of a time and place when he had hope for something more.

Something better.

But that hope died long ago. Seven years to be exact – a fucking lifetime ago – in Stardust, a quaint town nestled against the Sierra Mountains just thirty miles south of Reno, Nevada. Once the judge's gavel came down, the life Lynch always feared became his reality...in the state penitentiary, guilty of attempted murder.

A frustrated growl rumbled in his chest. He snatched up the nearby towel and dried his face.

Shit.

No use dwelling on things he couldn't change. He lived this life now. And his cellmate, Oscar, waited for him in the yard. And when Oscar wanted him somewhere, he went.

A small, bitter grin twisted Lynch's month. Oscar. *El Jefe.* Spanish for boss. Sounded like a character from a bad television cop show. But no one could dispute Oscar ran this cellblock. Nothing happened without his knowledge – or permission.

Lynch draped the towel over the sink, pulled his state issued t-shirt over his head then stuck his arms in the sleeves of the state issued chambray shirt. Buttoning it, he turned. A shadow filled his open cell door.

"You Oscar?"

The new inmate, his hands in his front jean pockets, didn't seem all that intimidating, but Lynch noted the ugly, irregular prison ink marring his forearms and the even uglier gleam in his dark eyes. A lifer.

Lynch reached back and grasped his discarded towel with a blasé shrug. "Nah. He's in the yard."

The guy eyed Lynch like a cat would a wounded mouse. "Name's Beck. Just transferred in and heard Oscar was the main guy on this block. Wanted to stop by and...make his acquaintance."

Bullshit. This meathead didn't want to make anyone's *acquaintance*. He wanted to establish his dominance by challenging *El Jefe*. Well he could try.

Lynch tightened his grasp on the terrycloth. "Like I said, he's in the yard."

A slow, nasty grin lifted the corners of Beck's mouth. "You his guppy? Maybe I'll make *your* acquaintance first. As a warm-up."

Lynch permitted his own lips to quirk up. "Have at. Fucktard."

Beck's smile disappeared and he pulled his hands from his pockets. A short, but no doubt deadly shank glinted menacingly in his right fist.

Well shit. It probably hadn't been the best idea to insult this guy, but live and learn.

Shifting his left leg forward, Lynch angled his body to make himself less of a target, his muscles tense. He wrapped the towel around his hand, knowing the cramped quarters would either save or kill. A crap shoot either way.

Beck weaved the shank back and forth. He feigned a thrust. Lynch responded with a sweep of his toweled hand, almost knocking the blade free.

Beck's eyes widened then tapered into slits. He adjusted his hold on the makeshift knife. "Guess this ain't your first rodeo."

Lynch didn't bother answering. He kept his gaze trained on Beck, ready for the next attack – when the unit guard, Johnston, appeared. "What's going on?" he demanded.

Beck quickly pocketed his weapon. "Nothing." He glared at Lynch.

"Right?"

Lynch refused to relax his bearing. "Right."

Beck backed out of the cell with a warning look. "See you later. Guppy."

"Count on it."

After Beck left, Lynch unraveled the towel and tossed it onto his top bunk. He looked at the guard. "You need something?"

"Yeah. Your lawyer is here."

Lawyer?

Lynch didn't have a lawyer. He'd fired his public defender a month into his incarceration. But maybe his mom hired him a new attorney.

He dismissed the thought as soon as it formed. With her beauty salon in Stardust, his mom struggled each month just to make her mortgage, so paying for legal counsel was out of the question. Plus, aside from a couple of Christmas cards, he hadn't had any communication with her, or anyone else, since he got inside. His choice. He lived in box now and having contact with people outside that box didn't benefit anyone.

Johnston blocked his access to the door. "You want to tell me what was going on between you and that new guy, Beck."

"Just inmate shit."

"Anything I need to deal with?"

"Nah. Oscar'll handle it."

"Riiight." Johnston moved to the side. "Just make sure Oscar handles it when I'm not on shift."

With a nod, Lynch exited his cell and headed down the narrow walkway, the guard right behind him. Other convicts moved to the side to make room.

"I don't remember you ever having a visit from your lawyer," Johnston commented.

"Once." Lynch stopped at the heavy unit door.

The metal hinges creaked in protest as Johnston opened it. "You remember the procedure?"

"Has it changed?"

With a small chuckle, Johnston shook his head.

"Didn't think so." Lynch descended the three flights of stairs.

Nothing ever changed in prison. Same schedule, same food, same shit-brown walls. If you were smart, you found comfort in the fixed routine. If not, well, you went a little batshit crazy.

All the way to the ground floor, Lynch felt the gazes of the sharpshooting guards on his head. That was something else that stayed the same in prison...you were never alone. Not ever.

At the bottom, he walked out into the lower yard. The April sun warmed his face. At least he thought it was April. Might be May by now.

Lynch sauntered across the expanse of dirt and gravel. Some convicts shot basketballs into net-less hoops while others lifted weights. Still others lingered in clusters for supposed protection.

He scanned the nearby area for Oscar even though he knew *Jefe's* usual post was the handball court on the far side. He needed to tell his cellmate about Beck. But warning him would have to wait until Lynch finished his visit.

Another guard, Morgan, met him at the strip-out room. After disrobing and spreading his ass cheeks for inspection, Lynch redressed then walked with Morgan down the hall to a semi-private room. Through the window, he saw a man and a woman sitting at the table, their backs to him.

The hairs on Lynch's neck itched as he walked into the room. Something wasn't right. The man sported a Marine buzz cut while the woman had her auburn hair drawn into a severe bun. Seeing their faces felt like Beck's shank had found its mark in his gut.

These two were either former military or feds. Probably both. Neither of them bothered to stand when he sat facing them, his palms flat on the tabletop. Morgan closed the door and took up his post at the window looking in.

"Mr. Callan," the woman said. "I'm Special Agent Emma Jarvis and this is Special Agent Sam Newman. We're with the FBI."

Lynch maintained a neutral expression and studied the first woman he'd seen in more than seven years. Attractive enough...if you liked the button-up. G.I. Jane type. Green eyes assessed him through black-rimmed glasses. She pursed her lips which gave her a pinched look. The firm set of her chin said she was probably a ball buster. He switched his gaze to Newman. "I was told my lawyer was here."

Newman folded his brawny hands on the table. "This meeting needed to stay as quiet as possible so as not to put a...damper on your life expectancy."

Lynch swallowed his snicker. Anyone who got a look at these two would know exactly who there were. "What do you want?"

"Your help," Jarvis said.

A smile split Lynch's face. "My help? In case you missed it, I'm in prison."

"We've missed nothing, I assure you," she replied dryly. "Not even the part about the man you tried to kill is the sheriff of Grant County. However, that doesn't change the fact we need your help."

Lynch tensed at the mention of Dell Albright. Though he and the good sheriff had grown up as classmates, they never hung in the same circles. Not unusual considering Dell's father had been sheriff twenty years prior to his son and Lynch's mom had been the old lady to the Streeter VP. Fact was, Dell hated him. A sentiment Lynch returned.

But Lynch never tried to kill Dell because if he'd *tried*, he'd have succeeded. His grin widened. "Get me outta here and I'll see what I can do to help you."

"That's exactly what we intend, Mr. Callan." She thumbed open a file.

Lynch sobered. "What does that mean?"

"It means we can arrange a new trial for you."

Distrust tightened Lynch's skin. "In exchange for what?"

"Your cooperation with your old biker gang, the 5th Streeters."

Lynch's smile returned. "Biker gang? Oh, you must mean the 5th Street *motorcycle club*. It's not a gang, though. Just a bunch of weekend warriors riding around on their tricked-out Harleys." He pulled his lips into a thoughtful frown. "I honestly didn't even know they were still around."

Jarvis flipped over a picture and pushed it toward him. A man's hideously bloated face looked up from under harsh autopsy lights. Lynch's stomach did a slow roil.

"This is..." Jarvis's voice hitched slightly. "Was Agent Olsen."

She turned over more photos. Lynch immediately recognized his best friend, Hez along with Rolo, the Streeter president and Flyer, the VP. There were other club members...Mick, Grunge, Picket. His mom. Plus Ennis and Tiny – when did those two go from being prospects to full-fledged Streeters?

Jarvis added more pictures...of his crew riding their respective hogs down Stardust's main street, his mom's beauty salon and the entrance to Rolo's bowling alley, which housed the clubhouse in the rear.

Nostalgia torqued his heart and clogged his throat. But he masked his feelings to focus on the faces of the people he didn't know. He supposed Agent Olsen populated the group, but he couldn't pick him out due to the disfigurement of the first image.

"Jerry...Agent Olsen," Jarvis continued, "had been undercover with the Streeters for over three years. He went missing last October. We feared the worst, then got confirmation a month ago when a fisherman on Pyramid Lake snagged Olsen's clothing and dragged him to the surface. Weights had been attached to his ankles, but not enough to keep the body from rising once it started to decompose." She leveled a hard stare at Lynch. "Jerry was a good agent. A good man. He left behind a wife and two young kids."

Lynch shifted in his seat. "My condolences, but what does any of this have to do with me?"

A short, neatly trimmed fingernail landed on Olsen's distended image. "This is the work of your *gang*."

"Even if that's true, I sure as hell don't know who did it."

"We realize you don't know who killed Olsen," Newman interjected, opening another file. "Not yet anyway. Things have changed for the Streeters since you've been gone. They're no longer a nickel and dime operation, growing and selling weed or extorting protection money from small businesses. They've moved into the big leagues. Smuggling heroin up from Mexico. Gun running." He pivoted the file so Lynch could read it. "And more."

Lynch leaned closer to examine the papers. "What am I looking at?"

"Missing person reports. Over two dozen young girls, some as young as twelve, have gone missing in Northern Nevada in the past six months. But that's just the tip of the iceberg. We discovered reports going back five years of teenaged, mostly white girls simply...vanishing. Some from as far away as Portland and Boise."

An acidic taste coated Lynch's mouth. He swallowed. "So?"

"So, Olsen learned a man, a Mr. Ian Blackwell, is behind the disappearances. He supposedly pays ten to twenty-five grand per girl, depending on her age and whether she's a virgin."

"And you haven't arrested this Blackwell dude because why?"

"Because no one knows what he looks like," Newman explained. "No pictures of him exist."

"But you're sure he's connected to these disappearances?"

"Yes. According to our sources in the Mexican Federal Police, Blackwell resells the girls to Luis Fuentes, a Columbian businessman headquartered in Mexico City. Fuentes is one mother of a badass. Not only is he a known human trafficker with international ties stretching from the Philippines to the Middle East, but he's also *the* go-to guy in this hemisphere for any dirt bag who wants to start their own private war. Fuentes can get anything and everything from C4 to AK 47s to missile launchers."

Lynch sat back. "Okay. Have your Federale friends take care of Fuentes. That'll cut the head off the snake and not only stop young white girls from disappearing on this side of the border, but should put a dent in the gun trade."

"It's not so simple. Fuentes is well connected in the local police forces. Every time a move is made on him, it ends in a blood bath – for the Federales. The FBI has formed a joint task force with the Mexican authorities in the hopes of back tracing to Fuentes from this side of the border. Agent Olsen was our point man."

"I still don't get what this has to do with me or the Streeters."

"Your hometown, Stardust, is ground zero for the trafficking operation. Which means the Streeters are involved."

An icy fist squeezed Lynch's heart. "No way...no fucking way would Rolo have anything to do with something like that."

"Believe it," Jarvis stated, "because it's true."

"So *you* say."

"So the *evidence* says," she countered, sitting forward. "I don't think you're grasping the gravity of this situation, Mr. Callan."

"Oh, I'm *grasping* it just fine, Agent Jarvis," Lynch bit out. He crossed his arms, causing Morgan to move to the door. Lynch placed his palms back on the table. "You want to spring me from this joint in exchange for ratting out my crew. Ain't. Gonna. Happen."

Jarvis glared. "We have more than enough evidence to bury, and I mean *bury,* your precious crew."

Lynch's heart rate spiked. "Do that and you'll probably never get

Blackwell. Which means you'll never get Fuentes."

"Oh, I'll get them. I'll get them both." Her smile lacked any warmth. "Eventually. In the meantime, I'll make do with the biggest consolation prize I can get my hands on." Her flinty gaze drilled his. "If you don't help us, I swear – on my life – not only will you spend the rest of yours behind bars, but so will everyone who's ever even remotely been affiliated with the 5th Streeters. Including your mother."

A deadly stillness blanketed Lynch. "You threatening my mom?"

"Call it motivation."

Narrowing his gaze, Lynch pressed his palms to the table so hard, the tendons bulged. And people claim criminals had no moral compass. He tilted his head. "Fine. Say I agree. Say you get me outta here. What's to keep me from flipping on *you* to this Blackwell dude and Fuentes?"

Jarvis's complexion flushed an angry red. "If you do, so help me–"

"But you won't, Callan," Newman interrupted.

Lynch swiveled his attention to him. "Really? What makes you so damn sure?"

"Because I've read your file more times than I can count, and I know nothing matters more to you than loyalty."

"If you know me so well, then you know I'll *never* turn on my crew."

"Not even to avenge one of their murders?" Jarvis asked.

Lynch snapped his gaze back to her. "Come again?"

Newman slid another photo of a gruesomely disfigured man across the table. "After finding Jerry's body, we dredged that part of the lake and discovered he wasn't alone. Jerry had been working a source inside the Streeters. Someone who had a serious issue with the club's new business model. This source agreed to help us find a direct link to Blackwell and ultimately Fuentes." He tapped the picture with a thick-set finger. "Recognize him? That's Flyer Gemstone. Shot once in the back of the head, execution style."

A roar filled Lynch's ears. Bile splashed his throat. He searched for Flyer's image from one of the other pictures. The lanky, half-breed Cherokee, who was the closest thing Lynch had to a father, stood next to his mom, his arm slung over her shoulders, beaming a smile like he'd just been told a joke. Anguish constricted his chest. He shoved the photo away. "I can't even be sure that's Flyer."

"It's him all right," Newman declared. "Now let me tell you what else I know about you. I know if given the chance to find out who killed Flyer Gemstone, nothing or no one will get in your way."

Holding Newman's gaze, Lynch clenched his jaw.

The agent squinted back. "Maybe you're willing to gamble we don't have enough to convict your mother along with the entire Streeter network, which we do. And maybe you can even live with the lie the Streeters aren't trafficking in young girls. But someone killing Flyer? Executing him?" Newman shook his head. "No. That requires retribution. Especially since he was more than likely killed by a fellow gang member."

Lynch sawed his molars together and maintained his stony silence.

Everyone who got patched into the 5th Streeters knew being a brother carried risks, including going to prison or dying. That was the chance you took to play the game. And as far as his mom went, she had the chops to fight her own battles. If he snitched to *save* her, she'd kick his ass six ways to Sunday.

But someone murdering Flyer? Newman had that right. Lynch would give anything – would do anything – to avenge him, or any of his brothers. Even if it meant betraying them.

He looked back at the grotesque photo these agents claimed was his mentor. Though logic demanded he shouldn't believe the horrific image was Flyer, in his gut...his heart...Lynch knew the awful truth.

A wave of heat flashed up his neck. He bowed his head. Flyer dead? Who killed him? A Streeter? Impossible. Brothers didn't kill brothers. Did they? But if Olsen's cover had been blown, and someone discovered Flyer had been helping the undercover agent...

None of this made sense. Just like the human trafficking allegations made no sense. Since when would the Streeters have anything to do with the buying and selling of young girls? Many of the men had daughters themselves. Hell, Rolo had three. It went against everything Lynch knew, or at least thought he knew, about these men.

But seven years had passed. People changed. God knew he had.

"So what's it gonna be, Callan?" Newman's voice broke into his thoughts. "Are you willing to have Flyer's death go unavenged? Or risk more girls being abducted? Shit's been brewing for a long time in

Stardust and it's all gonna hit the fan unless you help us."

Help them by becoming a snitch. A mole. How far was Lynch willing to go to get at the truth?

Determination lifted his head. "What will I have to do?"

Jarvis collected the photos. "Find out everything you can about the connection between the Streeters and the slave trade. Find out who Blackwell is and who killed Agent Olsen."

"Okay, but how will this work? Am I just gonna waltz outta here? As you said, I was convicted of trying to kill a sheriff."

"I'm a lawyer," she replied. "I used to work for the attorney general's office in DC, and I've been over your case file and the court records. All the evidence against you seems circumstantial at best. A first-year law student could have mounted a better defense than your public defender. It won't be hard to get a judge to sign off on a new trial."

Lynch gave her is best roguish grin. "Too bad I didn't have you as my attorney during the first go-around, counselor."

Her lips curled into a sneer. "While the evidence in *this* case seems sketchy, I'm sure you're guilty of other crimes that would earn you a lengthy prison stay." She closed the file with a slap. "You're a criminal, pure and simple. As far as I'm concerned, you deserve to rot behind bars."

Lynch couldn't fault her candor. He'd done more than his share of illegal acts, but that list didn't include trying to off Dell Albright. In actuality, his public defender hadn't been so much inept as Lynch refused to help mount a defense. Going to prison had been the only sure way to protect Shasta, the woman he loved, who also happened to be Albright's sister.

He'd been a goner the first time he stared into those root beer eyes. But with him a Streeter and her brother the sheriff, any chance at a relationship died before it began. Didn't stop him from having one with her. Guess love was blind. And fucking stupid.

Awareness tightened Lynch's skin. Once he got back to town, would he see her? He disliked how his pulse skipped at the prospect...a slim prospect. Shasta might not still live in the miniscule town of Stardust, though the thought of big brother Dell allowing her to leave seemed remote. Then there was the fact he'd been accused of trying to kill her brother. She could very well hate him, as she should.

But none of that mattered. The past needed to stay in the past. The only thing that mattered was finding out who murdered Flyer.

Jarvis stood. "I'll see about getting you into administrative segregation until you're released."

Lynch's stomach knotted. Ad Seg...he couldn't go into Ad Seg. He had obligations and debts to deal with before getting out...starting with warning Oscar about Beck. "Nobody said anything about me going into segregation."

She picked up her briefcase. "It'll be several days before I can make this deal happen and we can't risk your life by putting you back into the general population."

"But putting me in segregation *will* risk my life."

Her brow wrinkled. "That makes no sense."

"Not to you, but it makes perfect sense to me, and to every other convict. No one's been to see me since I got here and now suddenly my lawyer..." He mimed quotation marks in the air. "...pays me a visit and then I'm put in protective custody?" He shook his head with a humorless chuckle. "There'll be a torpedo gunning for me before supper tonight. Ad Seg or no Ad Seg."

"That's preposterous."

He hitched his shoulder. "That's prison."

She paused then shook her head. "It's too dangerous. I won't endanger this operation on a hunch."

"It's not a hunch. It's reality. But..." He stood and nodded to Morgan who moved to the door. "...it's your decision. Too bad I won't be around to tell you I told you so."

Jarvis huffed a breath. "All right. Fine. You go back to your cell, but," she jabbed her finger at him, "so help me God, Callan, you end up dead, and I'll kill you."

Lynch exited the room, a grin on his face. "I'll keep that in mind, counselor."

Chapter Three

WITH THE WIND cooling the sweat on her skin, Shasta Albright Dupree ran.

She often claimed she loved running because she needed the exercise and it gave her time alone to think. But the truth was she ran for the simple, sheer joy of it.

The isolated desert landscape of her favorite trail passed in blurry focus. The crisp spring air burned her lungs as her footfalls against the hard-packed dirt reverberated up her legs, through her torso and into her head. Her fanny pack bounced rhythmically against her hip. Nothing compared to a good, long run. It rejuvenated her soul. Granted her freedom – if only for a short period. The restrictions of being a mom and wife could be smothering at times.

It wasn't that she didn't dearly love her six-year-old son, Wyatt, because she did. She'd give her life for him. And then there was Graham, her husband, a truly awesome guy.

She'd known Graham her whole life, seeing he was her dad's best friend. He'd been the DA when her dad held the sheriff job. For over twenty years, they doled out their brand of law and order justice, with her father the law and Graham the order.

And when her world had careened dangerously out of control, Graham stayed right by her side. He'd been her rock. Her savior. Plus, he loved Wyatt like he was his own.

Shasta couldn't ask for a better life. She had a roof over her head, food in the fridge, a great kid and devoted husband. If not for the car accident shortly after their wedding, which left Graham paralyzed from the waist down, everything would be perfect.

Disgusted with her selfish thoughts, she raced up a sagebrush covered hill. She needed to stop complaining, even to herself. She should be grateful for what she had. Because she had a lot.

Her hands shook as her legs protested the uphill strain. But rather than decreasing her pace, she tripled her effort. By the time she reached the top, her brain was thankfully blank.

She danced in a circle, fist-pumping her hands overhead...her version of Rocky scaling the museum steps. She giggled at her silly antic.

A loud whinny halted her jubilance. She crouched low then scampered to the side of a boulder and peered into the ravine on her right. A small herd of wild mustangs grazed about sixty feet away. A roan-colored stallion stood watch over three mares, two of which looked pregnant. The stallion's ears jutted forward, his eyes wide. He pranced, his snout in the air trying to smell her location.

She immediately skulked along the rock surface until upwind of the herd. She peeked into the gulch again, glad she hadn't spooked the horses.

They were magnificent, so regal in their wildness. She extracted her cell phone from her pack, her lips curving upward. Wyatt would love a picture of them.

Sadness nicked her heart and her smile dipped. Seeing the wild horses reminded Shasta of her late father. Dad had nicknamed her "Mustang Filly" because growing up she'd been wild. No rule existed she didn't relish breaking, or at least bending. A tough position for the sheriff to be in, constantly defending his errant daughter's behavior. But Shasta's bond with her father had always been special, especially after cancer took her mom when she was nine. With older brother, Dell, off at college, that left the two rebel Albrights alone in Stardust.

Despite her transgressions – of which there had been many – her dad never came down on her too hard. He empathized with her defiant streak. With her need to be unfettered. Free, just like the mustangs.

Then, seven months after her sixteenth birthday, a hunting accident took him as well.

Shaking off the weepy memories, she zoomed in for a close-up of the stallion – when the sudden trill of her phone sent the herd galloping through the gully.

Crap.

She checked the caller ID and frowned.

Dell. Double crap.

Her brother, and boss, had lousy timing, ruining what would have been an epic shot. Why was he calling anyway? Today was her day off. Maybe no one at the sheriff's department could find the coffee filters.

She snickered at that thought, and sent Sheriff Dell Albright straight to voicemail then pocketed her phone. She swiped damp hair off her forehead and stood, gazing at the dust cloud left in the herd's hasty retreat. Maybe she could track them. Get another chance for a picture.

She started down the hill. With a bottle of water and a granola bar in her pack, she could easily stay out for the next hour or two. Another chime of her phone indicated she had a text. From Dell, naturally.

Where r u? Not running alone in the desert again?!? NOT SAFE!!

Shasta rolled her eyes. Her brother, the mother hen. She thought about ignoring him, but knew that wouldn't end well. He'd probably just call on the National Guard to comb the desert for her. She typed back...

What's up? Today's Fri, u no.

I no what day it is. He added a frowning face. *Adam called. Needs to meet.*

A shiver of revulsion traversed up Shasta's spine. She'd rather pet a scorpion than spend any time with the smarmy district attorney, Adam Murphy. She despised the lecherous looks he directed her way, when no one else was watching of course. She typed on her keyboard...

What does he want?

Dunno, but says it's important. When can you b here?

An hour, maybe sooner

Make it sooner. And B CAREFUL.

Shasta shook her head. What did Dell expect would happen? There wasn't another soul around for miles. Besides, she could take care of herself.

She slipped her phone back into her fanny pack and looked wistfully at where the mustangs had disappeared before reversing direction. She started an easy jog back to her car. So much for having a day to herself.

~*~

At just before eleven, Shasta walked into the stationhouse. It'd taken her longer to return to town than she originally thought. She just hoped Dell hadn't had a complete conniption fit.

A quiet squad room greeted her. Nothing unusual about that. Stardust was hardly a big crime-riddled city. She waved to the dispatcher, Joan, who sat crocheting at her desk, a headset balanced on her graying hair, then spied Dell in his window-lined office, talking with Adam – and Graham. Confusion knitted her forehead.

Graham should be on his way to Reno to catch the one o'clock flight to Vegas for a week-long business trip. Irritation tightened her shoulders. If her idiotic brother had called her husband because she was a little late, she'd have his hide. She headed for the office when Todd Weedly intercepted her between a narrow row of desks.

"Looks like someone needs a shower," he drawled, his gaze raking her from head to foot.

Shasta pulled to an abrupt stop, somehow managing not to scowl. The deputy, like Adam, made her skin crawl with his lewd looks and thinly veiled innuendos. While neither man ever said or did anything blatantly inappropriate, each time she came within twenty feet of them, she had to fight to keep from hurling. She needed a shower all right, but it wasn't because of her run.

She pasted on a smile. While *she* didn't like Todd, Dell did. Her brother hired him after all. "Yeah. Went for a run."

Todd hitched a hip on a desk, which made his leather gun holster creak, and nodded, his gaze fastened to her chest. She shifted, grateful she'd zipped her jacket up to her neck. "Anyway, I gotta go. Dell's waiting."

The deputy didn't move one iota while she sidled around him, careful not to touch his pant leg. She felt his stare on her as she hustled to her brother's office.

Dell saw her approach and his expression darkened. He pushed to his feet then grabbed his cane, which was never far away, and limped to the door. Any annoyance Shasta felt toward him dissipated. While her brother might be the biggest pain on the planet, she never doubted he loved her and worried about her. After all, he'd taken care of her since she was sixteen.

He opened the door. "Where the hell have you been? You said an hour *or less*."

"I know. I'm sorry." She breezed past him, bussing a kiss to his whiskered cheek. She then bent over Graham's wheelchair to do the same with his clean shaven one.

Her husband's powerful arms and shoulders bulged the seams of his polo shirt. He worked his upper body like a weightlifter to compensate for his lack of lower body strength. The dash of silver at his temples and his meticulously trimmed salt and pepper goatee were the only signs he was nearly thirty years her senior. She gazed into his pale blue eyes. "Shouldn't you be at the airport?"

"Yes, but when Adam called and said he had something important to tell us, I changed my flight to two-thirty."

"So my brother didn't contact you?"

His lips lifted in a weary smile. "Not this time."

Concern wiggled through her chest. "You feeling okay, honey? You look tired."

He patted her hand. "I'm fine. Got the start of a migraine is all. But don't worry," he added when she opened her mouth. "I took a pain pill and will sleep on the plane. I'll be right as rain once I land in Vegas."

She bit her lower lip. "Maybe you shouldn't go."

"Nonsense. It's just a headache."

"That can lead to blackouts. Maybe you should–"

"Shasta. Honey. Enough. All right? I said I was fine."

With a huff, she straightened and took her usual position behind his wheelchair, but Adam jumped to his feet.

"Here," he said. "You probably should sit down."

Her eyes widened. Adam being chivalrous? Not his standard MO. But he moved to lean against the wall, his arms and ankles crossed. Suspicion tap danced across her neck. Adam offered his chair without casting even one covert leer her way.

She tentatively perched her butt on the seat. "What's going on?"

Dell shuffled back behind his desk and sat heavily in his chair. "Yeah, counselor. Everyone's here now, so spill whatever this important news is."

Adam uncurled his stance with a cough. "I got a call this morning and wanted to tell you all myself."

Graham scrunched his eyebrows together. "Tell us what?"

The DA huffed a breath and shoved his hands into his pant pockets. "Lynch Callan is being released."

Shasta felt like she was being held underwater. No sound. No air. Stars danced in front of her eyes. She knew she needed to breathe, but her constricted lungs refused to work.

Lynch Callan – the man serving twenty-five years to life for trying to kill Dell *and* Wyatt's biological dad – was being released from prison? She sat in stunned silence while conflicting emotions bombarded her.

Joy hopscotched through her chest because she'd never believed Lynch guilty of trying to kill her brother in the first place. Just as quickly, though, dread clutched her heart. Had Lynch somehow found out about Wyatt? No, that wasn't possible. While everyone in Stardust assumed Graham to be the daddy, nobody knew the truth about Wyatt's parentage, not even her own husband. The singular saving grace about her having a firebrand reputation as a teenager was that her pregnancy shocked no one. Truth was, she'd only ever been with one man.

Thank God Wyatt inherited her dark brown hair. She prayed it didn't lighten too much when he got older. Wyatt also had blue eyes, same as Graham. Except her son's eyes bordered on the hypnotic, like Lynch's.

Finally guilt feasted on her conscience. If she hadn't been so rebellious, so damn reckless when she was younger, Lynch might not have ever gone to prison and Dell might not now be reliant on a cane to move, not to mention Graham being imprisoned in a wheelchair...

"Released?" Dell exploded from his chair then quickly grabbed the desk for balance. "How the *fuck* did that happen? He's not eligible for parole for at least another fifteen years."

Adam gusted another sigh. "He's not being paroled. A hotshot lawyer from the attorney general's office took an interest in his case. She petitioned a federal judge, and Callan's been granted a new trial. He's being released pending that trial."

"Jesus Christ." Dell spun away, and nearly toppled over. He gripped his tall chair back and inhaled a noisy breath. Anger vibrated his entire body.

Graham tilted forward as much as the restrictions of his wheelchair would allow. "Adam, what steps are you taking to keep

Callan behind bars?"

"Unfortunately, there aren't any steps I *can* take at the moment."

Dell turned around, his face an ugly, purplish red. "What the hell does that mean?"

"It means I found out about the situation just before coming here to tell you. But I believe this deal has been in the works for several days."

"Why do you think that?"

"Because Callan is getting out...this afternoon."

Dell's eyes bugged. "This *afternoon?*"

Adam glanced away with a nod, rubbing his neck. "Look, I understand this news is upsetting–"

"Upsetting?" Dell mocked. "I'm way past upset. Have you forgotten that bastard tried to kill me? He *shot* me. In the back."

Adam glowered. "I've forgotten nothing."

"Then keep that fucker locked up."

"There's only so much power I have in this–"

"What about petitioning for a stay?" Graham interjected.

Adam tore his angry gaze from Dell. "I plan to file with the Ninth District Court on Monday, but that's not going to keep Callan from getting out today."

Graham pursed his lips. "At least it's a start. The thing to focus on is what to do once Callan is actually back in town."

For the first time since Adam dropped the bombshell, Shasta piped up. "What do you mean?"

"What I mean, hon, is that we can't dismiss the possibility of Callan seeking retribution for his incarceration."

"Retribution? Against whom?"

"Well, me for one. His was the last case I prosecuted before..." His voice drifted off.

She reached over and grasped his hand. Graham hated any reference to his dreadful accident. He flexed his fingers around hers with a small smile then released his grip. She settled for resting her palm on his forearm. "Do you really think he'll come after you?"

"It makes sense to me."

"And to me," Adam concurred. He looked at Dell. "What about assigning Graham police protection?"

"That won't be necessary," her husband said. "I'll be in Vegas until next week. Hopefully you'll get that stay and Callan's taste of freedom will be brief. If not, we can discuss a security detail once I'm home. However, in my absence, Shasta and Wyatt will need one."

She jolted upright. "What? Me?"

Adam nodded. "Good point."

"I agree," Dell said. "I'll check the roster and assign someone to watch her."

"But why do *I* need protection?" Her voice sounded shrill in her ears.

Dell stared at her. "Because you're my sister."

"And my wife," Graham added.

Shasta looked from one to the other. "So?"

Graham tilted his head. "So, Dell and I are the two people most responsible for Callan going to prison. That potentially puts you in a dangerous situation."

"But..." Shasta frantically searched for a counter argument. "Having a deputy follow me around all the time would cost a lot of money." She glanced at Dell. "Wouldn't it?"

His expression hardened. "I don't care about the cost. You're my sister. And I don't want that bastard within five miles of you, or Wyatt."

"I may be able to help defer the expense," Adam offered. "I'll make a few calls when I get back to my office."

"And she should probably be at the stationhouse when not at home," Graham said. "Don't you think, Dell?"

"Yes I do." Dell scribbled on a notepad. "And there'll be no more jogging in the desert alone. And if she's not here, and if Wyatt's not in school, the two of them will be in lockdown at the house."

Dread welled in Shasta's chest, cutting off her voice. She couldn't go into lockdown. Be a prisoner in her own home. Unable to go out. Go running...

"Excellent," Graham said. "I know I'll rest easier knowing my family is safe."

Dell nodded. "It's settled then. I'll have–"

She slapped her hands on the chair armrests, and three sets of male eyes landed on her. "You're all being ridiculous. It's ludicrous to think I'm in danger."

Dell squinted. "What makes you so certain?"

"Because–" She stopped herself before saying *Lynch would never hurt me.*

If that come out of her mouth, it would lead to a bevy of questions. Questions she did not want to answer.

She'd hadn't breathed a word to another living soul about her connection to Lynch, and she wasn't going to now. Biting her lip, she pressed her fingers to her temples. She pulled in a slow breath. "When would this all have to start."

"Immediately." Dell went back to scrawling on his pad.

"But I have a spa date with Melissa in Reno this afternoon."

"Cancel it." Dell didn't even bother looking up.

Her jaw dropped. "I will not cancel. We've waited over three months for an opening."

Dell nailed her with a hard look. "Again, I don't care. You're not going anywhere without a police escort. Period."

"Oh, for heaven's sake. Lynch is on the other side of the state. Even if he drives a hundred miles an hour, he won't get here until late this afternoon. There's absolutely no reason for me to cancel my plans."

Graham took her hand. "Please do this. For me."

She couldn't say no to the stark plea in his eyes. Her shoulders drooped. "Fine. I'll cancel."

Dell threw his hands in the air. "Hallelujah."

She rounded on her brother. "But the only one *assigned* to me and Wyatt will be you."

"Why?"

She gave him her most wicked smile. "Because I intend to make your life miserable for your overprotective, Neanderthal attitude. I'm not helpless, you know. I can take care of myself."

Graham kissed the back of her hand and smiled. "We know, honey. Believe me. But that doesn't mean we don't worry about you."

She leaned over and kissed his cheek. "Apology accepted. Now if you'll excuse me." She stood.

Her brother sat taller. "Where do you think you're going?"

"Home, to cancel my spa date and take a shower. Unless you want me ripening up the air in your stationhouse."

Dell reached for his phone. "Fine. I can't go with you, but Todd can."

Todd? Ugh. She crossed her arms. "No."

Her brother's eyes ballooned. "*No?* You just agreed this was necessary."

"I also just made the point Lynch isn't within five hundred miles of Stardust. I think I'll be safe showering in my own home."

"But Callan isn't your only threat. The Streeters could come after you."

"They haven't in the last seven years. Why would they suddenly target me now?"

"Because Lynch is being released," Graham offered. "Sometimes it takes a catalyst like that to motivate them for revenge.

Shasta looked at Adam, who'd been abnormally quiet. His intent stare knotted her stomach. She toughened her posture. "Does anyone else know Lynch is getting out?"

He shrugged. The small movement reminded her of a rattlesnake shedding its skin. "Doubtful. I only received a call once Callan's lawyer knew I couldn't block his release. I doubt she'd risk telling a lot of people for fear the news would leak and they'd lose the element of surprise."

"In other words I should be fine."

"*Should be* doesn't mean you *will be*," Dell rebutted.

She shook her head. "You're not winning this argument, big brother. I'm going home, alone. But I'll be back in time for you..." She pointed her finger at Dell. "...to buy me lunch. A number four from Hopkins Deli, no mayo and extra pickles." She placed her hand on Graham's shoulder. "Call me when you get to Vegas?"

"Of course." He maneuvered his chair toward the door. "I'll walk you out. My taxi should arrive any time now."

Nodding, she looked over her shoulder at Dell. "Guess I'll see you later."

"Count on that, sis," he grumbled.

She glanced at the district attorney, barely suppressing another shudder. "Adam."

"Shasta."

The way he said her name scurried more icky goosebumps over her skin. She wasted no time escaping the stationhouse with Graham.

The handicap van was indeed waiting for her husband and once he was safely aboard, she waved and watched as it exited the parking lot. Once in the sanctuary of her car, she called Melissa and begged off the planned activity. Her friend sounded disappointed, but accepting. Shasta then inhaled a breath and texted *411* to Mark "Hez" Hernandez.

Hez had been Lynch's best friend since they were kids, and once Lynch went to prison, he became her confidant. But she hadn't had any contact with Hez in over two years. Her cheeks heated at the memory of what drunken mess she'd been that last time...

She shoved the image away and stared at the blank screen. What if Hez had a different number? How would she get in touch with him? She only had a small window of time before needing to be back at the station.

The answer came when her phone buzzed with the message *on my way*.

She tossed her phone in the passenger seat and turned the ignition key, wondering what Hez thought of her contacting him after all this time. Well, that couldn't be helped.

He needed to know Lynch was getting out of prison before it was too late.

Chapter Four

SHIT. SHIT. SHIT.

I can't believe my phone beeped with the message she's just sent the 411 text...the code for her Streeter buddy, Hez, to meet her. I knew I should've killed that bastard when I had the chance. If he lays one finger on her, I'll...

It's been over two years since Shasta met with Hez. Two years of me being stupidly complacent. No doubt the news of Callan's release prompted this rendezvous, that reality only fuels the anger pounding through my blood.

I know marriage to the "invalid" has been hard. She's so young and beautiful, she deserves a husband who can satisfy *all* her needs. But soon enough when she'll get everything that coming to her. She'll get *me*. She just needs to stay patient – and celibate. I'll be supremely disappointed if she doesn't.

I slammed my sedan to a stop, the sound of gravel spewing beneath the tires, but I don't worry about attracting attention because no one's around. I get out and head for the house. I'm so furious, the door key drops from my hand.

Once inside, I march past the sheet-covered furniture and into the back bedroom with the blackout curtains, ignoring the vile memories this place always elicits. I flip on the overhead light then sit at the lone desk and chair. I turn on my laptop and wait impatiently for it to boot up.

Sudden panic grips my chest. How long has it been since I last checked the equipment? The nanny cam in Callan's trailer is most likely still operational, but what about the camouflaged hotspot boosters on the light poles between here and there? What if the windstorm last month jarred the wiring? It'd only take one misalignment to send the signal in the wrong fucking direction.

Holding my breath, I stare at the blackened screen. Then, slowly, the interior of the shitty Winnebago comes into focus. Relief has me almost creaming my pants. Now I just have to wait to see what happens next.

I don't have to wait long as the door bangs open. Shasta walks in, with Hez right behind her.

He pivots her around and into a hug. My head practically explodes.

"It's been a long time, beautiful," he says. "To what do I owe the pleasure?"

Shasta moves away and my blood pressure lessens. "We need to talk."

Hez leans against the kitchen counter. "Okay. What's up?"

She crosses her arms. "Lynch is being released from prison this afternoon."

Jolting upright, Hez's mouth drops open. "No shit?"

"No shit."

"How did that happen?"

"Some fancy lawyer took on his case and got him a new trial." She glances away, her lips pressed together. "Thought you should know."

Hez runs a hand down his face. "Yeah. Thanks."

"Could you please collect my things?" she asks, her voice so quiet I almost don't hear it. "I'd do it myself, but I hafta get back to the stationhouse. I'm under some stupid lockdown."

Hez's eyebrows pop up. "How come?"

"Everyone thinks I'm in danger because Lynch is getting out." She shakes her head. "So will you get my stuff?"

"Of course. Text me a list and I'll put it all in a box. Where should I leave it?"

"Um...out behind the garage at the house. There's a bunch of other junk there so it shouldn't be noticeable if I don't get to it right away."

"I'll take care of it today. The box'll be there in the morning."

She shifted. "Thanks."

Hez moves from the counter. "You're welcome." He pulls her into a loose hug and I grip the desk edges, the tension building behind my eyes again. He releases her and kisses her cheek. "Promise you'll take care of yourself. Okay, beautiful?"

She smiles. "I promise."

I don't relax my posture until the trailer stands empty. Then slowly...ever so slowly...my body unwinds. I take a breath and unclench my grasp on the desk, but I'm far from calm.

If only Dell had died seven years ago when I shot him, Callan wouldn't be getting out of prison. No...he'd be on death row, or better, dead. It's more than what he deserves. What either of them deserve.

God...I hate both of them, but especially Callan. I didn't realize the extent of his corruptive effect on Shasta until it was too late. Until he'd stolen her from me. Stolen my son. Wyatt should have been *mine*. But he's not, and it's because of that fucker.

Now I have to exterminate Callan and her brother all over again – along with the kid...*Callan's* kid.

I know eliminating Wyatt will hurt Shasta, but it can't be helped. All vestiges of that bastard's influence on her life must be eradicated. I'll make it up to her, though. I'll give her more sons.

Better sons.

Long ago, I knew Shasta belonged to me. And no one would keep me from having her, not even her father. That hunting accident ten years ago? Daddy dearest never should have claimed I wasn't good enough for his daughter. Imagine that...*me* not good enough.

When Shasta should have turned to me for comfort and support, she turned to her brother and Callan. I needed to get rid of them. Too bad they didn't have the decency to *die*.

I stare into space. I've allowed myself to become distracted these past few years, building then maintaining my business relationship with Fuentes. I took my eye off of what's truly important...*her*. Maybe it's time to retire. To take her away. Far away.

The more I contemplate this, the more excited I become, and my dick responds in kind. I undo my pants, slip my hand inside and fist my cock.

Yes...

Since Callan's out, the timing could work to my benefit. I made him my patsy before, I can make him one again.

My erection hardens. God...sometimes I'm too brilliant for my own good. I'll tie up the loose ends here in Stardust while ensuring Callan takes the fall. Only this time around, he *will* get the death penalty. As will Shasta's brother and poor, little Wyatt.

The thought of justice finally being served on Callan fills me with schoolboy glee and I pump my hand faster. I close my eyes and picture Shasta kneeling before me, naked. I finger the tip of my dick, imagining I'm tracing it along her lips before I feed it inside her mouth. All the way. Until I touch the back of her throat. Her eyes water as she gazes up at me, adoration written on her face...

Very soon she'll be mine and mine alone.

Once and for all.

Chapter Five

LYNCH MARCHED ACROSS the lower exercise yard, Officer Morgan right at his elbow.

Nearby convicts paused in their workout routines to stare. The weight of their gazes pricked Lynch's skin. He focused on placing one foot in front of the other to keep from tripping. He still couldn't fathom he was actually being released.

Since the visit from Jarvis and Newman three days ago, Lynch half expected to get shanked in the shower. He definitely didn't expect to be making this walk. The only way he figured he'd leave this place would be feet first.

In the control room, the checkout procedure passed in a blur. He stood where told and signed on dotted lines. Garbled words filled his ears. Morgan ushered him through a set of mechanical doors, and Lynch found himself in the building's lobby.

He blinked at the sunshine streaming through the glass of the barless windows. This sunlight seemed different than what it had been just moments ago in the yard. This seemed brighter. Cleaner. Freer.

Morgan pulled open the front door and waited for Lynch to step over the sill.

Seventy feet of dirt lay before Lynch. No Man's Land. He never thought he'd live to see it from this angle.

"Let's go, Callan," Morgan prodded. "Up to the red line."

The red line was at the base of Tower One, and where Lynch stopped. Morgan handed the documents to the tower officer who verified everything one last time.

On the other side of the wire mesh fence, Jarvis and Newman loitered next to a sedan. Newman sported a gray polo shirt and black pants while Jarvis wore a light-colored blouse and khaki slacks with her hair down. Both agents wore sunglasses, but stared in his direction.

Lynch kept his eyes straight, his face devoid of expression. Sweat trickled down his back and beaded on his upper lip. Finally, the immense steel gate rumbled open.

Commanding his legs to move forward, soon the fifteen-foot tall, electrified fence stood behind Lynch. Stars clouded his vision. He hadn't realized he'd been holding his breath – probably since he exited his cell.

He inhaled slowly, savoring his first taste of non-incarcerated air in seven long years.

Free.

The word reverberated through Lynch's head. He was free.

Or was he? The reason behind his release crashed down on him. He had to inform on the Streeters. His crew. His brothers. His gut soured at that thought.

It's like the old saying went...freedom was never free. Seemed like he'd substituted one prison for another, minus the bars.

A car door opened. "Come on," Jarvis said. "We've got a long drive ahead of us."

Lynch grasped the backseat passenger handle and slid into the upholstered seat. A fake pine scent itched his nose. He buckled his seatbelt. Newman sat in front of him with Jarvis behind the wheel.

Newman twisted around to look at him, two flip-style phones in his hand, one black and the other silver. The agent held out the silver. "This is a burner and it doesn't leave your person. It's got GPS so we'll have a fix on you at all times."

Lynch took it. "GPS? As in military tracking shit?"

Newman's mouth kicked up. "As in military tracking shit."

With a shrug, Lynch wormed it into the back pocket of his Levis.

"Jarvis and I also have burners," Newman continued. "The numbers are programmed into your phone. When we call, we'll ask for Darren. If it's not safe to talk just say you've got the wrong number then get back to us within thirty minutes. Do *not*, under *any* circumstances, call anyone but Jarvis or myself on that phone." He handed over the black one. "This one's for general use."

Lynch rolled his eyes. "Two phones? Tracking me? Is this cloak and dagger shit really necessary?" He turned the second phone over in his hand.

"In a word, yes," Jarvis replied. "I've been working to bring down Blackwell and Fuentes's human trafficking operation for over five years. When Jerry...Agent Olsen...got into the Streeters, it looked like the opening we'd been waiting for. But it wasn't, and a good man paid the ultimate price. This time I'm not leaving anything to chance, especially something preventable like our burner phones getting traced."

Lynch chuckled. "Secret spy shit. I suppose the entire FBI's on speed dial too, huh?"

Jarvis and Newman shared a look, but said nothing.

Distrust narrowed Lynch's eyes. "What?"

Jarvis squirmed in her seat. "No one from the Reno office knows anything about this op."

"Why the hell not?"

"Because the last time we got within striking distance of Blackwell and Fuentes, we walked into a trap. We believe they have a person or persons inside the bureau."

Lynch sat forward. "So what happens if things go wrong?"

"They won't," Jarvis asserted. "They can't."

"But what if they *do*?" he persisted. "I've got my mom to consider in all this."

Newman torqued around in his seat again. "If you think you've been compromised, or if there's an emergency of any kind, text 411 to either me or Jarvis."

"Then what?"

"Then we'll deal with the situation," Jarvis replied.

"Deal with the situation?" Lynch repeated. "Christ. Why didn't you tell me this before?"

Newman arched an eyebrow. "Would it have made a difference?"

Lynch sat back and popped his tight neck muscles, directing his gaze out the window. Flyer's murder needed to be avenged, so no, it wouldn't have made any difference. "Just the three of us doing this thing? Great."

"I said no one local knows anything," Jarvis said. "But both Portland and Sacramento offices have been fully briefed and will be ready to move at a moment's notice should there be any trouble. We'll just have to...improvise until they arrive."

Lynch shook his head. "Whatever. When will we get to Stardust?"

"About six."

Newman glanced at Lynch over his shoulder. "You should maybe call your mom. She doesn't know you're out."

Lynch snapped his gaze to the agent. "You didn't tell her?"

"We couldn't chance the news leaking," Jarvis responded. "It might have jeopardized your release. I did, however, call DA Murphy this morning, but only because I'm required to notify the local authorities."

"DA Murphy? You mean Adam Murphy? How long's he been DA?"

"Since about six or seven years ago when Graham Dupree got into a car accident and ended up paralyzed from the waist down."

"No shit?"

"No shit," Newman replied. "Because he's permanently confined to a wheelchair, Dupree didn't think he could continue as the district attorney. Murphy stepped in and has been the DA ever since."

"Huh..." Lynch again stared out the window, not sure how he felt about Dupree being paralyzed. Maybe he should revel in the justice that the man who prosecuted him and sent him to prison now had to deal with his own personal imprisonment. One with wheels. But the best Lynch would muster was mild interest.

"And speaking of Dupree..."

Lynch looked at Jarvis's reflection in the rearview mirror. Even wearing sunglasses, he felt her sharp gaze.

"I want to make something perfectly clear, Callan. Your job is to find out who Blackwell is and help nail Fuentes."

Her terse tone flared his anger. "I know my job."

"See that you don't forget it." Her mouth stretched into a thin line. "You are *not* to go rogue and try to exact revenge on Dupree."

Lynch narrowed his eyes. "Relax, counselor. The former DA has nothing to fear from me."

"Or his family," she added. "You're to leave his family alone as well."

He redirected his stare out his window. "Or his family...not that I remember Dupree having any family."

"Well, he does. He married the sheriff's sister."

Lynch's insides went cold and he whipped his gaze back around.

"Shasta?"

Jarvis's posture snapped to attention. "You know her?"

Lynch schooled his expression. In the last seven years, he learned not to react to news, whether good or bad. If an inmate discovered a weakness, the consequences could be deadly. "I know *of* her. Everyone in Stardust does. She's an Albright after all." He hitched his shoulder. "I'm just surprised she married Dupree. That guy's old enough to be her father." He flipped opened his phone. "Now, if you don't mind, I'd like to call my mom."

He punched in the memorized number, but his thoughts were on Shasta.

She was married to Graham Dupree, a man in a wheelchair.

He didn't begrudge her finding someone to share her life with, and he certainly never expected her to wait for him because he was never supposed to get out of prison, but Graham Dupree? That didn't fit with the carefree spirit he once knew.

The ringing of his mom's phone yanked his thoughts from his former girlfriend. It rang four times before she answered.

"Yeah?"

The prick of tears burned his eyes at the husky timbre of her voice. Up to now, he hadn't truly believed he'd ever see her again. He coughed. "Ah...hi Mom."

A long silence met his salutation.

"Lynch?"

Her voice sounded so tiny, he could barely hear it.

"Yeah...Ma. It's me."

"Oh my God...*Lynch?*"

Her joyful shriek echoed in his head as the corners of his mouth lifted. "How ya doin'?"

"How am I doing?" Her tone changed dramatically. She no longer sounded happy, but pissed. "What the fuck kind of question is that? Why the hell are you calling me? Oh my God...are you in trouble? Hurt? What's going on?"

"It's okay, Ma. Really. I'm...uh...out."

"Out? What do you mean you're out? Out of where?"

"Prison."

Another pregnant pause. "*What* did you do?" she hissed. "Did you escape? Are you on the run?"

He laughed. "No, Ma. I didn't escape."

"Then what the hell is going on?"

"It's kinda a long story–"

"Good thing I've got lots of time for you to explain it," she shot back.

Lynch blew out a breath. "Okay, okay. I had a visit from a lawyer this week–"

"Lawyer? What lawyer? Since when do you have a lawyer?"

He grinned wider at her rapid-fire questions. "Do you want me to explain or not?"

"Fine," she huffed. "Explain."

"Anyway she came to see me and–"

"She? This lawyer's a woman?"

"Yeah." He stared at Jarvis's semi profile. "She's a woman." The agent pursed her lips. "And she petitioned for a new trial. I'm out until then."

"Really, honey?"

He swallowed the sudden thickness in his throat. "Really."

"Oh my God..." She wept into the phone.

Lynch stared hard at the back of Newman's seat to keep from breaking down too.

His mom sniffled loudly. "So you're coming home?"

"Yeah. We should be pulling in about six."

"Who's driving you?"

"My, uh..." He coughed. "Lawyer."

"You say you'll be home around six?"

"Give or take."

"Then I'm calling *everyone*. We're gonna have one hellraising, welcome-home party for you!"

"Ma, that's not necessary–"

"The hell it's not. My baby boy's coming home. If that isn't cause for a celebration, I don't know what is." Paper rustled on the line. She had to be making one of her famous lists. "Bring your lawyer, honey. I want to thank the person responsible for getting you out."

"I really don't want–"

"You never should've been convicted." Anger dripped from her words. "Fucking small town with its fucking small-minded people.

You were *innocent*. Fucking bastards railroaded you."

The conviction in her voice warmed his chest. "Thanks, Ma."

"So, your lady lawyer. Is she pretty?"

His mom dragged out *pretty* so it sounded like two words instead of one. Jarvis, pretty? No. Certainly good looking though. For a fed. Lynch gazed out the passenger window to the looming hills bordering both sides of the highway. "Guess some might think so."

"And would you be one who thinks so?"

He shook his head with a subdued chuckle. Leave it to his mom to tease him. The line suddenly crackled then went dead. "Hey, Ma...you there? Hello?"

"Lynch? Honey? Can you hear me?"

"Yeah, but I'm about to lose the signal so I guess I should hang up." He didn't want to. He wanted to keep talking to her all the way to Stardust just to hear her voice. Emotions pressed against his ribcage. God...he'd missed her. "I'll, uh, see you in a little while, okay?"

Another sob echoed in his ear. "Okay, honey. See you soon. I love you, Lynch."

"I love..." He cleared his throat. "Love you too, Mom."

He disconnected the call then pressed his thumb and forefinger to his eyes with a shaky breath.

"Hey." Using the rearview mirror, Jarvis stared at him. "You okay?"

Lynch straightened with a nod. "Fine. My mom's having a party tonight and wants you to come."

"That's nice of her," Newman said, "but we'll pass."

A smile played at Lynch's mouth. "A word to the wise, Agent Newman. It's not a good idea to tell my mother no. That has a tendency to piss her off. And that's something you really don't want to do." He settled into his seat and closed his eyes. "Wake me when we get there."

~*~

Five hours later, Lynch woke with a king-sized kink in his neck. Despite the pain, he couldn't remember sleeping so well or so hard while sitting upright. Of course not having to keep one eye open like he did in prison helped. He yawned loudly.

Newman glanced over his shoulder. "Good, you're awake. We're coming to Stardust city limits."

Lynch stared at the unfamiliar scenery surrounded by the all-too-familiar Sierra Mountains. "Is this Route 314?"

"Yes," Jarvis replied.

"When it go from two lanes to four?"

She smirked. "When you were in prison."

They passed the sign welcoming people to Stardust, Nevada, population ten thousand and twelve.

Ten thousand? When Lynch went inside, barely four thousand people lived here. Gas stations and fast food places dotted the side of the road. A subdivision, with expensive looking houses, occupied the field where he and his buddies used to play baseball. And instead of the stand of old-growth oak trees, a huge industrial park stretched out almost to the base of the nearest mountain. He remembered carving his and Shasta's initials in one massive trunk...

Everything had changed. The reality of all he'd missed hit him hard. But what the hell did he expect? For Stardust to remain in a time warp where nothing changed? He certainly hadn't.

A very different person rode into Stardust than who left seven years ago. A smarter person, for sure, and a more cautious one.

And a narc.

The car's GPS navigated them through Stardust. Soon, the neighborhoods became more recognizable. Lynch's pulse increased and his gut contracted when Jarvis made the final turn onto his mom's street.

Cars and Harleys lined the narrow avenue, with a conspicuous spot vacant right in front of the white and beige, single-story, clapboard house. Jarvis eased into the space and killed the engine.

Heavy metal music and raucous laughter spilled from the residence. At least this looked, and sounded, the same. Lynch climbed out, barely noticing his stiff muscles from hours of riding in a car. He gazed at his childhood home. Jarvis and Newman joined him.

Jarvis nudged his shoulder. "Remember to stick to the story about your release. No one can suspect anything else. Got it?"

"Got it."

Lynch licked his suddenly dry lips and led the way up the tiered front walk. The evening breeze raised the hairs on his skin. His heart thumped in time to the bass guitar. A fluttery sensation filled his stomach when he gripped the doorknob and twisted.

Half a dozen older versions of Streeter members, some with old ladies he remembered, some he didn't, stared at him from beneath a *Welcome Home* banner that stretched across the living room wall. Someone switched off the stereo. The resulting silence crashed down on Lynch.

Then a swarm descended on him.

Amid whoops and cheers, arms clasped him while hands slapped his back. Smiling and nodding, he accepted the boisterous welcomes when a shriek all but shattered his eardrums.

"Lynch!" A petite woman with short, frosted brown hair rushed forward and launched herself at him, nearly strangling him in the process. "You're home...oh thank God. Thank God. Thank God. Thank God."

He returned his mother's hug as the faint fragrance of her citrusy perfume filled his senses. He buried his face in her shoulder, blinking furiously at the sting in his eyes. His chest squeezed. When had she had gotten so small?

She pulled back and took firm possession of his hand. Tears ran down her cheeks as her soft blue eyes searched his face, like she couldn't believe he was there. He couldn't believe it either. Her gaze slipped to Jarvis. He'd forgotten the agent stood beside him.

He moved to the side. "Uh, Mom, this is my...attorney."

Jarvis extended her hand. "Emma Jarvis. It's a pleasure to meet you Mrs. Callan."

His mother shook it. "I've never been a Mrs., so call me Edie."

Jarvis smiled. "All right...Edie. And this is my associate," she indicted Newman who filled the doorway, "Sam Newman."

The agent nodded. "Ma'am."

Edie peered down her nose at him. Tough to do when you're five foot three and staring up at a man six foot plus, but Lynch's mom managed it just fine.

She huffed. "I'm no more a ma'am than I am a Mrs." She gave his "attorney" an appraising perusal. "You don't look like a stuffy lawyer type."

Jarvis laughed, an inviting tinkle which didn't sound the least bit forced. "I assure you I am a lawyer, Edie, though hopefully not the stuffy type. And Sam's a private investigator who'll help ferret out the truth about your son's case."

Lynch fought to keep his mouth from dropping open at the smoothness with which Jarvis lied.

"Good." His mother nodded once. "I'm glad *someone* finally realized my son's innocent of those charges." She turned a critical eye to Lynch. "Did they feed you in the last seven years?" Her palms rested on either side of his waist. "Look at this...you're no bigger around than a rail."

With a grimace, he shooed her hands away. "Ma," he protested. "Don't fuss."

"Don't fuss?" She planted her fists on her hips. "Don't fuss? I'm your mother, Lynch Abraham Callan. I'll fuss any time I please."

"Ah listen to the boy, Edie," a voice boomed. "And don't fuss."

Lynch would know the owner of that voice anywhere. He turned, and Rolo Pruett, the barrel-chested president of the Streeters, strode from the kitchen. Always a stout man, the seams of Rolo's cut jacket were stretched tighter than usual across his increased girth.

With his easy smile, big belly, white bushy beard and hairline which reached the top of his head, Rolo resembled a kindly Santa Claus. But anyone who underestimated him would regret that fatal mistake because under the loveable façade beat the heart of a ruthless gang leader.

Rolo enclosed Lynch in a manly bear hug. "Welcome home, brother," he whispered.

More tears gathered in Lynch's eyes, but he collected his wits and smacked the other man's back then stepped away.

Rolo offered his hand to Jarvis. "Rolo Pruett."

Jarvis's smile remained frozen as she shook it. "Emma Jarvis. And Sam Newman."

After shaking Newman's hand, Rolo draped his arm around Lynch's shoulders. "We can't thank you enough for bringing our boy home. There's a keg out back and burgers on the grill. We'd be honored to have you stay for dinner."

"Thank you," Jarvis said, "but it's been a long day and–"

"Have you eaten?" Edie asked.

"No, however–"

"It's settled." His mom commandeered Jarvis and Newman's

wrists. "You're staying." She marched them toward the kitchen. "This is a party, goddamn it. So we're gonna have *fun*."

Lynch smiled. Those poor agents...they never saw his mom coming. He turned to Rolo, but caught a glimpse of unruly, blond dreadlocks and scruffy beard. The lump in his throat increased as his composure again threatened to crack.

Hez lingered in the hallway.

Rolo followed his gaze and moved back. Hez came forward.

Always taller and thicker than Lynch, Hez looked even more so now. He grinned that lopsided grin of his and playfully punched Lynch's arm. "How's it going? Gotten laid lately?"

Lynch laughed and a tear ran down his cheek. "More often than you." He swiped a hand across his eyes with a sniffle. "Jesus, you're uglier than I remember."

Hez's face crumpled, and he clutched Lynch in a fierce hug. "God...it's so good to see you, man," he croaked.

"You too, brother," Lynch mumbled into his shoulder. "You too."

Hez eased away and brushed his thumbs across Lynch's wet cheeks. "Fuck...I need a beer."

Lynch choked out a half chuckle, half sob. "I need a whole fucking keg."

Rolo slung an arm over each of their shoulders. "Let's go take care of that." He ushered them through the kitchen and into the backyard.

An extra-long table, surrounded with a mishmash of lawn chairs and covered with a red and white checkered tablecloth, dominated the grass while a keg sat on the edge of the patio. The charred aroma of cooking meat saturated the air, whetting Lynch's appetite. Charlotte and Dawn, two old ladies who'd been with the Streeters since before he was born, manned the barbeques. Past the "ques" were card tables laden with every salad and side dish known to man.

And desserts. Good God, the desserts.

His mom hadn't relinquished control of either Jarvis or Newman and they patiently stood by as she introduced them to everyone. A small smile touched his lips. He'd given the agents fair warning his mom didn't take no for an answer.

Another horde of well-wishers swamped Lynch, with more embraces and a few cheek kisses. Rolo filled plastic cups from the tap. He handed one to Lynch and Hez then lifted his own in the air. "A toast!" the president bellowed.

Other cups rose.

Rolo looked at Lynch. "To coming home."

A chorus of "coming home" echoed. Lynch drained his glass in two gulps. God, he'd forgotten how good beer tasted. Since he hadn't eaten since lunch, the alcohol hit his system with a splash. He wiped the foam off his lip and held his empty out to Rolo. Chuckling, the president poured him another.

Lynch looked around the yard. It looked...smaller somehow. Smaller and different. Yet the same. Just like Stardust.

He coughed the heaviness from his throat. "Where's Flyer?"

It killed him to ask, knowing the answer, but to not question the absence of the VP would cause suspicion. And Jarvis instructed him to act normally.

Rolo's cheerful bearing dipped. He handed a fresh beer to Lynch. "Flyer...he, ah...left us, son."

"Left? Left to go where?"

Rolo rubbed the side of his nose. "He needed to go...ah...to Idaho to visit his pops."

"Or so he claimed." Bitterness rang in Hez's voice.

Lynch cocked his head. "I don't understand. What happened?"

Hez turned away, his mouth in a tight line, and swallowed more beer. Lynch looked at Rolo.

The president blew out a breath. "It was maybe a month after Flyer left when he sent a text to your ma. Said he'd been seeing someone else. For months. That they went to Idaho together and he...wasn't coming back."

Lynch pretended outrage. "What the fuck?"

"That's right," Hez spat out. "A goddamn Dear John text...you believe that shit? Fucking bastard. It tore your momma up bad, man. Real bad."

"Why that lying, cheating...fucker." Lynch hoped he'd nailed the right tone of indignation. "When the fuck was this?"

"Last Halloween," Rolo responded.

With a disgusted grunt, Lynch drank his beer, covertly peering at the president over the rim. Rolo sounded...sad. Not enraged like he should if a member actually *had* walked out on the Streeters. You didn't get to just walk away. Not without blood. Blood in, blood out. That's the motto. If you wanted to leave, you had to pay a price. A very stiff price. One Lynch never could've paid...

"You went after Flyer?" he asked.

"Hell yes," Hez snapped. "Junkyard and Tre went after him."

"Junkyard and Tre?"

"Junkyard Taylor and Tre Olsen," Hez answered. "Good guys, especially Tre. He got patched in a few years back. He rolled his—"

"Enough," Rolo said, authority edged his voice. "Edie will kick all our asses if she hears us talking about this. *This is a party*, goddamn it." He topped off the cups. "There'll be time enough later to catch up on all the club shit."

Lynch eyed the president. First he wasn't infuriated by Flyer's apparent desertion of the club and his mom, and now he didn't want to discuss it? Rather than press the point, he decided to let it drop. For now.

He turned and two men he didn't recognize, but both wearing Streeter cuts, sauntered up. A red haze blanketed his vision. The shorter of the two sported the VP patch on his jacket.

"So you're the prodigal son who's come home, eh?" the short one said with a snicker. "Name's Junkyard Taylor. This here's Bowyer." He held out his hand. "Congrats on getting out."

Lynch's scalp tingled like the first time he walked into the prison shower. Tats covered Junkyard and Bowyer's exposed forearms and necks. Instinct said they were not to be trusted. Were these two somehow involved in Flyer's death?

Rather than shake hands, Lynch drained his glass in a gulp then burped. Loudly.

The new VP lowered his arm, his gaze narrowing. "You got a problem, boy?"

Though the same height, Junkyard had a wiry build and didn't appear as muscular as Lynch. With gray streaking his reddish ponytail, Lynch doubted he'd have trouble taking him. By contrast, Bowyer was big and bald and kinda dumb looking. *He* could be trouble.

Lynch rolled his shoulders with a lazy shrug. "No...just want to enjoy the party with my brothers."

Junkyard cocked his head. "You don't think I'm your brother?"

Lynch handed his empty cup to Hez. "Grab me another, will ya, brother?"

"Uh...sure..." But Hez didn't move from Lynch's side.

Junkyard canted forward. "I'm waiting for an answer, boy. Don't you think we're brothers?"

"How should I know?" Lynch answered. "Just met you two seconds ago. You could be a lying, cheating, no-good motherfucker as far as I know."

A twitch flickered at the corner of Junkyard's eye. "Someone should teach you manners."

Lynch smiled a toothy grin. "And who'd do that? You?"

A slow nasty smile spread across the VP's face. "No. Him."

Junkyard stepped back as Bowyer advanced. Lynch tensed, ready for a charge, his hands balled into fists.

Rolo moved in front of Lynch. "Enough of this shit. Go cool off, Junkyard." He grabbed the back of Lynch's shirt. "You, come with me." He yanked Lynch to a vacant corner of the yard then released him. Hez trailed behind.

"What the fuck is wrong with you?" the president demanded.

Lynch adjusted his shirt. "Nuthin'."

"Like hell nuthin'," Rolo snapped. "You know better than to diss club officers."

"But *I* don't know Junkyard."

"But *I* do. Him and Bowyer." Rolo crossed his arms over his barrel chest. "Since when is my vouch not good enough for you?"

With a silent curse, Lynch blew out a breath. His personal feelings about Flyer, mixed with the beer, were making him stupid. And careless. He forced his body to unwind before meeting Rolo's gaze. "Sorry. It's just everything's changed. This town. Different Streeter members. A new VP. And I can't believe Flyer would leave like that. Leave my mom. They'd been together since I was in first grade. For him to throw away almost twenty-five years..."

Rolo's harsh expression softened and he dropped his arms. "I know it's tough, but things change, brother. People change. Even after all those years."

Lynch stared at the ground. "I suppose you're right."

"Of course I am." Rolo clapped him on the back. "Now if you're done being an asshole, we've got a little something to show you."

Curious, Lynch walked between Rolo and Hez to the detached garage he and Flyer converted into a bedroom for his sixteenth birthday. All his Streeter brothers, minus Junkyard and Bowyer – he doubted he'd ever think of those two as brothers – milled about on the cracked driveway, smiling and winking. Then everyone moved aside to expose an achingly familiar Softail Custom Harley. Lynch stopped dead in his shoes.

"We got her out of storage as soon as Edie said you were coming home," Mick volunteered, holding out the key. "It took most of the day, but me and Picket got her cleaned and tuned up."

Lynch took the key, swung a leg over the scooped, padded seat and trailed his fingertips along the handlebars. Nobody could nurse a long-neglected Harley back to healthy better than Mick. The chrome gleamed like it had been polished for hours. Not a single smudge was anywhere to be seen. "Great job, brother." He held his hand out to Mick. "Thank you."

"Well," Rolo urged. "Don't just sit there. Start her up."

Lynch inserted the key, activated the fuel petcock then pulled the choke out all the way. After turning the ignition key, he gently compressed the clutch lever and pressed the start button. The engine purred to life.

Everyone whooped and hollered as Lynch revved the motor, not caring his grin touched his ears. God...he wanted to hit the open road and ride. Ride far and fast. Feel the wind rush past his face and see nothing but open space. But Rolo motioned for him to cut the engine. Reluctantly, he complied and climbed off the bike.

Facing Rolo, what the president held in his hands had emotions strangling Lynch.

His cut.

Holy Jesus Christ.

Sudden clarity centered his mind and Lynch stiffened his spine as Rolo helped him slip on the jacket. He stroked his palms down the leather front. It felt like coming home.

Really coming home. Because he *was* home.

Moisture pressed at his eyes, but this time the beer had weakened his defenses, making him helpless against the onslaught of emotions. With a choked sob, he wrapped his arms around Rolo. Next came Hez who hugged Lynch tightly, his own shoulders quaking amidst the sniffles of the men surrounding them.

After Hez came Mick, then Grunge, then the other Streeter brothers. Lynch wept harder with each embrace. He loved this crew, this family, every single motley one of them. And he was dying inside because as much as he loved them, he had to betray them. For their own good.

Rolo wiped his nose. "All right...enough of this sappy shit. Let's get drunk."

Lynch nodded. "Sounds like a plan."

The group made its way to the keg when Jarvis interceded. "Excuse me. Mind if I have a word with my client?" Though the agent smiled, she looked far from happy.

Once alone, she pivoted so Lynch's back was to the yard. "Are you trying to screw this thing up before you even get started?" she hissed in a low voice.

Lynch narrowed his eyes. "What the hell you talking about?"

"I'm talking about your little show with that guy."

"Hey." Lynch jabbed his finger. "He's wearing Flyer's patch."

"I don't give a good goddamn," Jarvis fired back. "*No* one can suspect *any*thing, you understand me? Otherwise you could get yourself killed, along with me and Newman."

"Yeah, okay."

Jarvis scowled. "I mean it, Callan. If you want justice for Flyer, and not get dead, stick to the goddamn plan. Got it?"

"I got it," he ground out.

"Good. Newman and I are leaving. We'll give you the weekend to settle in and get the lay of the land. But time is short, so the sooner you bring us something actionable, the better. For everyone."

The agent strode to where Newman waited for her. Lynch mockingly saluted his "lawyer" then turned to see Rolo and Junkyard on the far side of the yard, away from everyone. The president flexed and rubbed his hands...his tell when the conversation wasn't to his liking. Lynch would give just about anything to know what they were talking about...

"Hey."

Lynch spun around. Hez stood there, two fresh beers in his hands.

His friend handed him a cup. "Everything okay? You seem a million miles away."

"Yeah...everything's just peachy." Lynch took a healthy swallow of beer, his gaze back on Rolo and Junkyard. "What can you tell me about our new VP?"

"Junkyard's a decent enough guy. Smart and dependable. Watch out for Bowyer, though. That motherfucker's crazy, especially with a knife. I saw him skin a live rabbit in less than a minute. He's got mad skills. Deadly mad skills."

"I'll keep that in mind. Where they from?"

"They ran with a crew up in Vancouver, Washington."

"How long they been in the club?"

Hez gave him a questioning look. "About five years. What's with all the questions?"

Lynch shrugged and loosened his stance. "Nuthin'. Just curious."

"You should know, Junkyard stepped up big when Flyer split."

Yeah, but was he responsible for Flyer's murder?

Lynch made a mental note to tell Jarvis about Mr. Junkyard Taylor. The feds had the resources to dig into the new VP's background.

Hez took Lynch's beer and set both cups on the ground. "Okay...time for my welcome home present." He pulled a nine-millimeter Glock from his waistband and held it out. "I kept her cleaned and oiled." He grinned. "I assume you're not supposed to carry, but..."

Lynch took the gift with a huge grin. "Yeah, fuck that." The pistol grip fit his palm perfectly...like having back a missing part of his arm.

He turned, pointed the barrel into the darkened corner of the yard and squinted down the sight. He wanted nothing more than to squeeze the trigger. Pop off a couple of rounds, if not the whole damn clip, but knew he couldn't. He lowered the weapon and slid it into his waistband. The weight at his lower back gave him comfort. He pulled Hez into a quick hug. "Thanks for keeping her safe, man."

"Anytime, bro." Hez eased away and pulled a joint and lighter from his pocket. "Time to get down to some serious celebrating." He lit the thin cigarette, inhaled then handed it to Lynch.

Lynch smiled. "Damn straight." He drew in a deep pull, but his lungs protested the invasion of smoke after so many years without.

He doubled over, coughing hard.

Hez thumped his back with a laugh. "You okay?"

Lynch straightened with his own chuckle. "Yeah." He gave Hez the doobie. "Shit...that's embarrassing."

"It's like riding and fucking, man. You might not have done it in a while, but it'll come back to you."

"Food's ready!" Charlotte announced to appreciative applause.

"Bout damn time." Hez threw his arm around Lynch's shoulders. "C'mon, brother. Let's eat."

His mouth watering, Lynch piled his plate high with more food than he'd probably eaten in the entire past month, then he and Hez sat at the table with his mom.

Rolo and Junkyard were still in conversation. The president leaned close to Junkyard, his finger in the VP's chest. Junkyard said something. Then all hostility leaked from Rolo's body. He gave a docile nod. Junkyard signaled to Bowyer and the two strode from the yard with cocky swaggers.

If Lynch hadn't seen it with his own eyes, he never would've believed anyone capable of making Rolo back down. But Junkyard had.

Rolo headed for the food line. When he saw Lynch watching him, he pasted on a wide smile. But it didn't fool Lynch. Something was seriously not right with the Streeters. And he'd bet the next twenty years of his life the trouble centered around Junkyard.

A few minutes later, Rolo took a seat next to Edie.

Lynch made a show of looking around. "Junkyard ain't staying?"

"Nah. He and Bowyer got business." Rolo picked up his burger.

"What kind of business?"

Rolo's gaze drilled him. "*Club* business."

"Thought you were gonna catch me up on the *club* business."

"Not tonight, son."

"Why not? I'm anxious to get back to things."

The big man sighed. "Because it's gonna take more than thirty seconds to fill you in on the last seven years."

"Tomorrow then."

Rolo shook his head. "Gonna be outta town until Tuesday. Now shut up and eat."

Lynch wanted to press the issue, but reluctantly, he dug into his meal instead. And soon he forgot everything except the explosion of flavor in his mouth.

Good God...had food ever tasted this good? He didn't think so, but it wasn't long before his belly wouldn't accept another bite.

His mother frowned at his half-empty plate. "Is that all you're eating? Didn't you like it?"

"Everything was great, Ma. Better than great. Really. Just full."

She opened her mouth, but Rolo cut her off. "Now what'd I say about fussing at him, Edie? The boy's been on a prison diet. It's gonna take time for his stomach to catch up to his eyeballs." He pulled a joint from his breast pocket. "'Sides, I bet he's leaving room for dessert." He lit the doobie then passed it to Lynch.

When he hesitated, Hez elbowed him. "Like riding and fucking."

This time Lynch didn't take as deep a drag and was able to hold the smoke in with a minimum of coughing. He gave the reefer to his mom who, after her toke, handed it to Hez. By the time the dope made it several times around, his body felt light and floaty. His mom cleared the plates and headed into the house. He looked at Rolo, nudging his head in her direction. "She okay?"

Rolo folded his arms on the table. "As good as can be expected I suppose. Hez is right. Flyer's leaving ripped her up good. But she's a tough old broad. She'll be fine." He leaned back in his chair with a wink. "So...you ready for dessert? Hez, go fetch the dessert."

"With pleasure." Grinning a shit-eating grin, Hez stood and walked to a darkened corner of the yard.

Lynch patted his belly. "I couldn't eat another thing."

"Oh, I think you'll make room." Rolo wagged his eyebrows, staring at something behind Lynch.

Confused, Lynch turned. Hez escorted two attractive, and similar-looking blondes, one on each arm toward him. Catcalls and whistles echoed in the air.

The girls wore hip-hugging jeans and midriff tops that nearly popped with their surgically enhanced tits. They were all smiles, and they were smiling right at him. He looked at Rolo who tipped his cup in salute.

The realization of the situation sent a rush of blood to Lynch's dick. All thoughts of Junkyard sped from his brain. Even Flyer became a ghostly memory as his jeans shrank two sizes.

Oh fuck yeah!

"In case you didn't notice, they're twins," Hez stated. He nodded to the girl on his left arm. "This one's Tamara and this one's Tabitha. They work at the Comstock Whorehouse." He winked. "Just like riding, right bro?"

Tamara and Tabitha stood on either side of Lynch, their voluptuous tits right at eye level. Their hands stroked his upper back and chest. His body tightened painfully.

Rolo jostled his shoulder. "Well, say something."

Lynch licked his dry lips. "Um...thanks?"

Everyone laughed.

"The garage is fully stocked," Rolo explained. "Clean sheets on the bed, food and beer in the fridge. And plenty of rubbers," he added with a lecherous grin to the twins.

Lynch stood. He wanted to act cool, like having two gorgeous hookers dropped into his lap happened every day. Truth was, his legs shook and his heart raced. And his cock felt ready to burst. He feared he'd blow his wad right then and there. He crooked his elbows to Tamara and Tabitha. "Ladies."

To thunderous applause and cheers, Lynch guided the girls into the single room apartment and the outside noise dimmed. The bedside light shed a warm glow over the room. Next to the lamp sat a bowl of foil packets. One girl turned down the sheets while the other took his hand and led him to the bed. She eased off his cut.

"So which one are you?" He placed his Glock on the nightstand. "Tamara or Tabitha?"

She paused in tugging his t-shirt from his waistband to look up. "Does it matter?"

One side of his mouth lifted. "No."

"Didn't think so."

His shirt dispatched, both girls then went to work on the buttons of his fly. His jeans were shoved to his knees, along with his boxers, and his engorged dick sprang free.

"Ohhh," one of them cooed. "Nice."

"Uh, huh," the other concurred, then her tongue teased his tip.

Small but determined hands pushed him onto the mattress. His shoes and socks were removed and his jeans shucked from his legs. He stretched out with his back against the headboard, one arm tucked behind his head with the other fisted around his cock, and watched the twins slowly disrobe.

Actually they disrobed each other. Maybe he should've been weirded out because they were sisters and caressing each other's tits struck him as borderline not okay. But with the beer and dope in his system, plus the adrenaline rush of today, Lynch would've been fine with them strapping on dildos and fucking each other's asses.

After the twins were naked – god*damn* they were smoking hot – they crawled onto the bed with him, one on either side of him. They started by kissing and nipping his hipbones, torturously making their way toward his aching package. Once there, they alternated between licking his dick and stroking it. With four hands and two tongues, he would've thought they'd get in each other's way, but they seemed well versed in teamwork.

One knelt between his parted legs and pillowed his dick with her boobs. Holy shit. It was like having his cock surrounded by a cloud. A soft, downy, perfect cloud.

The other worked up his torso. Her tongue swirled in his bellybutton before she kissed her way to his chest. She bit lightly on his nipple. She nibbled on his neck just below his ear. Goosebumps chased across his scalp. Straddling his lap, she thrust her breasts in his face.

He palmed one boob while twirling his tongue around the other pert nipple. Delicate fingers threaded through his hair with a moan. He sucked the tit deep into his mouth. Moist heat swallowed his cock, and his vision blurred.

The girl on top bounced and jiggled as the girl on the bottom deep-throated him.

Whatever control Lynch held over his body snapped. He came with a shout and torrent of cum. But he came too quickly. He wanted to savor this moment. Prolong it. Not come like a high school freshman during his first trip to a whorehouse.

Top girl climbed off him and he slithered to a prone position, his eyelids suddenly heavy. "Sorry," he muttered.

"No worries, lover. We'll be here when you wake up."

Chapter Six

AND THEY WERE. For two whole damn days, Lynch did nothing but sleep and fuck. Occasionally he ate, but not that much. His need for sleep and pussy seemed insatiable.

In prison, sleep was as prized a commodity as privacy, and just as impossible to get. You learned fast not to fall into a deep sleep around a bunch of inmates. Made for a short life.

As for pussy, you also learned to make do with what you had available while incarcerated. Or worse, learned to have someone make do with you.

On Monday morning, the third official day of his freedom, brightness against his closed eyelids forced Lynch from slumber. He cracked one eye. Sunlight streamed through the small, rectangular windows of the old pull-up garage door and across his face. The smell of cum and sweat hung the stale air. His dick pulsed with need, ready for action. He groped for a handful of ass or tit, but found nothing but empty bed next to him.

With a groan, he sat up, blinking to clear his vision. Both Tamara and Tabitha were gone. He squinted at the clock radio on the dresser across the room.

8:17 am.

A sudden and loud rattling turned his attention to the nightstand, and the cell phone on top. He leaned over to grab it. Someone at some point had been smart enough to plug it in to charge. The small screen lit up an unknown number.

Jarvis and/or Newman.

He answered.

"Is Darren there?"

He stretched out on the rumpled sheets. "All clear, counselor."

"Where the hell have you been?"

He frowned at her snappish question. "Where does the GPS on

this phone say I've been? Thought you knew where I'd be at all times."

"Don't get smart, Callan. You're not very good at it. I know you've been at your mom's. I also know you were instructed to answer whenever we call. I've been trying to get in touch with you since Saturday morning."

Lynch worked to rein in his temper. "You also said I could take the weekend."

She blew out a breath. "I had no idea if you were dead or what."

"Is that concern I hear in your voice?"

She snorted. "Hardly concern for *you*, Callan. My only concern is this mission. Speaking of which, what have you discovered about Blackwell?"

His turn to scoff. "What the hell do you expect me to do? Cop a squat and shit out information on this guy?"

"If necessary, that's *exactly* what I expect." Her tone held a steely edge.

"Sorry for ya, counselor." Sarcasm laced his words. "Things don't work that way."

"You better make them work otherwise you, along with all your biker buddies *and your mother,* will go to prison. Understand?"

Rubbing his eyes, Lynch bit back a scathing retort. He understood the stakes just fine...his freedom, and the freedom of everyone he cared about. "Look, I asked questions at the party and that raised eyebrows. You said not to do that, right?"

She sighed. "I know." She suddenly sounded very tired. "It's just two fourteen-year-old girls from Reno were reported missing."

Lynch sat taller. "When?"

"Friday night. They were walking home from a neighborhood market. Witnesses reported seeing a dark colored van cruising the area. No license plate."

"What time?"

"Around ten. Why?"

"Could be nothing, but Rolo had an intense conversation with Junkyard Taylor after you and Newman left, and Rolo definitely didn't seem happy about the outcome." Rustling filled his ear, like Jarvis jostled her phone.

"Who's Junkyard Taylor?"

"The new Streeter VP."

"The guy you had words with at the party?"

"Yeah. Him and his goon, Bowyer, came down from Vancouver, Washington about five years ago. Right about the time all those girls started missing. Like I said, it might be just a coincidence."

"I don't believe in coincidences."

Neither did Lynch. "Then Junkyard and Bowyer split."

"To go where?"

"Dunno, but Rolo said it had to do with club business."

"What else do you know?"

"That's it. I'm headed to the MC this afternoon to see what I can dig up."

"Good. I'll do the same on this end. We'll touch base later tonight. Oh, and you'd better answer my calls from now on."

He rolled his eyes. "Whatever you say, counselor."

The line went dead. Lynch laid in bed for another few minutes, taking in the reality of actually being out of prison. Up to this point, he hadn't had the chance to absorb his circumstances.

He was home, with his mom and his crew, but things were different. Christ, things were *hell-a* different. Like the fucked-up situation with the missing girls. And the more messed up shit with Flyer...

A knot formed in Lynch's throat at the thought of never seeing Flyer again. He shouldn't be dead. He should be in the house right now, arguing with his mom about stupid old man, old lady shit. But he wasn't.

And if it hadn't been for the dumb luck of some fisherman, the FBI never would have contacted Lynch. And he never would've learned about Flyer or his supposed "leaving" the Streeters.

No brother deserved to end up in Pyramid Lake, especially Flyer. He'd been a good man. A good brother. A good...father. Lynch blinked at the burn in his eyes.

In a brisk move, he scrubbed his hand over his face, his sorrow morphing into anger, then into rage. He'd ferret out the truth behind Flyer's murder, if it was the last thing he did. He owed the man that much. And if Lynch found out Junkyard or Bowyer, or even Rolo, had anything to do with Flyer's death...well...God help them. Because

Lynch sure as hell wouldn't.

He stood and padded into the small bathroom to pee. After the sex marathon, he figured a shower should be the next order of business. His first *private* shower in over seven years. His lips curved into a grin as he set the water temperature to nuclear.

Ninety minutes later, after using all the hot water and devouring half of his favorite casserole his mom left in the fridge, Lynch squatted beside his Harley in the driveway, an open toolbox to his right. While he didn't question Mick's job fixing up his ride, he nevertheless checked the oil and transmission lube. It was like reacquainting himself with an old lover. Relearning all her ins and outs. Remembering what she liked and didn't like.

The temperature was chilly even in the bright sunlight. His fingers and tips of his ears grew numb, but he didn't care. It felt amazing to be outside without a fence or guard tower anywhere in sight, hearing the low rumble of passing cars and the distant howl of a train whistle.

When he finished tinkering with his Harley, he closed up the toolbox and stowed it in the garage. He returned to his bike, intent on riding to the clubhouse to dig into recent Streeter activity, and saw five cars, two of them belonging to the sheriff's department, blocking his access to the street.

Lynch recognized most of the half dozen men milling around the vehicles from high school. While he didn't know the deputy sheriff, there was no mistaking Dell Albright as he leaned against the hood of one squad car. Wearing a sheriff's jacket and khaki pants, Shasta's older brother didn't look all that different from seven years ago, except maybe for the cane beside him. Dell grabbed it then made his way up the gently sloped driveway.

Conflicting emotions swirled through Lynch as Dell limped toward him. On one hand, Lynch's animosity toward Dell hadn't diminished in the years since they were classmates. On the other, seeing the physical toll taken on Dell generated sincere...empathy for the guy. Lynch remembered Dell as the state record holder for the hundred-yard dash. In high school, he'd been so athletic, and fast. But now...

Dell stopped, one hand on his cane, the other on his gun. "Morning."

Lynch stared into the mirrored sunglasses, both grateful and not because he didn't have his Glock on him. "Dell."

"It's Sheriff Albright when I'm on duty."

"So you're here in an official capacity?"

"Yep." Dell shifted and his mouth thinned. "I need you to come to the stationhouse."

Lynch's belly tightened. "Why?"

"So we can...catch up."

"Am I being charged?"

"No." Even with the sunglasses, Lynch felt Dell's deadly glare. "Unless you decline my request. Then I'll have something to charge you with."

Lynch observed the deputy and other men closing ranks around Dell. Six against one. Given the odds, he had no chance.

There'd once been a time in Lynch's life when he would've been stupid enough – when he would've said fuck it – and attacked like a madman, with or without a gun.

But that was prior to his prison education. In the joint, he learned hard, fast and in a fucking hurry it was better to surrender than fight a losing battle. Because fighting and losing held more consequences than simply capitulating. He pulled his cell from his pocket. "Mind if I call my lawyer and have her meet us there?"

Dell plucked the phone from Lynch's grasp. "You can call once you're there." He eased to the side. "Let's go."

~*~

Early Monday afternoon, Shasta blasted the radio as she drove along the highway. The snow-capped peaks of the Sierra towered in front of her. They looked so pretty this time of year, with the contrast between the white and the multiple shades of brown. In another month or two, the snow would be gone and the brown would become even more diverse. Off to her left, a red-tailed hawk hovered above a cow pasture, looking for his lunch. Despite the serenity of the scene, suspicion nipped at her.

Given how freaked-out Dell had been about Lynch's release on Friday, a feather could have knocked her over when her brother sent her to Reno for office supplies, alone.

Although she'd argued they had more than enough coffee, coffee filters, print cartridges and paper clips to last another month, Dell insisted she go, making her leerier.

And her brother spent the weekend on patrol which piled onto her mistrust. While he'd stayed with her and Wyatt at night, and assigned a squad car to watch the house during the day, that didn't explain why, with his bad leg, he'd spent hours in the tight confines of a car. She knew lack of movement increased his pain exponentially. So why had he submitted himself to that kind of agony, plus send her on this wholly unnecessary outing to Reno?

The timing between Dell's odd behavior and Lynch being released couldn't be ignored. But her brother wouldn't be so stupid as to do something to Lynch...would he?

She slowed her car and pulled onto the off ramp.

No. It was just a coincidence. Nothing more. Besides, Lynch had a lawyer who would ensure he didn't get harassed. Or so she hoped.

She decelerated more upon entering Stardust's city limits. Two turns and one stop light later, she pulled into a spot at the sheriff's department.

Usually the number of cars in the parking lot could be counted on three fingers, six if they were busy. But over a dozen vehicles populated the asphalt space. Very odd. She cut the engine, unclicked her seatbelt then grabbed the plastic bags from the backseat. She hustled up the walkway as the biting, northerly wind kicked up. It might be May, but the weather felt more winter-like than spring.

The interior temperature made the exterior temperature feel balmy. Everyone wore jackets while a few folks sported hats. And a number of extra people loitered in the squad room.

She stopped at the dispatcher's desk. "Joan, what's going on? Why isn't the heat on and what are all these people doing here?"

Joan, who wore fingerless mittens with a matching knitted cap and scarf, shrugged. "Dell said the furnace is on the fritz and I don't have any idea why everybody's here, but they've been going in and out of the Sheriff's office and the interview room all morning."

Shasta adjusted her hold on the bags. "Where's Dell?"

A burst of laughter turned her head. Her brother, along with several guys she remembered running track with Dell in high school, walked out of the viewing room. If she needed further proof something was amiss, this was it.

Shasta dumped the bags on Joan's desk. "Please take this stuff to the break room. I'll put everything away in a minute." She beelined across the room to where Dell stood, surrounded by his smiling friends. As she approached, his wide grin faded from his face.

He murmured something and everyone scattered like cockroaches in a flashlight beam. "Hey, sis," he said in a sugary tone.

She crossed her arms. "What's going on?"

His eyes widened in feigned surprise. "Nothing."

"Baloney." She pointed to the door he exited. "What's going on in there?"

Dell's amicable demeanor vanished. "Like I said, nothing." He reached for her arm, as though to lead her away, but she dodged his grip and rushed past him. "What the fu – Shasta...*wait.*"

Just inside the room, Shasta stopped so abruptly, Dell rammed into her. Stunned astonishment tore through her as she stared at the person standing on the other side of the one-way mirror.

Lynch Callan.

A *naked* Lynch Callan.

But before her brain could fully process that reality, it registered a bluish tint to his lips and the fact he visibly shivered. And all the odd happenings of the day fell into place...

Her "essential" trip to Reno. The furnace being on the "fritz." Her brother's friends populating in the squad room...

She whirled around. Dell stood there, his posse crowded behind him, and he almost looked sheepish. Almost.

"What the fuck have you done?" she demanded.

Dell's eyeballs practically jumped out of their sockets. In high school, Shasta could swear a sailor under the table, but it had been years since she uttered anything more profane than damn.

Her brother recovered enough to point to the glass. "Nothing that bastard doesn't deserve."

She leaned forward, unable to believe the words coming from his mouth. "Deserve? Did you just say he *deserves* this treatment?"

One of Dell's buddies piped up, "You know he does, Shasta."

She cut her gaze to him. "Am I talking to you, Allen? No? Then be quiet. In fact, get out." She waved her arms. "All of you. Get the hell outta here."

After a moment of shocked silence, the mob quickly backed out of the viewing room. Shasta slammed the door shut then turned.

A thunderous cloud had settled on her brother's face. "Just who do you think you are?"

"I'm your sister," Shasta shot back, "and apparently the only one in this room with a working brain." She tunneled her fingers through her hair and spun away, a growl snagging in her throat. "Jesus, Dell. Is this why you've been on patrol? So you could pick Lynch up and treat him like your personal freak show? How could you?"

"Are you actually defending that fucker? After what he did to me?"

"*This* is your answer? Petty revenge?"

"It's not petty."

"Then you admit you went looking for payback. Do you have any idea how stupid this is?"

"I did it to send a message."

"Really?" She cocked a hip. "What message? That you're an idiot?"

He glowered. "That he'd better not mess with me or my family." Dell sliced his gaze to the man behind the glass. "Because if he does, this will only be the beginning of the shit storm I'll cause him."

She blew out a harsh sigh. "You need to get him his clothes and release him."

"No."

Shasta's mouth dropped open. She stared at her brother, but it was like looking at a stranger. She knew Dell was bitter about the past, but the extent of his vitriol staggered her. To abuse his office and authority this way was *not* how her brother would act. She whipped out her cell. "I'll call the local newspaper and TV stations."

"And tell them what?" he goaded.

She narrowed her eyes. "That the sheriff of Grant County is trampling on someone's civil rights."

Dell's expression melted into anger. He grabbed for her phone then wobbled, caught off balance because of his cane. She easily evaded his grasp.

"No one will believe a convicted criminal over a sheriff," her brother stated.

"Not even with the support of that sheriff's sister?"

His stare turned icy. "You wouldn't..."

"I will, unless you release him. *Now.*"

"You'd side with him?" He jabbed his finger at the glass. "Instead of your own brother?"

"If my brother's acting like a total douche, yes. If he's thrown all his ethics and morals of the sheriff's position – *a position our father held* – into a dung heap, yes." She knew it was a low blow to bring up their dad, but she didn't care. She shook her head with a sigh. "Christ, Dell...you could lose your job. Think about the repercussions to your career. To Dad's legacy. You need to let him go."

Dell adjusted his stance. "And if I refuse?"

She waved her phone in the air. "Then I'll call the press. Either release Lynch or be prepared to be on the six o'clock news. Your choice."

A wound look flitted over her brother's face, then he glared. "I don't believe you'd do that."

"Believe it."

He flattened his lips and pivoted to the door.

"And Dell..."

"What?" he ground out not bothering to look at her.

"Get the heat back on."

Spine straight, he limped out, closing the door harder than necessary. Once alone, Shasta focused her attention on Lynch. She stepped forward and lightly touched her fingertips to the mirrored glass.

Tears burned her eyes. He looked thinner. Thinner, yet bigger. More rawboned. Sinewy.

Powerful.

The chairs had been removed from the room and he stood behind the bolted-down table, head high and wrists handcuffed. He cupped his genitals with both hands and glared at the mirror. Apparently he hadn't lost any volume *down there.*

He could've turned his back to garner a small measure of privacy, but that wasn't Lynch's way. To hell with the world, that was his motto.

His shaggy ash blond hair had lost the sun-streaked highlights she remembered from so long ago. And the scraggly beard covering his cleft chin looked darker than his hair. His collarbone jutted across his upper chest like some kind of weird, tribal piercing while his broad shoulders seemed broader or maybe it was because his waist appeared more narrow.

He carried the same tattoos...his mom's name, in a large cursive font embellished the front of his neck and a black Celtic cross, with a green shamrock in the middle, decorated his left shoulder. Another Celtic symbol adorned his left upper chest area while the Streeter tat...a snake slithering through the eyes of a skull...dominated his right shoulder with the words *Learn Through Pain* scrawled on that same forearm. And she knew a picture of Gabriel kneeling beside a crumbling cross inked his entire back.

He looked so different, yet so much like he had seven years ago. Especially his eyes. Those smoky blue eyes were the same. Still mesmerizing. The same eyes as his son...

Sudden flashes of Lynch's smile – of his kiss, his touch and more – bombarded Shasta. Of her body twined with his. Joined with his.

Her cheeks burned at the vivid memories...and her innocence at having fallen in love with a Streeter. She'd been innocent and so very dumb. He was a gangster. A criminal. And she could never share a life with a criminal.

Todd entered the interview room, a bundle of clothes in his hands, interrupting her unruly thoughts. A gentle whirling indicated the furnace was back on. Shasta waited long enough to see the deputy unlocked the handcuffs on Lynch's wrists before turning away. She wiped the moisture from her cheeks, inhaled a breath and walked into the squad room.

Everything appeared normal. No superfluous people. Just a typical afternoon. Dell sat hunched over his desk. In the break room, she put away the supplies, keeping a diligent eye out on the interview room door.

Soon, a woman Shasta didn't recognize, wearing form-fitting slacks, a white turtleneck and short denim jacket, marched into the Dell's office. By the woman's emphatic gesturing and finger pointing, Shasta figured she was upset about something. Her brother simply sat there, his face like granite.

The woman snatched up a leather garment – Lynch's motorcycle cut – and stormed from the office, and immediately into the interview room. She emerged again, Lynch right behind her, his Streeter jacket gripped in his hand. Despite his t-shirt being untucked, Shasta could tell his jeans rode low on his hips.

His angry gaze swept the squad room. She quickly ducked behind the door, her heart in her throat. Had he seen her? It made no sense to hide. In a small town like Stardust, they were bound to run into each other at some point. Still, she'd prefer that point not be today. A moment later, she peeked back around and watched the duo head for the entrance.

Just before he exited, Lynch threw on his cut. A defiant gesture considering gang colors and garments were prohibited in the stationhouse.

The woman placed her palm on the center of Lynch's back, and a wave of possessiveness scorched through Shasta.

Who the hell was she? Lynch's girlfriend? But how could he have girlfriend...he'd been in prison for the last seven years.

Maybe she was a convict bunny. Someone with a fetish for inmates. Maybe she and Lynch had started out as pen pals then moved onto to pals...with conjugal benefits.

Shasta pulled herself up short. She had no right to feel jealous of Lynch and another woman. Yet she did. A lot.

And that bothered her even more....

Chapter Seven

THE NEXT MORNING, after dropping Wyatt off at school, Shasta drove to the stationhouse, Dell in the passenger seat. Without the six-year-old's constant chatter, the quiet in the small car thudded against her eardrums.

She and Dell hadn't exchanged three words since yesterday afternoon. The last time she had defied him she'd been in high school...on Ditch Day when he'd grounded her from going to Lake Tahoe with her friends. While she hated being at odds with her brother, she refused to apologize. If anyone should say he was sorry, it was Dell. And fat chance of that happening.

But squabbling with Dell accounted for only part of Shasta's pensiveness. She'd checked behind the detached garage last night, as well as that morning, unable to locate the box of personal items Hez said he'd gather for her.

Not that there was anything of value. Just junk. Trinkets Lynch had given her or silly mementos she'd accumulated all those years ago. She'd stashed everything at Lynch's trailer because she didn't want either Graham or Wyatt stumbling across them. Now, with Lynch getting out, she didn't want him knowing she'd been at his place. Somehow that prospect made her feel wild, like she had been as a teenager. And she wasn't wild, not anymore.

She texted Hez before getting into the shower, but had yet to hear back. Once she got to work, she'd text him again. She pulled into Dell's parking space and killed the engine. Her cell twittered with a new message. But it wasn't from Hez. She typed a quick reply then unclipped her seatbelt.

"Who was that?" Dell asked.

She didn't bother looking at him as she reached into the back seat to grab her purse. "Graham."

"Everything okay?"

"Everything's grand. Graham finished his business early and will be home tomorrow." She got out then waited while Dell clumsily exited the car before hitting the door lock and turning.

"Dell!"

The shout turned them both.

Adam marched forward, stopping inches from her brother's face. Agitation billowed off the normally disciplined DA. "Just what the *hell* did you do?"

Dell leaned on his cane, his expression guarded. "What are you talking about?"

"What am I talking about?" Adam parroted. "I talking about the fact that after I spend all-goddamn day yesterday in federal court in Reno trying to get Callan back behind bars, I return to my office to find a myriad of messages from Emma Jarvis."

"Who's Emma Jarvis?" Shasta asked.

Adam dissected her with a disdainful look. "Callan's lawyer." He returned his glare to Dell. "She's threatening a lawsuit for illegally hauling in Callan then detaining him for over three hours without notifying her."

So the woman from yesterday was Lynch's his lawyer...

Shasta figured she should squelch her relief. Just because the Jarvis woman was Lynch's lawyer didn't mean they weren't involved. Though that constituted an ethical no-no, didn't it?

Dell puffed out his chest. "I had cause to bring him in."

"Really? And what cause did you have for putting him on display – naked?"

The starch evaporated from Dell's stance. "Shit. She told you about that?"

Adam snorted. "If she had, would you be standing here now? Or would your sorry ass be out of a job and facing serious misconduct charges?"

Dell frowned. "Then how'd you know?"

"You didn't exactly keep it a secret. Parading half the town through the interview room." Adam shook his head. "What in God's name were you thinking to pull such a dick stunt?"

Dell brushed a glimpse at Shasta, saying nothing.

The DA eyeballed her then glowered at her brother. "I get that you want justice. Vengeance even. But not this way, understand?"

Dell sighed with a nod. "Yeah, I understand. Won't happen again."

"See that it doesn't," Adam snapped. "I've worked too long and too hard to have you fuck things up now."

Dell's eyebrows shot up. "What things?"

A flush stained Adam's neck. "Nothing I'm at liberty to discuss. But when I can, you'll be the first one I brief." He turned then pivoted back. "Oh, and one more thing, Jarvis wants to interview both of you along with Graham for her investigation."

Alarm stiffened Shasta's posture. "Why me?"

Her stomach curdled under Adam's scrutiny. "Don't know. Don't care. Just give her your cooperation." He cut his gaze to Dell. "Both of you."

Shasta watched the DA stomped off.

I wonder what things Adam can't discuss.

"I wonder that too."

She jumped a foot at her brother's voice in her ear. She hadn't realized she'd spoken out loud.

Dell stared after Adam. "But what bugs me even more is why Callan's lawyer didn't rat me out completely about yesterday."

"Maybe because Lynch never told her the whole truth about what happened."

Dell grunted. "Oh, he told her all right."

"What makes you so sure?"

"Because it fits the pattern for a lowlife like him, and his lowlife attorney." Dell limped up the sidewalk.

She fell into step beside him. "What do you mean, the pattern?"

"They think they've got information on me that'll turn into some kind of a payday for them."

"Uh, they *do* have information on you. And, according to Adam, half the town knows it."

He paused in opening the entrance door to direct his most withering stare at her. "Thanks for the reminder."

She breezed past him. "You're welcome."

~*~

Lynch folded then placed clothing in his duffle.

"But why do you hafta leave?" his mother asked yet again. She paced the garage bedroom, wringing her hands. "You can't let that asshole sheriff run you out."

"He's not, Ma. I swear." He ducked into the small bathroom to gather up his toothpaste, toothbrush and deodorant. He didn't want his mom dealing with any fallout from his run-in with the sheriff, especially if he revealed the truth about what actually happened. But he didn't need any payback on Albright. It wouldn't restore his dignity. He'd probably only lose more of it. And the repercussions could land hard on his mom. He walked back into the bedroom and dropped the toiletries into his bag. "I just think I should stay at my trailer. It'll mean less heat for you."

"Harrumph." His mother plopped onto the bed. "I ain't worried about any heat." She plucked at the frayed quilt. "It's just been so...quiet around here since..."

"Flyer left?" he finished gently, checking his Glock then tucking it into his waistband.

Still focused on the quilt thread, she nodded.

Lynch eased onto the mattress beside her. "Did you notice anything strange about Flyer's behavior before he left?"

Her posture stiffened. "You mean other than him being a cheating, two-timing bastard?" Her shoulders stooped again. "No. But..."

"But?"

"He just seemed damned...depressed the six, eight months before he left. Disappointed somehow. Other times, he was so pissed, I thought he'd go on a statewide shooting spree."

A sad smile lifted Lynch's lips. Flyer did have one hellacious temper.

"And secretive," his mom continued, staring into space. "Good God, the man acted worse than a Cold War spy. Mysterious as shit and seriously neurotic about me."

"What'd you mean, neurotic about you?"

"He didn't want me going to the salon by myself or working late. At the time, I thought it sweet, him showing how much he loved me. Then he just left." Her voice hitched and she bowed her head.

Lynch wrapped an arm around his mother's quaking shoulders and hugged her tight. His heart broke. Flyer hadn't left. He'd been taken. "What can you tell me about Tre Olsen?"

She sat upright with a sniffle. "He and Flyer got real tight. I think that's the reason Tre and Junkyard were sent up to Idaho." She wagged her head. "Only Junkyard came back, though. Tre rolled his bike under a semi on the ride home. Such a shame to have lost him like that."

Not a shame, but murder. Same as Flyer.

"Ma, what you think of Junkyard and Bowyer?"

Her lips twisted in a smirk. "As an old lady for twenty plus years, it's not my place to judge club members. Especially the officers."

"But you must have an opinion."

"'Course I do."

He gave her an expectant look.

"Well, Junkyard's smart and oilier than a greased hog. Bowyer's just flat crazy. I don't trust either of them. And I don't think Rolo does either."

That surprised Lynch. "If that's true, then why the fuck is Junkyard the VP?"

"You'll hafta ask Rolo. What I can say is Rolo's taken up where Flyer left off being all kinds of paranoid about my safety."

Everything inside Lynch stilled. "Why's that, Ma?"

"Again you'll hafta ask him. In my opinion it's just stupid old men turning into stupid old *worrywart* women." She stared at his duffle. "Isn't there anything I can say that'll get you to stay here? Nobody's been at that trailer since you went inside. It's probably nothing but a shit-hole mess. I bet raccoons won't even live in it."

Forcing a chuckle, he kissed her cheek. "Okay, Ma. You win. I'll stay."

Her eyes lit up. "Really?"

He stood and started removing the items from his bag. "Really."

If Flyer, then Rolo, thought his mom was in danger, then she must have been.

Which meant she most likely still was.

~*~

Once he'd safety deposited his mom at her salon, Lynch rode to the outskirts of Stardust.

He had every intention of keeping his word and staying with her, but he also wanted to see for himself just what kind of a "shit-hole mess" his trailer was. Situated on the very edge of Bureau of Land Management land, there weren't any utilities because he squatted on federal property. But he had a gas-powered generator for electricity which made the fifth-wheel livable. However, with it vacant for so long, he could only imagine the disaster that awaited him. Raccoons no doubt would be the least of his worries.

Yet checking the status of his trailer was only part of his reasoning for going there. The other part – the bigger part – had to do with the momentary glimpse he'd gotten of Shasta the previous day, at the sheriff's office. And with the feelings seven years behind bars should've killed, but didn't.

Feelings of belonging. And love.

He'd never considered Shasta a piece of ass. Some girl to fuck then forget. No. Shasta Donahue Albright was anything but forgettable. Her daring, smart-mouthed, impulsive, yet romantic ways impressed the hell out of him. She'd been the best damn thing to ever come into his life.

Spending time with her was as easy as breathing, and just as vital. She taught him to laugh more and judge less. Her boundless zest for adventure astonished him. As did her bravery. She never hesitated to call him on his bullshit, notwithstanding his reputation as a known criminal. She made him want to be a better man.

A better man for her.

He'd even begun to naïvely think they could have a future together. That he could leave the Streeters and be accepted into her world of law and order. God, he'd been such a fool.

Still he wanted...no *needed*...to go where he and Shasta had rendezvoused. Where they'd found the privacy to share their deepest dreams, their worst fears, their first kiss. And more.

Lynch understood he couldn't go back. No one could. But maybe, just maybe, he could recapture an inkling of the innocence he'd once felt with Shasta.

If only for a moment.

He slowed his motorcycle to maneuver around the potholes on the dirt road leading to his trailer. A mix of Ponderosa and juniper pine trees rose up on either side of him. The brisk, clean morning air filled his lungs. He rounded the last bend and eased to a stop. There sat his house on wheels...in all its peckerwood glory.

While it needed a hard power washing and a major clearing of the slew of gigantic sagebrush which reached halfway up the siding, the thirty-foot trailer actually appeared in fairly decent shape. Confusion narrowed his eyes. How was that possible?

Considering the amount of time he'd been away, the place should have been a pile of debris. Unease tightened his gut. Had someone taken up residence in his place? Been squatting on his squat? Because no way, after being vacant for seven years, should his fifth wheel look this good.

He cruised to the far side of the trailer, cut the engine and swung his leg over the seat. He removed his helmet and gloves, slipped his hand under his jacket to grasp the Glock grip, then circled back around, surveying the area.

The surrounding foliage looked much denser than he remembered, but the birds twittered their carefree songs. Maybe nothing was wrong. Maybe his stint in prison had made him overly cautious. But he'd learned in prison not to disregard his gut. If you did, you ended up dead.

He edged to the trailer door and reached down behind the cinderblock step for his hide-a-key rock. He'd just extracted the key when the low rumbling sound of an approaching Harley had him ducking back next to his bike.

Flat against the aluminum, he peered under the trailer nose, and tightened his hold on his gun. Who the fuck followed him? Junkyard? Bowyer? Had his arrangement with the FBI been discovered?

The answer came as Hez steered into view, the tangle of his dreadlocks sticking out from under his half helmet. With a sigh of relief, Lynch emerged. Hez pulled to an abrupt halt, surprise plainly written on his face despite his sunglasses.

Lynch ambled over and slid his handgun back into his waistband. "What are you doing here, bro? You talk to my mom?"

Hez took an inordinate amount of time removing his glasses. "Uh...no. But when you weren't at her place or the clubhouse, I figured you'd be here. Thought you were staying with her."

"I am. Just came up here to scope things out." Lynch's gaze again wandered the vicinity. "You been staying here?"

Hez coughed, his complexion paling. "Why you asking?"

"Because the place looks in way better shape than I expected." He stared at his friend. "And definitely better than you. Anything wrong?"

"Nah. Wanna grab some breakfast? My treat."

Lynch furrowed his eyebrows. "Sounds great, but don't you hafta work?"

Hez shook his head. "Got called in over the weekend. I'm not back on the schedule until tomorrow." He shifted on the bike. "So, breakfast...how about Mert's Cafe?"

"Sure." Lynch tossed the trailer key in the air then caught it. "First I want to check the inside of this beast."

"Can't you do that later?"

He eyed his best friend. It wasn't like Hez to be so...edgy. "I could, but I'm here now. You sure nothing's wrong?"

"Yeah, it's all good." Hez fiddled with his sunglasses, not looking up. "Just hungry."

"Well, as my momma likes to say, you'll get fed soon enough." Walking to the trailer, Hez surprised him by grabbing his sleeve. Lynch hadn't heard him get off his Harley.

"C'mon, man." Hez sounded desperate. "Let's bail and get some grub."

Lynch shook off the hand with a scowl. "What the hell's wrong with you?" He inserted the key and opened the door. "This'll only take a minute." He stepped inside.

The first thing he noticed was how clean everything looked. No dirty dishes cluttered the sink or the small counter. Not his normal MO. He only ever did the dishes when he knew Shasta was coming over. And the last time she'd done that had been almost a week before he got arrested.

The second thing to snag his attention was the smell. It sure didn't smell like his trailer had been locked up for seven years. A slight floral scent, mixed with an earthy accent, teased his nose – and his subconscious.

Apparently Hez *had* been staying here, but didn't want Lynch to know. Weird considering whatever belonged to one belonged to the other. They were brothers after all.

Lynch pocketed the key, his gaze lighting on the built-in table, and the box on top. Curious, he opened the flaps.

And a torrent of memories battered him. Memories of Shasta.

The hodgepodge of items...everything from used wrapping paper, faded ribbons, a stuffed baby seal toy, a photo strip from a carnival photo booth, a red velvet necklace box...inundated him with flashes of her smile and fragments of her laugh.

With calculated calm, he picked up the jewelry box and flicked it open, but he already knew what lay inside. A silver heart-shaped pendant on a twenty-four-inch chain. An engraved rose embossed one side with the inscription *To S from L* on the other.

His gift to Shasta for her eighteenth birthday. The day he took her virginity.

Hez's bizarre behavior – his nervousness and insistence on going to breakfast – it all made sense now. As did the familiar and persistent flowery aroma in the air. It was the lingering fragrance of Shasta's perfume, mingled with the musky undertone of sex.

Sex she'd had with Hez.

Blood pounded in Lynch's ears and his vision clouded. Slowly he crawled his gaze to Hez who stood in the narrow doorway, a bright red staining his cheeks.

"I can explain."

"*Explain?*" Lynch fisted the necklace tightly in his hand. "Explain what? That you've been fucking Shasta?"

Hez's expression hardened. "It wasn't like that. We never–"

A feral bellow blistered past Lynch's lips as he charged. He plowed his shoulder into his friend's midsection, driving them both out the door. Hez hit the ground with a loud grunt. Lynch straddled his chest and pummeled his face.

His friend – his *best goddamn* friend and the man he'd asked to look after Shasta – had been fucking her while *he* sat in prison. There were some things brothers did *not* share.

Pain ricocheted up Lynch's arms with each delivered blow. Air scraped his throat. His pulse pounded. His hands turned numb from the punching, but he didn't ease off the beating.

Not one bit.

He reared up, ready to smash his fist clean through Hez's skull, but stopped. It finally sank into his fury-filled brain his friend wasn't fighting back. And at two inches taller and thirty pounds heavier, Hez could've easily pitched Lynch onto his ass.

Breathing hard, Lynch heaved himself off Hez and pressed his fist to his forehead. Something bit into his palm. He opened his hand to reveal Shasta's necklace.

Hez sat up. "Feel better?"

Lynch glared. "Don't fucking talk to me."

"You told me to look out for her."

"But not to *fuck* her."

"I told you, it wasn't like that." Hez spat out blood then dabbed at his lip. "Look, brother–"

Lynch scrambled to his feet. "I am *not* your brother. Brothers don't do what you did. They don't betray–"

Emotions clogged his chest. He refused to dwell on the cruel irony of his own deception to the Streeters and Hez's to him. The situations were different. Absolutely and completely different.

Lynch stared down at his former friend, his former brother. Blood trickled from Hez's nose, the cut over his left eye and his bottom lip.

Anger still heated Lynch's blood. But rather than continue to pound the living shit out of Hez, he pivoted, stuffing the necklace into the breast pocket of his cut as he marched to his bike.

"Where are you going?" Hez called after him.

Lynch grabbed his helmet. "Gonna return this necklace to its rightful owner."

A hand clamped onto his shoulder and whirled him back around.

Hez stood there. "I can't let you do that, man."

Something deadly snapped inside of Lynch. He whipped out his gun.

His former best friend's arms shot up. "Whoa, man. You're gonna shoot me now?"

"Thinking about it." Lynch adjusted his grip on the Glock. "Back off."

Hez shook his head. "I can't let you go. Not when you're this pissed."

Pissed? He light years past pissed.

Lynch's finger itched to squeeze the trigger. "I should gun you down like the mangy hound dog you are. You knew how I felt about Shasta. You were the..." His voice cracked, his eyelids suddenly hot and gummy.

Christ.

Scrubbing an angry hand across his face, Lynch pulled in a rickety breath. "You were the *only* one who knew about her. I *trusted* you."

Hez slowly dropped his arms. "Let me explain. Then, if you still want to, you can shoot me."

Lynch stiffened his arm. "Don't tempt me."

Tense seconds ticked by. Finally Lynch lowered his gun and smiled, a big I-couldn't-give-a-shit smile. "Fuck it. It doesn't matter. None of this matters." He dug the necklace from his pocket and tossed it into the dirt at Hez's feet. "Give it back to the skank next time you fuck her." He buckled on his helmet while throwing his leg over his motorcycle. He revved the motor.

Hez bent down to retrieve the trinket. "You got it all wrong, man," he shouted over the engine noise. "Seriously wrong."

Lynch popped the clutch and lurched his bike onto its rear wheel. Balanced on the single tire, he roared past Hez, kicking up gravel and small rocks in his wake. At the dirt road, he slammed onto the front wheel and raced down the hill. Too bad he couldn't outrace the feelings of deceit which flooded his veins.

He'd been right – he couldn't go back. Not ever. All he could do was secure the evidence Jarvis needed, then hope like hell he could move beyond all this drama.

Beyond Hez and Shasta and maybe even beyond the Streeters too. Because he didn't have a home in Stardust. Not anymore.

Chapter Eight

I STARE AT the computer monitor straining to hear what's going on outside Callan's decrepit trailer. Nothing intelligible. Just garbled sounds. I wish I'd been smart enough to install an exterior camera.

Not much surprises me anymore, but I sat in shocked silence watching the exchange between Callan and Hez. The revelation on Callan's face when he thought Hez had fucked Shasta...priceless. Fucking priceless.

Then for those two to start brawling put the cherry on my sundae. The situation couldn't have worked out better had I planned it myself. I can only hope they're killing each other right now.

A knock lands on my office door.

Christ.

I cut the laptop's volume. "What?" I snap.

The new blonde with the big tits and skinny waist sticks her head inside. She looks scared, and she should. It didn't end well for the last bimbo who displeased me.

"Sorry to interrupt, Mr. Blackwell...Junkyard Taylor is here."

"Fine." I wave her out. "Five minutes."

Once the door is shut, I increase the volume again in time to hear a roaring sound. What's that? A motorcycle? Silence fills the air and I tense in my chair. A few moments later, Hez stumbles into the trailer and grabs the box.

His face looks like someone beat him with a mallet. I can't help but smile as I close my laptop. I then pull sunglasses, a surgical mask and beret from a right-hand desk drawer. God, I hate this ridiculous getup, but can't chance anyone from Stardust discovering my true identity. Just like Batman. I chuckle to myself. As if Batman could ever be as brilliant as me.

After donning my costume, I hit the intercom button to my receptionist. "Send him in."

Moments later, Junkyard struts into my office. "Mr. Blackwell."

I frown at the dust coating his clothes as he slouches in the suede chair across from my desk, but harness my irritation. "Was the shipment delivered?" I remove a manila envelope from the center drawer.

"Yes, sir." Junkyard perches an ankle on the opposite knee. "Though Fuentes's man wasn't happy only three of the twelve-year-olds were cherries." He shakes his head. "Kids are fucking so early these days. Soon the only virgins to be had will be goddamn eight-year-olds.

I pause in checking the contents of the envelope. "Then we'll get goddamn eight-year-olds. You got a problem with that?"

Junkyard sits taller. "No sir."

I toss the envelope onto the desktop, watching him snatch it up like a shark feasting on chub. "Were there any problems?"

Junkyard thumbs through a thick stack of twenties. "No," he mumbles, his focus on counting his booty. "Wait...there was one thing."

Annoyance tightens my skin. "What one thing?"

"Nothing with the delivery," the moron says in a rush. "It's just Rolo Pruett threw his back out on the ride down here. He's probably gonna be laid up for a couple of days. Stupid old man. I don't know why we just don't put him out of his misery."

"Because that's not what *I* want." I raise an eyebrow in silent challenge.

Junkyard blinks then clears his throat. "Of course, Mr. Blackwell. Whatever you say."

Damn straight.

I swivel my chair. "Put Pruett in the usual Motel 6 and have one of the men stay with him. I want the rest of you back in Stardust tonight." I glance at the list on my desk. "The Idaho crew has four girls ready to go, Oregon has eight and Washington has another half dozen." I set the paper aside. "I want as many girls for this next shipment as possible so get on it, understand?"

Junkyard stands. "Understood."

He leaves and I open my ledger, making several notations then checking the balance sheet.

While the last few shipments haven't been as profitable as I would have liked, that shouldn't interfere with my plan of ending my business dealings with Fuentes. I anticipate the Columbian will be less than pleased with my decision, but it can't be helped. It's time I prioritized my life.

I close the book with a sigh. Yes...in another month, two at the most, I'll be on a sunny, tropical beach.

With Shasta by my side.

Chapter Nine

ON TUESDAY EVENING, the breeze fluttered through Shasta's hair as she waited with Wyatt and Graham for the handicap van to show up outside the Reno airport.

"How could your brother have allowed you two to come to Reno alone?" Graham's repeated question grated her nerves. "I thought we agreed it wasn't safe." He glanced over at Wyatt. "Under the current circumstances," he added in a tight whisper.

Shasta swallowed her groan. She squatted down to be eye to eye with Wyatt who clutched the bag containing his prized purchases from the train store. "How about you go to the curb and let us know when you see our cab coming? But don't go into the street, okay?"

"Okay, Mom."

Once the six-year-old stood out of earshot, she pivoted to her husband without rising. "One, I never agreed to anything like that and two, we weren't alone. Melissa and Aiden were with us."

"That's hardly a comfort." Graham adjusted the ever-present blanket on his lap. No matter how hot the temperature, he always kept his mangled legs covered. "I can't believe you'd be so irresponsible, Shasta." He massaged his forehead.

Concern for her husband supplanted any irritation she felt. "You got a headache?"

He frowned. "I didn't until finding out you and Wyatt came here without an escort."

Her annoyance flared to life and she shoved to her feet.

She wasn't an errant teenager any longer, but a grown woman. She hated that Graham sometimes treated more like a daughter than a wife. "You're overreacting. Nothing happened."

"This time," he retorted. "What about next time?" He shook his head, his lips in a thin line. "Forgive me, but I need to know my wife and son are safe."

Her exasperation dissolved. *Of course* he'd be concerned for their welfare. How selfish of her to be cavalier about his anxiety.

She knelt back down, took his hand, and gazed into her husband's tired eyes. "I'm sorry I worried you. And I promise to be more careful in the future." She squeezed his fingers. "Can you please let this go?"

Though he didn't look happy, Graham nevertheless nodded, patted her hand then released it.

She smiled. "Thank you."

"Mom, I think I see the van coming," Wyatt called.

"Thanks honey," she answered as she straightened.

"Say, sport." Graham motored himself forward. "Show me what you got at the train store."

After they were all situated in the cab, with Wyatt on the small pull-down seat right next to Graham's wheelchair, Shasta settled into for the ride home. She listened while her son chatted away, telling his dad about all his new toy train parts.

But they weren't toy trains, she reminded herself. Model trains. Wyatt got huffy when she made that mistake. Graham recently introduced the hobby to him which gave father and son something to share.

A sad smile played at her mouth. In every way, Graham was Wyatt's dad, except for DNA. But no biological father could be more supportive or affectionate.

Shasta stared at the passing landscape and wondered, not for the first time, what her life would have been like had her brother not been shot. Had Lynch not gone to prison.

When she'd been younger, she often daydreamed of marrying Lynch. Of reforming him and having a life with him. Of being with him.

Her eyes drifted shut as her intimate muscles pulsed in long-neglected need. Though it had been years since she'd been with Lynch, she could still feel his hands on her skin. His lips and tongue...

"Shasta, honey, you okay?" Graham's voice yanked her from the erotic fantasy.

She sat straighter. "Um...yes." She pasted on a smile. "Just tired."

Graham gave her a quizzical look before turning his attention back to Wyatt.

Shasta redirected her gaze out the window. Good God...what was wrong with her? Fantasizing about Lynch Callan? That's the last thing she should be doing. Whimsical musings weren't productive. They only served to undermine her carefully crafted control. Control she didn't dare let slip.

She had a great husband. No, a *really* great husband. If celibacy was the price for a wonderful father for Wyatt and a generous partner for her, then so be it.

Just as the sun set, the van pulled into the driveway of their white, two-story, colonial. The house had been in the Dupree family for two generations, with the ground floor remodeled to accommodate Graham's wheelchair. The den, dining room and half the living room had been transformed into an oversized bedroom and home office for him. Shasta and Wyatt's rooms were upstairs.

She gathered her purse and Graham's suitcase while the hydraulic lift lowered her husband, Wyatt on his lap, to the ground. She caught a bit of their whispered conversation, something about playing with the new train pieces and delaying bedtime.

She turned to inform the duo there'd be no delay in bedtime on a school night when a movement by the garage snagged her attention. A familiar-looking figure paused so only she could see him then ducked behind the building. Her pulse rate spiked.

Hez.

What the hell was he doing here? He knew better, especially with Graham and Wyatt home.

"Mom?"

Wyatt's voice skipped her heart, but she managed not to yelp. "Yes?"

"Can I stay up a little later tonight? Please?"

Her planned veto dashed from her brain. If the boys were occupied, she could discover why Hez lurked about. "All right. But just thirty minutes. Deal?"

Wyatt hopped off Graham's lap. "Deal! Thanks Mom."

As Graham paid the driver, Shasta headed for the kitchen door. After making quick work of unpacking Graham's suitcase, then making certain he and Wyatt were entrenched in model-train-land, she hurried outside. She rounded the garage to find Hez, his back to her and his shoulder shoved against the weathered siding.

"What the hell are you doing here?" she hissed. "Are you crazy?"

Hez unbent his posture and turned. A small gasp escaped her mouth. The diminishing daylight couldn't hide his bruised, battered face. One eye was almost swollen shut with nasty contusions coloring both cheeks. And his lips looked three times their normal side. "What happened?"

He opened his mouth then grimaced when his lip started to bleed. He gingerly swiped it with his finger. "Ran into a couple of fists."

She stepped forward, her hand outstretched. "Do these fists have an owner?"

He dodged her touch. "Yeah, Lynch."

Her insides went cold and her world tilted. She pulled in a lungful of lilac-scented air and held it, feeling her heart pound against her ribcage. "Lynch?"

Hez nodded, staring at the ground. "He showed up at the trailer before I could get your stuff." Slowly he met her gaze. "Sorry, beautiful."

"You said he's staying with Edie."

"He is." Hez rolled his shoulder. "But he wanted to check out his place. Didn't take him long to figure out you'd been spending time there. 'Specially once he found this." He held up her silver necklace then dropped it into her palm.

The treasured piece of jewelry felt cool against her skin. "And Lynch did..." She gestured to Hez's face. "...that?"

"Yeah." Hez fingered his black eye. "He was pretty pissed."

"Didn't you explain things?"

"He wasn't all that interested in listening. Just punching."

Tears filled her eyes. It was her fault Lynch beat the daylights out of his best friend. Just like so much else was her fault. "God...I'm so sorry, Hez."

He shrugged again. "You're not to blame, beautiful."

"Yes I am."

He shook his head, caressing his thumb down her cheek. "You're not." He dropped his hand, picked up a small box at his feet and handed it to her. "Here's your stuff."

"Thanks." She shifted, not sure what to say. "Where's your bike?"

"I parked a couple of streets over and cut through the yards."

"Smart."

"Yeah. I gotta go."

He turned and made his way through the trees. She watched him until the twilight closed in around him then trudged back to the house, her heart heavy in her chest.

~*~

Just before eleven Wednesday morning, Lynch rolled his bike into the weathered and cracked asphalt parking lot of the Stardust Bowling Alley – the front for the 5th Streeters clubhouse.

With all the crap of the past few days, first getting hauled into jail and then the shit with Hez, he hadn't had the chance to stop by until now. Since Rolo should've returned yesterday, Lynch figured he needed to find out just what the fuck his crew had been up to.

He climbed off his ride, pushed his sunglasses to the top of his head then strode to the double glass doors. Inside, he blinked against the sudden dimness. The steady sound of bowling balls crashing onto synthetic resin lanes, followed by the rumble as they traveled toward their ten-pin targets, transported Lynch back to the time when his only concern had been trying for the perfect three hundred score.

To his right, the same half dozen slot machines occupied the same shallow, grungy alcove. Several geriatric ladies played video poker while being watched over by a circling, hazy cloud of cigarette smoke and a bored change person. Lynch walked past the restrooms until the narrow corridor widened into the concourse and the eighteen lanes, all of which were in use. A bowling league, obviously.

The equipment counter and snack bar were to the left with people milling about. On the far side sat the lounge bar. Lynch spied a Streeter cut sitting on a stool, engaged in a conversation with the cute blonde bartender and smiled.

Grunge, the middle-aged, pot-bellied club treasurer, hit on anyone with tits, despite the fact his old lady would snatch any other female bald. Lynch edged up behind the older member, his finger to his lips when the girl saw him approach. Without warning, he clapped the treasurer on the shoulder.

Grunge swung around, his harsh expression dissolving when he saw Lynch. "Well, shut the front goddamn door. 'Bout goddamn time you showed up here." He stood and lugged Lynch into a quick hug then put him at arm's length. "Heard Albright hauled you in the other day."

Lynch's jaw fell. "Shit...news travels fast."

"Indeed it does, brother, 'specially in this town. So what the fuck did he want?"

"To rattle my cage, I guess."

"You okay?"

"Yeah. I'm fine."

Grunge play-slapped the side of Lynch's head. "Then what the hell took you so long to get here, brother? Forget where this place was?"

Smiling and rubbing his cheek, Lynch slipped onto the neighboring stool. "Jesus, man. I've been out for less than a week. Give a guy the chance to get some sleep, will ya?"

Grunge gripped his shoulder with a laugh. "And some pussy, right? I saw those two with you on Friday night. Damn fine snatches. Am I right?"

"You are." Lynch arched an eyebrow at the bartender whose ample breasts threaten to spill out the top of her scoop-necked t-shirt. She didn't look old enough to drink let alone tend bar. Probably an off-shift girl from the Comstock. "And what's your name?"

She wiped the bar with a flirtatious wink. "Josie. What's yours?"

He allowed a slow grin to spread across his face. "Lynch."

"What can I get you...Lynch?"

"Coffee, please...Josie."

Grunge snorted. "Coffee? Fuck no. This calls for tequila." He slapped the bar. "Set us up with the good stuff, my darlin' Josie. And don't bother with the fucking limes or puny shot glasses."

Josie nodded, placed two tumblers on the bar and grasped a bottle from underneath. Lynch couldn't believe the label as she expertly poured the generous shots.

Holy mother... Patrón Añejo.

Since when could Rolo afford to serve anything but Jose Cuervo?

Grunge clinked glasses with him. "Welcome home, brother."

While the treasurer downed a healthy gulp, Lynch took a moment to just breathe in the scent of the alcohol. A woody aroma mixed with vanilla and raisins teased his senses. He took a sip, allowing the smooth, sweet taste to roll around on his tongue before swallowing. The pleasant burn warmed his chest.

Grunge picked up the bottle and his glass then stood. "C'mon. Let's take this to the back. Don't need any of these loser bowlers thinking they can have the good stuff."

Lynch grabbed his tumbler and rose while Grunge moved to the door marked "Private," the official entrance to the Streeter inner sanctum.

Josie reached across the bar. "Promise you'll come tell me good-bye when you leave, okay Lynch."

He flashed a grin. "It's a promise Josie." Following the treasurer, he crossed the threshold, and his feet stumbled to a halt.

Everything looked so...opulent. Not a word to describe the hard-bitten members of the Streeter MC.

Another bar, this one oak, still dominated the right side of the room. But instead of the wood surface looking dull and lifeless, it gleamed brighter than the gaudy, gold-plated mirror behind the row of liquor bottles. The ratty couches and armchairs Lynch remembered had been swapped out for what looked like a floor exhibit from an upscale furniture store. And the numerous mismatched, threadbare rugs had been replaced with seamless, wall-to-wall carpet. Even in his heavy boots, he could feel the plushness beneath his feet.

Just where had the club gotten this kind of money? The answer soured the sweet taste of Patrón in his mouth.

But the far more disturbing thing Lynch noticed were the dozen "brothers" populating the expensive furniture and shooting pool at the two tables off to the left. Brothers he didn't recognize, yet they all wore Streeter cuts.

Some stared at him. A few others glared. Lynch ignored them as he trailed Grunge to a couple of vacant easy chairs which flanked a small lacquer table.

Lynch sank – and sank and sank – into the over-stuffed cushions. Fuck. He'd never sat in anything so luxurious. He worried he'd rip the expensive upholstery.

Grunge splashed more tequila into his tumbler then set the bottle of the table. "Hang here a sec. I'll be right back." He headed for the meeting room door.

Scanning for a familiar face, Lynch sipped his drink. No Ennis, Tiny or Mick. No Hez either, a good thing. Angry resentment still scorched Lynch's blood that his supposed best friend had been fucking Shasta. He stretched his neck. It popped loudly in his ear.

But he needed to forget Hez and concentrate on his mission...get the necessary information for Jarvis and find out who killed Flyer.

His gut quivered. Expensive stuff and men he didn't know from Adam. Something wasn't right. And the sooner he found out what, the better. For him and his club.

Grunge plopped into the adjacent chair and handed him a wad of bills. "Here ya go. This should hold you for a while."

Lynch took the bundle and did a quick count. Three grand. His gaze rocketed to Grunge's. "What the hell...I've never seen such a payout."

"That's cuz we've never been involved in such a motherfucking sweet deal before."

"What kind of deal? Robbing banks?"

"Nothing that complicated, or dangerous." Grunge poured himself more tequila with a chuckle and smug grin.

Lynch frowned at the man's silence. "So spill. What the fuck's been going on since I left? First the Patrón, then the fancy furniture shit. Now this..." He held up the money. "And who are all these guys?"

"Most of 'em came down from Vancouver with Junkyard. But don't worry." The treasurer settled into his chair. "They're good. Junkyard vouched for them."

"And they got patched in? Just like that? On the word of one guy?"

Grunge scowled. "Yeah, just like that. Junkyard's the one responsible for the cash in your hand. If he says these boys are good, they're good."

Lynch tempered his anger. He couldn't get caught up in his suspicion of the VP. If he did, he'd never find out anything. "So what's this mother-fucking sweet deal?"

Grunge shifted in his chair. "Can't tell you, bro."

Lynch's jaw dropped. "Why the hell not? Don't you trust me? I thought we were brothers."

"We are, man. We are. If it were up to me, you'd be read in on the whole operation, but it ain't up to me. It's Rolo's call. Sorry."

"So you're saying Rolo has a problem with me?"

"No." Grunge scrubbed a hand down his face. "Shit...it's just since

Flyer split, everyone's been on edge. You can understand that, right?"

"Except I'm not Flyer, am I?" Lynch countered. "I'd never do anything to hurt this club." And he wouldn't. His current actions were designed to *help* his crew...

"I know, brother." Grunge blew out a sigh. "But if anyone found out I told you–"

"Nobody's gonna find out shit."

Grunge pinched his lips together, giving Lynch a gimlet stare. "If this blows back on me..."

"It won't. You have my word."

"Fine," Grunge grunted. He took a swallow of Patrón, glanced around then sat forward. Lynch matched his posture.

"The deal is...pharmaceuticals."

Lynch arched an eyebrow. "Pharmaceuticals?"

Grunge nodded.

"All this..." Lynch waved his hand. "...is because of some pills?"

"Not just pills. Grade-A pharms, man. Everything from antibiotics to morphine to beta blockers, whatever the hell those are." Grunge's eyes gleamed brightly in the muted light. "Junkyard's got an inside guy at a drug manufacturing plant in Canada who puts together little care packages for us. Junkyard and a few of his guys ride up there and bring back a non-descript van. Then a different team of brothers accompany it to Vegas. From there, another crew takes the product south."

"South? To where? Mexico?"

"Sometimes, but mostly the stuff goes to whoever will pay the most. The black market on this shit is huge, man. Fucking huge."

"But don't drug companies have super intense security?"

"Yeah, they do, which is the beauty of this scheme. Because Junkyard's guy is on the in-inside, he can pull the shit before it gets on a truck. If nothing's logged, then nothing can go missing."

"And the Streeters are the distributors?"

Grunge shook his head. "We're just an escort service. The distribution, and most of the risk, is on others. It's the perfect deal." He knocked down his tequila then poured another. "Perfect, I tell ya. Just fucking perfect."

Lynch fingered stack of money, his lips pursed. "So how'd I earn this cash? I've been gone for seven years. Won't Junkyard get pissed

I'm mooching off his score?"

"If Junkyard don't like it, he can take it up with Rolo. He said to cut you in. 'Sides, there's plenty more where that came from."

That piqued Lynch's curiosity. "How much more?"

"Average of five grand." Grunge's face split into a grin. "Per brother."

Lynch felt his eyes bulge. "Five Gs...*each*?"

Grunge settled into his chair. "Did I not say one sweet, motherfucking deal?"

Lifting his tumbler back to his lips, Lynch took a moment to collect his jumbled thoughts.

No way could the black-market trade in pharmaceuticals pull in this kind of money. Not even if every country south of the Rio Grande bought the illicit drugs, which most couldn't even afford. No. The true source of this newfound wealth was from the trafficking of young girls. Just like Jarvis and Newman claimed. Lynch needed no further proof of Streeter involvement. But just how many of his true brothers knew the facts about *where* all the money came from?

Lynch set his glass down. "Where's Rolo? I suddenly feel the urge to give him a big hug. Maybe even a kiss. On the lips."

Grunge threw back his head with a hearty laugh. "I'd pay to see that. Too bad Rolo ain't back yet."

"But he said he'd be home on Monday."

"Business in Henderson is taking longer." Grunge shrugged. "No big thing."

Lynch gently swirled his drink, mentally cataloging all this new information for the FBI. If he could find out the schedule for the next run, that'd be even better.

He again took in the surroundings. "All we do is play escort for these pharms? No more protection money or selling weed?"

"Some, but not much." Grunge stretched in his chair. "Junkyard also has connections in the gun and smack trade, but the Vancouver boys handle most of that. Leaving the pharm angle, which is way safer, easier and cleaner, to us." He nodded his head to the money on the table. "As you can see, this setup is very profitable."

Lynch picked up the roll of bills and turned it over in his hand. "So why are Junkyard and his guys the only ones who go to Vancouver?"

"It's Junkyard's guy, and he only wants to deal with him."

"How often do these runs happen?"

"Depends. Couple times a month."

"Rolo on a run this past weekend?"

"Nah. Other business."

"What other business?"

"Dunno. I wasn't on the need-to-know list."

Lynch heard the suspicion in Grunge's voice and sat back, his ankle perched on the opposite knee. "So when's the next run?" Silence answered his question. He met the other man's guarded gaze and hitched his shoulder with a self-deprecating grin. "If I make this..." He held up the wad. "...for just breathing, I gotta wonder how much I'll get for being an active participant."

Grunge relaxed. "We're not read into the details until the night before. Rolo and Junkyard keep all that info tight to the vest. And they keep the route under wraps till the last minute, too. Don't want anyone getting ideas about doin' something stupid, like trying to rip off the club."

Lynch nodded sagely. "Smart." He downed the rest of his tequila. It burned his gullet.

So Rolo knew about the shipments in advance. Did that mean he also knew what the cargo actually contained? God...that thought made him sick. He stood. "Well, I gotta jam, brother. Gotta meet my fucking lawyer."

Grunge grinned up at him. "That lady lawyer of yours definitely is fuckable, ain't she?"

With a wink, Lynch offered a tight smile. *Oh, brother...if only you knew the truth about my fuckable lady lawyer.*

He turned, and came face-to-face with Junkyard and Bowyer.

Junkyard glowered, almost like he didn't think Lynch had the right to be in the clubhouse. Lynch loosely hooked his thumbs in his belt loops and glared right back.

The VP looked down at Grunge. "What's going on?"

The treasurer straightened his posture at the terse question. "Nothing. We're just catchin' up."

Junkyard's gaze slashed back to Lynch. "Catchin' up with what?" He stepped forward.

Lynch held his ground. "Stuff. Something wrong with that?"

One corner of Junkyard's eye twitched. "Maybe."

"Which is...?"

The unfinished question hung in the air like a rattlesnake ready to strike. Everything seemed to stop.

Finally Grunge cleared his throat and got to his feet to stand between Lynch and Junkyard. "Hey, let's remember we're brothers."

After another tense moment, the VP eased away as a smile curved up his mouth. A mean, threatening smile. "Sorry, man Grunge is right. We are brothers. Let me buy you a drink as an apology. Go grab some new glasses, will ya Grunge?"

"Uh..." Grunge seemed unsure if he should leave. "Okay."

Junkyard settled into the chair Lynch vacated while Bowyer took up Grunge's.

Lynch extracted his Harley key. "Thanks, but I gotta get going. Lawyer shit."

Junkyard nodded. "Speaking of shit, what you wanna do about Albright taking you in?"

"What can we do?"

"All kinds of things."

Lynch tugged his ear. "You know, if anything happens to Albright, I'll be the first one the cops come looking for."

"What's the matter?" Bowyer mocked. "Scared you'll end up back in the joint? Wuss."

Lynch snorted. "Spoken like someone who doesn't know what the fuck he's talking about."

Bowyer pulled back his lips, baring his teeth. He stood, but Grunge returned with fresh glasses and Junkyard rested his hand on Bowyer's arm. The pit bull sat down.

Junkyard poured a shot. "There's more than one way to get back at the sheriff." He lifted his glass and glared at Lynch over the rim. "But don't worry your pretty head. You just go off and have fun with your lawyer. We'll take care of everything."

A shiver chased up Lynch's spine at the menacing tone, but he turned and left, a lead ball of dread settling in his gut. He needed to tell Jarvis and Newman about Junkyard's threat to Albright so they could warn the good sheriff. Lynch didn't know what the VP planned to do, but he knew it wouldn't be at all pleasant.

Chapter Ten

SHASTA PAUSED AS the words and numbers blurred before her eyes.

Since her brother and husband continued to be paranoid about her safety, her parttime job had turned fulltime. But on an average day, she barely had enough clerical work at the stationhouse to keep her busy. So her darling brother had "volunteered" her to input years of hand-written police files into the new computer database. The work made tedium sound thrilling. But at least it *was* work versus doing nothing. Because, like it or not, she was stuck here for the foreseeable future. And she did not like it one bit.

She stretched her neck then went back to her mundane chore.

"Mrs. Dupree?"

The female voice brought up Shasta's head, and her insides chilled. Lynch's lawyer. Dressed in beige pants and a white blouse with just the right hint of lipstick and blush, she looked elegant yet professional.

Shasta sat straighter, painfully aware of her drab t-shirt and lack of makeup. "Yes?"

The woman smiled, but the amiable gesture didn't reach her green eyes, and extended her hand. "Emma Jarvis. I'm representing Lynch Callan in his bid for a new trial."

Shasta shook her hand, unsure if she should admit she already knew Ms. Jarvis, and her mission in Stardust. "How can I help you?"

"Is there somewhere we can talk?"

"Um...sure." Shasta pushed away from her desk. "We can use the conference room–"

"What the hell is going on?"

Her brother's voice pivoted her. "Oh...Dell...this is–"

"I know who she is." He shifted his weight, trying not to lean on his cane, and aimed a glare at Jarvis. "What do you want?"

The corners of the lawyer's eyes squinted slightly. "To ask Mrs.

Dupree a few questions on behalf of my client."

"My sister doesn't know anything about your client." Contempt dripped from Dell's words.

Jarvis arched one perfect eyebrow. "I'd like to decide that for myself, if you don't mind, Sheriff."

"I do mind. Counselor." The last word sounded like a sneer. "You're not asking my sister anything unless Adam Murphy is present."

"This isn't a deposition so it's not necessary to involve DA Murphy."

"I beg to differ. My sister isn't talking to you without legal counsel."

Jarvis's expression hardened. She placed her black briefcase on the desk with a thud. "All right. I had hoped to keep things off the record, but if not, I'll arrange for a court stenographer to be in attendance. That way everything will be official, and on the record."

Animosity zinged between Dell and Lynch's lawyer like static electricity. Shasta gripped her brother's arm. "Adam said she wanted to talk to me so let's just get it over with. Okay?"

He slid his gaze to her then back to the attorney. "Not without me in the room with you."

Jarvis gave a tight smile. "Fine. That way, I can interview you after your sister."

Shasta led the way to the conference room. She took a seat, with Dell beside her. Jarvis sat across from them.

Several edgy moments passed while Jarvis retrieved a file, a legal pad and a pen from her briefcase. After slipping on black-framed glasses, she peered at Shasta over the rim, her hand poised over the paper. "Mrs. Dupree, do you know my client, Lynch Callan?"

Shasta's heart dropped into her stomach. How to answer that question with Dell sitting right next to her? She twisted her wedding band with a hopefully casual shrug. "I know *of* him."

Jarvis's mouth twitched. "Let me rephrase the question. Have you ever *met* my client, Lynch Callan?"

The hawkish glint in the other woman's eyes indicated she already knew the answer. Shasta weighed the option of lying. As Jarvis said, this wasn't a deposition so she wouldn't face any perjury charges. But if Lynch had already told his lawyer about their...relationship...things could get sticky if she lied, especially with her brother present. She swallowed the tightness in her throat. "Yes. We've met."

Dell whipped his head around to stare at her. "What? When?"

Jarvis saved Shasta the embarrassment of having to reply. "Sheriff, please." The attorney frowned. "I'll ask the questions." She redirected her gaze to Shasta. "What were the circumstances of you meeting my client?"

"He...uh...helped me out of a...situation. Once."

"And the particulars of this...situation?"

Shasta wet her lips. "I don't see how any of that can be helpful."

"I'll be the judge of what's relevant to my client's case. Now when did you two meet?"

Shasta twined her fingers. She didn't understand how her meeting Lynch could be of any use to Jarvis. But if the chance existed it *could* help, she had to go for it, Dell's reaction be damned...

"It was about seven years ago." She studied her hands in her lap, feeling her brother's hot stare boring into her. "I was still in high school at the time."

Silence ballooned in the room.

"And, Mrs. Dupree?" Jarvis prompted.

Shasta blew out a breath. "And I got into a minor traffic accident." She boosted her shoulder. "Your client helped me."

Jarvis scribbled on the pad. "Were you injured in this accident?"

"Oh, no nothing like that." Shasta heaved another sigh. "I backed into his motorcycle with my brother's truck," she blurted.

"*You what?*"

Shasta flinched at Dell's shout. She turned to him. "It happened a long time ago. Just a couple of months after Daddy died. You remember what a mess I was then." She covered her brother's hand with hers. "It was Ditch Day my junior year. You'd grounded me from my truck and I retaliated by taking yours. I accidentally backed it into Lynch...I mean..." She glanced at Jarvis who seemed enthralled with the story. "...your client's motorcycle."

She looked back at Dell, but he stared at the table, the muscle in his cheek repeatedly popping. She tightened her hold on his hand. "Please say something."

His gaze snared hers. "I remember that day. My truck was found on the far east side of town. *You* took it?"

She briefly closed her eyes with a small nod.

"But the window and steering column were busted. Did you do that too?"

"No. That was Lynch. Since I took your spare key, he said you needed to be...convinced someone stole it."

Dell's mouth hung open. "Why that motherfu–"

"Why did my client help you, Mrs. Dupree?" Amusement tinged Jarvis's voice. "Did he know you were the sheriff's sister?"

"Yeah, he knew." Shasta rolled her lips together. "He said he wished he could've seen Dell's face when he realized his truck was gone. Making sure he never found out who took it would be the next best thing." She gripped her brother's hand with both of hers. "Please don't be mad. Like I said, it happened a long time ago."

Shaking his head, he scoffed a small laugh.

"After that initial meeting, Mrs. Dupree," Jarvis said. "Were there any other occasions when you met my client?"

Shasta held the lawyer's gaze and willed starch into her spine. No way would she reveal – in front of her brother – how much her world changed that fateful day. How she stopped being so reckless because of Lynch's friendship. How he altered her perspective on everything from school to her father's death. How he helped her gain control over herself and her emotions. How she fell in love with him.

Dell could never know the truth because if he did, it wouldn't take long before he realized the truth about Wyatt. And she wouldn't risk that. "No."

Jarvis cocked one eyebrow and Shasta held her breath. If Lynch had confessed all to his attorney, she prayed the good lawyer wouldn't out her. That she understood the dire consequences if she did...

Stars swam in Shasta's vision, but she didn't look away.

Finally Jarvis nodded once and closed the folder. "Thank you for your time, Mrs. Dupree. I won't keep you any longer." She handed a business card to Shasta. "If I have any other questions, I'll be in touch."

Shasta slowly released the air in her lungs and fought to keep from slumping in relief. Somehow she managed to stand on watery legs and walk from the conference room, leaving Dell to be interviewed next. At her desk, she sank into her chair and studied Jarvis's business card.

The simple yet graceful design mirrored the attorney. Emma Jarvis seemed like an excellent lawyer, which was a good thing. Lynch would need a first-rate one to clear his name. And it probably wasn't a bad idea for Shasta to know a high-quality lawyer too. For what, she didn't know. But she slipped the business card into her wallet anyway, then resumed her task of entering the police files into the computer.

~*~

At two in the afternoon, Lynch sat hunched over a cup of coffee in the back booth of the local diner, waiting for his "lawyer."

Immediately after leaving the clubhouse that morning, he texted her about needing to meet. Funny thing, Jarvis pushed him off until now. He lifted the warm brew to his lips. After all her bullshit pressure, he would've thought she'd be more interested in what he had to say. Guess not.

The bell over the door tinkled. He looked up, hoping to see Jarvis, but an elderly couple walked to the counter and sat. He exhaled an irritated sigh and switched his gaze out the window.

Mert's Diner stood at the far end of Main Street and across from Stardust's only park. Since it was mid-afternoon on a workday, no one took advantage of the nice day other than a few moms with young kids in strollers. That's why the man in the business suit reading a newspaper caught his attention.

He looked familiar, but it took a moment for Lynch to recognize him. Adam Murphy. Why would the DA be sitting alone on a park bench at this time of day? Some kind of weird stress relief therapy?

The answer came when Sam Newman ambled up and parked his ass at the opposite end of the bench. A few moments later, Murphy folded the paper and placed it on the bench. He then stood and sauntered off.

Lynch sipped more coffee and watched as Newman rose, scooped up the paper and headed in the opposite direction.

Not a very clandestine handoff, but then how many people would actually take notice? A small town like Stardust didn't fit the profile for a lot of cloak and dagger shit. Still, he wondered what Murphy had passed to Newman...

His musings were interrupted when Jarvis slid into the seat across from him. He set his cup down. "Glad you could make it, counselor."

She frowned as she put on her glasses.

The waitress stopped at their booth. "What can I get you?" she asked Jarvis.

Jarvis pulled a pad of paper and a pen from her bag. "Coffee with cream please."

The waitress nodded while warming up the contents of Lynch's mug and walked away.

He rested his arm on the back of the seat. "Where's Newman?"

"Reno. Been there the past couple of days."

Lynch glanced back out the window to the now empty bench. Had Jarvis seen Newman? Did she know he'd met with Murphy? Was something going on they weren't telling him? Suspicion danced along his neck.

"So, Callan, tell me what you found out."

Clearing his throat, he eased forward. Despite his misgivings the agents might not be on the up-and-up about everything, they were still his best bet for finding out the truth about Flyer's murder, and ultimately for helping his crew. "I'm not sure, but something's definitely hinky with the Streeters." He paused as the waitress placed a cup and saucer in front of Jarvis and poured coffee into it. Again alone with Jarvis, he canted closer to the agent. "I went to the clubhouse and spent some time with Grunge, the treasurer. It appears there's been a huge influx of money into the club."

"What makes you say that?" she jotted on the paper.

"There's all this new, fancy furniture and primo booze. Real top-shelf shit. There's also a butt-load of new members...all brought in curtsey of Junkyard Taylor."

Jarvis squinted. "Is that all you've got? A few new bodies and some liquor and furniture?" Shaking her head, she pulled off her glasses.

"No, that's not all I got. I was also given a wad of cash that wouldn't choke a horse, but it'd do damage to a Great Dane."

"How much?"

"Three grand."

Jarvis tapped her pen. "And that's not a typical payout for the

Streeters?"

Lynch scoffed. "Are you kidding? You and Newman had it right, we're a nickel and dime outfit. Or at least we used to be. A couple of times a year we'd get a big score selling weed in the Bay area that would tie us over, but nothing that would dole out three thousand to a brother just getting released from prison."

Interest sparkled in Jarvis's eyes. "Did this Grunge say where the money was coming from?"

"Black market pharmaceuticals."

"Pharmaceuticals?"

Lynch nodded. "Supposedly Junkyard has an inside guy at a drug company in Vancouver. The story is, he and a couple of his guys go pick up the drugs, using vans, then escort the vehicles to Reno. Some of the brothers then usher the vans to Vegas where yet another crew takes over and takes the cargo south of the border."

"And you think those vans don't contain drugs, but young girls?"

"Makes sense, right?"

"Yes, it does. How often do these shipments happen?"

"Usually a couple of times a month."

"When's the next one?"

"I don't know. Only Rolo and Junkyard know the when, where and route until the night before."

She stared at him over the rim of her glasses. "Rolo Pruett? Guess this means your friend is involved after all."

"Not necessarily. Rolo could be as duped as anyone else."

She shook her head. "All this money, and no one questions where it's coming from? Do they all honestly believe it's from the illegal distribution of pharmaceuticals?"

"Look...my guys are blue-collar. Living payout to payout trying to provide for their families. With this kind of money on the line, they're not gonna ask a lot of questions."

"Or none at all." Jarvis sighed. "What else can you tell me?"

"Junkyard also has his hand in the gun and heroin trade. That might be the connection to Fuentes. And he was pretty pissed Grunge told me all this shit."

Silence swallowed the next few moments as Jarvis finished her notes. "All right." She removed her glasses. "I'm leaving tomorrow for a couple of weeks in DC, and here's what I need from you...find out when the next shipment is, the route and the number of people in the escort."

He cocked his head. "That's all you need from me?" He barely contained his laugh. "Counselor, there's *no way* I'm gonna find out any of that info."

"Why not?"

"Because Junkyard doesn't trust me. A feeling that's mutual."

"Find a way around that."

"And how would I do that?"

"Be creative. Put that criminal mind of yours to work. I expect results by the time I get back." She gave him a hard stare. "Just remember, a lot of young girls – and your mother – are depending on you."

He bit back a scathing retort as she scooted from the booth. He reached out his hand to stop her. "There's one more thing..."

She paused, an eyebrow raised.

"I think Junkyard plans to retaliate against the sheriff for hauling me in earlier this week.

"Retaliate how?"

"Dunno. But you might wanna give him a heads up."

She nodded. "I'll have Newman handle it...thanks."

With that, his lawyer walked out.

~*~

Two days later, on Friday afternoon, Lynch eyed the cue ball up behind the eleven. "Corner pocket." He drew back his stick and smacked the white ball. It collided with the eleven, but at an angle. The red-striped globe bounced off the rail and careened to the center of the table. He bowed his head. "Shit."

Mick laughed. "How could you miss such an easy shot, brother? You must not have had much practice time while you were inside."

Lynch uncurled his body then picked up his beer. "Not in the least."

Mick examined the table while chalking his stick. "You'll be back to your pool-sharking self in no time, I'm sure. In the meantime, though..." He indicated the four ball. "Four in the side pocket." The purple orb sailed in. "I intend to take full advantage." Grinning, Mick straightened and re-chalked his stick.

Lynch smiled and tipped the bottle to his lips, but he took barely a sip. He'd been nursing the same beer ever since he got to the clubhouse that morning while keeping his ears open for information about any future "pharmaceutical" shipments. With Jarvis out of town for a while, he had some breathing room, but not much.

So far he'd heard nothing about the pharms, but he'd heard plenty from the trio at the other table about an upcoming run of AK-47s. He filed the information to tell Newman the next time he met him.

Watching Mick line up his next shot, Lynch thought back to what he'd seen in the park between Newman and Murphy, along with dear Agent Jarvis. He wanted to believe he could trust the agents, but years as a Streeter had made him inherently cynical any trustworthy relationship could exist. Still it didn't make a lot of sense for them to spring him from prison just to screw him over. Of course maybe they wanted him as a fall guy. If this operation tanked, an ex-con would be the perfect candidate for blame. In any case, he needed to stay on top of the situation...feed Jarvis and Newman just enough information to keep them happy, and him out of prison.

Mick finished the game with an eight-ball bank shot to a corner pocket. "Want me to rack 'em again?" he asked.

"Abso-fucking-lutely," Lynch answered, pulling out his wallet. He handed a twenty to Mick. "I need to redeem my reputation. Plus win back some of my money."

"What's this I hear? Lynch Callan losing money while playing pool?"

Lynch looked over as Rolo approached. He also noted Junkyard and Bowyer stood at the bar. Though the president wore a wide grin, he looked haggard. He hugged first Mick then Lynch.

"What the hell happened to you?" Lynch asked. "You look like you were dragged for ten miles on a dirt road."

Rolo scowled. "Thanks, brother." He sprawled into a nearby armchair with a not-so-quiet groan. "Been a long trip is all. Mick, how 'bout you fetch another round?"

Mick laid his stick on the table. "Sure thing, boss."

Lynch joined Rolo. "Heard you were in Henderson."

"Who'd you hear that from?"

Lynch paused in sitting. "Was it a secret?"

Rolo grunted. "No."

"From Grunge." Lynch sank into the cushions. "He also gave me your welcome-home present. It's been a long time since I've seen that many Ben Franks."

Rolo smiled. "No need to thank me, son. You earned it."

"How? By being locked up for the last seven years? It feels like charity."

The president frowned. "It ain't no goddamn charity. You earned it by being a brother, brother." He huffed. "I would've thought you smart enough to remember that."

"*I* remember being a brother who pulled his weight for his payouts. Not goddamn handouts."

Rolo's scowl deepened, but he said nothing.

"C'mon, brother," Lynch implored. "I gotta do something more than shoot pool and drink. It's making me bat-shit crazy."

"I woulda thought you'd like the vacation."

"Vacation from what?" Lynch rubbed his hands together. "I've had seven years of vacation."

Rolo sighed. "I suppose you have. All right, if it means so much to you—"

"Here ya go, boss." Mick returned, three beers in hand, followed by Junkyard and Bowyer.

"Mind if we join you," the VP asked, pulling up a chair.

"Not at all." Rolo's jolliness sounded forced.

Lynch flopped back in his seat. *Christ.* Just when he thought he'd get some answers, Junkyard shows up. And with his pit bull no less. Didn't that guy go anywhere without Bowyer? Who knew when Lynch would get another chance to talk with Rolo alone.

Rolo lifted his drink. "To a job done."

Lynch tipped his beer to his lips. "What job?"

"A motherfucker that is now over," Rolo answered. He shifted in his chair with a grimace. "I know I look youthful and all, but I'm getting too old to do these long rides."

"Since when is a ride up from Henderson a long one?"

Junkyard scoffed. "You ask a lot of questions, don't you?"

Lynch glared. "And if I do...?"

An uncomfortable silence descended.

"Well...?" Lynch prodded. He didn't like the look that passed between Rolo and Junkyard. He glanced at Mick who suddenly studied his lap with intense interest while Bowyer smirked. He set his bottle down with a thunk and stood. "I am done with this bullshit."

"What the fuck's your problem?" Rolo demanded.

Planting his hands low on his hips, Lynch glowered back. "My problem is ever since I got back, I've been on the outside looking in. And I'm sick of it. Either I'm a brother or I'm not."

"I vote for not," Bowyer sneered.

Lynch lowered his arms and balled his fists. "What did you say, fucktard?"

Rage melted Bowyer's face like a wax statue. He shoved to his feet and lunged. The other three men jumped up. Junkyard grabbed Bowyer while Mick did the same with Lynch.

"*Goddamn it,*" Rolo roared. "I'm too fucking tired for a goddamn pissing contest." He rubbed his palm down his face then aimed an angry stare at Lynch. "Club meeting. Tomorrow. Eleven am. You wanna pull your weight around here, then don't be late. Happy?"

No, Lynch wasn't happy. He'd be happy if he got to pound the living shit out of Bowyer and Junkyard. But this would do. For now. He relaxed his stance. "Yeah."

"Good." Rolo flopped back in his chair and picked up his beer. "Now get the fuck out before you cause another ruckus."

With a final glare to the VP and his pit bull, Lynch left.

Chapter Eleven

STARING AT THE monitor, I watch Callan stomp from camera range.

I hate I can't hear for shit in that damn clubhouse. With all the goddamn money I spent to ensure I kept an eye and ear on the Streeters and the only place I get good audio is in the meeting room. But even though I couldn't hear the words, I heard Callan's body language loud and clear.

His intense conversation with Pruett started a tick pulsating behind my left eye. No doubt that fucker had pumped Pruett for information, just like he had that idiot Grunge. Information about what, I don't know. Thank God Junkyard and Bowyer had walked up, ending the conversation both times.

Callan looked so pissed as he left, I had to smile. When he and Bowyer almost came to blows, even better. That's a matchup I'd love to see, especially with Bowyer wielding his knife.

I switch the feed to the stationhouse and see Shasta sitting at her desk. When the new station was built three years ago, no one suspected hidden cameras and microphones would be strategically placed throughout, allowing me to monitor everyone. Especially my Shasta.

I zoom in and caress my fingertip over her face. She is so beautiful. A shiver of pleasure dances up my spine. It won't be long before I'll be touching her for real. Holding her. Kissing her. Making love to her.

I frown as Todd Weedly struts up and perched his hip on her desk. Like the Streeter MC, the only decent audio I get in the stationhouse is in the more confined spaces like Albright's office, but I turn the volume all the way up and strain to hear what's being said.

"You sure you don't want to go to lunch with me," Weedly says.

Shasta nods without looking up. "Need to finish this, but thanks for the invite."

Weedly leans close to her. "You've been bent over those files all week, Shasta. Maybe it's time you were bent over something...or *someone*...different for a change."

Shasta snaps up her head.

Weedly stands with a chuckle. "Let me know if you change your mind about lunch." He saunters off.

I glare at the screen, feeling my pulse thump in my head.

I've never considered Weedly a danger to Shasta, but then he's never been this blatant in his innuendos toward her. And that pisses me off. A lot. I suppose it's possible I'm just being overprotective because Callan's out and is making my life miserable. Still the suggestion Shasta would allow Weedly to fuck her curdles my blood.

I close my eyes and steady my breathing. This is *Todd Weedly,* a simpleton who's absolutely *zero threat* to me or Shasta. It's ludicrous to afford him more significance than he's worth.

Calmer, I open my eyes and smile. No way will anyone but me touch Shasta.

Not ever again...

Chapter Twelve

SATURDAY MORNING, LYNCH grabbed his key ring off the dresser then exited his bedroom in his mom's house. "C'mon, Ma. You 'bout ready? My meeting starts in an hour."

"Then go," Edie answered from her room. "I can drive to the salon on my own." She appeared in the small hallway, putting on earrings. "Been doing it for years, you know."

"I know, but now I'm home I want to spend as much time with you as I can." He grinned when she rolled her eyes before disappearing back into her room.

He heard her long-suffering sigh followed by a resigned, "Fine."

"Awesome. I'll go start your car."

"Yeah...yeah."

Still smiling, he walked outside...and saw Hez leaning against the hood of his mom's Camry talking with Grunge.

Guilt nipped Lynch at the purplish bruises covering most of Hez's face. He shook off the sensation, the bastard deserved that beating and more, then stomped down the porch steps. "Why the hell are you here?"

Grunge immediately backed away while Hez maintained his lazy posture. "Thought it was time we had a conversation."

"I've got nuthin' to say."

"Good, cuz you've got nuthin' I wanna hear. But you *will* listen to me."

"What's going on?" Edie asked, from behind.

"Nuthin'." Lynch opened the passenger door. "Let's go."

"Mrs. C," Hez said. "Is it okay if Grunge here escorts you to the salon? Lynch and I have a few things to discuss."

Lips pursed, Edie slid her gaze between Lynch and Hez then shrugged. She closed the car door Lynch held open, walked around to the driver's side and slid behind the wheel. Grunge climbed on his bike and trailed after Edie as she drove away.

Lynch watched the Toyota until it vanished. He crossed his arms and glared at his former best friend. "All right. Talk."

Hez stuffed his hands in his back pockets. "What happened between Shasta and me is not what you think."

"Don't tell me what to think," Lynch ground out through tight lips.

"Look...I did as you asked. I kept an eye on her. Nothing more. I didn't even talk to her. After you'd been inside for a couple of years, I was following her back from Reno and she got a flat tire. It was like a hundred degrees and who knew how long it'd take for anyone to get to her. Plus she had her kid in the car." Hez blew out a breath. "So I stopped and helped."

"And she repaid you by fucking you, right?"

Hez narrowed his eyes. "Keep being a dick and I'll pound the shit outta you. No, she didn't fuck me. She baked me cookies."

"Chocolate chip?"

"Yeah. Just like she made you." Hez shook his head. "After that, she'd text me whenever her old man was gone. She'd get a babysitter for the kid and we'd...hang out at your trailer. It was innocent. We never did anything more than talk."

Lynch snorted. "Talk about what?"

"You mostly."

Lynch tucked his chin back in surprise. "Me?"

"Yeah. She asked about everything from us growing up together to how you were doing in the joint. And I swear to God I never did more than kiss her cheek."

"But something happened to change that, right?"

"Right." Hez's shoulders rose on a deep inhale as his gaze lifted to the swaying treetops. "Around the fifth anniversary of her brother getting shot, she asked me to meet her. When I got to the trailer, she was a mess. Crying and so drunk on her ass, she could hardly stand. She kept saying it was all her fault."

"What was her fault?"

"Beats the shit outta me. I held her. Tried to comfort her...and..."

Lynch clenched his jaw so tight he thought his molars cracked.

A blush crept over Hez's cheeks and he huffed a breath. "She kissed me and I...uh...kissed her back." He forced a chuckle. "I mean I'm only human, right?" His small smile died. "We got into some pretty heaving petting and she was making these gurgling noises..."

A growl caught in Lynch's throat.

Hez scrubbed a hand down his face. "I figured things were going full steam ahead. I whispered her name, and she whispered...yours." He shook his head. "When she realized what she'd said, she lost it completely. Nothing I did calmed her. Finally she passed out and I left." He scuffed his shoe through the dirt. "Haven't seen or heard from her since, until she told me you were getting out."

Lynch stared at the ground, his hands on his hips, taking a moment to process his emotions.

On one hand, he felt grateful Hez hadn't betrayed him, yet on the other, remorse consumed him. He *never* expected Shasta to languish. Especially for him. After all, he'd been convicted of trying to kill her brother. He always assumed she moved on, and she had. With a man in a wheelchair.

Hez shifted. "You gotta believe I wouldn't hurt you like that, man. I love you."

Lynch glanced up. "But you have been staying here, right?"

Hez rubbed his neck. "Yeah...me and the twins use your place when they're off shift from the ranch."

Lynch nodded. Tears burned his eyes as silence settled in the space around him and Hez. Not an awkward silence, but a clean one. Like he'd just gotten back his best friend. He cleared his throat. "You, ah, wanna grab some lunch before the meeting?"

A crooked grin creased Hez's face. "Yeah, I do. Mert's?"

"Sounds great."

Lynch turned, but Hez gripped his shoulder, pivoted him back and enfolded him in a monster hug. Lynch clutched him tightly for a moment as a tear eked from his eye. He slapped Hez once then stepped away. The other man sniffed and wiped his nose.

"Enough of this shit," Lynch said with a smile. "Let's go eat."

~*~

From his seat against the wall, Lynch watched the club members file into the meeting room.

Time was when the brothers all sat at the same table with the prospects delegated to the perimeter. But now only the officers sat around the massive oval table.

Lynch crossed his arms, his knees wide and snarled under his breath. He wasn't no goddamn prospect...

Hez elbowed him, a question on his face. Lynch relaxed his posture with a small shake of his head. He needed to keep his cool and not give away his personal feelings. No matter how hard.

When the door closed, Rolo smacked the gavel on the oak surface. "Order."

The din of voices quieted.

While Rolo went through his version of Robert's Rules of Order, Lynch fought his impatience. Who gave a fuck about the secretary or treasurer reports? When the hell would they get to the brass tacks of the meeting? Finally the discussion moved onto old and new business. He perched his ankle on the opposite knee, his hands folded in his lap, hoping to give the impression of detachment, but he hung on every word spoken.

Everything from forming an alliance with a Latino gang in Sacramento to guaranteeing the safe transport of guns to opening new distribution lines in Seattle for heroin was hashed out. Lynch catalogued the names and dates in his memory. The information might come in handy in the future. But he heard nothing about any pharmaceutical shipments.

Rolo struck the gavel. "If there's nothing else, meeting's adjourned. See Junkyard for your assignments."

Lynch stood. "I'm out," he said to Hez then headed for the door.

"Yo...wait a minute there, brother."

Lynch turned and saw Junkyard grinning at him, as was Bowyer and two more of Junkyard's crew. Cocking his head, Lynch moved closer. "Yeah?"

"Don't you want your assignment?" Junkyard asked.

Lynch narrowed his eyes. "Okay."

"Good." Junkyard wiped the smirk off his face. "Old Man Perry's behind on his protection money. Why don't you go collect it?"

All Lynch could do was stare.

Junkyard rolled back on his heels, his mouth pulled into a thoughtful frown. "I know it's been a while for you..." Bowyer snickered, followed by the other two morons, and Junkyard's attempt to keep a straight face failed. "But the old man's bones should be brittle enough that if need be even you could break them."

The foursome dissolved into fits of laughter.

Lynch glared at the VP. "Let me get this straight...you want me to lean on Old Man Perry?"

"Yeah," Junkyard chortled. "Figured you needed something simple to do."

Lynch looked at Rolo, who didn't meet his gaze. "You approved this?"

The president shrugged. "You said you wanted to pull your weight and the old man's behind."

"But I'm not a pimple-faced prospect looking to get patched in."

"You want something easier?" Junkyard's pit bull taunted.

Blood pounded in Lynch's ears as he squared off with Bowyer. The atmosphere in the room changed. Became tenser. Lynch didn't know what would happen, but if he got the chance to beat the fuck out of Bowyer, he'd take it.

"Knock it off, both of you," Rolo snapped, heaving to his feet. The president gave Lynch a hard look. "Your assignment is Old Man Perry, got it?"

"No."

Rolo skewered him with a glower. "What?"

"I haven't fought and bled for this club to be relegated to shaking down a ninety-year-old man." Lynch stalked toward the door.

"Where the hell you going?" Rolo asked.

"Vacation."

~*~

The week passed in a bored haze for Lynch. He'd been out of prison for two weeks...funny how one monotonous schedule could be so easily replaced with another.

Every morning, he took his mom to her salon then spent the day hanging at the clubhouse with the hope of garnering some tangible information about any future "pharmaceutical" shipments. A hope that faded more with each day.

He was treated like a pariah. Correction. He'd be lucky to be treated as well as a pariah.

No one talked to him about anything more substantial than the weather. And whenever he got within five feet of a group, the discussion abruptly ended. The only bright spots were the facts he'd gotten back some of his skills at the pool table and Jarvis wouldn't be back in Stardust for another week. But once she did return, she'd want a report. A report that, with the current circumstances, would be mighty thin.

The nine ball sank into the closest corner pocket after Lynch banked it off the far rail. He chalked his stick and rounded the table, looking for his next shot. At just before noon on a Sunday, only a few Streeters populated the clubhouse, and none wanted to challenge him to a game. He lined up the cue ball behind the two when his cell buzzed.

Hez.

Smiling, Lynch flipped open the phone, put it on speaker then bent back over the table. With all the crap he'd been going through, it was a relief to have his best friend back. "Yo, brother."

"Where are you?"

The hushed urgency in Hez's voice snapped Lynch upright. He grabbed his cell and put it to his ear. "Clubhouse. What's wrong?"

"Junkyard plans to nab Shasta as payback against the sheriff."

Lynch's stomach dropped through the floor as a cold sweat broke out on his forehead. "When?"

"Now. They've watched her since Albright hauled you in, but she's under twenty-four, seven police protection. Except her old man left with the deputy and she just headed out for a run."

"How do you know all this?"

"I'm one of the guys keeping an eye on her. You know...spying on the spies."

Lynch hurried from the clubhouse. Later, he'd thank Hez for his brilliance in keeping watch over Shasta, but right now, he needed to get to her before anyone else. "You with Junkyard now?"

"Yeah...him and Bowyer and a couple others. We're over at Mert's Diner waiting on a text from Spunky who's following her. Once she leaves the town limits, we're riding."

"So you think she'll take the Miner Trail into the desert?"

"Yeah."

Shit.

The outside, muggy air felt like a brick wall. Lightning lit up the western sky. Lynch threw his leg over his Harley seat. "Is Rolo there?"

"Nah. Haven't seen him all day. I don't think he knows.

"Any chance you can stall?"

"Doubtful. Junkyard's got a real mean glint in his eye. Once he hears from Spunky, not much is gonna stop him."

"Just five minutes." Lynch's bike roared to life. "That's all I need."

"I'll try. But you better hurry, bro."

Lynch disconnected the call and sped from the parking lot. He didn't need to be told to hurry because he knew exactly what was at stake. Shasta's life.

He'd been stupid to think Junkyard would take revenge on Albright himself. No...the VP didn't have the stones for something like that. He'd want an easier target. A softer one.

Shasta.

Lynch's gut clenched. He didn't doubt Junkyard would kill her, but first she'd be raped. Probably multiple times by multiple men. His insides twisted harder. Egged on by terror, Lynch gunned the motor and rode faster through the streets toward the north side of town.

The Miner Trail...an ambusher's wet dream. Tall, sandy berms lined the path which made for countless spots perfect for getting the drop on an unwary jogger. But maybe Junkyard didn't want to work that hard. The BLM had constructed a small picnic and rest area in the shade of several Ponderosa Pine trees where the trail branched off into dozens of others. With its easy access for motorcycles, perhaps that's where he intended to nab Shasta.

Or perhaps not.

Perhaps Junkyard already had her at his mercy.

Heart in his throat, he prayed that wasn't the case.

~*~

Perspiration trickled down Shasta's forehead and cheeks. She'd been jogging at an easy tempo, but the overcast, humid weather had her sweating profusely. A few fat raindrops splashed her shoulder as she sucked in a deep breath of sweet air.

It wasn't the grimy, oily smell of precipitation on asphalt streets. This was the cleaner, fresher scent of rain in the desert. Add in the fragrant perfume of the sagebrush, and it all worked to assuage her guilt at having lied to her husband.

With Graham receiving a call about an emergency meeting in Vegas first thing Monday morning, one of the deputies assigned to them needed to drive him to the airport. The other officer had accompanied Wyatt to a classmate's birthday party. Rather than have her brother called in on his day off, Shasta promised to stay in the house until the deputy returned, but hadn't. She couldn't give up the chance to go for a run. It had been weeks since she felt this kind of freedom.

But she vowed to make it a quickie. She had to. Wyatt was due home at three. Plus she couldn't chance Dell discovering her defiance.

A jagged bolt of lightning gashed the darkening sky. Seconds later, thunder rumbled in the not-too-far distance. Suddenly the sky opened up, releasing a deluge of rain. Typical Nevada weather...one second a few splatters, the next a freaking downpour.

Instead of turning back, she increased her pace determined to get a run in, albeit a short one. The rest stop was just around the next bend. She'd take cover until the cloudburst ended, which shouldn't be too long.

Another clap of thunder sounded, closer this time. A blur whizzed past her on the right. She turned just as a hand covered her mouth and a muscled arm circled her waist. The whiff of damp leather teased her senses right before she was yanked backwards against something rock-hard.

Then her feet no longer touched the ground.

Her instincts kicked in. She wrestled for escape, but her assailant easily carted her behind an enormous clump of sagebrush and dropped her onto the wet dirt. She rolled away only to have a heavy weight pin her face down.

Despite the terror gripping her, she forced herself to think. To remember her self-defense lessons. She took shallow breaths through her nose. She needed to fight just enough to convince whoever was on top of her she was trying to get away. Then she'd feign passing out. Hopefully he'd drop his guard, allowing her to run.

She diminished her resistance and after a long moment, the heaviness holding her captive lessened a bit. She trundled onto her side and drove her knee upwards. It connected with something pliable. A pained grunt penetrated the thrashing in her ears.

She tucked her arms to her chest and rolled three more times, then surged to her feet. A powerful grasp cut short her freedom. Again, she was tossed to the soggy ground. The impact whooshed oxygen from her lungs. She continued to twist and torque, scratch and kick anything and everything as she somersaulted with her attacker.

"Goddamn it, Shaly," a gruff male voice hissed low. "Settle down."

She landed on her back and strong hands gripped her upper arms, shaking her...hard.

"Shaly – I said to settle down."

Shasta ceased her struggles. No one called her Shaly except...

She swiped rain off her face and stared into hypnotic, smoky blue eyes. A tiny squeak slipped past her lips.

Lynch.

Anger overrode her confusion. She slapped his chest and shoulders. "What the fu–"

He again covered her mouth with his hand as he pulled a handgun from the back of his waist. She felt her eyes widened, but he held the barrel to his lips.

That's when she heard men arguing – and they were very, very close.

"So where the fuck's that Dupree bitch?" one demanded.

Horror shafted Shasta's chest. Panic must have shown on her face because Lynch gathered her close, shielding her.

The feel of his hard body pressing into hers peaked her nipples and swirled heat through her belly.

Good God. What the hell was wrong with her? She coerced herself to concentrate on the conversation rather than her innate reaction to Lynch.

"Think she turned around because of the rain?" a second man grumbled.

"Hell if I know," the first voice griped.

"Maybe one of the others grabbed her."

"Maybe. Fuck. I ain't got no goddamn signal out here. Jesus...Junkyard's gonna be pissed if we missed her. He wanted her on the shipment to Vegas next week."

"Should we look for her?"

Lynch tensed, his gun poised.

"Look where? Anyone'd be crazy to be out in this shit. I'm soaked through. Don't know why Junkyard wants her in the first place. She's old and has a kid, for crissakes. No money to be made with her."

"Yeah, but if Junkyard wants her, that's all we need to know. C'mon, let's go back. Maybe we'll get lucky and find her ass."

Sloppy footsteps trailed off, and Lynch slowly rose onto his knees. When she followed suit, he placed his hand on her shoulder and leaned close. "Stay put. I'll make sure they're gone."

She shook her head. "No, I–"

His hand again covered her mouth, his gaze narrowing. "Do *not* argue," he hissed. "Stay put."

She glared back. She didn't need him telling her what to do. But those men were looking for her. *Specifically* for her...so she remained on the wet ground.

Lynch shrugged off his cut and laid it over her. In a half-crouch and gun in hand, he prowled away to the right.

Shasta curled into Lynch's jacket, her knees to her chest trying to get warm. She clamped her jaw tight to keep her teeth from clicking.

A monstrous clap of thunder rented the air. The ground shook. She pressed her hands to her ears and squeezed her eyes shut.

Why hadn't she stayed home? Why had she insisted on going for a run? She was *so* stupid. God only knows what would have happened if Lynch hadn't shown up. A thought that had bile burning her throat.

A hand gripped her shoulder.

She scuttled away, finding a good-sized rock in the process. She scrambled to her feet and spun around, prepared to bash in someone's brains...but it was Lynch.

With his hair plastered to his head and his t-shirt clinging to his torso, he looked like hell. And she almost wept with relief.

"C'mon. Let's go."

If she weren't cold and scared, she might question where exactly where they were going. As it was, she allowed him to lead her to his waiting Harley.

He retrieved a spare helmet from his pack, placed it on her head and fastened the buckle. He threw his leg over the seat, helped her mount up behind him then slowly rode down the jogging trail.

She huddled to him, working to calm her breathing and pulse.

She was safe. Lynch was taking her home. And she might not ever leave again.

Chapter Thirteen

DRIVING THROUGH THE sheets of rain, Lynch became increasingly concerned about the weather. Wiping out in the middle of nowhere during a ferocious thunderstorm with Junkyard's goons after Shasta was not a good scenario.

He squinted, but barely saw anything past his bike's front tire. The very real possibility of getting caught in a flash flood tightened his gut.

He veered west and headed in the direction of the Bentley ranch. It'd been abandoned since before he went to prison. With luck, parts of the outbuildings still stood.

Wetness soaked him to his marrow, but he took comfort in Shasta's body pressing into his. She was safe, thank you, God, but was also shivering. Bad. And not just from being wet and cold. Shock had to be setting in. He needed to get her someplace warm and dry, and soon.

At the derelict barn of the Bentley farm, he lowered the kickstand and cut the engine. He climbed off, but Shasta grabbed his sleeve. He leaned close to hear her over the storm.

"Why are we here?"

"Can't ride in this."

"But I need to get home."

He shook his head. "Too dangerous." He held out his hand. "C'mon."

For a moment he thought she'd refuse, but she gripped his fingers and he helped her alight. He shoved his shoulder into the door to open it. She hurried inside while he muscled his Harley across the threshold. He hauled the door closed.

The smell of dank hay itched his nose as the rain pelted the roof. His clothes clung to him like a sopping second skin. He pulled off his half helmet and shook his head. Water droplets sailed everywhere.

Shasta's hands trembled so badly, she fumbled with the chinstrap. He brushed away her fingers, removed the helmet and set it on the bike seat.

Rain dripped from her face and hair. She looked like a kitten saved from drowning.

She wrapped her arms around her middle, visibly shaking. "Jesus...I'm cold." Suddenly she groped at her waistband. "Shit...I lost my phone." With her frantic movements, she almost toppled over. "God*damn* it."

"Hey..." He steadied her. "We can't do anything about your phone right now. Here..." He retrieved a dry shirt and zip-up sweatshirt from his pack. "Put these on. It'll help warm you up."

She shied from the offered clothes. "What about you?"

He quirked a grin. "I'll be fine. I've got more meat on my bones than you."

Not meeting his gaze, she slipped off his cut, took the t-shirt and pulled it over her head. She then donned the sweatshirt and zipped it to her neck. "Thanks." She re-crossed her arms, but she continued to shudder.

Without conscious thought Lynch enclosed her in a hug and rubbed his hands along her back. His body immediately reacted to her nearness. To how her soft curves fit against his hard planes. To her spicy, musky scent.

He cleared his throat and eased her away. "Better?"

She nodded, her brown eyes staring up at him. Her pupils darkened and her gaze lowered to his mouth. She licked her lips. A groan lodged behind his breastbone. His cock swelled.

Against his better judgment he cupped her cheek. He couldn't help himself. After years of having nothing but brutal harshness in his life, to touch something this supple, this beautiful was too tempting to ignore.

She leaned into his palm and her eyelids drifted shut. He traced his thumb under her chin. Her mouth opened on a silent moan.

Lynch needed no other enticement. He dipped his head.

One kiss, he told himself. That's all. He wouldn't take more. Just a chaste kiss to recall what he'd once had with this woman.

He lightly touched his lips against hers. He fought the primal urge to ravage her mouth. But like a man lost in the desert for seven years, the first sip of sweet water proved his downfall.

He crushed her to him, his palm behind her head holding her in place for his plundering tongue. He swept through the savory recesses of her mouth, over and over and over again.

If she'd protested in any way, shoved him back or turned her head, he would have stopped. But she didn't. Her nails bit into his biceps and her gurgled moans rang in his ears. She seemed to crave this kiss as much as him...

His hands traveled down to her luscious ass and hoisted her up. A squeak vibrated deep in her throat then her sleek legs wound around his waist. Not relinquishing control of her mouth, Lynch knocked her helmet to the ground and perched her on the hammock seat.

He broke the kiss and grasped the pull tab of the sweatshirt zipper. With purposefully slowness, he lowered it. He bore his gaze into hers, giving her the chance to stop him. She just stared at him with eyes so huge, so round, he thought he'd die within their rich brown depths.

Once the jacket hung open, he flicked it off her shoulders then skimmed the wet t-shirt up her torso. She lifted her arms and he pulled the shirt over her head.

He snagged her wrists. "Keep 'em up, kay?"

Her delicate throat muscles labored as she nodded.

Lynch ghosted his palms over her sports bra then wormed his fingers under the bottom. Still holding her gaze, he tugged it up. She licked her lips and her arms quivered slightly, but didn't lower. Within seconds, her breasts were bared. He devoured them with his gaze.

They were flawless. The perfect size with two perfectly pearled nipples.

He outlined one areola with his finger. Her body trembled. He shifted her position so she laid prone on the seat, her feet near the handlebars and her head resting on the passenger cushion.

He kissed her again. His balls ached and his cock pounded at twice his heart rate. His hand molded around one breast. The satiny feel sent another shaft of hunger through his blood.

He kissed her eyes closed before nipping his way to her ticklish earlobe. Goosebumps erupted across her skin and her body arched toward him. His mouth journeyed down her delectable flesh to lick the velvet hollow of her neck, then down farther to a rigid nipple. Her body went completely still, almost like she'd stopped breathing, as his lips closed over the puckered crest.

Lynch stroked his tongue over the peak while his hand skimmed across her flat belly to the snug waistband of her jogging shorts.

Shasta braced her heels on the handlebars and elevated her hips. Lynch pulled while she wiggled. At last, he peeled the offending garment off one leg then the other, along with her running shoes. He replaced her socked feet to the outside edge of the handgrips.

Air back up in his chest as he feasted on her spread before him in all her naked glory. Her skin held a slight rosy hue and her earthy, sexy scent filled his senses. Her nest of pussy hair tightened the knot in his belly. He never dreamed he'd see her like this again.

Once more, he gently gripped her wrists and placed her hands on the passenger seat. "You best hold on, Shaly," he croaked.

She swallowed again, her fingernails curling into the leather.

Using his body to keep her from falling to the ground, he leaned over and took command of her lips in a raw, scorching kiss. He poured every ounce of pent-up desire – seven fucking years of pent-up desire – he felt for this woman into that kiss.

When his need for oxygen overrode his need to consume her mouth, he dragged his teeth down her neck to a taut nipple. He suckled her deeply while cupping her mound, his fingers teasing through her wet folds, his thumb circling her clit.

Tension quaked her legs. She widened her knees. But he didn't delve into her canal. Not yet. He wanted to revel in her writhing body. In her puffy gasps of air that was his whispered name.

He paid homage to the other breast then finally turned his attention lower. He ringed his tongue around her bellybutton and nipped each hipbone.

He snaked his hands under her upper legs to hold her steady as his fingers parted her folds. He immersed his face between her thighs.

Her taste hadn't changed, not in seven years. It was still the freshest, purest, most intoxicating flavor known to man. He lapped at her delicate skin while his middle finger pressed deep into her slit. Her feet came off the handlebars which opened her even more for his questing mouth and probing finger. He closed his lips over her clit, worrying it slightly with his teeth.

And she exploded.

God.

It took all his self-control not to come in his jeans. He loved the sound of her strangle cries. Loved how her hips bucked and her intimate muscles fucked his finger. Loved the taste her succulent juices on his tongue.

But he wasn't satisfied. Not by a long shot.

He sucked her clit into his mouth and tunneled a second finger into her slick channel. He twisted his digits high and hard, grazing her g-spot to prolong her orgasm. To wring out every last morsel of her pleasure.

She shuddered and quaked, and pure male pride streaked through him. Even after seven years, he knew her body so well. Knew how to give her this kind of pleasure. The ultimate pleasure between a man and a woman.

Lynch withdrew his fingers then stroked her clit with gentle licks to soothe her down from her climax. But her convulsions continued. As did her hitching breaths. He looked up at her, and dread tightened his shoulders.

Both arms were folded over her face, still he saw the tears tracking down her cheeks.

Realization clicked in his brain.

She'd reacted the way she had because it had been years since any man touched her. Because she was married to a man in a wheelchair.

Regret carved a hole in his heart. He straightened and tenderly gathered her into his arms. She shook her head and brushed away his hands, but he insisted. He sat on the seat, Shasta cuddled on his lap, and awkwardly draped the sweatshirt to cover her nakedness. She crossed her arms over her breasts and wept into his shirt.

He rocked her and murmured low, the words incoherent in his own ears. He traversed his hands back and forth across her back, desperate to alleviate her anguish, his earlier lust forgotten. The only thing that matter was Shaly, and making sure she was okay.

She cried for a long time. Long enough for the rainstorm to cease and for sunlight to peek through the holes in the barn rafters. She took a deep, stuttering breath then eased away from him. The moisture brightening her eyes landed another hard blow to his heart.

She knuckled moisture off her cheek. "Sorry."

"No...I'm the one who's sorry." He caressed hair from her forehead. "I shouldn't have allowed anything to happen between us."

"It's not like you did it alone." She sat up, drawing the sweatshirt tighter around herself like armor. "Is it still raining?"

He set her on her feet. "No."

"Then I should go."

His eyebrows veed. "Not by yourself."

"Oh, please. I'll be fine. Those guys are gone."

"No they're not. They've been watching you for weeks."

Blood leaked from her cheeks. "Watching me? How do you know that?" Her eyes widened. "Wait...do you *know* them? Were they Streeters?"

Lynch picked up her discarded clothes and shook off the stale hay, mentally kicking himself. He couldn't tell Shasta the truth, that might put her in greater danger, not to mention jeopardize the FBI operation. But to say nothing would fuel her curiosity. He handed over her top and shorts. "Probably." He turned to retrieve her shoes and helmet and give her some privacy.

"Probably? Don't you know who's in your own club?"

He heard fabric rustling. "Not anymore. There's a lot of guys in the crew I don't know, and don't trust."

"Like Junkyard?"

"Yeah. He's the new VP."

"It sounded like he had me targeted. Why?"

"Retribution for your brother taking me into custody."

"But I didn't have anything to do with that."

He heard the distress in her voice. "Doesn't matter. Not to guy like Junkyard."

"And the shipment thing they were talking about?"

"You don't want to know."

She stepped in front of him, pulling on his sweatshirt. Even with messy hair, swollen eyes and a slightly blotchy complexion from crying, she looked beautiful.

"Same with the money?" she asked.

"Same with the money." He held out her shoes.

She slipped into them, but didn't bother with the laces. "Are you taking me home?"

He shook his head while stowing his damp clothes. "Can't risk Junkyard's guys seeing me. I'll drop you at the Grab-n-Go on 314. You can use Felix's phone to call someone to pick you up."

She puffed a grim laugh. "Dell's gonna freak when he hears about this."

Lynch seized her upper arms, ignoring her startled yelp. "No one can know about this, Shaly. Especially your brother."

"But Dell's the sheriff–"

"I don't care. You tell no one. If you do, you could be in more danger."

"Okay. Okay. I won't say anything." She shrugged her shoulders and he released her. "So those guys get off scot free?"

"No." He handed her the spare helmet then donned his own and buckled the strap. "I'll handle the situation." He straddled his bike.

She fastened her chinstrap. "Handle it how?"

"Don't worry about it and don't say anything, understand?" He extended his hand to assist her onto the seat behind him. "There's one more thing..."

She paused and met his gaze.

He gave her his best scowl. "No more running in the desert by yourself."

She rolled her eyes.

He tightened his grip on her fingers. "I mean it, Shaly. It's not safe."

Her nose wrinkled. "You sound like Graham."

He stared at her. A blush stole across her cheeks as she shut her mouth with a click of teeth. She averted her gaze and settled onto the bike. He slowly motored the Harley out of the barn.

The licorice aroma of rain-pounded sagebrush hung in the air. Sunshine streamed through the dark clouds, arcing a rainbow across the sky.

Maneuvering around the puddles, Lynch couldn't help but notice how Shasta held herself away from him. Her husband was the eight-hundred-pound gorilla situated between them. No doubt she regretted what happened. He didn't. He couldn't. He'd never regret being with her.

But he did hate that he hurt her. Hated that he hadn't been

stronger. That he'd surrendered to temptation and took advantage of her.

Most of all, though, he hated she was married to another man.

~*~

While Lynch navigated the back streets toward the Grab-n-Go, Shasta worked to stay detached. To not dwell on the erotic experience she shared with Lynch. Impossible when orgasmic aftershocks continued to ripple through her core.

How could she have cheated on Graham? Yes, she'd been scared and cold and Lynch had been a beacon of stalwart strength. But that wasn't an excuse. And neither was the fact it'd been years since any man touched her.

She squeezed her eyes shut to blot out the memory of his kisses. Of his hands and mouth on her...in her.

Her chest constricted and she fought to breathe. It felt like she was drowning. Drowning in a sea of guilt.

Some people might say she had the right to have a normal sex life, given Graham's inability to perform. But she was not such a person. Her husband was the most decent, caring man she knew. In the face of all Graham had done for her and Wyatt, the least she could do was remain faithful. Apparently she couldn't. She swallowed a sob.

In less than ten minutes, Lynch parked his bike across the road from the convenience store, behind several over-grown juniper bushes. He kicked down the stand, but kept the engine idling then offered his hand to help her alight from the Harley.

She took off his helmet and sweat jacket, setting both on the passenger seat. Lynch kept his gaze straight ahead, his jaw clenched tight. She removed her hair band, threaded her fingers through the tangled locks and redid her ponytail.

When he maintained his stony silence, she walked toward the store.

"I'll stay here until you get picked up," he said. "You gonna call your brother?"

Her stomach rolled. In the aftermath of everything, Dell learning of her little excursion slipped her mind. He'd find out eventually, but she could maybe postpone the inevitable.

She didn't bother turning around. "I'll call Todd, one of Dell's deputies."

Not waiting for a response, she hot-footed across the road and pulled open the Grab-n-Go door. The bell chimed as the air conditioning raised shivers on her skin.

Felix, the owner, paused in restocking candy at the register when she entered. His eyebrows arched high. "Holy shit, Shasta. You get caught in that gully washer?"

"Yeah, and I lost my cell. Can I use your phone to call for a ride?"

He reached behind the counter and handed her the cordless receiver. "Of course."

"Thanks." Shasta moved to the window, her back to Felix, seeking out Lynch by the bushes. She saw nothing. Todd picked up on the second ring.

"Hallo?"

"Todd...hi. It's, uh, Shasta Dupree."

"Well...hell-oh." He sounded much too pleased with himself. "To what do I owe the privilege of this call, on my day off no less?"

"I need a favor."

Todd's chuckle crawled over her skin. "Isn't that interesting?" he drawled. "*You* needing a favor from *me*. And I bet I know what your favor is." He gave another creepy chortle.

And Shasta's remaining composure splintered. "Oh, for the love of all that's holy, Todd," she hissed. "Can you please, for one bloody, goddamn minute, *not* be the biggest douche bag on the planet?"

Despite her best efforts, her voice cracked. She willed away the tears burning her eyes.

"Hey..." Todd's voice sounded clearly different. "I was just joking around. What's wrong?"

She rested her forehead on the glass. "I'm at the Grab-n-Go on 314. Can you come get me?"

Silence answered her question, then...

"*Jesus Christ*," Todd exploded. "What the hell are you doing there? Where the fuck are the goddamn officers assigned to you?"

She fingered the display sign for thirty-weight motor oil. "Graham had a last-minute meeting in Vegas so one drove him to Reno. The other one went to a birthday party with Wyatt."

"That doesn't explain how you ended up out on 314."

"I went for a run and got caught in the downpour."

"Are you shitting me? I'm calling the sheriff."

"*No*, Todd, *please*. I realize what I did was irresponsible and wrong, but don't call Dell."

"He needs to know."

"And he will. I promise to tell him. Just please...come get me."

Todd sighed. "Okay. But tomorrow, I *will* talk to the sheriff about this. Understand?"

"Yes. Thank you, Todd."

"See you in a minute."

Chapter Fourteen

SO WHERE THE fuck is she?

I clench my hands to keep from heaving my laptop across the plane's cabin. Can't do that. It'll just bring the unwanted attention of the first-class attendant. And I've got enough goddamn problems already...like not knowing Shasta's whereabouts.

Fuck!

I have access to every manner of surveillance paraphernalia known to modern man, yet I don't know where she is. If I hadn't arranged for the invalid to go to Vegas, she never would've left the house. But I needed the worthless blob of skin for that stupid impromptu meeting tomorrow. Goddamn it to hell anyway.

When I saw Shasta leave via the external camera at the rear of the house, I didn't think it would be an issue. GPS trackers have always been installed on her phones. Who knew I'd lose her signal? Now I'm flying at thirty-five hundred feet and can't do a fucking thing about it.

The fasten seat belt sign comes on in preparation for our descent. Shit.

I quickly switch my monitor back to the outside cameras at the cripple's house. Still nothing.

My chest squeezes. What if something happened to her? What if she needs my help and I can't get to her? She's my whole world...everything I've done, I've done for her. For us. What will I do without her?

The attendant tells me to put my computer away. I scowl at her terse tone. Fucking whore. If she knew who I was, she'd be *much* more respectful.

I reach to close the lid when a cheery red, two-door Camaro comes into the picture. I know that car, and its owner. But it's confirmed when Todd Weedly gets out. As does Shasta.

My heart jumps into my throat at seeing she's safe. But then my stomach burns. Just what the *fuck* was Todd doing with her?

The attendant tells me again to power down. I absently nod while zooming in on Shasta's face.

Her clothes are disheveled...her cheeks look pale and her eyes swollen, like she'd been crying. Todd comes around the hood of his car and says something to her. She smiles. He pulls her into a hug.

I see fucking red.

How *dare* he touch her.

The whore's back, sounding even more testy about my laptop. I give her a harsh look then switch off the appliance. But I can't forget what I saw.

Todd embracing Shasta. Why was she crying? Had Todd done something to her? If he did, he was dead.

Oh. My. God.

Did Todd bang her? My thought is not just no, but hell no. With all the equipment I've got watching Shasta, she can't tinkle without me knowing about it.

My pulse stutters.

Except for the past two hours, I had no clue where she was or what she was doing. Had she been with Todd during that time? Had she fucked him?

Staring out the plane window, I drum my fingers on my laptop lid. I might not know what's been going on between Shasta and the good deputy, but I do know this...

Todd Weedly must die.

Chapter Fifteen

THAT NIGHT, LYNCH rode his Harley seven miles south of Stardust, to Rolo Pruett's house.

Flat alfalfa fields stretched out from the single-lane, dirt road then collided with the steep peaks of the Sierra Mountains. Rolo's grandfather had bought the six-hundred-and-forty-acre parcel, the best farming soil in Grant County, back in the 1950's. The land had long since been sold, but Rolo still owned a small acreage with a house and barn. The relative seclusion often came in handy when the Streeters had to deal with...sensitive topics.

Lynch rolled his bike through the gate and cut the engine. He surveyed the area as he peeled off his gloves while swinging his leg over the seat. Rolo's hog sat next to a small compact car in the open garage. After removing his helmet, Lynch marched up the walk to the ranch-style house. He paused before knocking.

Since Shasta drove off with Deputy Weedly that afternoon, Lynch fought to subdue his rage over her attempted kidnapping. Fought and failed. He visualized his hands around Junkyard's neck...squeezing. The weasel's beady eyes bugging from their sockets.

His vision blurred and he took a breath. Shasta was safe, that's what he needed to focus on. He compressed his lips. But if he found out Rolo was somehow involved in the botched abduction...

Lynch rapped his knuckles on the front door twice. He needed to keep his shit together and not let his emotions rule because he was about to attempt the mother of all bluffs.

After a few moments, a gorgeous teen-aged girl dressed in an oversized t-shirt and Capri pants opened the door. With her striking black hair and brown, almond-shaped eyes that harkened back to the family's Mexican, Italian ancestry, Lynch assumed this was Rolo's youngest daughter, Vivian....

He smiled. "Vivi, right?"

Wariness narrowed her gaze and she angled herself behind the door. "Can I help you?"

"I'm an associate of your father's. From work." Early on, Rolo taught his girls to not question when a "work" associate came to the door. "Is he around?"

She looked Lynch up and down then called over her shoulder, "Dad...some guy's here to see you." With that, she turned and walked away, leaving the door open.

Lynch accepted the unspoken invitation and entered the house. Rolo came in from the kitchen, a dishtowel in his hands.

"Brother." Rolo's face split into a wide grin. "What brings you here? Not that it ain't great to see you." He tossed the towel on the dining table. "Want a beer?"

"No thanks. We need to talk. In your office."

Rolo's expression sobered. Without a word, he turned and headed through the kitchen, past the washer and dryer and down the narrow hallway at the rear of the house. Lynch followed. In the small, paneled room, the older man plopped into his padded chair behind the desk while Lynch closed the door.

Rolo eyed Lynch. "What's going on, brother?"

Lynch sat in the only other chair in the room, opposite the president. "Grunge told me about the black market pharms we've been escorting down to Vegas."

Rolo scowled. "When'd he tell you that?"

"A few days after I got home." Lynch braced his hands on his knees. "But we both know there ain't no pharms in those vans."

It sounded like Rolo swallowed his tongue. He coughed and sputtered, shooting upright in his chair, his palms flat on his desk. "What the hell are you talking about? What else could possibly be in the vans?"

"Don't play stupid." Lynch leaned forward. "Since when do the Streeters traffic in young girls?"

Rolo darted his gaze to the closed office door then to Lynch then back again to the door as though looking for an escape. There wasn't one.

The president feigned a chuckle. "You've got a wild imagination, brother, I'll give you that."

Lynch drilled Rolo with his stare. "Are you honestly gonna sit there and *lie* to me?"

Rolo's chin dropped to his chest as he expelled a long, low breath. "How'd you find out? Grunge doesn't know anything. None of our guys do."

Easing back, Lynch let out his own quiet sigh of relief. "But Junkyard's guys know plenty, don't they? And some of them tend to run their mouths. I overheard lots in the past week at the clubhouse."

"Goddamn it." Rolo shook his head. "I told Junkyard it was a matter of time before someone found out about this shit."

Disbelief veed Lynch's eyebrows. "That's all you got to say?"

"What you want me to say?"

"How about *why*?"

Rolo glanced away. "You wouldn't understand."

"Try me."

The president rifled his gaze back to Lynch. "To what end? You think you can help?" He scoffed. "No one can help. They've got me by the fucking balls."

"Who has you by the balls?"

Rolo flattened his lips.

Lynch scooted to the edge of his seat. "Okay, so maybe I can't help you, but my lawyer can. She's–" He bit back the rest of his words before saying something stupid. He cleared his throat. "She used to work for the Justice Department and maybe she's still got connections there. I'll bet a dollar for a dime *she* can help. You just need to tell me what's going on."

Rolo's shoulders deflated like a week old, helium balloon. He suddenly looked so...old. "Fine." He blew out another sigh. "It was about six years ago when my middle girl, Carolyn, got diagnosed with leukemia."

A chill raced through Lynch. "Jesus, man. I'm sorry."

A small grin curved up Rolo's mouth. "She's been cancer free for two years now. Going to college down in Vegas. A sophomore."

"Good for her."

"Yeah, but it was real tough for a while. The chemo and radiation made her so sick. She never complained much, though. Then the bills started piling up." Rolo's chuckle held no humor. "With pot getting legalized in California and online gambling becoming popular, the profits for the club have been cut by more than seventy percent. What little money we still made on protection was barely enough to feed our families. So me paying thousands for doctor and hospital bills wasn't doable. I burned through my savings then mortgaged my house then the bowling alley. But it wasn't enough. We were on the brink of having to forgo any more treatment for Carrie..."

"But?" Lynch prompted.

Rolo shrugged. "Junkyard came to town. He said Stardust was the perfect location for running guns and smack from Mexico up to the Northwest and Canada. At the time I thought he was the answer to my prayers. Literally. He had his own crew and just needed a home base plus the occasional muscle. In exchange, the club got a fat thirty percent. For basically doing nothing. It was a no-brainer when I brought the offer to the table. The vote was unanimous."

"Then things changed, right?"

"Right. About a year into the arrangement, things were going pretty well. Carrie's bloodwork looked good and while the brothers weren't exactly rolling in money, everyone had enough to live decent. I thought we'd weathered the worse then Junkyard said he had a new proposition for the Streeters. One that would be even more lucrative. Not seeing the harm, Flyer and I met with him." Rolo rubbed a hand down his face. "That's when Junkyard dropped the bomb about what this new proposal would...involve."

"Trafficking in young girls."

Rolo nodded. "I looked at Flyer and knew his answer was my answer. We said no."

"How'd Junkyard take that?"

"Not well, but Flyer and I stuck to our guns. Hell...even if we took this idea to the table, we knew it'd get voted down."

"But that wasn't the end."

Rolo slowly shook his head. "Junkyard said his boss wanted to meet for the chance to convince me to change my mind."

"Who's the boss?"

"A complete whack-job named Ian Blackwell."

Lynch worked to keep his expression neutral. "Whack-job? How so?"

"The guy's a total germaphobe. Wears a doctor's mask, huge sunglasses and some kind of asinine French hat."

"So you met with him?"

"Yeah. Rode to Henderson with Junkyard. That's where he's based."

"Flyer with you?"

"Nah. Blackwell insisted on just me. We get to an industrial park that's out in the middle of fucking nowhere and ride into a huge, barren warehouse. It must've been a ninety plus degrees in that place. I was sweating my balls off, and there stands this guy in a long trench coat, mask, sunglasses and stupid hat."

"Blackwell?"

"Blackwell. At first I worried I was about get offed, but it wasn't me they intended to kill." Rolo stared into space. "When Blackwell turned, all the lights in the joint switched on. In the middle of the concrete floor stood a table, like they use for surgeries, with a naked girl strapped to it."

Lynch's stomach dropped. "Who was she?"

"No clue. She couldn't have been any older than my Carrie. God...she looked so fucking scared. That's when I noticed Bowyer stood to the side. Sharpening his knife." Rolo swallowed, the sound echoing in the deadly quiet office. "Bowyer started with her toes and peeled away her skin one layer at a time." He turned blank eyes to Lynch. "They didn't bother gagging her, I guess cuz they knew no one would hear her. Her screams were like nothing I'd ever heard before. So shrill and piercing. Such agony and pain. I never want to hear that sound again."

Lynch wiped his sweaty palms on his pant legs as his gut cramped harder.

Sweet Jesus.

Rolo shifted his gaze to a spot on the wall. "After I puked up every meal I'd eaten for a week, Junkyard handed me a manila envelope containing pictures of Roxie, Carrie and Vivi. Blackwell said if I didn't go through with the new deal, the next girl on that table would be one of them."

Bile splashed up Lynch's throat.

Oh...sweet, sweet Jesus.

Forget about being held by the balls. These guys had Rolo by the throat.

The big man looked back at Lynch. "But I told Blackwell it wasn't up to me...that the table had to vote, and no way would the Streeters choose to be a part of this. We might be criminals, but we had hard limits. That's when Junkyard came up with the pharms angle."

The expanding silence smothered Lynch.

Rolo Pruett was as hard and calloused as any gangbanger. He'd never be accused of having a moral compass because morality and criminality didn't mix. But what he witnessed in that warehouse – and the ominous threat to his daughters – would test even the most depraved individuals.

Lynch took a breath, hoping to quiet his riotous belly, and looked at Rolo. "But Flyer didn't buy the pharmaceutical story."

"No. When I told him about that girl, he agreed to keep his mouth shut. Life pretty much went back to normal until..."

"Until?"

"Tre Olsen joined the club." Rolo blew out another somber chuckle. "*He* turned out to be a goddamn fed. I must've been getting old because I didn't see any of the signs till it was too late."

"What do you mean too late?"

Moisture brightened Rolo's eyes. "Olsen got Flyer to flip on the club."

Lynch's body tightened. "Flyer didn't go to Idaho, did he?"

"No."

Though Lynch knew the answer, he still had to ask the question. "Was he killed?"

Rolo sat up and gave Lynch a beseeching look. "You hafta understand, Flyer had turned into a fucking narc, and that couldn't be allowed. He needed to go. For the good of the club."

"You mean for the good of a payout."

Rolo's expression transformed into a vicious scowl. "You think it was about some goddamn payout? The lives of my daughters were at stake. Are *still* at stake."

Lynch reigned in his burgeoning temper. "Did the vote at least go to the table?"

"It couldn't. It'd lead to too many questions."

"So you played judge, jury and executioner?"

"*Goddamn it.*" Rolo slammed his fist on his desk. "Do you honestly think I'd willingly allow Flyer to be..." His voice cracked and he bowed his head. "I tried to reason with Junkyard...he said there was no other way." The big man wiped his nose with a sniffle. "I loved Flyer, but it was either him or my girls," Rolo said in a quiet, tortured voice. He looked Lynch square in the eye. "I didn't have a fucking choice then, and I don't have one now."

Lynch understood family was everything to a man. He'd do whatever it took to keep his mom safe. Given the grim circumstances, he couldn't blame Rolo for his decisions. But Lynch still had a job to do. "What can you tell me about the scheduled shipment next week?"

A beefy shoulder rolled up. "Nuthin'. Junkyard doesn't tell me anything until a few days before. Wait...how do *you* know about it?"

"As I said, Junkyard needs to close ranks with his crew," Lynch lied. "Do you know where the girls are being stashed?"

Rolo squinted. "Why you want to know that?"

"I'll tell Jarvis. Hopefully she can use her federal connections to stop Blackwell."

"That won't stop him. Hell...it'll just piss him off, and you don't want that, trust me."

Lynch could only stare at the man sitting across from him. "That's it? You plan to just keep doing what you're doing? Keep sacrificing other people's daughters to save your own?" He shook his head. "I understand your predicament, brother, but this is not how the Rolo Pruett I once knew would act. *That* man would find a way out. If not to save those innocent, young girls then to avenge Flyer's murder."

Rolo scrubbed both hands down his face. "I'm not that man. Not anymore."

"Then I'll be that man. Just tell me where the girls are being held."

"*I don't know*. Like everything else, Junkyard doesn't tell me shit."

"You'll have to find out."

"But my girls–"

"Will always be in danger so long as Blackwell is still breathing. Your only move is to help bring down that sick fuck."

Rolo's posture crumbled. "It won't be easy. That bastard has spies everywhere. I don't know who to trust anymore."

"Trust me." Lynch stood and braced his hands on the desk. "And I'll do everything I can to keep your girls safe. I swear to God I will."

The two men stared at each other. The naked vulnerability in the president's eyes clogged the air in Lynch's chest. What he was asking this man to do defied every innate instinct a father could have.

Finally Rolo drew in a breath and reached for a pen. "We have three stolen passenger vans we rotate between shipments." He scribbled on a piece of paper. "We also steal license plates to ensure the registration stickers are up to date." He tore off the paper and handed it to Lynch. "These are the current numbers for the vans."

"Who else knows this information?"

"Anyone who paid attention would know."

Lynch swallowed the lump in his throat. "You said you weren't that man, but you paid attention, brother. You knew there'd come a time when you'd hafta step up." He held the slip of paper between his index and middle fingers. "You are that man."

Shaking his head, Rolo lumbered to his feet. "If you say so, brother. But what do you plan to do about Junkyard? If he gets wind of what we're trying to do–"

Lynch turned to the door. "Don't worry about Junkyard. If it's the last thing I do, I'll put him in the ground. Permanently."

~*~

The next morning, Shasta rubbed grit from her eyes then watched milky light slowly brighten her bedroom curtains.

She'd spent a restless night, sleeping only in brief snatches. The fact someone in the 5th Streeters had targeted her weighed heavy on her mind. But the events in the barn with Lynch weighed even heavier on her heart.

The powerful memory of her dual orgasm pooled warmth to her pussy, and welled tears in her eyes. In a fit of frustration, she tossed off the bedcovers.

She couldn't change what happened between her and Lynch. All she could do was redouble her efforts to be the kind of wife Graham deserved. A devoted one.

Her more immediate dilemma – what to tell Dell. She'd promised Lynch not to say anything about the Streeters attempt to kidnap her, but she also told Todd she'd confess to leaving the house without an escort. How much could she reveal without revealing everything?

She'd chickened out on saying anything last night when Dell came over to spend the night, going to bed early with a headache. Today, though, she had to pay the piper. She knew as pissed as her brother would be at her for going against his wishes, it would be a million times worse if he heard it from Todd.

With her resolve at least somewhat fortified, she slipped on her robe then padded downstairs. She flipped on the overhead fluorescent light in the empty kitchen. The stove clock read 5:20.

So where was Dell? Still in bed? Very unusual for her brother. She pivoted to retrace her steps down the hall when a knock landed on the backdoor. She tensed. Who could be here at this hour?

She grabbed Dell's backup revolver from the cupboard over the fridge, eased to the side of the door, grateful to see the deadbolt in place, and carefully separated the window blinds. Two officers, wearing uniforms, stood on her back stoop. "Yes?"

"Mrs. Dupree? I'm Officer Hays and this is Officer Larson. We're with the Reno Police Department Gang Unit."

"What can I do for you, Officer Hays?"

"We saw your light come on and wanted to let you know we were here."

"Where's my brother?"

"He got called into the station."

"Why?"

"We don't have that information. We were told to keep watch then take you and your son to work and school. But if you need anything, please let us know." With that, Hays tipped his hat to the closed door then he and Larson strode down the three steps to the backyard.

Shasta rested her back against the wall as a sudden iciness hit her chest. Had Dell really been called into work? If so, why hadn't he told her himself? Or had something happened to him?

Panic gripped her throat. Given that the Streeters had targeted her...

She grabbed the house phone and punched in her brother's cell number.

He answered in the middle of the first ring. "Can't talk."

She ignored his brusque tone, and the relief that weakened her legs. "What the devil is going on? Reno PD at my house? What am I supposed to say to Wyatt about them?"

"That's the least of my worries at the moment."

"But–"

"Goddamn it, Shasta. Once, *just fucking once,* will you please do as I ask without a shitload of drama?"

She wrapped her arm around her waist as tears pricked her eyes, more frightened than hurt by her brother's nasty words. "Please tell me what's going on. You're scaring me."

He sighed into the phone. "I'll explain everything once you get here, okay?"

"Okay." Her voice sounded like a tiny squeak in her ears.

"Gotta go." The line went dead.

Shasta replaced the receiver then set about her normal morning routine. Making coffee, drinking coffee, fighting to get Wyatt up, fixing him breakfast...

Through it all, she functioned on autopilot, unable to shake the ominous feeling that something bad, awful even, had happened. But she wasn't finding out what until she saw her brother. After what seemed like hours, she finally shooed her son into the back of the cruiser.

Thankfully Wyatt seemed much more interested in asking the officers how many bad guys they'd put in jail rather finding out why they were driving him to school. And once Officer Larson agreed to be Wyatt's show and share, no doubt because he'd been assigned to stay with the six-year-old all day, the first grader bounced like a kangaroo on crack.

Still, the knot in the pit of Shasta's stomach grew the closer she and Officer Hays got to the station. When she saw the parking lot packed with both Reno and Carson City police cars, along with a number of unmarked, black sedans, her insides went on full revolt. She swallowed the bitter coffee bile burning her throat, quickly exited the car and hurried to the entrance.

Inside the building, her feet stumbled to a halt. Uniformed policemen and what she assumed were plain clothes officers sat at desks either with a phone to their ear or staring at computer monitors. She zeroed in on Dell's office, seeing her brother talking with Adam.

"It's just horrible." The dispatcher, Joan, stared at Shasta with red-rimmed eyes.

Shasta stepped closer. "What's going on?"

Joan dabbed her nose with a sniffle. "He's dead."

Lynch?

Shasta couldn't catch her breath. "Who?"

"Todd."

Her knees buckled, but Shasta caught her balance and stared at the older woman. "Oh my God...when?"

Joan shook her head. "I don't know any details. All I do know is that they found him early this morning, shot in the head."

Shasta wrapped her arms around her middle, her thoughts a jumbled mess. Todd dead? She'd just seen him the day before, and he hadn't been the creepy, slimy Todd she abhorred. He'd been chivalrous and supportive. Worried about her welfare.

And now he was dead.

The automatic doors swishing open whirled her around. In marched a troop of men, all wearing flak jackets embossed with FBI and carrying assault rifles. Following behind was Lynch.

Momentary joy shot through Shasta's chest before she realized his hands were bound behind his back, and two more enormous officers flanked him.

Lynch flicked a glimpse in her direction then stared straight ahead, his mouth set in a grim line. Reality spiked her blood pressure. Lynch was being arrested? For killing Todd?

No. No. No.

That made no sense. No sense at all. After Lynch was so adamant yesterday about her *not* being alone, he wouldn't have hurt Todd, especially since the deputy helped her out.

Seeing Lynch disappeared into the interrogation room spurred Shasta to move, and she marched straight to Dell's office.

Unmindful that her brother was on the phone, she burst through his door. "Why did you arrest Lynch?"

Dell's eyebrows slashed together in a ferocious scowl while Adam actually looked amused.

"Thanks for the update," Dell said into the receiver then hung up. Daggers shot from his eyes. "What the hell ever happened to knocking?"

She ignored his reprimand. "Tell me why you arrested Lynch."

"I didn't. The FBI did."

Adam coughed, a small grin still on his lips. "As entertaining as this loving exchange between brother and sister promises to be, I need to get to Callan's interview."

Once the DA left, Shasta honed her attention back on Dell. "Why did you call the FBI?"

"It's standard procedure for the feds to take over the case when a law enforcement officer is murdered."

"But Lynch didn't kill Todd."

"And you know this how? From your extensive training as a cop?"

Her brother's jeer slapped her face, but she stared him down.

He glanced away with a tired sigh. "Look...they found Todd's body at Callan's trailer. They had no choice but to bring him in."

Blood drained from her cheeks as she sank in the chair across from Dell. "Lynch's trailer?"

Dell scrubbed both hands down his face. "Yeah."

For the first time Shasta noticed his ashen complexion and the lines marring his features. He'd just lost his deputy, and friend. God...she felt like such a shit. "Hey."

He met her gaze.

"You okay?"

With a nod, he sat taller and shuffled through the papers on his desk. "I'm fine."

"You sure?"

"I said I was fine."

Hearing that tone, she knew better than to push. "What else do you know about Todd?"

"Not much. The feds don't want the particulars leaked, but there was an anonymous tip early this morning around three saying where the body of a deputy sheriff could be found. They also found a nine-millimeter Glock in Callan's motorcycle pack when they arrested him. That's the same caliber used to murder Todd."

She wilted into a chair. "Really?"

"Yeah. And if the ballistics on the recovered nine-mil matches the gun used to kill Todd, the case against Callan will be a slam-dunk."

A slam-dunk? Shasta's stomach dropped through the floor. She needed to tell her brother about what happened yesterday, her promise to Lynch be damned. If the Streeters truly had been after her, maybe one of them saw Todd pick her up at the Grab-n-Go and killed him for interfering. It might be the only way to save Lynch now...

"I need to tell you—"

Dell's phone interrupted her words. "Albright." After listening for a moment, he waved her from his office.

"But I need to talk to you," she mouthed.

Frowning, he shook his head. She crossed her arms, her own jaw set.

"Hang on for a second," Dell said into the phone. He covered the receiver with his hand. "This is official business."

"But I—"

"Close the door on your way out."

She narrowed her eyes, but he scowled right back, one eyebrow arched. After a long moment, she stood and walked out.

If her dear brother thought this conversation was over, he was *so* wrong. She'd prove Lynch had nothing to do with Todd's death if it was the last thing she ever did.

Chapter Sixteen

SITTING IN INTERROGATION, his hands folded on the table and his posture relaxed, Lynch observed the two men across from him as they straighten their respective stacks of papers, rifled through them, then straightened them again.

Silence soaked the room, but he didn't mind. He knew this tactic...make the suspect sweat with an extended quiet.

Since getting handcuffed, no one had said a word to him. And he responded in kind. He didn't have a clue what was going on, and didn't bother asking. He was just grateful to have on his clothes.

Luckily, he'd seen the black sedans pull up in front of his mom's house and quickly shot off a couple of texts. One to Hez telling him to take care of Ma that day. The second to Newman. With Jarvis out of town, he hoped her "associate" would be able to do something if he got detained. Otherwise, God only knew when Lynch would get released.

Finally the guy to his right spoke, "Mr. Callan, I'm Special Agent Granger and this is Special Agent Coleston. We're with the FBI. Would you mind enlightening us to your whereabouts last night between the hours of midnight and six am?"

"Not at all," Lynch replied with a nonchalant shrug. "Once my lawyer, Emma Jarvis, gets here I'd be happy to...enlighten...you about anything you want."

No recognition of Jarvis's name flickered on either man's face. Was that because these two were the world's best actors or did they really not know a fellow agent? Lynch's stomach tightened. If they didn't know Jarvis, then they didn't know about his deal with her. But then she'd warned him the Reno office wouldn't be in the loop...

Granger turned to Coleston. "He wants his lawyer. You know what that means."

Coleston nodded. "He's guilty." The agent shoved a picture across the table. "Do you know this man?"

Lynch said nothing, not lowering his gaze.

"This is Deputy Todd Weedly. Found murdered early this morning. Shot in the back of the head."

Icy fingers squeezed Lynch's throat. Todd Weedly...the guy who picked up Shasta yesterday at the Grab-n-Go. If Lynch hadn't followed Weedly's car back to her house and seen her walk inside, he might have feared something had happened to her. He pushed the photo back, still not looking directly at it. "Haven't had the pleasure."

"Interesting," Granger interjected, "considering we found his body next to your trailer."

Lynch's pulse skyrocketed and his stomach contorted, but he kept his expression dispassionate. "I said I want my lawyer."

Coleston extracted another photo from a file and held it up. It was of a nine mil Glock. "You got out of prison a couple of weeks ago?" He glanced at the picture. "This was found in your motorcycle gear."

Lynch swallowed his snort. How dumb did these two think he was? If he had shot someone, would he seriously have kept the weapon, or left the body next to his trailer?

"A parolee in possession of a gun will get him a seat on the first bus back to prison," Coleston continued. "And if the gun killed a law enforcement officer in cold blood, then that parolee will spend what's left of his life in solitary twenty-three hours a day. But..." He tented his fingers, "...you save us the trouble of *proving* you murdered Deputy Weedly, and we'll not only see to it you go into gen pop, we might even be able to take the death penalty off the table. But this offer is only good for the next five seconds."

Lynch clamped his jaws together and glared as Coleston made a show of looking at his watch.

"Time's up."

The agents collected their pictures and files then stood, but Granger paused to lean close to Lynch's ear.

"I'm really glad you're as stupid as you look, Callan," he said. "I'll have a front row seat to your date with a needle."

Lynch stared at his reflection in the one-way mirror, maintaining a stoic exterior while the agents left, but the knot in his stomach increased. With this evidence, his name *would* be on a return ticket back inside before the day ended if something didn't happen, and happen real fucking soon.

If Lynch went back to prison, what would happen to Jarvis's op? To his club? His mom?

Shasta...?

Someone had to be framing him. It was the only explanation. Question was who...

It didn't make sense for Junkyard or another Streeter to go to this effort if they wanted to eliminate Lynch. A bullet to the head was faster and infinitely easier, not to mention foolproof.

No. Someone either couldn't get rid of him the swift, simple way...or they wanted him to suffer. Then there was the fact Weedly had driven Shasta home. Could be a coincidence, but Lynch didn't believe in coincidences. His gut said Shasta was involved. But how – and was she in danger?

The idea of an unknown person threatening her curled his hands into fists. He would kill anyone who harmed Shasta. With his bare fucking hands if necessary. His murderous thoughts were disrupted when Newman hurried into the room.

Lynch never thought he'd be happy to see a fed, but he sure as shit was now. "Thanks for coming."

"I didn't really have a choice." Newman held the door. "C'mon...let's go."

Shock jolted Lynch's heart. "I can leave?"

The agent nodded. "That's what I said."

"But how?"

"I'll explain later. Right now, let's just get out of here."

In no mood to argue, Lynch stood and preceded Newman out of interrogation. Feeling every set of eyes on him as he strode across the squad room floor, Lynch kept his gaze fixed on the main entrance. In his peripheral vision, though, he noticed Granger and Coleston in what appeared to be a heated discussion with Adam Murphy. He also caught a glimpse of Shasta sitting at a desk. While she looked drawn and pale, relief warmed his chest at seeing her.

Once outside, he turned to Newman. "How'd you managed to get me released? Neither of those FBI guys seemed to know Jarvis."

"That's because they don't. My car's over here."

"So I'll ask again...how'd you get me released?"

"I made a deal with the DA." Newman hit the key fob of a black Toyota.

"DA Murphy? How'd you pull that off? They think I killed a deputy."

"I know. I also know you didn't."

Lynch pulled up short. "How the hell do you know that?"

"Get in the car and I'll tell you all about it."

"Tell me now."

Newman opened the passenger door and fixed Lynch with a glare. "Time's running out so get in the damn car."

Warning bells clanged in Lynch's head. This whole situation was too sketchy by half. He crossed his arms. "No."

Newman looked left then right – then pulled his weapon. "Get in the fucking car."

"So now you're gonna shoot me in broad daylight?"

"If that's what it takes to get you in this car, yes."

Lynch stared Newman down. As pissing contests went, this one was a tough call for Lynch. Capitulate by getting in the car and God-only-knew what would happen to him. Or stand here and maybe get shot.

Finally Newman lowered his gun. "Oh for Christ's sake...I'm not your enemy. The ballistics on the nine-mil recovered from your stuff matches the gun that killed Weedly."

Despite the warm breeze, a cold shiver hit between Lynch's shoulder blades. He dropped his arms. "I take it Granger and Coleston don't know this."

"Correct. But they're gonna find out soon and you need to be somewhere else when they do."

"Does Murphy know about the ballistics?"

"Yes."

Lynch's mouth fell open. "And he signed off on releasing me? How does that square?" Realization knotted his gut. "Did you blow my cover with the DA?"

"Oh, for the love of God..." Newman holstered his weapon and slammed the car door shut. "It's protocol to bring in a local for an operation of this size, so, yes...Murphy knows you're working with us."

"What the fuck? If word leaks out about my involvement, I'm dead."

"Relax. Murphy has every incentive to keep your connection secret. He's been working on a RICO indictment of the Streeters since he became DA, but the investigation was stalled, until you came into the picture and started doling out information about the gun and drug shipments."

"I never agreed to be a part of any RICO bullshit."

"I know. That's why you weren't told, but Jarvis and I don't give a fuck about that. We care about getting Blackwell and ultimately Fuentes, which trumps whatever a small-minded, power-hungry DA wants. I did, however, tell Murphy that unless he intended for his precious case to go tits-up, he'd better find a reason to have you released before that ballistics report became common knowledge." He reopened the door. "*Now* will you get in the car?"

Stunned, Lynch slid into the passenger seat while Newman stomped to the driver's side and got behind the wheel. If Lynch had any lingering doubts about Newman, or even Jarvis, they were gone – for the most part. He clicked his seatbelt into place. "How is it you're convinced I didn't kill Weedly?"

Newman started the engine and backed out of the parking slot. "For one because there were no fingerprints on that weapon. None. Inside or out. Doesn't make much sense for you to wipe it down, including the bullets, then leave it in your motorcycle pack. And two, the GPS on your phone said you were at your mom's house all last night."

"Maybe I left the phone behind."

The agent gave Lynch a sidelong look. "Did you?"

"No."

"Didn't think so."

Lynch glanced out the window. "Where are we going?"

"Gonna stash you in a hotel in Reno until we can figure out this mess."

"But what about my mom? It's not safe for her to be alone."

Newman eased to a stop at a red light. "I've instructed a team to keep an eye on her."

"Can we at least swing by her place so I can grab some clean clothes?"

The agent hauled a duffle up from the backseat. "Already taken care of. And here are two new burner phones." He handed over silver and black cells.

"Same as before? The silver is only for you and Jarvis?"

Newman nodded. "Our numbers are programmed in."

Lynch stowed the silver in his jean pocket and switched on the black one. "I don't suppose I can tell anyone where I'm going?"

A sardonic grin twisted Newman's mouth. "You suppose correctly. No one is to know anything, got that?"

"Yeah...I got it." Lynch punched in Hez's number.

It took four rings before his best friend answered, "Yeah?"

"Yo, brother. It's me."

"Hey...you got a new phone?"

"Uh...lost my other one. Listen, I need a favor."

"Anything, brother. You know that."

"I need you to stay with my mom for the next couple of days."

"Oh?" Curiosity flourished in the single word.

"Yeah. And I need you not to ask any questions."

Silence met that statement. "Okay, but what do I tell your ma?"

Lynch glanced at Newman. "Tell her I'm tied up with pretrial and lawyer shit and that I'll be outta town for a while. Tell her not to worry and that I'll call her."

"You can count on me, brother." Hez paused. "And take care of yourself. Okay?"

His best friend always could tell when something more was going on. "I will. And thanks."

Lynch disconnected the call then looked inside the bag. It was a jumbled mass of t-shirts and jeans, underwear and socks. And nestled on top of the heap sat a cannon of a Remington 44 magnum handgun, with a box of ammunition. He looked at Newman. "What's this?"

"My backup."

Lynch molded his palm around the grip. "*This* is your backup?"

Not taking his gaze from the road, Newman answered. "It's my *un*official backup. But I figured you'd need to be armed...with an untraceable gun...in case."

"In case what?"

"Whatever. Suffices to say, I'm not willing to take any chances. Be careful with her, though. The recoil's a bitch."

Lynch picked it up. Weighty, but comfortable. A good fit for his hand. He shook his head. Obviously he was much deeper in the weeds than he could have ever imagined. He replaced the weapon and zipped the bag closed. "I guess so long as we're sharing, there are a few things you probably should know about yesterday."

"Yesterday?"

"Yeah. I stopped a couple of rogue Streeters from kidnapping Albright's sister."

Newman swung his head around to stare at Lynch. "How'd that happen? She's got twenty-four, seven protection."

"Shasta, Albright's sister, slipped the detail and went for a run by herself."

"How'd you know this?"

"Got a tip. And I got to her before the others did."

"And you're sure they were Streeters?"

"Positive. They mentioned the Streeter VP, Junkyard, by name. They also said Junkyard wanted her on the next shipment."

The car swerved. "Shipment of girls?" Newman asked.

"Makes sense. They also commented Shasta, Albright's sister, was too old."

"What else can you tell me?"

"Not much. I confronted Rolo last night about the human trafficking."

"You think that was smart?"

"I needed to know what he knew."

"And?"

Lynch sighed. "Rolo's been in on the trafficking from the beginning, though not by choice. His daughters were threatened."

"Did he say when the next shipment is?"

"He didn't know. Guess Junkyard doesn't give out that info until right before." Lynch removed the slip of paper from his jean pocket and placed it on the center console. "But he did have the plate numbers on the vans they're using."

The car veered again. "Are you fucking kidding me? The license plates numbers? That's good work, Callan. Damn good work."

Lynch studied the passing scenery. "Thanks. Think there might be a deal for Rolo in exchange for his cooperation?"

"That'll be Jarvis's call, but if Pruett has good intel, maybe."

"She still in DC?"

Newman nodded. "Taking a redeye back tonight. Once I get you squared away, I'll send her a confidential email with all the new information. She'll probably have a fucking coronary."

"What's gonna happen next?" Lynch asked after a long pause.

Newman sighed. "Honestly...I don't know. But remember how I said shit was about to hit the fan here? You'd better duck and cover because it appears a serious storm is brewing."

Lynch stared out the window.

Tell me something I don't know...

~*~

Though Shasta didn't know the man who accompanied Lynch from the station, the fact Lynch hadn't been handcuffed had to be a good sign. Tears welled in her eyes, but the reality of Todd's death severely tarnished her relief.

For the first time since hearing the news, grief bubbled up. While Todd hadn't been one of her favorite people, she never wished him dead.

An oppressive gloom hovered over the squad room as everyone worked quietly and efficiently. And intently. Little wonder since the case involved the death of a fellow officer.

Shasta was assigned coffee-making duty, which was fine with her. Since Lynch wasn't in custody any longer, she didn't feel panicked to relay the events from Sunday to her brother. Telling Dell could wait until later, as could any repercussions. So when his shadow fell over her desk, she was more than a little surprised.

"We need to talk," he snapped.

"Um...okay. I was about to make some more coffee—"

"It can wait." He gripped her arm and pulled her from her chair.

She yanked away. "Let go of me."

He scowled, but complied. "In my office. Now."

Her gaze darted to Adam who stood next to Dell's desk, watching the exchange, his expression unreadable. She brushed a hand down the front of her shirt. "Fine." She marched into the office and crossed her arms.

Dell shut the door then limped to his chair, but didn't sit. He punched several keys on his laptop. "Come here. I want you to see something."

She moved to stand beside her brother. The screen displayed a grainy picture of the Grab-in-Go entrance. A few seconds later, the hood of a red Camaro came into view. Then Shasta watched herself exit the store and climb into Todd's car.

Rolling her lips together, she glanced at Dell. He looked furious...no surprise there. "I can explain."

"I sincerely hope so," Adam said, perching a hip on Dell's desk, his hands laced together in his lap. "The time stamp on that surveillance video says 3:10 yesterday afternoon. What were you doing at the Grab-in-Go by yourself? Where were the officers assigned to you?"

"Graham got called to Vegas for a meeting that morning so one drove him to the airport while the other went with Wyatt to a birthday party." She hitched her shoulder. "I went for a run, and got caught in the downpour."

Dell drew a hand down his face. "Jesus..."

"This is what I wanted to talk to you about earlier," she said in a rush. "But with everything that's going on, I thought it should wait."

"It can't wait now," Adam declared as he straightened. "The FBI will want to interview you."

Her mouth dropped open. "Why?"

"Because you're one of the last people to see Weedly alive." Adam closed the laptop. "They'll need your statement to help establish a timeline for yesterday."

"Oh...all right." She placed her hand on Dell's arm. "Please don't be upset."

"Too late for that." Her brother's mouth formed a thin line. "I can't believe you took such a risk. You have no idea what the Streeters are capable of."

"Actually, I kinda do." She moved to the front of the desk and sat in a chair. "There's something else I need to tell you." She looked at Adam. "Both of you."

Surprise on their faces, Adam leaned against the wall, his hands in his pants pockets while Dell eased into his chair.

She clasped her hands together in her lap. "On my run, I'd just gotten to this side of the picnic area on Miner Trail when..." She inhaled a breath. "...Lynch grabbed me."

Dell shot to his feet. "*What?*"

"But it's not what you think–" she began.

"*Goddamn it.*" Dell jabbed his finger at Adam. "And you let the bastard walk outta here."

Adam glared back, his mouth pulled down in a nasty frown.

"It's not what you think," she said again. "Lynch wasn't there to hurt me, but to help."

"Come again?" Dell asked, leaning both hands on his desktop.

She nodded. "It's true. He tossed me behind a large clump of sagebrush." She tightened the grip on her hands. "That's when I heard these other guys talking."

Adam cocked his head, his eyebrows drawing together. "What other guys?"

"I'm pretty sure they were Streeters, though Lynch didn't recognize their voices."

"What were they talking about?"

She swallowed. "Me. It sounded like they'd been watching the house because they knew I'd left and where I'd gone. They mentioned a guy named Junkyard and stuff about a shipment."

"Shipment of what?" Dell asked.

"I don't know. But they also said this Junkyard guy wanted me...on the next shipment."

Deafening silence met her last statement. Dell looked ready to either throw up or spit nails. In contrast, Adam seemed angry with his jaw clenched tight.

"What happened after that?" the DA inquired in a curt voice.

Relieved to have the burden of secrecy off her shoulders, she sat forward. "The men left and Lynch took me to the Bentley place where we waited out the storm." Her cheeks heated at the memory of being in the barn and she stared at her lap. "Then he insisted on taking me to the Grab-n-Go so I could call someone for a ride."

"And you called Todd instead of me," Dell uttered in a low voice.

"Because I knew you'd be upset."

"Damn straight I'm upset. Do you have any idea just how dangerous – and dumb – your actions were? Jesus...you could've been seriously hurt."

"I understand, believe me. But the more important point is Lynch didn't murder Todd."

Dell snorted. "That's quite the stretch."

"No it's not," she insisted. "He protected me from those other men and refused to leave me alone during the storm. He took me to the store and even waited until Todd picked me up. It doesn't make sense for him to kill someone else who helped me."

"Criminals aren't known for making sense," her brother responded drily. "But this is all a moot point as Callan's no longer in custody." He shot another glower at Adam.

The DA checked his watch then picked up his briefcase. "I have another meeting, but it's like I told you and your fed buddies, until there's concrete evidence directly linking Callan to your deputy's death, like ballistics, we don't have enough to hold him."

"Bullshit," Dell argued. "Todd's body was found next to his trailer for crissakes."

"True. But there was also a distinct lack of blood."

"We've held other suspects on a lot less," her brother grumbled.

"Also true, but those other suspects never got hauled in *for no good reason* like you did before with Callan. I won't risk a lawsuit." With that, Adam opened the door and left.

Once alone with her brother, Shasta looked at Dell. He stared into space, the ever-present trough between his eyebrows even more prominent. "Can I get you anything?"

He jolted slightly. "No...um, yes." He nudged his coffee mug across the desk. "A cup from a fresh pot, if you don't mind. By the time I get to the break room, all that's left is grounds."

She stood and took the mug. "I know. It's a wonder that poor coffee pot hasn't given out completely. It's never seen this much use. I was thinking we should maybe replace it with an industrial-sized maker, but then figured we'd wouldn't see another case like this again."

The words were out of her mouth before she thought them through. *Of course* they'd never see another case like this because this one involved the murder of a deputy. Of Todd.

Shasta covered her lips with her hand. "Oh God...I'm sorry..."

He waved her off with a sympathetic look. "It's okay."

She gave a weak smile. "I'll get your coffee." Turning to the door, she paused. "What did Adam mean when he said there was a distinct lack of blood?"

Dell blew out a breath. "It's possible Todd was killed somewhere else and his body left at Callan's trailer. But," he added quickly when she opened her mouth, "that's not proof he didn't murder Todd."

Her eyes widened. "Are you serious? Why on earth would Lynch–"

The phone rang, cutting off her argument.

"Albright," Dell said into the receiver. "About damn time we got the report. What did you find?" He grabbed a pen and pad. As he listened, his expression grew more thunderous. He struggled to his feet, his hand on the desk for support. "Are you kidding me? And why the hell did this take so long? Delayed because of what? Oh, Christ...never mind." He banged his phone down, grabbed his cane and hobbled out from behind his desk.

Shasta seized his sleeve. "What happened?"

Dell shrugged off her hand and flung open his office door. "Granger!"

An agent, looking every bit enraged as her brother, stomped across the squad room. "We just got the news. There's an APB out on Callan."

"Get units to his mom's house and the bowling alley. Sonofabitch!" Dell pounded his fist on the door jamb.

She gripped his arm and pivoted him to face her. She'd never, ever seen her brother this livid. "Tell me what happened."

"Callan's gun matched the one that killed Todd. And the one that shot me seven years ago."

Chapter Seventeen

MY DOCTOR HAS lectured me about my blood pressure. He says I need to exercise, meditate and cut down on the red meat and cigars. What a crock. What I *need* is to have employees who aren't unqualified fuckups.

I take a deep breath then hit speed dial number eight. Junkyard answers before the second ring.

"Mr. Blackwell. I wasn't expecting to hear from you."

He sounds nervous...as well he should.

"Junkyard, my boy," I force cheeriness into my voice. Cheeriness I don't feel because I want to strangle this asshole through the phone line. "I have a question. Do I pay you well?"

"Why yes, Mr. Blackwell, you do. Very well."

"Good. Good. And what do I ask in exchange for paying you well?"

"Um...to do what you need done, sir."

"Excellent. So tell me, Junkyard..." I pick invisible lint off my jacket. "...have I ever said to do anything with the Albright woman?"

"The...Albright woman?"

"Yes. The sheriff's sister. Have I ever even mentioned her to you?"

"Um...no sir."

"Then tell me *why the fuck* you went after her on Sunday."

"Well...I...ah..."

"Spit it out man." Blood pounds at my temples. "You did have a reason, didn't you?"

"Yessir, Mr. Blackwell...I had a reason."

"Can't wait to hear it."

"Well, you see, sir...the sheriff, who's her brother, arrested a Streeter. Going after his sister was payback."

"Payback? Because Albright arrested a Streeter? Lynch Callan to be specific. Since when are you paid to give a flying fuck about Lynch Callan?"

"Um...it's the principle. Something like that needed retribution."

"So you willingly sacrificed everything because of some petty vendetta?"

"I apologize, Mr. Blackwell. I didn't think it'd–"

"That's your problem, Junkyard. Thinking. You're not paid to think, but to do as I say."

"Understood, sir. Won't happen again."

"See that it doesn't because if it does...if anything happens to Shasta Albright..." I lower my voice to a harsh whisper. "...you will answer to *me*. Am I making myself perfectly clear?"

"Y...y...yessir. Perfectly clear."

"Good." Calmer, I reached from my cigar box and snip off the end of a fat Cuban. "Now I do have a job for you," I say around the stogie as I light it.

"What's that, Mr. Blackwell?"

I puff for a few moments then blow out a billow of smoke. "Kill Callan."

"But he's in police custody."

"Not any longer. He's out and I want him dead."

"How'd he get released? We set him up just like you said to."

"Yes, but you fucked that up too, didn't you?"

"I did? How...sir?"

"Because you didn't kill the deputy at Callan's place."

"So?"

I'm surrounded by idiots.

"*So,* there wasn't a blood pool at the trailer. It's obvious Weedly was killed somewhere else and his body dumped."

"But the gun–"

"Yes, yes. You planted the gun. Bully for you. I was willing to let the justice system play out for my amusement, but not anymore." *Especially since he'd been with Shasta during the storm.* "Now I want Callan eliminated. Immediately. Think you can handle that?"

"Of course, Mr. Blackwell. Of course."

Now the moron reminds me of an over-eager Labrador, so willing to please.

I thumb through the papers on my desk. "Good. Callan's at the Flamingo Star Hotel in Reno under the name Garret Wilson."

"Flamingo Star...Garret Wilson...got it. I'll take care of it, Mr. Blackwell."

"See that you do." I perch my cigar in the ashtray. "Fuck this up, and I will end you. Got that?" I hang up before he can respond.

Chapter Eighteen

STRETCHED OUT ON the hotel bed, clad only in a towel, the 44 Remington by his side, Lynch flipped through the late night TV channels.

Newman had dropped him at the hotel around one that afternoon, with instructions to sit tight until morning. As promised, Lynch called his mom and she'd been more pissed about Hez staying with her than about Lynch being gone, though she finally, and thankfully, accepted both.

Despite knowing his mom was safe, he was wound tighter than a rice rocket hyped up on NOS fuel because try as he might, he couldn't get what happened with Shasta out of his head. Her taste and smell. The way her body had reacted to him. Those little moans of hers...

His dick tented the towel. Again. Shit. He needed another shower.

He realized it was madness to dwell on that event, but he felt powerless to stop himself. He feared if he stopped thinking about it, he'd lose the memory – and he couldn't allow that. He would need every second of those glorious moments to keep him company in the endless years to come...since he wasn't staying in Stardust.

Sitting alone in the hotel room had given Lynch the time and perspective to come to an important decision. Once this shit-whole investigation mess with the Streeters and the FBI was done, and providing he wasn't dead or back in prison, he'd take his mom and leave Stardust. Start over someplace new. He had to. For his sanity. But, more importantly, for Shasta.

She was married, had a kid and definitely didn't need him being as a constant reminder of their past. She deserved better.

Better than him.

Frustrated, and still horny, he switched off the television then the nightstand lamp. He rolled onto his side, determined to ignore his aching erection. At the rate he was masturbating, he'd probably peel the skin off his dick. He wrapped his hand around the handle of the gun and closed his eyes, only to have Shasta's beautiful image float behind his lids...

In prison, Lynch never allowed himself to fall into a deep sleep. That was a sure-fire prescription for disaster. But after just a few weeks out, he'd gotten soft. He didn't hear anything until his door clicked open.

He tightened his grip on the magnum and rolled out of bed, away from the door. Thank God he'd latched the security lock because it gave him just enough time to scuttle across the room and behind the floor-to-ceiling oak bureau before whoever was outside his room kicked their way inside.

Rapid muzzle flash from automatic weapons joined the intense hallway light streaming into the darkened room. Bullets annihilated the space on the bed where Lynch had been a nano-second earlier.

He cautiously peered around the dresser and made out two shooters standing in the doorway. Balancing his arm against the wood edge, he fired.

Christ...Newman hadn't lied about the recoil as his arm wrenched upwards. He crouched low as bullets pelted his barricade. Bits of wood embedded in his arms, legs and face. Without looking, he pointed his gun at the intruders and fired, emptying the barrel.

An eerie silence followed, then Lynch heard muffled, fading footsteps like someone running on carpet. He chanced another look at the door to see a body on the floor. With care, he stood and crossed to the unmoving form. His mind whirled.

Newman had said no one would know where he was staying. So how the hell did these guys find him?

Frantic shouts and fast approaching sirens jarred him into action. He tossed the gun on the bed, grabbed his jeans from the nearby chair and pulled out his phone. He hit speed dial number one, praying Jarvis was back in Reno because there was no way he'd call Newman.

As the phone rang, he stuffed his legs into his denims. Her voicemail message answered.

Fuck.

He left a cryptic message saying where he was and she'd better get here ASAP then hung up. He could only hope to God she arrived before he landed in jail, this time with the key thrown away.

~*~

Lynch sat in a chair, wearing only his jeans, and patiently allowed a female EMT kneeling beside him to take his blood pressure while a male EMT hunched over and swabbed the cuts on his face with antibacterial wipes. The medicine burned like a mother, but Lynch kept his attention on the tall, balding detective who tapped a small notebook with a pen.

The once good-sized room had shrunk with all the various security personal and cops cluttering the space. Some took pictures of the busted door frame while others combed the demolished bed, collecting spent shell casings as the body of the dead would-be assassin was wheeled from the room.

The tapping stopped and the detective frowned. "And you're positive you can't think of a reason why you were attacked, Mr. Wilson?"

Lynch inwardly groaned. Asking the same fucking question four different ways wouldn't change his response. "Yeah...I'm positive."

"And you don't know this man?" He showed Lynch his phone, and the picture of the dead Hispanic.

While Lynch did recognize the guy from the clubhouse, he didn't know his name. He shook his head.

"He's a member of a local gang."

"I still got nothing."

"All right, Mr. Wilson, let me ask you this–" The detective's cell rang. He checked the ID then held a finger up to Lynch. "Excuse me a minute. Duncan," he said into the phone.

The male paramedic put a butterfly bandage on a cut over Lynch's right eye and the woman released the blood pressure cuff.

"BP's normal," she said, her gaze on Lynch's bare chest a beat or two too long. She packed the equipment and stood. "You sure you don't want to go to the hospital?"

"Yeah. I'm fine," Lynch replied absently, watching Duncan who abruptly straightened his posture. The detective closed his phone then said something to a behemoth uniformed cop.

"Okay," the male EMT said, snapping off his rubber gloves and yanking Lynch's attention from the officers. "Follow up with your regular physician if those cuts get infected."

"Will do."

The paramedics left. The detective jotted in his notebook again then he and the officer turned. And the hairs on Lynch's neck stood at attention.

Shit, shit and triple shit.

He had a bad feeling about that phone call, especially since both cops now rested their hands on their weapons. But rather than show weakness, he went on offensive. "Are we done?"

Duncan grinned. "'Fraid not, Mr...." He looked at his notes. "...Wilson. We need to go everything one more time."

"What's there to go over? I was sleeping when two guys busted into my room, guns blazing. I don't know who they were or why they were after me."

"Right...and this?" The detective picked up the bagged 44 mag from the table.

"A friend loaned it to me."

"And the name of this...friend?"

Lynch scoured his brain for an answer, but came up empty. All he knew for sure was he couldn't tell Duncan anything even remotely close to the truth.

A commotion in the hallway and a loud woman's voice ruptured the tense silence. Then Jarvis plowed into the room.

With her hair a tousled mess and lines marring her face, it appeared she hadn't seen sleep in more than twenty-four hours.

Duncan raised his hand. "Sorry, ma'am, but this is a crime scene."

"My name is Emma Jarvis. I'm a lawyer and that man is my client."

Duncan pivoted back. "You called your lawyer? Way to look guilty."

Jarvis stepped in front of Lynch. "Kindly refrain from speaking directly to my client." She glanced around the room then focused her stare on the detective, her arms crossed. "Care to fill me in Detective...?"

"Duncan. And not at all, counselor." Disdain dripped from the words. "Seems your client shot a man to death tonight."

"It also seems, detective, from the shattered door frame and obliterated bed, the shooting was justified."

Duncan scowled. "He's also wanted in the murder of a deputy sheriff in Grant County."

Jarvis cocked her head. "Correct me if I'm wrong, but Grant County isn't your jurisdiction. If you insist on charging my client for what happened here, I'll need a few minutes – in private – to confer with him."

The detective's frown deepened. "Fine," he bit out. "Everybody out." He glared at Jarvis. "We'll be outside."

Once the room was cleared, Jarvis directed her laser stare to Lynch, her arms still crossed. "You want to tell me what the hell happened while I was in DC? What's this about a deputy sheriff being killed?"

"Didn't Newman fill you in?"

"That little tidbit must've slipped his mind."

Lynch rubbed both hands down his face. He'd never felt so exhausted before in his life. "The body of one Todd Weedly was found last night next to my trailer. Shot in the back of the head."

Her jaw dropped. "What?"

"Yeah...and if that wasn't bad enough, a nine mil Glock was found in my gear. It's a ballistics match to the gun that killed Weedly."

"Jesus Christ." She plopped onto the non-destroyed side of the bed.

"And apparently no fingerprints were on that Glock. Not even the bullets."

Jarvis massaged her temples. "So you're being framed." She dropped her hands and looked at him. "Any idea by whom?"

"No." He leaned forward. "But I do know the only other person who knew where I was and under what name was your partner, FBI Special Agent Sam Newman."

"You're saying Sam set you up?" She shook her head. "No way. I trust Sam with my life."

"You got a better explanation?"

"Not at the moment, but I can't believe Sam's behind this."

"Still maybe we should keep him out of the loop for a while."

"Too late for that. I texted him after I got your message. In fact, I'm surprised he wasn't here when I arrived."

"Really? I'm not."

As though on cue, Newman walked into the room. He stopped abruptly. "Holy Christ..." He turned a befuddled gaze to Jarvis and Lynch. "I saw all the cops in the hall...what the hell happened?" He stepped closer. "You okay, Callan?"

"Oh...now you're concerned?" Lynch jeered.

"Where have you been?" Jarvis demanded as she stood. "I texted you over an hour ago."

"Yeah...I was...otherwise engaged."

"Doing what?"

A stain crept across Newman's face. "I needed to blow off some steam so I went to the Comstock Whorehouse, and left my phone in the car."

"Seriously?" Jarvis shook her head with a disgusted grunt. "Who else knew about this hotel and Callan's cover name?"

"No one."

The silence drew out long and slow as Jarvis and Lynch simply stared at Newman.

Realization dropped Newman's jaw. "Wait...you think I had something to do with this?"

"You just said no one else knew where I was," Lynch said.

"No one but you and me and..." His voice drifted off.

"And?" Jarvis asked.

"Adam Murphy." Newman ducked his head and propped his hands on his hips. "Adam fucking Murphy. It was his idea to use the Flamingo Star hotel and the cover name Garret Wilson." The agent snorted. "He played me. He fucking played me with all that RICO crap. Jesus...how goddamn stupid of me."

"If Murphy's behind this, then the whole operation is compromised," Jarvis said low.

"Yeah..." Newman gusted a breath. "Christ..."

Lynch sat on the bed. "You really think Murphy's behind this shit? Seems a stretch for a smalltime DA."

Jarvis waved her hand to the room. "How else do you explain your late-night visitors?"

"I dunno. Maybe he's being blackmailed like Rolo."

Jarvis narrow her eyes then looked at Newman. "What else do you know about Murphy?"

"Not a whole helluva lot," Newman confessed.

"Dig into his background and finances. Quietly," Jarvis directed. "And keep a discreet eye on his activities too."

"You got it."

"There's one more thing you two should know," Lynch said. "The dead shooter was a Streeter."

Both agents swung their gazes to him "You sure?" they asked together.

"Very. He's one of Junkyard's minions."

"Holy shit–" Jarvis paced between the shot-up bureau and the bed, her fingers combing through her hair. "If the gang's gunning for you..."

"*They're* not gunning for me, counselor," Lynch interjected. "Junkyard is."

She stopped and rubbed a hand across her forehead. "In any case, the first thing is to get you someplace safe."

"I'm all for that. Whatcha you got in mind?"

She tapped her lips with her finger. "We won't move you, but keep you right here at the Flamingo Star."

Lynch stood. "Is that a good idea?"

"Makes sense," Newman added. "Keeping you here might be the last thing anyone would suspect. Besides, with the shootout, the security is going to be amped up big time."

Jarvis nodded. "My thoughts exactly. But how can we make sure someone's not watching the hotel? They'll see if he leaves. And what the hell are we going to do with all the local LEOs in the hallway?"

Newman pulled out his cell. "I might be able to take care everything with one call." He punched in a number while walking to the other side of the room.

Jarvis looked at Lynch. "Still think he set you up?"

Lynch watched Newman as he spoke into the phone, too softly to be heard. "I'm reserving judgment."

"If it makes you feel better, I won't be leaving your side for the foreseeable future."

He allowed a slow grin to crease his face. "I didn't know you cared, counselor."

She scoffed. "About you? I don't. I care about cleaning up this mess then getting back to the work of ending Blackwell and Fuentes."

~*~

The roaring clap of seven rifles firing made Shasta flinch.

Standing next to Graham's wheelchair, amidst the mourners at the Lady of Snow cemetery in Reno, she pressed a shredded tissue to her teary eyes and stared at the flag-draped casket.

Another boom of gunshots broke the quiet.

She never knew Todd had been in the National Guard, or that he served two tours in Iraq. She also didn't know he was divorced with a twelve-year-old daughter. Seemed there was a quite a bit she hadn't known about the late deputy.

One last blast of gunfire sounded, then a bugler played *Taps* as the flag was reverently folded and handed to the weeping parents.

Shasta bit her lip to stem the sob in her throat, but her tears weren't from grief so much as remorse. She should have been nicer to Todd. While his often disturbing and inappropriate innuendos had creeped her out, maybe she'd misjudged him. Maybe he'd actually been a decent guy. She watched the coffin being lowered into the ground. Now she'd never know.

She waited patiently in line with Graham to express sympathy to the grieving family. Her husband shook Mr. Weedly's hand, leaning closer to whisper something. The older man grinned slightly with a small nod. Leave it to her husband to know just what to say.

Graham achieved another a tiny smile when he spoke to Mrs. Weedly. All Shasta could muster was a lame, "Sorry for your loss."

Finished with the condolences, she walked beside Graham as he traversed the bumpy ground toward the paved path. Adam joined them.

"Graham...might I have a word?" The look he sent Shasta curdled her stomach.

Graham looked back at her. "I'll meet you at the van."

"All right." She bent down and kissed Graham's cheek.

As she strolled toward the parking lot, she saw Dell, wearing his dress uniform and trying not to lean too much on his cane, chatting with several other officers from the surrounding departments. Despite their sunglasses, she could see the sorrow engraved on their faces. When one of their own went down, they all mourned. She gave a small wave to Dell, who excused himself and fell into step with her.

"How ya doing, sis?"

She sighed. "Okay. Relieved Graham's home." She stopped at her husband's custom-built van. "If it's all right with you, I won't be coming in today. Or for the next couple of days." She swept hair off her forehead. "I think I'll take Wyatt out of school early, too. I just want to hug him. Like a lot."

Dell's mouth twisted in a grin. "I don't blame you." His smile vanished. "I'm also glad you're planning to stick close to home. You should know we haven't been able to locate Callan."

Shasta tilted her head. "Why would I need to know that?"

"Because of what happened on Sunday, I want you to be on your guard. And to call if he contacts you."

"You honestly think he'll contact me?"

"He most likely won't, but I want you prepared."

She shrugged. "Whatever you say."

He kissed her forehead. "As it should be." He dodged her elbow with a chuckle. "I gotta get back to the office."

Dell left while Graham cruised up. He hit the fob and the van lights blinked. She slid open the van door and pushed the button to activate the hydraulics.

"What did Adam want?" she asked.

"To give me an update on the Streeter situation."

Her husband's brusque tone didn't surprise her. Graham wasn't one to wear his heart on his sleeve, but he cared deeply about anyone working in law enforcement. Todd's death had to be hitting him hard.

Graham wheeled himself onto the square platform, pushed another button and was lifted into the van. He then pivoted into position behind the wheel. She closed the door and hoisted herself into the passenger seat.

He started the engine and through a series of hand joysticks which controlled the gas and brake pedals, he pulled from the parking space and drove slowly from the memorial park. At the street, he turned left and waited at the stoplight.

"I thought maybe tomorrow we could come back to Reno and get your broken phone replaced," he offered out of the blue.

Icicles sprouted in her belly and she rubbed her arms. "Oh, that's not necessary."

"Of course it is. You can't live without your cell."

She compelled a modest laugh past her lips. It sounded tinny in her ears. "Sure I can. We've got the landline at the house which is all I'll need since I'm not going anywhere." *And I didn't break my phone in the first place...* Another forced chuckle. "Besides, I don't want to bother you."

"It's no bother, sweetheart." The van moved through the intersection when the light turned green. "We can go to lunch while we're in town. That new Indian restaurant. Make a day of it."

"Lunch is a wonderful idea, but couldn't we take care of my phone now rather than making another whole trip back to Reno?"

"We'll need the SIM card from your old cell."

"Why?"

"To transfer all your contacts and pictures." He glanced at her. "You'll want those, right?"

Her head spun, and she grappled for a counterargument, but nothing came to mind.

"Shasta...honey...is something wrong?"

She stared at her lap. "I don't have the SIM card."

"Oh? Why not?" He pulled to a halt at another stoplight.

She angled slightly away from him as her silence mushroomed in the cab.

"Honey...is it because you didn't break your phone like you said?"

She swung her head around to stare at Graham. He gazed at her with an unreadable expression. "What did Dell tell you?"

He looked back at the street and eased onto the gas. "Your brother? Nothing. However, Adam told me about your little outing on Sunday."

Annoyance poured over Shasta. "Why would he do that?"

"Maybe because he figured I'd be concerned about my wife."

"I didn't want to worry you."

A derisive chuckle puffed from his mouth. "I'm your husband. It's *my job* to worry about you."

"I know." She reached over and touched his arm. "I'm sorry."

He smacked the steering wheel with his palm, clearly and uncharacteristically agitated. "Damn it...do you have any idea how lucky you were nothing happened?"

She bowed her head, her hands folded tightly in her lap, as images from the barn hijacked her thoughts. She'd rather be staked to a rattlesnake nest than hurt Graham.

"Nothing did happen, right honey?"

She shut her eyes at the unease in his voice and prayed for the seat to swallow her whole.

"Did Callan rape you?" The steely edge to Graham's voice promised retribution.

She yanked up her head. "*No.* Nothing like that happened."

He gave her a sharp look. "But something did happen."

Crap.

She swallowed hard. "Nothing happened. I swear."

Turning the van southward onto State Route 314, he stared straight ahead, tension rippling along his jaw line. She gazed at the passing casinos of downtown as the uncomfortable silence prickled her skin. But she felt powerless to alleviate it.

After several miles, he finally broke the quiet. "Shasta, honey, I'm neither blind nor stupid to the fact you have certain...needs. Needs I'm incapable of–"

Tears welled in her eyes. "Graham, *please...*"

"Let me finish." He sighed. "I know ours was never a love for the ages, but over the years I've come to care deeply for you, and for Wyatt. And I'd like to think you feel the same about me."

She covered his hand gripping the steering wheel. "I do feel the same. I don't know what I'd do without you."

His smile didn't reach his eyes. "Me neither. However it's like I said...I'm not ignorant of reality. I don't know if you've sought out physical relationships with other men...God knows no one could blame you for having an affair–"

"I'm not having an affair."

"I appreciate you saying that, but if you were to have a tryst, I know you'd be extraordinarily discreet. But to sleep with a dangerous man like Lynch Callan–"

"I did not sleep with him," she asserted firmly. "I'm not sleeping with *anyone.* I really wish Adam hadn't said anything to you because I'm fine. Lynch didn't hurt me. And I've learned my lesson not to go out alone until the whole new trial thing is settled. Can we please not talk about this anymore? Today has been upsetting enough with Todd's funeral."

"Of course, honey...I'm sorry."

He offered her his hand, palm open. She immediately twined her fingers with his.

He brought her hand to his mouth, kissed the back of it then rested it on the arm of his wheelchair. "We could still come back to Reno for lunch tomorrow, if you want."

"If it's all right with you, I think I'd rather stay home. Maybe we could keep Wyatt home too. Just have a family day. How does that sound?"

His smile looked more relaxed. "Perfect."

Chapter Nineteen

BLOOD POUNDS BEHIND my eyeballs.

"No, you imbecile," I snarl into the phone. "*All* the vans have been compromised. You need to get a new vehicle for this delivery...I don't care. Something that'll accommodate the shipment...Spare me your opinion and just do as I say. I want that shipment on its way here as soon as possible, understand? Good."

I hang up then pause to rub the pressure at my temples. For a moment, I fear I'm about to have a stroke – just like my doctor predicted. But the tension eases and I inhale a deep breath. Now that transportation for the shipment has been dealt with, I can move on to the next thing.

I slip the small cassette cartridge into the manila envelope, seal the flap and scrawl the address across the front with my left hand. At this point I can't allow something as pedestrian as my handwriting being recognized to railroad my plans.

This consignment of girls is the biggest yet. Over two dozen with most of them cherries. Hopefully that will lessen the blow when I tell Fuentes I'm quitting. To be honest, the Columbian has become a demanding diva, making me glad this is my last deal with him. And the payout will be quite substantial. Combined with the money I've already stashed in a Cayman account, there'll be more than enough for me to disappear. With Shasta, of course.

I've got the ideal getaway place picked out, too. A small isle that's part of the Marshall Islands in the South Pacific. Nothing but sun, sand and Shasta for the rest of my life.

Thinking about my future puts a smile on my face. I stand, envelope in hand and sauntered into the warehouse.

The sound of flesh hitting flesh accompanies the echoing click of my heels while I stroll across the concrete floor. I savor the sight before me. Suspended between two columns by piano wires wrapped around his wrists, Junkyard's feet dangle just inches from the substantial pool of his blood. A shirtless and sweating Bowyer lands another punch to Junkyard's blackened midsection using weighted gloves. The soon-to-be-former Streeter VP doesn't react. As I approach, Bowyer steps back.

I bend forward and peer into Junkyard's distorted face. His eyes are so swollen, I can't be sure he's conscious. It wasn't like I didn't warn him of the consequences should he fail me. And fail me he did. More than once.

First he tried to hurt the love of my life, then he fails to eliminate Callan. But to repeatedly use the same license plates on those vans? Epic disappointment. And I hate to be disappointed.

I pick up the cattle prod from the nearby table and zap Junkyard in the ribcage. His head lolls up with a hoarse moan. He doesn't even try to shift from the painful current.

"Ah, good. You're awake." I replace the instrument then turn to Bowyer. "Take him back to Stardust, finish him off and bury him somewhere outside of town that'll be easy to find."

"Puheeze," Junkyard mumbles through bloated, chapped lips. "On't ill me."

I cluck my tongue. "So pathetic...begging for your life. But you've been a constant disappointment to me, dear boy. Perhaps it's my fault for having been so lenient. But no longer. I can't afford any more mistakes. It's time for you to go."

Junkyard feebly shakes his head. "Nooo..."

"Don't despair," I tell him. "Your death won't be in vain. In fact, it should ultimately lead to my victory."

I nod to Bowyer who punches Junkyard in the face, knocking him out cold. I grab a clean towel and wipe my hands. "Once you've disposed of the body, wait a couple of days then report him missing." I toss the towel back on the table. "In the meantime, pick up Rolo Pruett's daughters and bring them and their father here. The Streeter president needs a lesson about the dangers of crossing me. Lastly, find Callan."

"How? No one's seen him in days."

"Use your imagination. Bribe every cop in Northern Nevada. Use his mother as leverage. Just find him."

"Want me to take care of him when I do?"

"No. He needs to suffer before I personally put a bullet in his brain. Oh, and mail this from anywhere in Stardust." I hand him the envelope.

"What's this?"

"The beginning of the end for Lynch Callan."

Chapter Twenty

LYNCH DESPISED HIDING. When playing hide and seek as a kid, he always insisted on being "it" because he loathed the hiding part. For him hiding translated into cowardice.

Yet for six days, six long fucking days, he'd been locked in a hotel room with Jarvis...hiding. He'd rather cut off his left nut, with a rusty knife.

But as bad as hiding was, not being able to leave the room proved worse. Even in prison he'd had the freedom to go to the yard for some exercise. Not here. Not safe, or so he was told...repeatedly.

Good thing the room was slightly bigger than average. It permitted him to set up a small workout station between the two queen beds where he could do jumping jacks or squat thrusts along with various pushups and sit ups. Jarvis didn't seem to mind his activity as she kept herself sequestered to her bed and the small table next to the window, piled high with papers as well as her computer.

She had some new high-tech hotspot gadget which allowed for a secure internet connection so she could work. It also gave him the opportunity to talk to his mom each night. All-in-all, Lynch really couldn't complain too much about the situation, but he still wasn't happy.

He just finished his fourth set of tricep pushups when Jarvis slapped her laptop closed.

"Goddamn it."

He scooted his butt onto his bed. "Problem counselor?"

She glared at him. "Yes. Finding those stolen passenger vans is taking forever."

He wiped his sweaty face with a towel. "Even with the plate numbers?"

"Even with the plate numbers."

"Maybe you can't find them because they're not being used."

"No such luck." She tapped a stack of folders. "At least two dozen girls have been reported missing from the northwest in just the past month."

Lynch whistled low. "Two dozen?"

"Yeah. And the clock is ticking for them." She reopened her laptop and went back to typing.

He studied her as she adjusted her glasses and squinted at the screen. With her hair slicked back from her shower and dressed in a t-shirt and Capri pants, she looked more like a college student than a federal agent. Except for the gun holster hooked to her waistband.

"Maybe you should take a break," he suggested.

"Maybe," she responded as she switched her focus to an open folder.

"Newman should be here soon with some lunch, right?"

"Uh huh."

Shaking his head, Lynch went back to the floor for one last set of pushups then he'd jump in the shower. He'd say this about the two federal agents...they kept their word.

Somehow, and Lynch had no idea how, Newman managed to get rid of the local cops from the night of the botched assassination attempt as well as procure a room at the Flamingo Star under yet another false name. And Jarvis had said she wouldn't leave his side, and she hadn't.

A knock thudded on the door.

Lynch and Jarvis vaulted to their feet. Gun in hand, she motioned him into the bathroom. He rolled his eyes, but complied knowing the futility of arguing. If they'd been discovered, being in the bathroom would do no good.

He peered through the cracked door. Jarvis checked the peephole, unbolted the lock and turned the knob. She stepped back, her gun still raised, as Newman came inside. Only after the deadbolt had been resecured, did she lower her weapon.

"Clear. You can come out."

Lynch existed the bathroom, noting Newman's empty hands and the agent's grim expression. "Something happen?"

"Yeah." Newman rubbed the back of his neck. "There's been another murder."

Lynch's gut contracted. "Who?"

"Junkyard Taylor."

"Taylor?" Jarvis sounded as shocked as Lynch felt. "When?"

"The body was discovered in a shallow grave yesterday afternoon on the north side of Stardust. And he was tortured by someone who knew what they were doing. The ME put time of death at sometime late Wednesday night."

Jarvis holstered her weapon. "Wednesday? That's four days ago."

Newman nodded. "I know."

"Why the hell did it take so long for you to get that information?"

"That I don't know, but that's not the real interesting part."

"Oh?" Jarvis smirked. "And what's the interesting part?"

"A cassette recording showed up in Sheriff Albright's mail on Thursday." He leveled his gaze on Lynch. "A recording that has you threatening Taylor."

An icy blast hit Lynch's stomach. "Me?"

"Him?" Jarvis moved stand beside Lynch. "That's not possible. He's been with me."

Newman nodded. "Again, I know. But listen to this." He extracted his cell, pressed a button and held it up.

Lynch immediately recognized Rolo's voice – and the last conversation he'd had with the president. *"Don't worry about Junkyard."* Lynch heard himself say. *"If it's the last thing I ever do, I'll put him in the ground. Permanently."*

Newman clicked off the phone.

"That's hardly a smoking gun," Jarvis stated.

"True, but with this evidence, the search for Callan has quadrupled." Newman sighed. "And to top it off, Albright's scheduled a press conference for tomorrow afternoon, where he plans to name Callan as a person of interest in Taylor's murder."

"Shit," Jarvis muttered. "That'll make things messy. You said the cassette was mailed. Forensics get anything off the envelope?"

"Nope. And before you ask, the postmark said it was mailed from the post office in Stardust. So that's a dead end."

Jarvis smirked. "You're just full of good news today, aren't you? Did you at least have something new on Murphy?"

Newman shook his head. "The guy hasn't put so much as a toenail out of place. And his financials are squeaky clean." He took out a small notebook from his pocket and flipped through the pages. "He's divorced with no kids. Makes sixty-eight thousand a year, has a mortgage, two car payments and owes thirty-five hundred on his Visa card." He closed the book. "Like I said squeaky clean."

Jarvis paced to the window, her head bowed and arms crossed. "Shit, shit, shit..."

"Got any ideas?" Newman asked.

Lynch sat on the bed. "Um, I hate to be the one to point this out, but the cops coming after me isn't the worst thing about that recording."

Jarvis turned to look at him. "What are you talking about?"

"That conversation with Rolo was also when he told me about the plate numbers. So if the cops know I threatened Junkyard..."

Her eyes slammed shut. "Then whoever sent that tape probably knows Pruett spilled about the plates. *Shit.*" She went back to the table. "No wonder we weren't able to locate those vans. God*damn* it."

"But all might not be lost, counselor."

Jarvis snapped her gaze to Lynch. "What the hell do you mean?"

"It means whoever has those girls will now hafta find another means of transportation. And fast. They'll be improvising which should make them careless." Lynch nudged his chin to her computer. "Use your agency voodoo to do a search on recently stolen vehicles. Everything from passenger vans to SUVs to semi-trucks."

Jarvis shook her head. "Using my agency connections will compromise this op."

"It's already been compromised. Doing this secret agent shit hasn't worked. Murphy, Blackwell or whoever's behind this, has been one step ahead of us the entire time."

"What are you suggesting?"

"That we go straight at the fucker."

She snorted a laugh. "Go straight at him? How?"

"Use me."

"Come again?"

"You use me," Lynch repeated. "March me into Albright's office and tell the good sheriff I've been working with you all along. Come clean about everything. With you vouching for me, that should clear me of any murder charges."

"Then what?" Newman asked.

"Hopefully it'll cause a shit storm with everyone trying to deal with me which might give you the chance to find the girls."

"You're taking a huge risk, you know that, right?" Jarvis asked. "There's no way we'll be able to keep that kind of news under wraps. Your involvement with the agency will come out and you'll most likely end up with a bullet in the head. Courtesy of one of the Streeters."

"Maybe, maybe not. The only reason this scheme has worked this far is because none of my brothers knew the truth. Once they know the facts, they'll be on my side."

"Another gamble."

"One I'm willing to take." Lynch stood. "Besides, I'm sick of hiding like a rat in a trap. If it's my time to go, then I want to face it. Head on."

Jarvis looked at Newman. "Whatcha think?"

The agent brushed his hand over his buzzed hair. "I think it's dicey as hell, but I don't see an alternative."

"Me neither," Jarvis conceded. She glowered at Lynch. "All right, Callan, we'll do it your way. But God help us – and you – if this plan goes south."

"Look at it this way, counselor, could things get worse?"

~*~

Shasta leaned into the backseat to release Wyatt's seatbelt. The first grader banged open the door, but she snagged his arm. "Nah, uh, young man." She slipped the strap of his backpack over her wrist, closed the door and hit the lock.

"But Mom...I want to see Uncle Dell."

"And you will." With a firm grip on her son's hand, she ushered him up the sidewalk. "But it's like I told you this morning, Uncle Dell is very busy so you will *not* run around like a crazy person. You'll sit quietly at my desk and not bug him or anyone else. You read me?"

"Aw, Mom." He tugged at his hand.

"Don't 'aw Mom' me." She pulled to a stop and bent down, giving Wyatt her best stink eye. "If you don't behave, I'll have Mrs. Hinckley watch you for the rest of the week. You want that?"

Wyatt's mouth flattened into a mulish line, but shook his head.

Shasta stood. "I didn't think so. C'mon...I'll get you a glass of lemonade." She started walking again, Wyatt compliant by her side.

Ah the joys of conference week when kids got dismissed early from school with more bottled-up energy than they, or their parents, knew how to handle. And today was just the first day of early release...

Under normal circumstances, it wouldn't be an issue for Wyatt to hang out at the stationhouse in the afternoons. But these circumstances were far from normal.

The investigation into Todd's murder continued at full throttle. Though the local police and sheriff deputies had returned to their regular duties, the conference room still overflowed with the half a dozen FBI agents assigned to the case. The last thing anyone needed, especially Shasta, was for her darling son to be a royal pain to the men and woman searching for the murderer.

Approaching the front entrance, Wyatt gave a hard yank of his hand, and broke free.

With a devilish grin, he sprinted to the door. "Race ya, Mom."

"Wyatt – *no*."

Shasta hurried after him, entering the building in time to see Wyatt bulldoze into a pair of jean-clad legs. The resulting impact bounced the six-year-old back into her.

"Oh my gosh," she gushed. She juggled the backpack while recapturing Wyatt's wrist. "I'm so sorry about that. Wyatt, apologize to the..."

Her voice trailed off when she stared at the man Wyatt rammed into.

Lynch. His gaze darkened as it swept over her face and ever-so-quickly down her body.

Confusion froze her brain, and her thoughts. What on earth was he doing here? Dressed in a chest-molding, white t-shirt and low-slung jeans, he held his cut in his right hand. Did he not think someone would recognize him?

Her pulse rate zoomed and her breathing quickened. She clutched the short sleeve of his shirt, glancing quickly around the squad room. Any second someone would spot him and slap cuffs on him. "What are you doing here?"

"Mrs. Dupree?"

Shasta dropped her hand and spun toward the female voice. Lynch's lawyer strolled up. "Oh...um...Ms. Jarvis."

"Actually it's Special Agent Jarvis. I'm with the FBI."

Air choked Shasta's throat. "The FBI?"

"Yes ma'am. Mr. Callan has been assisting me and Special Agent Newman," she pointed to the man beside her who'd left with Lynch the morning after the discovery of Todd's body, "in an investigation."

Bewildered, Shasta looked back at Lynch, noting his relaxed stance, his left thumb hooked in his belt loop. "An investigation?"

He winked as a small, crooked grin lifted the corners of his mouth.

Wyatt turned his gaze up to Shasta. "Mom...what's a vestigation?"

Shasta covered Wyatt's mouth with her hand. "Not now, honey."

Wyatt immediately twisted away. "What's a vestigation? What's FBI?"

She looked down at her son. "I'll tell you in a minute." Shasta refocused on Lynch and Jarvis "Does my brother know about this?"

Lynch's grin grew larger. "He does now."

"Oh..." Shasta glanced at Dell's office where he stared back, looking extremely pissed. She met Jarvis's gaze. "What about Adam...I mean DA Murphy? Does he know?"

"We're on our way to his office now. If you'll excuse us..."

"Of course." Shasta maneuvered Wyatt to the side.

"What's that?" Wyatt pointed a small finger at Lynch's cut.

"My jacket." Lynch held it out in both hands.

Wyatt studied it for a moment. "How come it don't got no sleeves?"

"Why doesn't it have sleeves?" Shasta automatically corrected.

Lynch looked at his cut. "It came this way when I got it." He squatted in front of Wyatt. "Think I should take it back?"

The first grader gave a solemn nod. "Jackets are supposed to have sleeves."

Chuckling, Lynch stood. "Yes they are."

"Come on, Callan," Jarvis said. "We need to go." She nodded to Shasta. "Mrs. Dupree."

"Ms...Agent Jarvis."

The agents and Lynch existed the building while Shasta guided Wyatt toward the break room. But on the way, her legs wobbled and she nearly fell.

Oh my God...Lynch saw Wyatt.

She leaned on a desk, a hand to her forehead.

"Mom...Mommy...you okay?"

Straightening, she forced a smile and nodded. "I'm fine, honey. Let's get you that lemonade."

In the break room, she situated Wyatt on a tall stool and retrieved a glass from the cupboard, her thoughts reeling.

Had Lynch noticed any family resemblance? His behavior indicated he hadn't, but that didn't make her feel better. In hindsight, she'd been damn lucky father and son never met face to face before now. She poured the yellow liquid and set it on the table.

Wyatt grasped the paper cup both hands. "Mom, who was that man?"

"Um...someone Mommy and Uncle Dell knew a long time ago. Careful not to spill, okay?"

"What's FBI?"

"A special kind of policeman." She cut up an apple, more to give her something to do than to feed Wyatt. He'd had lunch less than an hour ago.

"So that man's a policeman like Unca Dell?"

She paused in placing the apple slices on a plate. Lynch assisting in an FBI investigation? What investigation, and for how long? Was this the real reason behind his release from prison? Was this investigation dangerous?

Wyatt pulled at her hand. "Is he a policeman, too?"

"In a way, yes." Plate in hand, she sat next to Wyatt. "Here, honey."

He looked at the offering, a slight frown on his mouth. "Mom, can I play Doodle Jump on your phone?"

"Sure." She set up the game then absently nibbled on a piece of fruit, watching Wyatt concentrate on the tiny screen.

She knew the older Wyatt got, the more he'd favor Lynch. Already, his hair bleached out in the summer. Besides the memorizing blue eyes, dad and son also shared the same strong chin and Roman nose. It'd be just a matter of time before everyone in Stardust knew who fathered Wyatt, including Graham. But would that be such a bad thing? Wasn't it time the truth came out? Didn't Lynch deserve to know he had a son? Didn't Wyatt deserve to know his real father? She wasn't a child any longer. She should take responsibility for her past actions.

And if Lynch now worked with the FBI, did that mean he'd given up his unlawful, biker ways? That he'd decided to walk the straight and narrow? To be respectable? And if true, didn't that also mean she could be with him?

Realization shrank her vision down to nothing as pain sawed through her chest.

Shasta cradled her head in her hands, her eyes shut, fighting the sudden onset of vertigo.

Oh. My. God.

She still loved Lynch.

Even after everything – his criminal past, the accusations against him, the seven long years of him being in prison – she still loved him. Still wanted to be with him. To have a life with him.

But what about Graham? Could she be so selfish, so cruel as to leave him? For Lynch? Is that how she repaid the man who did so much for her and Wyatt? Who'd helped and supported her for the last seven years? Who saved her from her reckless youth?

No. It wasn't.

Graham once suggested they relocate to Vegas where his security firm was based. But she'd been cool to the idea of leaving Stardust. She claimed small town living would be better for Wyatt than a big, impersonal city. If she were brutally honest, though, her wanting to stay had more to do with wanting to keep the memories of Lynch alive in her heart.

Not any longer, especially if Lynch remained in Stardust.

She sat taller, her decision made. When Graham called tonight, she'd discuss moving to Vegas. She just hoped it wasn't too late...

Chapter Twenty-One

DUE TO A family emergency, Streeter Bowling Alley will be closed until further notice.

Lynch stared at the handwritten sign hanging on the glass door, his hands on his hips.

After going to the DA's office, and being told Murphy would be in a Reno courtroom all day, he, Jarvis and Newman drove to the Streeter MC to confront the president about a few things.

Since when did Rolo shut down the lanes on a Monday for any occasion other than Christmas, Thanksgiving or New Year's? And a family emergency? Lynch didn't think so. All the Streeters knew the alley business in case something like this came up.

He spun and marched back to the sedan where the FBI agents stood waiting. "Something's not right." He gripped the backdoor handle. "Let's head over to Rolo's house."

Jarvis heaved a sigh. "I've got better things to do than chauffeur you around. I still say putting out an APB for Pruett is the best call."

Lynch climbed into the backseat. "But I want the chance to look Rolo in the eye and ask him myself what the hell is going on."

"Fine." Irritation laced Jarvis's voice as she slid behind the wheel.

The only conversation on the drive into the country was Lynch's terse directions. He knew the agents were unhappy, but didn't care. He needed to hear first-hand from the Streeter president how the fuck their private conversation ended up recorded. And in the hands of the cops. As much as he maintained – and wanted to believe – Rolo was innocent, the evidence said otherwise.

"This is it," he stated.

Jarvis slowed the sedan, turned right and eased to a stop. If Lynch had a funny feeling before, his internal alarm system jumped to full alert. There weren't any cars in the carport and Rolo's hog was also missing.

Lynch supposed father and daughters could be out, but out where? He exited the car and stared at the house. The curtain fluttered in the large picture window then metal flashed in the sunlight. He ducked. "Gun!"

A barrage of bullets peppered the sedan, shattering glass and puncturing tires. Both Jarvis and Newman scrambled through the passenger door and slammed it shut, their guns drawn.

Jarvis glowered at him. "Got any other smart ideas, Callan?"

Lynch scowled back. "Yeah...gimme a gun."

She pulled her backup revolver free of its holster and handed it to him. Lynch took aim over the trunk and fired. The agents did the same using the hood as cover. The gun barrel in the window jerked into the air.

Lynch knelt. "I'm gonna try to get around back. Cover me."

Jarvis nodded, adjusting her stance. "On three. Three...two..." She and Newman leaped up and unloaded their clips. "Go, go, go, go, go!"

Crouched low, Lynch raced to the left, behind an oak tree. He paused for a heartbeat then scuttled from his hiding place. Bullets ricocheted off the dirt, scurrying him back to safety.

Heart pounding, he peeked around the tree – and just about got his head blown off for the effort from a second shooter in the kitchen window. He hunkered down again, swallowed the dryness in his throat and counted to five. At five, he darted out, shot four rounds at the small window then dodged back.

A surreal silence pressed against his eardrums. He shifted position so he could see the car. Jarvis stared at him from behind the sedan. The agent nodded once and slowly stood, her weapon trained on the house. Lynch rose as did Newman. Guns at the ready, they advanced.

On the porch, Jarvis took position on one side of the door...Lynch and Newman on the other. She tried the knob. When it didn't turn, she retracted her hand and Newman kicked it in.

"Federal agents," she called.

No response.

She nudged her head to Newman who slid through the doorway opposite her. Lynch followed them into the house.

A mess of broken glass, wood splinters and couch stuffing, along with busted picture frames cluttered the floor. Bullet holes marred the walls. A body laid under the window, bleeding from several wounds to his upper chest and head. Lynch recognized him as Virgil...one of Junkyard's lackeys. Using her foot, Jarvis swiped the AK47 away from Virgil's lax grip.

Newman moved down the hallway as Jarvis and Lynch approached the kitchen.

Another shooter sat sprawled on the linoleum next to the table, the blood stain on his t-shirt spreading by the second, but still conscious. Cam...another Junkyard henchman. Cam feebly tried to point his assault rifle at Jarvis using one hand.

Jarvis stiffened her arms and aimed her pistol right at the guy's head. "Federal agent. Drop your weapon."

With a defiant stare, Cam continued to lift his gun.

"Don't do it," she warned.

Cam glared harder, but didn't have the strength to raise his weapon. It clattered to the floor. She kicked it out of reach then bent down and removed the Glock from his belt. Cam's eyes rolled back into his head.

Lynch squatted beside him and gripped his shirt. "Where's Rolo?"

Cam centered his bleary gaze on Lynch. "Go to hell," he slurred. His eyes closed as his body sagged.

Lynch stood. "You first."

Jarvis holstered her gun. "Would've been nice to keep one of them alive to question. You know either of them?"

"Yeah. This one's Cam and the other's Virgil. Both part of Junkyard's crew."

A loud ringing erupted from Cam's body. Jarvis pulled out a rubber glove, leaned over and extracted a cell phone. It rang again then stopped.

She checked the ID. "Blocked call."

Newman came in. "Bedrooms are clear."

"Clear here too," Jarvis replied, setting the phone on the table. "Better call in this shit show, Sam, and get some of the agents assigned to the Weedly case out here. We're gonna need help processing the scene. If possible, have the guys try *not* to let the sheriff know what happened. At least not yet." She looked at the disarray with a sigh. "The paperwork on this will be brutal enough without Albright going ballistic."

Newman grabbed his phone and went back into the living room.

The cell on the table rang again. Twice.

Jarvis shot her gaze to Lynch. "A signal?"

Lynch shrugged. "Hell if I know, but it makes sense."

"Once the tech guys in Reno get it, they might be able to back-trace the call." A thump from the back of the house had the agent redrawing her weapon. "What's back there?"

"Rolo's office."

Her eyebrows arched as she inclined her head for Lynch to lead the way. He crept down the short hallway, Jarvis right on his ass, and stopped outside the closed door. The agent stood on the other side.

He knocked once. "Rolo? Brother? You in there? It's me."

A muffled sound answered.

Jarvis held up three fingers and nodded to the knob. Lynch wrapped his hand around it, the brass slightly cool against his sweaty palm.

Two fingers. He turned it.

One finger, he threw open the door, crashing it into the wall.

"Federal agent," Jarvis said again, her body plastered against the wall for protection and her gun pointed inside the room.

Lynch craned his head around the door jamb. The bright afternoon light hitting the west window illuminated a shirtless and bloodied Rolo, gagged, sitting in the chair beside his desk, his hands bound behind him. A quick glance indicated no one else.

Lynch slipped Jarvis's backup revolver into the waistband of his jeans and hurried to the Streeter president. The stench of body odor, antiseptic and decaying flesh made his eyes water.

Rolo looked beyond rode hard and put away wet. Bruises colored his cheeks and jaw while both his eyes were so swollen, Lynch didn't think he could see. Blood oozed from the multitude of cuts on his torso, arms and face. And he'd been shot in the right shoulder with the injury crudely doctored. A bottle of rubbing alcohol along with a container of salt sat on the desktop.

"I'll get some water and call for an ambulance," Jarvis said, walking out.

Lynch carefully pulled the gag off Rolo's mouth. "What the hell happened, brother?"

Rolo licked the dried blood on his lips. "Bowyer and a couple of his goons showed up." His voice sounded hoarse.

"And they did all this? What the fuck for?" Lynch extracted his knife and cut the zip-ties holding Rolo's wrists.

"Wanted my girls." With his arms free, nothing kept the big man anchored to the chair. He slid to the floor with an agonized groan.

Lynch caught him and propped him against the front of his desk, but he sagged to the side. "Easy, brother..." Lynch knelt beside Rolo. "I've got you. Gonna just sit you up. What's wrong with your legs?"

"They broke 'em." Rolo held up his badly misshaped hands. "Knuckles too." He glanced at the door. "Did your lawyer just say she's a fed?"

"Yeah. Both her and Newman are with the FBI. Where's Bowyer now?"

"Dunno. What the fuck you doin' with the FBI?"

Lynch peeled the dressing from Rolo's shoulder. Pus caked the bullet wound. He grimaced at the reek of infection. "You're a smart man. Figure it out."

Rolo tipped his head up, anger glinting in his slotted eyes. "Thought something was up the way you got out. Too fucking easy. You're working with the goddamn feds. Shit..."

"Me working with the feds is the least of your worries. Why did Bowyer want your daughters?"

"'Member the young girl I told you about? The one in the warehouse?"

Lynch's stomach squeezed. "Yeah."

"That's why." A croaky chuckle pushed past his lips. "But didn't tell 'em shit. Pissed Bowyer off huge. Pour salt...alcohol on me. Still didn't tell 'im nuthin'."

"So where are your girls?"

The president's mouth quirked up as his posture flagged. "A place nobody's knows. Not even me."

"I don't understand."

"Me neither...till I found it...found it all over the house..." Rolo's voice drifted off and his eyes closed, his chin lolling down to his chest.

Lynch jostled his uninjured shoulder. "Stay with me, brother. You found what all over the house?"

Rolo jerked with an incoherent mumble, but didn't regain

consciousness.

Jarvis reentered the room with a towel slung over her arm and carrying a basin. "Paramedics are on their way. Here's a clean rag and some hot water. How is he?"

"Bad." Lynch took the water, dipped the cloth in it then wrung it out. "They tortured the shit out of him, but didn't want him dead." He gently swabbed sweat from Rolo's forehead.

"Did he say anything?"

"Yeah, that Bowyer was behind this. Guess he wanted his daughters."

"Did he get them?" Apprehension rang in Jarvis's voice.

"Don't think so. If they had, I doubt Rolo'd still be breathing." Lynch cleaned the cloth then dabbed at the cuts on the president's chest. "He also babbled about something he found all over the house."

"Probably meant the surveillance equipment Newman discovered piled in a bedroom. By the looks of things, every room in the house had been wired with cameras and microphones."

Lynch's jaw fell open. "No shit?"

"No shit." She pointed to the ceiling.

He looked up. Holes of various sizes had been cut into the drywall.

Jarvis squatted on the other side of Rolo. "And what do you want to bet this isn't the only place that's bugged?" She shook her head. "That's how Blackwell managed to stay one step ahead of us. And how your conversation about Junkyard got recorded. That bastard is one cunning SOB."

"Jesus." Lynch plopped onto his butt and scrubbed his hand down his face. "I knew Blackwell was dangerous, but goddamn..." He looked at Jarvis. "He really plays for keeps, doesn't he?"

She nodded, her features grim. "Yes. But so do I."

Rolo moaned.

"Brother?" Lynch sat taller and patted his cheek. "You hear me?"

The president groaned again.

"Hang in there, 'kay? Ambulance is on the way."

Rolo wagged his head. "Can't..."

"Can't what?"

"Can't go...hospital."

"But you have to. You're in bad shape, man."

Rolo dragged his tongue along his lower lip. "No...my girls...can't have 'em find me." His eyelids slowly slid up then down as he visibly fought to focus on Lynch. "Gotta die."

"You're not dying." Lynch swiped the damp rag over Rolo's forehead again.

"Not yet...you...kill me."

A wintery wind blew across Lynch's heart.

Rolo did not just ask him, Lynch Callan, to kill him, did he?

"What did you say?"

"Kill...me...please. For my girls..." Rolo labored to swallow. "If alive, they'll find me. Please brother...can't let Bowyer have 'em."

"We'll get Bowyer and Blackwell. I swear we will. Then everyone'll be safe."

"Can't risk it." Moisture seeped from Rolo's swollen eyes. "Can't do it myself...too weak. You gotta...please. Don't make me beg."

Lynch bowed his head.

Christ.

He understood Rolo's fear because if he did survive, his daughters *would* eventually reach out to their father. That's how tight knit they were as a family.

He also knew Blackwell wasn't only cold-blooded and ruthless, but brilliantly cagey. No guarantees existed he'd be caught this time, if ever. And if that fucker lived, Rolo's girls would never be truly be out of danger.

Still...kill Rolo? A man he'd known all his life? There had to be another way. But given how merciless Blackwell was, he couldn't think of it.

He pulled the gun from his waistband.

"Here..."

Lynch looked up. Jarvis held out the nine mil she'd taken from the kitchen shooter and a rubber glove.

He stared at her. For the first time since meeting the FBI agent, he read compassion in her green eyes. Mutely, he donned the glove before accepting the gun.

Jarvis glanced at Rolo then rose. Without another word, she left.

Lynch pressed the Glock muzzle to Rolo's heart.

Tears trickled down the president's cheeks. He smiled. "Thank you, brother. I'se got 'nuther favor."

"Wh–" Lynch coughed the emotion from his throat. "What's that?"

"Cut's on the chair. Take patch." Rolo's eyes coasted close. "You were right...never shoulda done business like we did. Need to make it right. Promise you'll make it...right." He slumped to the floor.

Through his own file of tears, Lynch hunched close to the other man's ear. "I promise, on my honor, I will make this right."

Rolo's smile grew then faded.

Shutting his eyes tight, Lynch pulled the trigger.

During his life, Lynch had fired plenty of guns – hell, he'd even killed a few men in the process – but this discharge sounded different. It resonated in his head. His heart.

He gulped back a sob as the acrid smell of gun powder filled his nose. His chest ached. He should've been able to help Rolo. Should've been able to save him. But he couldn't. Just like he couldn't save Flyer...

He banged the nine mil to his forehead. A noise from behind whipped him around.

Jarvis stood there, a plastic evidence bag in her hand. "I'm sorry about your friend, Callan, but backup's almost here. I can hear the sirens." She plucked the gun from his grasp and dropped it in the bag. "We need to move. C'mon."

Lynch nodded and shoved to his feet, stripping off the glove. He stuffed it in his back pocket then rounded the desk and grabbed Rolo's cut off the chair. With a few expert slices, he removed the president badge. Gripping the worn piece of fabric in a tight fist, he gave a final look to Rolo before following Jarvis to the front of the house.

In the living room, Newman knelt by the gunman under the window, snapping pictures with his phone. He stood, his gaze sliding from Jarvis to Lynch then back. "All done?"

"Yes." Jarvis handed him the evidence bag. "Put this with the other weapons. Let's get this scene processed fast. The sooner it's done, the less questions there'll be."

"You got it." Newman placed the bagged handgun on the shot-up easy chair with the AKs. He looked at Lynch. "Sorry, man."

"Uh..." Lynch cleared his throat. "Thanks." He held up the black cell. "I'm...uh...gonna call my mom. Tell her what happened."

Jarvis nodded, then she and Newman shifted through the surveillance cables piled on the sofa. Lynch walked into the dining room, hit speed dial number three and gazed out the window. It rang twelve times before he disconnected the call. Strange that his mom didn't pick up. She was home, given she didn't work on Mondays. But maybe she went to the grocery store and couldn't hear her phone. He tried Hez's...

Again no answer.

He shivered at the sensation of a spider crawling along his neck. Just because his mom and Hez weren't picking up didn't mean something was wrong. They could be at the store. He'd talk to Jarvis about heading over to his mom's house as soon as possible.

The sound of a keening siren broke into his thoughts. He reentered the living room to see an ambulance pull to an abrupt halt by Jarvis's car and two paramedics jump from the vehicle. They grabbed their equipment, hustled up the walk and into the house.

"Three bodies," Jarvis told them. "All DOA. One here, one in the kitchen and one in the rear."

A medic checked Virgil's pulse while the other went to the kitchen. The wail of more sirens announced the arrival of two dark FBI sedans, and a sheriff's cruiser.

Jarvis gave a sharp look to Newman. "I said to *not* let Albright know about this."

Newman frowned. "I didn't have much control over the situation."

"Shit..." She glanced at Lynch. "Stay here."

He shrugged and she headed out the door. She spoke to the arriving agents while Dell hobbled toward her.

The sheriff leaned on his cane, his feet planted apart. "Why the hell didn't you call me? If you were raiding Pruett's house, I had the right to be informed. This is my goddamn county."

"It might be your county, Sheriff," Jarvis retorted, waving the agents into the house, "but it's *my* investigation. And, for the record, we weren't here on a raid. We wanted to ask Mr. Pruett a few questions."

Dell barked a laugh. "Right. You wanted to ask a known gang leader, someone you claimed less than an hour ago in my office is involved with the trafficking of young girls, a few questions."

Jarvis pursed her lips. "It's the truth."

"Fine." Dell elbowed past her. "I've got a couple of questions to ask Pruett myself."

She raised her hand. "You can't. He's dead."

The sheriff did a double take. "Dead?"

Jarvis nodded. "And if you promise not to interfere, you can see for yourself." She shifted to the side.

Using both his cane and the rail, Dell awkwardly mounted the stairs. Entering the house, he glared at Lynch, then pulled to an immediate halt with a low whistle. "Jesus...what a mess. How many guys were in here?"

Jarvis stepped carefully through the debris. "Two, plus Pruett. He's in the office in back...tortured then shot dead."

"Tortured? Why?"

"We surmise they wanted his daughters."

Dell sent a quizzical look to Jarvis.

She gestured to the surveillance paraphernalia cluttering the sofa. "The whole house has been bugged, we assume at Blackwell's directive, which means he knew Pruett planned to help us."

"Wait...what?" Dell shook his head like he couldn't believe her words. "Pruett was going to *help* you?"

"That's right. No doubt his daughters were going to be used as...punishment for his disloyalty. And if Blackwell had Pruett's house wired, it's a safe bet he didn't stop there. I've called for sweeper teams to check the stationhouse, the DA's office, the Streeter clubhouse along with the courthouse."

"You think my station's bugged? The courthouse? The DA?" Dell blinked. "That's crazy."

"Not to me. To me it makes perfect sense."

Dell stared at the agent like she'd sprouted horns. "Are you hearing yourself?" He spread out his arms. "*None* of this makes sense. You're in Stardust, lady. Stardust, Nevada. Not New York or London or Paris. All this James Bond shit with hidden listening devices doesn't happen here."

Jarvis planted her hands on her hips with a scowl. "I don't know what to tell you, Sheriff, because it *is* happening here. Furthermore, it's highly likely someone on the inside is involved."

The sheriff's eyes bugged from their sockets. "Someone on the inside? As in my department?"

"Or perhaps at Murphy's office."

"Murphy?" Dell shook his head. "You're certifiable."

"Think about it, Sheriff. The surveillance equipment is only part of the story. Someone has been manipulating the circumstances...like framing Callan for the murder of your deputy and Junkyard Taylor. Anyone capable of that, had to be privy to the investigation details."

A scathing grunt flew from Dell's mouth. "You'd believe upstanding public servants are involved, but not this guy." He jutted his cane at Lynch. "He's guilty as hell. I should arrest his ass right now."

Jarvis dropped her arms. "I'm not going to bother arguing. But remember this, Sheriff...so long as Callan's working with the FBI, he's out of your jurisdiction."

Glowering, Dell leaned close to Lynch's face. "This isn't over. You won't be able to hide behind the FBI's skirts forever. When they're gone, I'll still be here, waiting for you to fuck up." He left the house and made his way down the steps, his gait unsteady, but his spine rigid.

Lynch looked at Jarvis. "Mind taking me to my mom's? She's not answering her phone."

"You got things here?" she asked Newman.

"Yeah. Go," the agent answered. "The CS unit should be here inside of thirty minutes. I'll hitch a ride back with them after they're done with the scene."

"Sounds good." Jarvis extracted her car key. "Once I get back to the station, I'll start the paperwork. C'mon, Callan. Let's go."

Chapter Twenty-Two

GODDAMN IT.

I stare at the monitor. I'm supposed to be spying on the stationhouse, but for the last twenty minutes, all I've seen is static snow.

It's not possible my carefully hidden equipment was discovered. Simply *not possible.* No one, not the FBI and certainly not Albright, is smart enough to have figured out my system.

Of course, Pruett did stumble across the gear in his house, but that had been sheer, dumb luck. And Pruett's been on ice ever since, so no way could he blab to anyone else...

Still concern wiggles through my gut. The guys Bowyer assigned to keep the good Streeter president alive, yet extremely uncomfortable, have yet to call. I dismiss my worry. Those two buffoons are just that...buffoons. Not that Bowyer's exactly a brain surgeon, but at least he knows how to follow orders. Unlike Junkyard.

Ah...dear Junkyard. I gave the man too much credit. I really thought he had more on the ball. Oh well...lesson learned. I won't take anything for granted again. I know now to give instructions a three-year-old could follow...like Bowyer...

Find Pruett's daughters then contact me. Find Callan's mother then contact me. Do X then contact me. Do Y then contact me. Simple, straightforward. No chance for any more fuckups. This is how I'll know everything is fine. It wouldn't dare be any other way.

Despite my self-confidence, though, I squint harder at the screen, demanding it obey my command and *show me something.*

If I were in Stardust right now I might be able to surreptitiously inspect the equipment and possibly troubleshoot any hitch. But I'm stuck in San Diego, thanks to the meeting I have with Fuentes in a few hours.

As suspected, the Columbian was not enthused about our business partnership ending. However, I appeased him by agreeing to sell my residual supplies of drugs and guns at cost. I hate letting everything go at rock bottom prices, but I don't want to suffer the man's Latin temper.

I've only seen Fuentes pissed once, and that had been more than sufficient to convince me the man has ice in his veins. He's single-minded in his business pursuits. Nothing else matters, not even family. I heard he killed his own daughter when she tried to leave the family business.

Good thing this next batch of girls is primo. Snatches fit for a king. Or a Saudi prince. Or an African warlord. And it's the biggest shipment yet. Twenty-three, and the majority are virgins. Once it's delivered, it'll be time for me and Shasta to sail off into the sunset.

My phone chirps. Probably the buffoons finally checking in.

"What?"

I don't mask my irritation. They need to know they fucked up.

"Mr. Blackwell?"

It's Bowyer. He shouldn't be calling...I've already spoken to him once today, and everyone's under explicit directions to keep the phone use to a minimum. The wiggle of worry in my gut becomes a cramp.

I rub the pressure building at my temples. "What do you want? You know the rules."

"Yeah, but I'm thinking there's a problem over at Pruett's place."

"What kind of problem?"

"My guys, Virgil and Cam, didn't answer my text like they was supposed to. Have you heard from them?"

I massage the space over my left eye. "No."

"Whatcha wanna do?"

I sigh. "Have you found Callan's mother?"

"Nah, uh. Hez ain't talking yet."

"*Yet*?" The tension inside my skull increases to the point my vision blurs. "You've been at him for two days."

I can almost hear Bowyer shrug his shoulders. "He's being stubborn."

Expelling an angry breath, I prop my elbow on the desk, my hand to my forehead. The silence tightens around my head like a vise.

"If you want, Mr. Blackwell, I think I could–"

"No." I snap. "Don't think. You're not good at it." I blow out another frustrated sigh. "Clean up the mess there, then lay low. I'll be flying in late tonight to Stead Airport. You'll need to pick me up."

"What about Callan's mom?"

"Forget her, and Callan. Your job right now is to do nothing, understand?"

"Yessir, Mr. Blackwell."

"Good."

I disconnect the call then knead my neck's rock-hard muscles. Just when I thought things were going my way...when I thought I'd finally get my revenge on Callan...

Goddamn it.

But if I've learned nothing, it's patience. Callan *will* get everything that's coming to him. I swear to God he will.

Chapter Twenty-Three

LYNCH KNEW THE moment he saw his mom's house something wasn't right. The front window blinds were closed.

And she never, ever closed them.

He leaped from the moving car and dashed up the walk steps before Jarvis could slam the sedan into park.

"Callan...wait!"

Like hell he'd wait. His mom could be hurt. Or worse.

On the small stoop, he pulled the revolver from his waistband and tried the doorknob. Locked.

A metallic taste filled his mouth. He groped for his house key. Inserted it...turned it...then...

A hand yanked at his shoulder.

Jarvis, her weapon drawn.

Daggers flew from her green eyes before she directed her stare to the door and adjusted her grasp on her gun. She nodded. He threw open the door.

"Federal agent!" she yelled.

No response.

Lynch slipped along one side of the living room while Jarvis edged down the other. The sofa and bookcases had been moved away from the walls, like someone went on a serious hunt and seek mission. She motioned him into the kitchen while she continued toward the hallway and bedrooms. He inched forward, one cautious step after another, and peered around the archway leading into the kitchen...

What he saw heaved his stomach.

Hez, strapped to a chair, naked, his head bowed. Blood covered his chest. A car battery sat on the counter with cables running from it to different parts of Hez's body.

Lynch rushed forward. "Jarvis...in here." He knelt beside Hez. "It's okay, brother," he soothed. He pulled out his knife and sliced the ties holding Hez's wrists and ankles. "I'm here. Everything's fine now."

But as he said the words, Lynch knew nothing was fine. That nothing would ever be fine again. He didn't have to see the slash across Hez's throat to know his best friend was dead.

He caught Hez when his lifeless body slid from the chair, cradling him tight.

Jarvis tore into the room. "What the...oh my God..." She moved closer. "I'll call for an ambulance."

Lynch looked up. "Don't bother."

Her cheeks paled, but she turned and spoke quietly into her phone.

Lynch smoothed Hez's mop of blond dreadlocks from his face. Tears burned his eyes and throat. Anguish, the intensity of which he never knew existed, welled up from his soul. But he forced it down.

He wouldn't fall apart. He couldn't. He needed to think. *Think.*

Rolo had been tortured to learn the whereabouts of his daughters. So why would Hez be...

A cold fist gripped Lynch's heart.

"Jarvis!"

The agent instantly appeared. "Backup's on the way."

He gently laid Hez on the floor. "They were looking for my mom."

The agent's forehead pleated. "Your mom?"

"Yes." He stood. "That's why they tortured Hez. To find her."

"Do you think they found her?"

"I don't know, but there's only one place where she could stay hidden." He hurried past Jarvis, down the hall and into his mom's bedroom.

The furniture all sat at odd angles, just like in the living room. His breath came in raw gasps as he opened the closet door and tossed out all the shoes on the floor.

"Callan...what in hell are you doing?"

He ignored Jarvis. On his hands and knees, he gripped the far corner of the carpet and wrenched it up, exposing the particle board subfloor – and the hidden door.

"Mom! Mom, can you hear me?"

"Hello?"

Though muffled, he couldn't mistake his mom's voice. He grabbed the O-ring handle and hauled up the door.

Dressed only in her robe, with smudges on her ashen cheeks and forehead and her hair a tousled mess, his mom stared up at him with wide, terror-filled eyes.

Had he been on his knees, Lynch's legs would've crumpled. He extended his hand and hefted his mother from the underground crawlspace.

He enveloped her in an awkward, yet fierce hug, his face buried in her neck. She shivered and her teeth clicked. He felt the cold from her body seep into his.

"Grab the comforter off the bed," he instructed Jarvis as he trundled backwards, his arms wrapped securely around his mother.

Outside the closet, he hoisted her into his arms then set her tenderly on the bed. Jarvis draped the throw over Edie's slender shoulders.

Lynch tucked the quilt tight to his mom's tiny frame then squatted down. "You okay?"

Her head wobbled. "Thirsty..."

Jarvis turned. "I'll get some water and call for that ambulance."

He swiped strands of hair from his mother's cheek, worried at her pale complexion. Jarvis returned and handed Edie a glass. She stared at it with glazed eyes.

"Let me." Lynch shifted onto the bed, took the glass and carefully tipped it to his mom's lips. "But just a little, kay?" After a few sips, she slanted her face away.

Jarvis knelt down next to Lynch. "Can you tell us what happened here, Edie?"

His mother's brow crinkled. "Do I know you?"

Jarvis smiled. "Yes...I'm a friend of your son's."

"You know Lynch?"

Jarvis flicked her gaze to him then back to Edie. "Yes, I am. We met several weeks ago. Don't you remember?"

Edie shook her head and tried to stand. "Flyer's gonna be home soon so I need to start supper. Lynch...let me up."

Lynch's stomach churned as his mom fought to break free from his hold. "It's okay, Ma. Flyer said we were eating out tonight."

She quieted with a small smile. "Oh, that's nice."

He stood. "I'll be right back, Ma. I'm gonna...ah...talk to my friend here."

Edie patted her uncombed hair. "Do I look okay to go out?"

He smiled down at her through watery eyes. "You look beautiful."

Nudging his head to Jarvis, he and the agent moved to the bedroom door. "Something's not right with her," he whispered.

"Paramedics are on their way," Jarvis replied.

"From Rolo's?"

The agent shook her head. "From Reno."

Lynch glanced over his shoulder. His mother rocked slightly, humming to herself. His gut twisted. He looked back at Jarvis. "I don't want to wait that long."

She studied Edie then pulled her key fob from her pocket. "I'll drive."

~*~

Lynch gave Agent Emma Jarvis credit – the woman knew how to drive.

She accomplished the normally thirty-five-minute trip from Stardust to Reno in a record sixteen minutes, and in rush hour traffic no less. Of course the strobe lights and blaring siren on her car didn't hurt.

In the busy ER, she flashed her badge and a wheelchair instantly appeared to hasten Edie into an exam room. His mom no sooner got settled on the gurney when the attending physician came in, the FBI agent right behind.

A nurse gave Lynch a clipboard of admittance forms then ushered him and Jarvis into the hall. He stood by the nurse's station and wrote in the answers, grateful for the tedious distraction. It beat the hell out of thinking about the last three hours.

Rolo and Hez were both dead, and his mom was now in the hospital.

Planting his left elbow on the counter, Lynch rubbed the ache spanning his forehead as the words on the page ran together. A Styrofoam cup materialized.

He looked up. Jarvis stood there, a second cup in her hands.

"You okay?" she asked.

No, but he nodded anyway, picked up the coffee and took a sip of the bitter brew.

Her phone chirped and she checked the ID. "Be right back." She walked to the end of the corridor, the cell to her ear. "Jarvis."

The nurse relieved Lynch of the clipboard, leaving him to stare into space. Thoughts tumbled through his head...

What if he hadn't gotten to his mom when he had? What if she hadn't gotten into that crawlspace? What if–

"Hey..."

He whirled around to see Jarvis.

"Any news?" she asked.

"Not yet."

"Well, I found out something interesting." A grim smile touched her mouth. "That call was from the sweeper team. They found surveillance equipment throughout the Streeter clubhouse and the sheriff's department. But surprisingly not at Adam Murphy's office."

"That *is* interesting."

Jarvis nodded. "And the DA never showed up in court today."

"Really? What do you figure that means?"

"Nothing good, that's for sure."

The curtain of his mom's cubicle zipped open, ending their conversation.

The doctor exited, a chart in his hand. "Mr. Callan?"

"Yes."

"I'm Doctor Nickels."

"How's my mother?"

Nickels checked the chart. "She's badly dehydrated and suffering from hypothermia. We've wrapped her in some heated blankets and are giving her IV fluids. How old is she?"

"Fifty-two."

The doctor wrote on the chart. "Any history of cardiac issues?"

The hair on the back of Lynch's neck stood at attention. "Cardiac issues? You mean her heart? What's wrong with her heart?"

"Her pulse is irregular and her blood ox is in the low nineties. Probably the result of the dehydration and hypothermia. I'd like to keep her overnight as a precaution."

"Okay."

"Your mother's...resistant to the idea."

Lynch set his jaw. "If you think she should stay, then she's staying."

Nickels clicked his pen and stuffed it in his pocket. "I'll make arrangements to have her taken up to the third floor." He stepped to the side. "You can see her."

Lynch hurried into the exam room to see his mother, nearly smothered in hospital covers, sitting on a gurney and looking extremely pissed. Rhythmic beeping came from the monitor next to the wall and clear tubes ran from her nose.

"Lynch Abraham Callan..." she wheezed.

Abraham.

Despite the breathy quality to her voice, a bit of Lynch's apprehension eased. She seemed like her fiery self.

"...I am *not* staying in this goddamn hospital." She stared at him, daring him to defy her.

He kissed her cheek and wormed his hand through layers of material until finding her fingers. "But the doc says you need to stay."

"Bullshit." She angled her chin. "Just wants to pad his paycheck."

"He does not. He's worried about you." Lynch held his mother's flinty gaze. "As am I. So do me the favor of not being a royal pain in the ass about this. Otherwise, I'll give the staff permission to hogtie you to the bed. Got it?"

She yanked her hand back. "But I want to *go home.*"

Lynch darted his gaze to Jarvis who stood by the closed curtain and uncurled his posture.

Edie looked from him to the agent. "What?"

He sighed. "You can't go home, Ma."

"Why the hell not?"

Jarvis stepped forward. "Mrs. Callan—"

Edie glared. "What'd I say about calling me Mrs.?"

"All right. Edie. What can you tell me about the last few days?"

His mom squinted harder. "Why you want to know?"

"Because I'm an FBI agent."

Edie's mouth dropped open. "You're a what?" She swiveled her head around to stare at Lynch. "She's a what?" Her voice rose in volume and pitch.

"An FBI agent, Ma. Calm down, okay?"

"You calm down," she snapped. "You said she was a lawyer."

"I am a lawyer," Jarvis answered. "But I'm also an agent with the Bureau. Now, please...what do you remember?"

"I thought—"

"Ma," Lynch interrupted. "Whatever you thought was wrong, but I'll explain it to you later. Right now, you need to tell Agent Jarvis what you remember."

His mother's features twisted. "Agent Jarvis," she harrumphed. "Fine...after work Saturday night, Hez and I stopped for takeout pizza on the way home. We were gonna spend the night watching movies and relaxing. I'd just finished a shower when he busted into the bathroom then stuffed me in that rat hole, telling me not to make a sound. What the fuck happened anyway?"

"Some men came to your house," Jarvis said. "That's why Hez put you in the crawlspace."

His mom's face scrunched up again. "Some men came to my house? What'd they want?"

The agent's shoulders rose in a big inhale of breath. "We think they wanted you."

"Me?" His mom blinked. "Why me?"

"We're not entirely sure, Edie, but we're going to find out."

"How long was I down there?"

Lynch took her hand. "It's Monday night, Ma."

"*Monday*?" Edie shook her head as though to clear it. "My God..."

"Edie," Jarvis said gently, "can you tell us anything else? Did you hear anything while you were in the crawlspace?"

"Can't hear shit down there. Used to be a root cellar before the master bedroom was added." A distant smile played at her mouth. "Lynch and Hez used to hide there to avoid doing their chores." Her smile waned as her forehead creased. "By the way, where is Hez?"

Lynch tightened his hold on his mom's hand. "He's...uh...not here."

"I can see that. So where is he?"

He coughed the emotions from his throat. "Listen, Ma...let's not talk about Hez right now. Is that all you remember from Saturday night?"

His mom stared at him. Lynch knew that look. It was the same one he got whenever he'd been foolish enough to try dodging her question.

"Why don't you want to talk about Hez? Did something happen?"

Time ticked by with the only sound the incessant monitor beeping.

Realization lit Edie's eyes. "Something *did* happen, didn't it? To Hez?"

Lynch bowed his head. Shit...he'd wanted to spare his mom this pain. At least for a little while. How stupid of him. His mom was too savvy, too stubborn, for that bullshit.

He tightened his grip on her hand and met her watery gaze. "Hez is dead."

She released a pained gasp. "Dead? How?"

Lynch swallowed hard. "He was murdered."

"By the men who came to the house?"

"Yeah."

Edie looked at Jarvis. "And they wanted me?"

"We believe so," the agent replied.

His mom stared at her lap. "But Hez didn't tell them where I was so they...killed him?" She lifted agony-filled eyes to Lynch. "So he's dead because of me?"

"No," he claimed with conviction. "Hez is dead because a sick bastard killed him."

A sob broke from his mother's mouth and she angled her face away. Lynch hitched his hip onto the flimsy mattress and wrapped his arm around his usually stoic mother, fighting to control his own emotions. Tears burned his throat. He cast a desperate look to Jarvis.

The agent looked on the verge of breaking down herself. She cleared her throat. "Your son's right, Edie. You're not to blame for what happened."

His mom lifted her head. "But if Hez hadn't–"

"No buts, Ma. You hear me." Lynch hugged her tight. "If Hez hadn't done what he did, he'd still be dead. And so would you."

Edie huddled into his side, her shoulders quaking.

Jarvis's phone trilled again. She snatched it from her pocket. "I'm sorry..." She quickly ducked behind the curtain.

Lynch held his mom as she clung to him like a lifeline. Instead of succumbing to his own grief, he focused on his rage, and how he would make Blackwell...Murphy...Bowyer...all of them pay. Pay dearly for what they'd done to his family.

Soon, his mother's breathing became steady and even. He carefully laid her down then stood. For a moment he just stared at her.

Her hair splayed across the pillow in a matted mess. Not her normally coiffed do. She looked so...frail, like she'd shatter if she sneezed too hard. He tiptoed into the corridor.

Jarvis stood by the nurse's station, her arms crossed and head bowed.

"Hey."

Jarvis jerked up her head, her expression grave. "Hey. How's your mom?"

"Sleeping, which is probably a good thing. Was that call from Newman?"

"No, the Portland office. Your idea to check for stolen passenger vans paid off. A Sky Limo van was reported missing from the airport late yesterday afternoon."

"That's good news, right? Now you know what to look for."

"Except the vehicle's no doubt been painted with the GPS disabled, so we have no way of tracking it. Roadblocks have been put in place on the highways heading out of Portland, but they could have slipped past." She rubbed a hand across her forehead. "And this means we're back to square-fucking-one."

"What can I do?"

"Get me information on that damn van," she snapped. She threaded her fingers through her hair with a sigh then glanced at him. "Sorry."

He shrugged. "Have roadblocks been put on the freeways coming into Nevada?"

"Yes." Jarvis stalked the width of the corridor, dodging a nurse and orderly who went into his mom's cubicle. "But if Blackwell's guys feel boxed in, they could cut their losses and just eliminate the girls. We *have* to find that van." She pulled to a stop. "Do you know of any Streeter hideouts that could be used for keeping the girls?"

Lynch crossed his arms and leaned his shoulder against the wall. "In Oregon? No. All the stashes I know of are on this side of the state line. But..." He straightened. "...some of my brothers might know."

Jarvis arched her eyebrows. "You think it's a smart move to actually bring in the MC?"

"For the sake of those little girls, there really isn't another choice, is there?"

She shook her head. "No. What do you need from me?"

"How about everything you've got on Blackwell and the case so far? The more concrete evidence I can give the club, the better."

"I've got an extra copy of the file in my car."

Lynch nodded as the curtain of his mom's exam room opened and the orderly pushed out the gurney. His chest tightened painfully as he gazed at his mom, curled into a ball on her side like a small child. He watched her get wheeled down the hall toward the elevator.

Jarvis cleared her throat. "Just let me know when you're ready and I'll take you to a hotel for the night."

A humorless chuckle brushed past his lips. "No offense, counselor, but I'm not going to another fucking hotel. I'm going back to Stardust."

"And stay where? Your mother's house is an active crime scene."

"I'll stay at my trailer."

"Alone?" The agent shook her head. "That's a seriously bad idea. Especially since we can't locate Murphy. He or one of his guys could be waiting for you."

Rage clouded Lynch's vision. "I hope they are. I'd love to get my hands on..." His words trailed off and he blinked at the fresh surge of tears.

"Look..." The agent placed her hand on his shoulder. "I know what you're going through, but vengeance isn't the answer."

He shrugged off her touch. "I don't think you've got a fucking clue what I'm going through, counselor. You lost one man, Olson. I've lost three brothers and my mother's been threatened. My entire *family's* threatened. Vengeance might not be the answer, but it's a fucking good start."

She pursed her lips. "It's still a bad good idea to be at your trailer...or anywhere...alone."

"Nothing's gonna happen to me. I just need some time alone to think and get drunk."

Jarvis blew out a breath, clearly not happy. "All right then." She extracted her keys. "C'mon...I'll drive you back." She started down the corridor.

Lynch grabbed her arm. "Not necessary. I'll call a prospect to come pick me up." He released his hold. "But I do have a favor. Stay with my mom."

"Why?"

"Because I need to know she's safe."

Jarvis's forehead pleated. "Of course she's safe. She's in the hospital."

"But I can't take any chances. Will you stay?" He glanced away then back at the agent. "Please."

She sighed again. "Okay."

"Thanks."

Jarvis headed toward the elevator and punched the button. "Don't thank me yet, Callan. You haven't gotten my bill." With that, she disappeared.

Chapter Twenty-Four

SHASTA SLOWED HER car, staring at the yellow tape surrounding Edie Callan's house. No lights were on, but a patrol car sat in the driveway with the silhouette of two officers inside. She hit the gas and continued on her way.

By the looks of things, Lynch wasn't at his mom's house. So where could he be?

She still couldn't fathom half of what she'd heard at the station. Not only had Lynch been working with the FBI since he got released from prison, but someone tried to frame him for murder. Twice. Once for Todd's death, and then for the guy named Junkyard Taylor. The same Junkyard Taylor who'd tried to have her kidnapped.

But that wasn't all. Now the Streeter president, Rolo Pruett, was dead...and so was Hez...and Lynch's mom had been hospitalized.

She rubbed her fingers over her puffy, gritty eyes and refocused on her driving. She realized trying to find Lynch was the epitome of a dumb idea, but she had to do *something*. He'd just lost two people he cared dearly about and almost his mom. Shasta needed to know he was okay.

She drove her compact up the dirt road to Lynch's trailer. Probably a fool's errand. What were chances he'd be there? In all likelihood, the FBI spirited him away to an undisclosed, secure location. But with Wyatt safely asleep with Dell at the house and Graham still in Vegas, what did she have to lose by checking for herself? So she'd said her goodnight to her brother then snuck out.

She knew this might be her one opportunity to see Lynch. Graham had been quite alarmed at the recent turn of events and planned to cut his trip short. She told him it wasn't necessary, and almost had him convinced to finish up his business when Wyatt said something about going fly fishing this weekend. Which meant all the equipment needed to be assessed. So Graham would return home tomorrow morning. And that meant she had only tonight.

Shame badgered her as she circumvented the many potholes in the road, but she refused to let remorse deter her. She intended nothing more wicked than talking with Lynch. Holding him and being held...

Fresh tears surged to her eyes. Hez had been her friend too.

She rounded the last bend and her headlights shone on the fifth wheel, along with the familiar motorcycle parked in front. A light illuminated the trailer's windows from the inside, and her stomach did a flip-flop. Shaking off her sudden nervousness, she pulled alongside the motorcycle, cut the car engine and climbed out. Even with her jacket, the evening breeze raised goosebumps on her skin. She hustled to the door, but it swung open before she could knock.

Lynch stood there, his body partially blocked by the door, a gun in his hand. The light behind him threw his face in shadow. Tension pulsated off him in waves.

"What the fuck are you doing here?"

She folded her arms across her chest at his gruff tone. "I heard what happened today." More tears filled her eyes, but she couldn't fall apart. This wasn't about her. Yes, she grieved for Hez, but he hadn't been her best friend since kindergarten...

She tossed her head and gazed at Lynch's backlit features. "I just wanted to make sure you were okay."

"I'm fine. Go home." He closed the door.

She put out her hand and tried to look past him into the trailer. "Are you alone? No FBI?"

"No FBI."

That surprised her. "Is it safe for you to be alone?"

"Safer than asking a bunch of questions," he snarled. "Get the hint, Shaly?"

Yes, she got the hint...didn't mean she'd take it. She angled her chin. "Aren't you going to ask me in?"

He gusted a grunt and stepped back, leaving the door open. She quickly entered in case he changed his mind. "How's your mom?"

He placed the revolver on the counter next to a bottle of liquor. Bourbon...awful stuff, and Lynch's alcohol of choice when he was hurting.

He gripped the bottle and tipped it to his lips. "She's fine, just like me," he mumbled before taking a long swallow.

Though he was drinking, Shasta knew he wasn't drunk. At least not yet. She licked her lips and turned her attention to the surroundings. A heap of cables and wires sat stacked on the table. "What's all this?"

Lynch stared at the pile with a half-hearted shrug. "Nothing important." He set down the bourbon and faced her. "Why are you here, Shaly? Really?"

"Like I said, I wanted to make sure you were okay."

"Like I said, I'm fine."

But his red-rimmed eyes and splotchy cheeks said otherwise. She swallowed her building sob and reached for him. "I'm so sorry about Hez."

His expression crumbled as he veered from her touch. He hunched his shoulders, a fist pressed to his mouth. She wrapped him in a loose hug.

His arms wound around her waist like banded steel. He buried his face in her neck while his body shuddered. She smoothed his hair with her palm and cooed.

He eased back enough to claim her mouth in a brutal mating, like he wanted to purge his sorrow. His teeth clashed with hers and his whiskers burned her delicate skin. She cleaved to him and weathered his rough treatment.

As violently as it started, Lynch yanked her away. His fingers bit into her arms while his ragged breathing echoed with hers. He released her and moved back. "You need to go."

She shifted forward. "I'm not going anywhere. You need me."

"What about your husband, Shaly?" Lynch crossed his arms and leaned against the table. "Think he'll mind me..." He boldly raked his gaze over her body. "...needing you?"

She mimicked his stance, ignoring his transparent attempt at guilt. "Let me tell you about my husband. He's kind and generous, and one of the strongest men I know. And he *doesn't* need me. I don't think he's never needed me. Even with his disability..." She lifted a shoulder and switched her gaze to the floor. "Maybe it's the difference in our ages, but I always thought marriage meant more than simply being taken care of. It should be more." She looked at Lynch. "I want...no I *need* to be needed. And by more than just my son."

She took his hands and uncrossed his arms. "I know you're hurting...I hurt too. We both loved Hez..." Her voice hitched and tears pressed at her eyes. She cleared her throat. "Will Graham be happy I'm here? No. But that can't be helped. You need me. And I need you. Right now, in this moment, I'm exactly where I should be."

His fingers contracted around hers. "What are you suggesting?

She tilted her head. "We could hold each other."

His eyes darkened. "And if I want more than hold you?"

She released his hands and moved between his legs to cradle his face in her palms. Staring into his magnetic eyes, she realized her naïveté at thinking she wouldn't sleep with Lynch tonight. Though that hadn't been her objective, she couldn't deny the inevitable. She couldn't deny she loved Lynch.

That she'd always loved him.

And while she cared dearly for Graham, the depth of her feelings for her husband could never be as profound as the ones she held for this man.

She leaned closer and whispered her lips over his. A growl rolled from Lynch's chest into hers, but he accepted her invitation and returned her kiss.

Unlike before, this union was tentative, more of an exploration. Thoughtful and sweet and loving. His arms enfolded her, in a gentle embrace. It harkened back to when Lynch first kissed her. He held her like he feared she'd break. He deepened the kiss and she sighed into his mouth.

Spirals of need coiled low in her abdomen as his velvet lips traveled to the sensitive spot just below her ear.

"Be sure about this, Shaly," he murmured against her skin. Tingles raced across her scalp and warmth pooled in her panties. "Be very sure."

In answer, she eased away, toed off her shoes and removed her jacket. She pulled her shirt up and over her head then reached behind to flick off her bra. Her nipples peaked at his hungry, devouring gaze. She reached out her hand. He took it and she led him through the narrow kitchen to the bedroom in back.

Inside the minuscule, but tidy room, she helped him dispatch his shirt. She caressed her palms across his chest, relishing its silky feel.

She traced her finger along the Celtic design on his chest and pressed a kiss there. She then continued her exploration down to his waistband.

She undid the fly of his jeans while he did the same with her pants zipper. The actions were measured, controlled. Not like the adrenaline-induced frenzied encounter at the Bentley farm. Only when she stood before him as naked as him did he touch her. Really touch her.

His large hands spanned her waist, drawing her near until her body adjoined his from chest to groin, the evidence of his arousal tucked securely against her belly.

He captured her lips in a smoldering, scorching kiss. One that made her burn. Burn with the fire of wanting...needing...more.

His mouth journeyed to the hollow of her throat, kissed and nipped her collarbone. She flexed her fingers into the muscles of his shoulders to hold him closer. He urged her down onto the neatly made bed.

His sinewy body covered hers. How she loved the heavy feel of him pressing her into the mattress. Then he kissed her again. Long, drugging kisses that awakened every one of her nerve endings. She kissed him back amid her mounting urgency.

She encouraged him to roll over without breaking contact with his lips. Her legs on either side of his torso, she swept her tongue through his mouth while rocking her hips and dragging the length of his cock along her intimate folds. His groan mingled with her moan.

She left his lips and kissed her way down the breadth of his chest, pausing to tease his nipples. She moved lower, across his flat stomach to kneel between his legs.

Wrapping her hand around his girth, she looked up at him. He stared back, not moving...like he'd stopped breathing. She gave him a small smile then opened her mouth, and took him in.

She remembered when she'd insisted Lynch teach her to perform oral. He'd been almost embarrassed. But she'd persisted because she wanted to be the best for him.

She used her hands in tandem with her mouth then flattened her tongue and deep-throated him. She swallowed to lessen the gag reflex, but also to maximize his pleasure. His hips thrust, pushing him deeper into her mouth while his hands mussed her hair. Her cunt contracted as her clit throbbed.

He tightened his hold on her hair and hauled her back up his body. He easily tossed her onto her back, swallowing her surprised squeak. His tongue commandeered her mouth as he palmed her pussy. He inserted two fingers. And just like that, ecstasy exploded throughout her body.

Lynch continued to fondle her, his mouth never leaving hers, while her orgasm slowly ebbed. When he kissed her neck and shoulder, then her breast, she knew his intention. But as nice as that would be...she had to have more. She didn't want to just take from him. She wanted to give to him everything.

She grabbed his ear.

"Ow, Shaly...that hurts."

She ignored his protest and brought him nose to nose with her. "No oral."

His eyes ballooned. "But–"

"No buts. I want *you*, Lynch. Inside me."

He shifted on his haunches. "Will you regret this in the morning?"

She sat up, her legs on either side of him, touching him as intimately as she could without actual intercourse. "If I do, that'll be on me. Not you."

He climbed off the bed. "I can't let you do this."

She clamped her legs tight around his hips to keep him stationary and glared. "You can't *let me*? I'm an adult, Lynch Callan, fully capable of making my own decisions. Stop trying to protect me all the damn time and make love to me." Sudden fear slammed into her and she loosened her leg muscles. "Unless you don't want to..."

He drew his hand down his face with a barked laugh. "Not want to? Christ, Shaly..." He gestured to where their bodies met. "In case you didn't notice, I'm harder than steel."

"It's settled then." She meshed her mouth with his to prevent any more complaints.

She poured all her emotions – the heartache of past mistakes, the joy at being with him now, the love...all her love...she felt for this man into her kiss. Little by little his arms enclosed her in a hug and he kissed her back. His cock twitched against her pussy and she laid back, taking him with her.

He broke away. "What about rubbers?" His voice sounded raspy. "I don't think I have any."

She reached over, pulled out the nightstand drawer and groped around then pulled out an open box. "Ta da."

He lifted up. "Those have probably been here since before I got sent to the joint. They're years past their expiration date."

"Oh please." She extracted a foil wrapper and tore it open with her teeth. "Those dates are more like guidelines." She quickly rolled the condom on his pulsating dick. "They're fine."

Not that it mattered if they weren't, but Shasta didn't say that.

She threaded her fingers through his hair and kissed him again. He grasped his cock and caressed it through her wet folds to lubricate her canal. He nudged her opening with his hard tip then settled into her cradle.

"Tell me if I hurt you," he whispered against her lips.

She nodded even though she'd do nothing of the kind. Bit by bit, he pushed into her. Joined with her. Made them one.

Tears gathered in her eyes, though not from the fiery pain as her pussy walls stretched to accommodate him. No...her tears were from the sheer beauty of this moment. A moment she never believed she'd experience again with Lynch.

But she was. And she'd be forever grateful for it.

He moved with leisurely confidence, kissing her senseless.

Her desire mounted. Grew bigger, stronger...then even bigger and stronger. With no respite. Like she was dying from wanting him.

The mattress bounced and the springs protested. He tore his mouth away, straightened his arms and powered into her. Then he abruptly stopped.

His finger grazed her cheek, and came away wet. "I'm hurting you."

She shook her head which cascaded tears into her hair. "It's not that."

"What is it then?"

A frustrated growl gurgled in her throat. The last thing she wanted to do at this moment was *talk*. She dug her heels into the back of his legs, grabbed his ass cheeks and shoved her hips upward.

He held himself away. "Tell me why you're crying, Shaly."

"Because of you...and me..." A small sob escaped. "Because of *us*.

Don't stop. Whatever you do...please don't stop."

The concern lining his features softened. He lowered onto his elbows and cupped her face. He brushed his thumbs gently under her eyes and kissed her tenderly...so tenderly...her heart sighed.

He resumed his thrusts. An easy rhythm. Leisurely and languorous. But soon he gained momentum. As did her climax. It escalated. She squeezed her thighs to encourage a faster pace.

His intense stare burned into hers. Consumed her. Set her ablaze. Demolished her.

Her hips bucked and writhed and her internal muscles tightened...tightened...then tightened even more until finally clenching around him in a heart-stopping, epic orgasm that spiraled pleasure through every cell in her body.

Seconds later, his tempo turned uneven and jerky. He released guttural roar and she felt him pulse deep inside her womb.

He rested his face in the curve of her neck, his harsh breathing echoing in her ear. She stroked his shoulders and upper back while his body continued to shudder.

He rolled to his side and nestled her securely next to him. His hand glided up and down her arm. "Good God, Shaly...what the hell were you thinking to come here tonight?"

A short giggle burst past her lips. "I'm not sure I was thinking at all."

He snorted. "True that."

She heard the hurt in his voice and rose up to look at him. "Or maybe I was thinking, given all that's happened lately, I wanted to feel alive." She caressed her finger along his jaw. "And I wanted to feel alive with you."

His Adam's apple bobbed. "What will you tell your husband?"

"What I choose to tell Graham, or not tell him, isn't your concern."

He cuddled her to his chest and went back to stroking her arm. "If your brother finds out about this, he'll fucking kill me."

"He never found out anything about us before. He won't now."

His hand stilled. "I want you to know I didn't shoot Dell. I wasn't even in Grant County that night."

She hoisted herself onto her elbows, her eyebrows knitted. "I never thought you did shoot him. And if you weren't here, where were you?"

"In Yerington."

"Yerington? Doing what?"

"Visiting a former member, Ox LaBlaze."

Her stomach tightened. "Wait a minute...are you saying you had an *alibi* for the night Dell was shot?"

"Um...yeah. I guess."

"You *guess*? How come your lawyer never said anything about an alibi at your trial."

"Because I never told him."

Shasta bolted to a sitting position. "Why the hell not?"

"It would've been too risky."

"Too risky?" She slapped his bare stomach.

"Hey!"

"You were on trial for trying to kill a law enforcement officer...specifically my brother. What could possibly have been riskier than that?"

Lynch outlined her collarbone with a fingertip. "It was a judgment call, okay?"

"A judgment call?" Despite her anger, his feather touch paraded shivers up her neck. "What does that mean?"

He coaxed her to lie down. "That maybe we should talk about this later."

She reared back up. "You said *former* member. I didn't think there was such a thing as a former Streeter."

He trailed his hand down her arm. "There is...if you're willing to pay the price."

Another procession of goosebumps erupted on her skin. Her nipples puckered. She pushed his hand away, refusing to be distracted. "What kind of price?"

His gaze fastened onto her beading peaks and she crossed her arms. He frowned. "A really high one."

"Such as?"

He flopped against the headboard. "Such as when Ox fell in love with a widow from Yerington. She owned a bakery and had a couple of teenaged kids. And she absolutely rejected the MC lifestyle. No way was she cut out to be an old lady, not to mention she didn't want her kids exposed to our...less than legal activities. But Ox loved her. So he came to the table and asked permission to leave. The vote was yes...if he chopped off his left index finger."

"My God." Shasta's stomach rolled at the savage condition. "What'd he do?"

Lynch hitched his shoulder. "To the best of my knowledge, he's the only nine-fingered baker in the state."

"And you went to see this Ox guy why?"

"Hey you hungry?" Lynch rolled off the bed. "I'm not sure what's here to eat, but—"

She grabbed his wrist and pulled him back. "Why did you go see him?"

He settled one foot on the floor with his other leg bent and on the mattress, rubbing his forehead, saying nothing.

Realization barreled into her. "You wanted to leave the Streeters? Why?"

He peeked at her with a small grin. "I had my reasons. Or I should say...a reason."

Air caught behind Shasta's breastbone. "*I* was the reason? Seriously?"

His forehead puckered. "Why so surprised, Shaly? Don't you know how I feel about you?"

Her pulse rate kicked up a notch as her mouth suddenly went dry. "How you feel about me?"

"Yeah." He traced his thumb under her chin. "I love you."

Adrenaline flashed through her body. "You..." She swallowed. "Love me?"

Cupping her cheek, he nodded. "Probably since you ran over my motorcycle."

Tears sparked her eyes and she ducked from his touch. In all the time she'd spent with Lynch, he never uttered those words. Neither of them had. But she knew she loved him...she just wasn't stupid enough to assume Lynch loved her back. He couldn't. He was a Streeter.

She cleared her throat. "How come you never said anything?"

"Because you were young, Shaly. Too young to get tied up with someone like me. It would have only ended in disaster for you."

"Why tell me now?"

His sigh sounded heavy. "I don't really know."

Silence mushroomed in the tiny space. "So what price did Ox tell you?" she finally asked.

"The conversation never got that far. But Ox did say..."

"What?"

Lynch blew out another breath. "That the odds were the club would never let me leave. And definitely not for the daughter and sister of a sheriff. Ox also said if our...relationship was ever discovered, you'd in all likelihood be killed."

Shasta covered her mouth as icicles stabbed her chest.

"On the ride back from Yerington," Lynch continued, "I made the decision to break it off. I wouldn't chance anyone finding out about us. I wouldn't chance you getting hurt."

She reached for his hand. "*I'm* why you didn't tell anyone you had an alibi?"

He shrugged. "If Ox testified, the reason why I went to see him could've come out which might've put you in danger. Another risk I wasn't going to take. When I got arrested, I thought it was divine intervention or some shit." He chuckled, a grave sound. "I'd go to prison and you'd be safe. And then there was the added bonus that if you figured I tried to kill your brother, you'd hate me."

She shook her head, powerless to comprehend his words. "It's because of me you were locked up for seven years." Tears pooled in her eyes. "How is it you don't hate me?"

Smiling, he caressed the wetness from her cheeks. "Weren't you listening, Shaly? I love you." He canted closer and brushed his mouth against hers. He shifted back. "You thirsty? Want some water?"

She could only nod.

He kissed her nose. "Be right back."

Watching him go, she laid down, suddenly unable to remain upright.

She buried her face in his pillow, inhaling his musky scent. Elation spiraled through her heart.

Lynch Callan loved her. *Her.*

Just as quickly, though, a sob formed in her throat. Lynch had been willing to give up everything for her. Shit...he *had* given up everything...his freedom. And what had she done in return? Nothing. Not a damn thing.

She hadn't fought for him seven years ago when she *knew* he'd been innocent. All these years she lied to herself claiming she'd been too distraught over Dell's shooting and Graham's accident to come forward. But the ugly truth was she'd been too gutless. Too weak. Just like she'd been too cowardly to admit the real identity of Wyatt's father.

While she couldn't give Lynch back those seven years, she could give him his son. And maybe Lynch would still love her. And maybe he'd find it in his heart to forgive her. And maybe, just maybe, they could have a life together. The three of them...

Lynch padded into the bedroom. "Here ya go." He held out a plastic cup.

She sat up. "Thanks." She took the offering and a small sip then placed the water on the nightstand. "Uh...listen...there's something I need to tell you."

He settled on the mattress and held her hand. "First I want you to make me a promise."

"What's that?"

"That you'll be happy."

Confused, she tilted her head with a small giggle. "O...kay."

"I'm serious. You've got a husband and kid. You need to focus on your life with them."

"But I thought we'd...you know...be together. Now."

His smile looked sad. "You know that won't work, Shaly."

"Why not?"

"Because I'm a criminal."

"I don't care about that."

"You should. The Streeters might still come after you. But even if they didn't, you'd hafta give up everything. I can't leave this life, Shaly, so you'd hafta leave yours."

"I know. And I would. For you."

He squinted. "You sure about that? You'd be turning your back on all the people you love, Your brother, your husband...your son."

Cold fingers skittered down Shasta's spine. "Wyatt?"

"Otherwise he'd be part of the Streeter life. The Streeter code. You want that?" Lynch set his jaw. "One way or the other, you'd be sacrificing him."

She pulled her hand from his and folded her arms across her

middle. "Why are you doing this?" Tears of frustration burned her throat. "You said you loved me."

"And I do, which is why I need you to see reason. I live a dangerous life. One you, and Wyatt, aren't meant for." He took her hand again. "In your heart, you know I'm right."

She bowed her head, but he tucked his knuckle under her chin forcing her to meet his mesmeric gaze. "So promise me."

Shasta closed her eyes. Moisture eked from the corners.

He *was* right, and that reality broke her heart.

She couldn't abandon Wyatt any more than she could serve him up to the Streeters. She had no choice but to walk away from the man she loved.

Stiffening her shoulders, she opened her eyes. "I promise. I also promise not to ever forget you."

Smiling, he eased her down onto the mattress.

~*~

Lynch kissed Shasta with every scrap of love he felt for her. If he'd been stronger, or better, he would've turned her away when she showed up at his trailer. But he was neither that strong nor good.

Maybe with both Rolo and Hez dead, Lynch sensed his own time could be running short. If the Streeters didn't kill him for his involvement with the FBI, he might very well wind up another casualty of Blackwell's nefarious network. But, if by some miraculous miracle, Lynch lived to see the week's end, he'd make good on his vow to take his mom and leave Stardust. Go somewhere far away, with a warmer climate. Possibly Florida.

One way or the other, he'd never see Shasta again. And he was okay with that. She had the right to live her life without the threat of him or the Streeters fucking up things. As for tonight, he just wanted one final time with her. Something he could remember in the long, lonely years ahead of him.

He skimmed his hand along the silky soft skin of her neck and down to a fleshy breast. The nipple pearled against his palm. She moaned into his mouth.

He left her lips and worked his way to a beaded peak. He whipped his tongue over the crest, feeling it turn marble hard, while his hand tweaked and pinched the other.

She moaned again and bowed her back, shoving more of her

delectable tit into his mouth. Her fingers tangled in his hair and pulled him up where she kissed him with abandon.

He slid his hand across her taut stomach to her pussy hair. He fingered through the mesh until finding and exposing her clit.

He slowly ringed the responsive nub. Her legs widened as her hips arched into his touch. A raspy gurgle emanated from deep in her throat as he delved his fingers into her channel, finding her hot and moist and ready. For him.

Her hand wandered down his torso to wrap around his throbbing dick. She circled her thumb over the tip, spreading the pre-cum. She caressed his length. He instinctively thrust to the cadence of her strokes. Pressure built in his balls.

He broke the kiss, groped for the condom box and ripped open a packet then quickly donned the rubber. He reclined on his back and encouraged her to straddle his hips. With her towering over him, he gripped his cock and she slowly descended, taking him to the hilt.

He placed his hands on her waist to guide her movements until she found her own rhythm. She bent forward and kissed him, her tongue parrying and thrusting in time to her hips.

Shasta increased the tempo and Lynch soon became embroiled in a firestorm of passion set to consume him.

He stared into her face, curtained by her tousled hair. Her half-lidded eyes gazed back. Her short nails bit into his shoulders. Her harsh moans reverberated in his ears along with the sound of slapping flesh.

His fervor kicked into overdrive. He angled onto his side, cushioning her head with one arm while scooping her top leg into the crook of his other elbow...and drove into her without mercy.

The force in his balls reached titanic heights. He knew only a matter of seconds remained before he came. But he didn't want to come alone.

He wormed his hand down and tapped her clit. Her eyelids slid shut as her mouth formed a perfect *o*. He felt her inner muscles latch onto his dick. He buried his face in her neck and gave himself over to the glorious rush of pleasure.

Endless moments passed as his body continued to quake. He rolled to his back, Shasta cuddled on his chest, her hot breath cooling his sweaty skin.

An acute sense of peace shrouded him. Peace at having finally revealed the truth of his feelings to her. And also peace at knowing, no matter the outcome between Blackwell and the FBI, with him gone from Stardust, Shasta would be safe.

He couldn't ask for more than that.

~*~

The next morning, Lynch stared at the early morning light flickering across his trailer ceiling.

He'd spent most of the night awake, just holding Shasta while she slept. He didn't want to squander his remaining time with her by sleeping. Rather he tried to commit to memory everything he could about her...

The way her lashes fanned out on her cheeks. The way her face scrunched into a pout whenever he jostled her too much. The way she snored softly...

Just before dawn, he'd dozed off. When he woke, she was gone.

For the best. No awkward silences or stumbling good-byes. He didn't know if he'd see her again. Hell...he didn't know if he'd see the end of the week.

The jangling of his cell disrupted his thoughts. He hoisted himself onto an elbow, nabbed it from the bedside stand and checked the ID. He flipped it open. "Morning, counselor."

"Callan..."

The distress in Jarvis's tone cascaded ice through Lynch's chest, freezing his heart. He shot to a sitting position. "What happened?"

"Your mom..." The agent's voice caught. "She...uh...coded at two-thirty. They were able to bring her back, but she coded again at three-ten...then at three-forty. She just kept coding..." Jarvis cleared her throat with a sniffle. "About five minutes ago, the doctor called it."

He clutched the small phone with both hands. "Called what?"

A muffling sound filled his ear then Jarvis came back on the line.

"I'm sorry, Lynch. Your mom is dead."

Chapter Twenty-Five

LYNCH'S PHONE JINGLED again with Jarvis's ringtone. And he ignored it. Again.

After getting the news about his mom, he'd gotten on his bike and rode. He didn't know to where...just as far away from civilization as possible in as short a time as possible. He ended up somewhere northeast of Stardust, staring across the sagebrush dotted, desert dunes.

His heart felt carved out. First Flyer, then Rolo then Hez...

And now his mom.

Christ.

His mother – the woman who gave him life and who'd always loved him no matter what – was dead. Just thinking those words increased the pressure behind his breastbone.

He'd read about the five stages of grief...denial, anger, bargaining, depression and finally acceptance. Horseshit.

The truth couldn't be denied while bargaining wouldn't get you anywhere. Depression was a worthless emotion, and acceptance? Like hell he'd accept what had happened.

Anger he understood, but he didn't feel something so mild as anger. Rage...blind and seething...that he felt in spades.

There should be a sixth stage. Vengeance.

Cold, calculating vengeance.

He cracked his neck muscles, but the gesture did nothing to alleviate the building tension in his head. He didn't blame Jarvis or the doctors for his mom. He knew everyone had done their best. No...the focus of Lynch's hateful ferocity lay with one man.

Blackwell.

So many people had suffered, and would continue to suffer, until someone stopped that fucker. Until someone put their hands around the goddamn bastard's neck and squeezed. Squeezed until Blackwell gasped his last breath.

He would be that someone. *He* would exact the necessary retribution. His vow to Flyer, Rolo, Hez...and his mom. Starting right fucking now.

Lynch rode back to Stardust like a man possessed. He dodged the sparse traffic on the highway at a breakneck speed, not worried about the cops. He relished the thought of a confrontation. A release for his pent-up wrath and devastating sorrow.

At the town limits, he slowed his bike and maneuvered through the streets until reaching Grunge's house. The treasurer had been in the Streeters as long as Rolo and Flyer. If Lynch could trust anyone, it'd be him.

The quiet neighborhood set his nerves on edge. It seemed almost too quiet. Lynch rolled to a stop in front of the aging duplex. Grunge and Charlotte lived on one side and their daughter, Melody, lived on the other with her three kids. Lynch killed the engine while swinging his leg over the seat.

He retrieved the envelope containing the FBI file from his pack and headed for the door. It opened before he was halfway to the porch.

"Yo, brother." Grunge stood in the entryway, a Glock visible in his right hand. He darted his gaze up and down the street then back to Lynch. "Am I ever glad to see your sorry ass." He moved to the side, tucking the gun into the front of his waistband. "Where the hell you been? I've been trying to reach you for days."

"Yeah...sorry."

Grunge pulled him into a brief hug. "You know what's been going down, right? Junkyard's dead and nobody's seen Rolo or Hez since last week."

Lynch coughed as he released the treasurer "Um–"

"Say..." Grunge peered outside. "Where's Edie? You didn't leave her alone, did you? Shit's getting weird 'round here so we need to keep everyone safe."

Lynch swallowed. Hard. "Ma's...uh...with Hez."

"Thank God for that." Grunge shut the door. "I've been freaking the fuck out. Good to know you, your mama and Hez are okay." He gripped his shoulder. "You heard from Rolo?"

Anguish closed Lynch's throat. He removed the president patch from his pocket.

"What the hell..." Worry and anxiety etched Grunge's face. "How'd you get this?" His voice trembled.

Lynch struggled for control. His composure hung by a very thin, very frayed thread. "Rolo gave it to me." He gulped down his sob. "Yesterday...when he died in my arms."

Grunge's head jerked back as tears formed in his eyes. "Rolo's dead? No way."

"It's true, brother. Is there somewhere we can talk? In private."

"Uh...yeah...out back. Charlotte's in the bedroom watching TV with the grandkids. I'll tell her to keep them inside. Meet you in a minute."

On stilted legs, Lynch walked through the modest house to the backyard. Lilac bushes lined the eight-foot, cinderblock fence, the perfect barrier for privacy and security. He ambled over to the picnic table situated under the massive oak.

The aroma of freshly mowed grass hung in the air as the sun shone brightly in the pristine blue sky. It seemed like a perfect spring day, except it wasn't. The tragic events from yesterday swirled around him like a deadly undertow, threatening to drag him under.

In a burst of enraged anguish, he punched the tree trunk once, twice, three times. Pain roared through his hand and wrist. Good. He needed something to focus on rather than the grief eating his heart. The back door banged open and he pivoted.

Grunge carried two steaming mugs in one hand and a bottle of Crown Royal in the other. He sat on one side of the table. Lynch sat across from him.

The treasurer poured a generous amount of whiskey into both cups, slid one to Lynch then lifted his in the air. "To Rolo."

Wrapping his aching fingers around the mug, Lynch drank deeply.

"And Junkyard," Grunge added.

Lynch set his drink down with a thud.

Grunge shook his head and drew a hand down his throat. "Christ...Rolo and Junkyard."

"That's not all, brother." Lynch blinked tears from his vision. "My mom and Hez..." He sawed his molars together. "...are also dead."

It was like lightning hit Grunge. His body went rigid then

slumped. "*What the fuck?*"

Lynch could only nod.

"Who the fuck would do all this shit? A rival club?"

"Not another MC. Just one man. Ian Blackwell."

"Blackwell?" The treasurer sniffed and dug a kerchief from his pocket. "Never heard of him."

Lynch's grief morphed into rage. "He's a blackmailing, sadistic bastard who's had his hooks in the Streeters for years."

Grunge shot Lynch a frown. "Ain't nobody had their hooks in this club. Not ever."

"This guy has. Thanks to his minion Junkyard, and *his* minions Bowyer, Virgil, Cam and I don't know who the hell else."

Grunge frowned. "Watch what you say about fellow brothers, brother. Besides Junkyard's dead too–"

"And nobody deserved dying more."

Grunge's scowl deepened. "If Junkyard had a hand in this, how come he's dead?"

"I don't know," Lynch bit out.

"But you *do* know he was involved, along with the others?" Grunge squinted. "What's your proof?"

"This." Lynch opened the envelope and extracted pictures of Rolo and Hez's tortured bodies, placing them on the table.

"Jesus..." Grunge's face paled. "Holy Jesus Christ." He cradled his head in his hand then shoved the photos away. "Those prove nuthin'. Anyone coulda done that."

"Virgil and Cam were at Rolo's house. Plus before he died Rolo *told* me they did this to him."

"And why would they do that?"

"To get his daughters. We figured Blackwell wanted Ma too. That's why Hez got tortured."

Grunge sat taller. "Who's we?"

"What?"

"You said *we* figured. So who's we?"

Lynch shifted in his seat. "Me and Jarvis."

The treasurer cocked his head. "Your lady lawyer? What she got to do with this?"

"A lot, actually." Lynch held the other man's stare. "She's an FBI agent."

Shock registered on Grunge's face. An instant later, the shock dissolved from his expression. "You saying you're working with the goddamn FBI?"

"I'm saying the FBI came to me in prison and asked for my help."

"Yeah, right," Grunge scoffed. "Help in ratting out your brothers." He slid his hand to the right.

Lynch snaked out his arm and grasped Grunge's wrist. "Left hand, brother. Nice and easy."

Curling his lips, Grunge lowered his left hand under the table and slowly lifted his Glock using just his thumb and index finger. Lynch took the weapon, placing it next to him then released Grunge.

"Now what?" Grunge mocked.

"Now you're gonna listen to me." Lynch pulled more documents from the envelope.

"Never figured you for a fucking rat."

Lynch ground his teeth together, refusing to be baited.

"Just tell me why," Grunge sneered. "Was it to get outta prison? Is that why you ratted on your crew? Your brothers?"

"No." Lynch placed another photo on the table. "It was because of him."

Grunge barely glanced at the picture. "And who the fuck is that?"

"Flyer."

For the span of several heartbeats, all emotion drained from Grunge's face. Then scorn twisted his expression. "Bullshit."

"No bullshit. It's Flyer. His body was found in Pyramid Lake a couple months ago. The DNA tests prove it's Flyer."

"DNA tests?" Grunge scoffed. "Riiight. Performed by the feds. I don't believe you."

Lynch leaned across the table. "You'd rather believe Flyer left my mom for some skank in a skirt? You knew the man better than that."

Anger and dread warred on Grunge's face. Finally realization and resignation took hold. He dropped his gaze to the photo and fingered the edge. "Christ..." His voice hitched. "Flyer..." The treasurer bowed his head, his shoulders quaking.

Lynch tightened his jaw, waiting for Grunge to compose himself.

The other man blew his nose with a loud sniffle. "Why would anyone do that to Flyer?"

"Not anyone. Blackwell. And he did it because Flyer was working with the FBI too."

The treasurer's mouth fell open. "The hell you say."

Lynch placed another picture on the table. "With Special Agent Jerry Olsen to be exact."

"Tre?"

"Yeah."

Grunge rubbed both hands down his face then looked at Lynch. "You still ain't said why."

"Because of these." Lynch laid out the missing person reports. "You see, brother, all those shipments the Streeters escorted over the past five years weren't of black market pharms, but young girls."

Rifling his gaze to Lynch, Grunge narrowed his eyes. "What the shit you saying now?"

"That those vans were used to transport kidnapped girls south of the border where they were sold to a Columbian named Fuentes."

Grunge shook his head with a dour smile. "Quite the story."

"Did you ever once look in one of those vans?" Lynch countered, and Grunge glanced away. "So you don't have fucking clue what was inside. All you did know was you got a good payday out of it. And that, unfortunately, was the plan."

Lynch went on to recount Rolo's story about the girl in the warehouse – and older man's complexion whitened even further – as well as the attempts on his life and the discovered surveillance equipment in the various locations.

Finished, Lynch sat back, took a healthy swallow of his cold, whiskey-laced coffee and pushed the Glock across the table. Grunge didn't move for the gun. He just stared at it.

Empathy nipped Lynch. He knew how his brother felt...shocked, repulsed, ashamed, but sugarcoating things wouldn't change the facts of what the Streeters had done. And ignorance was hardly an excuse.

Finally, Grunge met his gaze. "So what do we do now?"

"We do what's necessary to take out that motherfucking Blackwell."

"Fine." Grunge narrowed his eyes. "But once all this shit's done with, the table's gonna decide your fate for having worked with the feds."

Lynch nodded and shoved to his feet. He knew better than to

argue. He also knew no reason would be good enough for betraying the club. Because that's what it was. A betrayal.

But as long as he got Blackwell, Lynch didn't give a fuck about anything else.

~*~

After scouring Grunge's house top to bottom for hidden cameras and microphones, and not finding any, Lynch and the treasurer decided they'd confide only in those Streeters who'd been in the club prior to Lynch's prison stint. That meant Mick, Picket, Ennis and Tiny showed up an hour later, their families in tow.

One of the good things about MC old ladies, they knew not to ask questions. They cloistered the kids in the bedrooms to watch TV or play video games then stayed in the living room drinking coffee while the men congregated out back.

Though Lynch worried how his fellow Streeters would respond to his collaboration with the feds, knowing Grunge had his back, at least for the time being, eased some of his trepidation. He quickly summarized the horrible deaths of Flyer, Rolo, Hez and his mom...no reason in belaboring events which couldn't be changed. Yet the overwhelming reaction of other men's grief and sorrow as they looked at the graphic photos of the murders and their murmured words of condolences jumped tears to his eyes.

Then Lynch admitted his FBI connection with Agent Jarvis.

As expected, angry insults and hostile threats flew, but Grunge quickly pointed everyone toward achieving vengeance for their fallen brethren rather than crucifying Lynch.

"So how do we get this fucker?" Mick asked.

"Yeah," Picket concurred. "I'd like to attach a car battery to his withered nuts." He eyed Lynch. "Among others..."

Lynch focused on Mick rather than Picket. "We get him by finding those girls. According to Jarvis a passenger van was stolen from the Portland airport over the weekend."

Mick shrugged. "Don't those have lojacks?"

"Yeah, but this one's been disabled."

Tiny sat forward. "Portland?" He glanced at the other men. "Didn't Junkyard say he had a sister in Portland?"

"He sure did," Grunge said. "A half-sister. What the fuck was her name...Anita? Amanda?"

Tiny snapped his fingers. "Amelia! Amelia Kruger."

"How the fuck you remember her last name was Kruger?" Picket asked.

The big man rolled his shoulder. "It's my ma's maiden name."

Lynch nodded while jotting a note on a slip of paper. "Good...I'll tell Jarvis."

Mick rapped his knuckles on the table. "And I'll ask again, goddamn it, how do we *get* Blackwell? The feds have been after him for how long...without success. So suddenly we're gonna be able to take him down? How?" He wagged his head. "If the girls are found, he's gonna figure it was us who helped the FBI. What's to keep him from coming after us and our families?"

"What do you suggest?" Grunge demanded. "That we sit on our asses and not do anything to save those girls?"

Mick blew out a breath. "We just gotta weigh the risks."

Lynch leaned back in his chair. Shit. Mick had a valid point. Helping the FBI would not only put the Streeters in danger, but everyone they loved too. Unless...

He folded his hands on the table. "Mick's right. The danger to your families will be huge. That's why, after we've made sure the bowling alley clear of any surveillance equipment, you'll everyone and go into lockdown at the club until this shit is done."

Grunge squinted. "And you'll be where?"

"With Jarvis, making sure whoever's responsible ends up in custody or dead. Preferably dead."

Picket scoffed. "You expect us to hide like little bitches?"

Lynch glared. "I expect you to take care of your families. Heard your old lady's pregnant so maybe you should think about her instead of getting all butthurt."

Red stained Picket's face as he dropped his gaze.

Lynch stared each of the other men square in the eye. "What's left of my family is sitting at this table. And I'll do *whatever* it takes to protect them."

"You could end up dead," Grunge commented in a low voice.

"Yeah, I could." Lynch didn't blink. "Your point?"

The treasurer rolled his shoulder. "Making an observation is all. What you need from us?"

Lynch pushed a pen and small pad of paper to the treasurer. "The names and numbers of the guys in Junkyard's crew."

Grunge picked up the pen. "The rest of you get everyone over to the clubhouse. There's enough supplies to last two weeks." He eyed Lynch. "Think this shit'll be over by then?"

"Hopefully it'll all be over in two days."

Grunge nodded then started writing. As the men dispersed, Lynch stood and pulled out his cell. It showed a half a dozen missed calls from Jarvis. He punched in the agent's number.

She answered before the first ring ended. "Where the hell have you been?"

Her testy tone raised his own ire. "Easy, counselor. I've been meeting with the club and I've got new information. Junkyard had a sister, Amelia Kruger, who lives in Portland. She might know something."

"I'll have Sam follow up with the Portland office. Right now, I need you to come in."

Lynch walked to the far corner of the yard. "I can't. The MC's going into lockdown at the club which means I'm the only one left to go after Blackwell."

"You don't understand...we've got a serious problem."

He gave a derisive laugh. "Only one?"

"Where you were last night, Callan?"

"At my trailer, like I said I'd be."

"Anyone with you?"

His pulse quickened. "Why you want to know?"

"Just answer the damn question."

"I was alone," he lied. "What's going on?"

Jarvis sighed into the phone. "A jogger discovered three bodies this morning by the Stead airport, bound and shot execution style. Still waiting on two of the IDs, but one came back as a Jack Martin. You knew him as Bowyer."

For a moment, Lynch couldn't breathe. Whether from elation or dread, he didn't know.

"The ME put time of death at around one a.m.," Jarvis continued. "Are you sure you were alone last night?"

"Am I a suspect?"

"Calls made to and from the burner phone found on Bowyer's body traced back to your mom's house. Plus, Rolo Pruett named Bowyer as one of the men who came to his house." She paused. "If no one can verify your whereabouts, it's like I said...we've got a serious problem."

"Who's not answering the question now, counselor? Do you think I'm involved?"

Silence filled his ear.

Jarvis blew out another breath. "Honestly? No. But I have to ask, did you have anything to do with what happened to Bowyer and the other two?"

"No."

"Guess that leaves one of the other Streeters."

Lynch shot a quick glance over his shoulder. "No one knew anything about Bowyer or any of this shit until this morning."

"Well I'm all out of suspects then."

He stood taller. "Maybe not. Have you located Murphy yet?"

"No. Why?"

"If he's really Blackwell, he could've killed Bowyer."

"And why would he do that?"

"Maybe he's cutting his losses."

"It's possible, but I still need you to come in. Albright's been read into the entire case file, including Bowyer's possible role in torturing your friends. With him now dead, the good sheriff wants to put out an APB. On you."

Dipping his head, Lynch rubbed his neck. *Shit.*

"It'll be a lot easier if you come in versus them bringing you in," Jarvis added.

"All right. I'll make sure everyone's set over here then I'll come in."

"Make it quick. I don't know how much longer I can stall Albright."

"Understood."

~*~

Shasta pulled her car into her driveway, turned off the ignition and grabbed the takeout bag in the passenger seat along with her purse. She got out, her heart thrumming in her chest.

She hadn't felt this...happy...since before her father died. But that's exactly how she felt. Happy, and very grateful. Grateful for last night. Grateful because she'd experienced one final time with Lynch.

He'd given her so much...had forfeited so much for her...the absolute least she could do was grant his wish that she focus on her husband and son, and be happy.

And the first step in her future happiness would be to carve out more alone time for her and Graham. Starting today. She'd hoped to surprise Graham by meeting him at the airport that morning, but couldn't get away from work. So she bought his favorite lunch instead. While not a spectacular start, at least it was a start.

She bounded up the front porch stairs and opened the front door. Soft jazz music greeted her. "Graham...honey..." She dropped her purse on the entryway table. "I'm home."

The music stopped, replaced by the quiet mechanical hum of her husband's wheelchair. He appeared in the archway to his office, slash, bedroom. Concern lined his face. "Hey...what are you doing home? Everything all right at work?"

She closed the front door with her foot. "Everything's fine." She leaned down and planted a quick kiss on his mouth before heading for the kitchen. "And lunch brings me home."

"Lunch?" He followed behind her. "But I thought it was an early release for Wyatt and he and I were going to the cabin to get the tackle boxes ready for Saturday."

"It is and you are. I just asked Melissa to pick him up for a play date with Aiden so we could spend some time together." She placed the bag on the table and turned. "That okay?"

"Of course. This is just..." He shrugged. "A surprise."

"A nice surprise, I hope."

He grinned. "A great surprise."

She smiled back. "Good. I told Melissa we'd be over around three to pick him up. You two will have plenty of time to sort through all those fishing reels and lures." She removed Styrofoam containers from the bag.

"Very true." Graham wheeled closer. "So...is lunch what my nose thinks it is?"

"It is indeed. Chicken fried steak and garlic potato salad from Mert's."

"Forget great surprise. This is awesome. But what did I do to deserve Mert's famous chicken fried steak and garlic potato salad?"

Shasta retrieved two plates from the cupboard. "Can't a wife bring her husband lunch?"

"She most certainly can. What can I do?"

"Grab the iced tea from the fridge?"

"Coming right up."

While her husband got the pitcher and poured two tall glasses, Shasta plated their lunches. She waited until Graham had positioned his chair at the table before situating his lunch, along with silverware and a napkin, on his place setting. She sat herself and raised her glass. He arched his eyebrows, but mimicked her action.

"To more surprises," she said, clinking her glass with his.

His moustache twitched. "I'll drink to that." After taking a swallow of tea, he cut into his steak and forked the portion into his mouth. His eyes closed as a groan rumbled in his throat.

"Is it hot enough?" she asked. "Or do I need to warm it up in the microwave?"

He cut off another slice. "It's perfect." He jabbed his knife at her plate. "But find out for yourself."

She complied and the next few minutes were occupied with eating. She refilled both their glasses. "Listen, I've been doing a lot thinking lately..." Her voice drifted off as an unexpected case of nerves hit her.

"And?" He scooped a mound of potato salad onto his fork.

She inhaled a breath. "And I think we should move to Vegas."

Graham's eyes widened, his fork hovering in mid-air. Shasta shifted in her seat, but held his gaze.

Clearing his throat, he put the utensil on his plate and wiped his mouth with his napkin. "You've always been against moving to Vegas. Why the change of heart?"

She toyed with her knife and hitched her shoulder. "It's like I said, I've been doing some thinking. Your business is in Vegas and it's stupid for you to travel so much when we could just as easily live where you work."

"But what about wanting Wyatt to grow up in a small town?"

"Maybe I was wrong about that. And how could I judge anyway? I've only ever lived in a small town. How would I know if that's better or worse than living in a bigger city?"

Graham peered at her. "What about your brother?"

"What about him?"

"You two have never lived more than a two-minute drive from

each other."

"I know. And maybe it's time that changed too." She gave her shoulder another roll. "I mean it's Vegas, right? Not the other side of the universe. It's not like I'll never see Dell again." She reached over and covered Graham's hand with hers. "I'm not saying I don't have doubts about moving, because I do. But we could try it for...say...the summer to see how it goes."

Her husband pulled his hand away then folded his arms on the table and leaned forward, his gaze penetrating hers. "What's going on, Shasta? Really?"

"I've been doing some–"

"Thinking. You've said that." He sat back, his mouth pulled into a frown. "Does this have something to do with Lynch Callan?"

Shasta's stomach bottomed out. "Why would you ask that?"

"For one, the timing. I can't help but assume you wanting to leave Stardust is related to him being out of prison. Do you feel threatened by him or any of his gang associates?"

Relief weakened her muscles. "No...it's nothing like that."

"Then what *is* it?"

She offered her hand again and he held it. She traced her thumb over his knuckles. "To be honest, it's been since Todd's death. Guess I'm worried about having regrets."

"Regrets?"

She nodded. "Regretting all the time you have to spend away from us. Away from Wyatt. Regretting not being more...adventuresome." A small shudder quaked through her. "Lord knows I was more than adventuresome when I was younger. I was downright reckless. And maybe I've compensated too much for that. Gone too far in the opposite direction." She chewed her bottom lip, staring into her husband's eyes. "I guess what I'm trying to say is I want to live a fuller life. A life with my husband and son and maybe even..." She switched her gaze to her plate. "...another baby."

Graham went stone still beside her. Shasta wondered if he was even breathing. She didn't know how long they sat there, in absolute silence. By inches, she raised her gaze.

His face appeared completely blank. She read no shock or joy or...any emotion whatsoever on his expression. She waited, her heart thumping in her throat, for him to say something.

Anything.

Finally he blinked. "You want another baby?" His question echoed with uncertainty and astonishment.

She gripped his hand with both of hers. "Yes. Very much."

He dipped his head slightly. "With...me?"

Her mouth curved upward in a nervous smile. "Of course with you, silly."

"But you know I can't."

She tightened her grasp on his fingers. "We could use in-vitro fertilization. I've done some research–"

Graham tucked back his chin. "You did research on in-vitro? When?"

"A couple of years ago."

"You never told me that."

"I know." She rolled her lips. "It was the summer before Wyatt started kindergarten. I think I suffered a mild form of empty-nest syndrome."

"And now? Why the sudden interest in another baby?"

She stiffened her spine. "It's not so sudden, Graham. I've always wanted more kids."

"Yet you've never mentioned that fact."

"Maybe because I wasn't sure how you'd react. Or maybe..." She sighed. "...because I wasn't a hundred percent sure myself."

"And now you are sure?" He sounded less than convinced.

"Yes."

Graham's brows drew together. He extracted his hand from her hold, planted his elbows on his chair arms and steepled his fingers. "I must confess, Shasta, this all strikes me as...odd. To say the least. Moving to Vegas. Having a baby."

"Things might be a little out of left field."

"*A little*?" He chuckled then sobered. "I like the idea of moving to Vegas, but a baby?" He shook his head. "I'm too old for a baby."

"Nonsense. You're not too old. And think of how great it'd be for Wyatt to have a little brother or sister to pester and protect. I know Dell is a major pain in the butt, but I wouldn't change having him as my big brother for anything in the world." She took his hand again. "I know you didn't have a brother, but you were close to your older cousin, weren't you?"

"Very. Until he died."

"Then you understand the special bond that exists between siblings. Just promise you'll think about it, okay?"

He smiled. "All right. I promise to think about it."

Shasta jumped to her feet and wound her arms around his neck. Tears welled in her eyes. "Thank you," she whispered against his neck.

Laughing, Graham returned her hug. "I didn't say yes, only that I'd think about it."

"I know." She settled into her seat. "But you also didn't say no."

Graham picked up his fork holding the forgotten heap of potato salad and resumed eating, as did Shasta, though she didn't taste anything. Her chest and heart felt so full. So happy. A chance existed she and Graham would have a baby, and she'd take that any day.

Once the lunch dishes were stacked in the dishwasher, she leaned against the table and checked her watch. "Guess I should mosey back to work."

Graham tossed the dishtowel onto the counter. "Any chance you can play hooky for the rest of the afternoon? We could pick up Wyatt and head to the cabin. The three of us."

She smiled. "Ohh. I love that idea. I've got some paperwork to finish, but it shouldn't take too long." She bent over with her best pouty, beseeching expression. "Would you mind terribly waiting?"

He pulled his mouth into a mock frown. "Well, I don't know..."

"Pretty please?" She batted her eyelashes.

He laughed. "Of course I'll wait. It'll give me the chance to get caught up on everything that's been happening since I've been gone so much this past month."

"It's settled then." She kissed him then straightened. "I'll get my purse and we can go."

Less than ten minutes later, Graham steered his van in the handicapped spot at the stationhouse and cut the engine. Shasta unclipped her seatbelt and got out while he maneuvered his chair to the hydraulic lift. She waited for him to exit the vehicle then ambled up to the entrance alongside his wheelchair. Inside, she waved to Joan and walked to her desk while Graham headed for Dell's office.

The squad room didn't look much different than it had over the last week and a half. Dark-suited FBI agents still sat at random desks working Todd Weedly's murder case. Shasta crammed the paperwork she'd finish tomorrow into a drawer as her husband approached.

"Perfect timing." She grabbed her purse and stood. "I'm all done."

"Yes, but it appears I'm not."

"What are you talking about?"

Graham placed his elbows on his armrests and sighed, an uncharacteristically fierce scowl on his face. "Seems Adam decided to take a last-minute vacation leaving your brother in a lurch, legally speaking."

Shasta raised her eyebrows. "That doesn't sound at all like Adam."

"I know. But he did. In fact he didn't even call in. He texted his secretary. And with everything that's been going on." Graham shook his head. "What an ass."

"So what's this got to do with you?"

"There's a suspect in interrogation with his lawyer and your brother wants me in on the interview. An assistant DA is on his way from Reno, but Dell thought so long as I was here..."

Shasta squinted at her brother's office. "He could take advantage of you."

"Something like that. But I told Dell you and I had plans for the afternoon and that you'd have to okay this."

She sighed. "How long do you think?"

"Hard to say. It's a murder charge."

Her breath caught. "Murder? Did they find who killed Todd?"

"No. This has to do with something that happened last night. So what do you say?"

"I say my brother is awful for imposing on you." She placed her purse back on her desk and pulled out the files from the drawer. "But I can see this is important to you." She sat down. "And I really should finish my paperwork anyway."

Graham grasped her hand and pulled her close for a chaste kiss. "Thank you," he murmured before releasing her. He pivoted himself around. "This really shouldn't take too long. Like I said another DA is in route."

She watched her husband wheel toward the interview room, a smile on her face. Her chest felt all...fuzzy. Normally Graham would have done the interview without a second thought to any plans he might have had with her and Wyatt. The fact he'd asked for her input thrilled her. With luck she and her husband and their son would still be able to spend part of the afternoon together.

Graham opened the door to the interrogation room and swung it wide enough to accommodate his wheelchair. Shasta caught a glimpse of familiar blond hair, and her body went rigid...like she'd been flash frozen.

Was that Lynch?

No...it couldn't be. Graham had said this was a murder case. And Lynch couldn't possibly be in custody for murder. Could he?

She must've misunderstood or she didn't see what she thought she saw. But she needed to check it out...just to be sure. On unsteady legs, she stood and walked toward the viewing room.

She slipped inside and three agents turned from the one-way mirror to look at her. With her hand on the door, she gave them a wan smile, and was about to turn tail, when she noticed the wastebasket overflowing with discarded Styrofoam coffee cups. Mustering confidence she didn't much feel, she grabbed the basket as Agent Jarvis's voice came over the speakers.

"You don't have an ounce of solid evidence. It's all circumstantial."

"That may be true," she heard Graham say, "but it's more than sufficient to convince a judge to hold Mr. Callan for twenty-four hours."

Reaching out her hand, Shasta steadied herself against the wall. Lynch *was* the suspect. She cast a fleeting look to the agents in the room. They all stared at the mirror, ignoring her. She stayed very quiet and listened to the conversation...

"A lot can happen in twenty-four hours to a guy in lockup," her brother mocked.

"Are you threatening my client?" Jarvis demanded.

"Cut the lawyer client crap, will ya?" Dell retorted. "You're an FBI agent."

"*And* a lawyer. Wanna see my degree?"

"What I want is Lynch Callan back behind bars."

"That's enough," her husband interrupted.

Thank God Graham's in there...

"Let's review the facts, shall we Agent Jarvis?" Graham continued. "Jack Martin, aka Bowyer, was a member of the 5th Street biker gang and a known associate of your client. And your client quite probably blames him for the deaths of Rolo Pruett and Hez Hernandez. Given the fact Mr. Martin and two other Streeters were murdered around one a.m. last night and your client doesn't have an alibi, you can-"

Shasta didn't hear the rest. She barreled from the viewing room and straight into interrogation. "Wait-"

Dell, Jarvis and Lynch jumped to their feet at her abrupt entrance.

"*Jesus*," her brother roared, stabilizing himself with a hand on the table. "What the hell are you doing in here?"

"Lynch is innocent."

Graham veered his chair around to face her. "Shasta, sweetheart, you need to go."

"But I'm telling you Lynch didn't kill anyone last night."

"And you know this how?" Jarvis asked.

Shasta looked at Lynch. He slumped in his chair, a hand on his face.

"Because I was with him."

Chapter Twenty-Six

THE RESULTING QUIET flayed Shasta's eardrums. She wrapped her arms around her middle to mask her trembling.

Dell's mouth fell open, and he stumbled backwards into his chair. "What did you say?"

"I said I was with Lynch last night. All night." She rolled her lips together. "And he was still sleeping when I left his trailer this morning at five-thirty."

Jarvis cleared her throat into the yawning silence. "Well...seeing as my client now has an alibi, we'll be going." She picked up her briefcase. "C'mon Callan."

Shasta shifted to the side, staring at the floor, as Jarvis and Lynch walked out. Her brother stood, grabbed his cane then hobbled to the door. He paused beside her, but said nothing. Then he too left, leaving her with her husband.

Graham wheeled himself until he sat directly in front of her. She inched her gaze up to meet his. The anger and hurt in his eyes twisted her stomach.

"Is this why you suddenly wanted a baby?"

"What? No—"

"You were hoping to pawn off another one of your mistakes onto me, weren't you?" His caustic tone ripped at her heart.

Tears gathered in her eyes and rolled down her cheeks as she vehemently shook her head. "No, Graham. I swear."

He winced and rubbed his fingers to his temples.

She squatted down. "Another headache? Here...let me." She reached for him.

He jerked away. "Don't."

She clasped her hands together at his snarled command.

Graham lowered his hands. Tension rippled along his jaw line. "Ask your brother for a ride home. I'm going to the house to get some things then I'll stay at the cabin until further notice." He grabbed the knob.

"But what about your afternoon plans with Wyatt?"

He hesitated.

She awkwardly shuffled toward him. "I understand you're angry with me. Furious even, and you have every right to be. But please don't take it out on Wyatt."

Graham heaved a breath. "Fine. I'll still pick him up and take him to the cabin." He sliced his gaze to hers. "*Without* you."

She bowed her head while her husband wheeled himself from the room. She plopped onto her butt, her face buried in her hands.

What in God's name did she just do?

~*~

Lynch trailed behind Jarvis from interrogation and into the sheriff's office. He grabbed his cut off a chair as the agent closed the door and leaned against it, her arms crossed.

"If you had an alibi for last night, why the hell didn't tell me?"

He popped his tight neck muscles. "I had my reasons."

She shoved from the door. "Yeah. Like protecting the reputation of another man's wife." She shook her head with a small laugh. "And here I didn't think gangbangers had ethics."

"Well apparently some of us do," he ground out. "Can we go now?"

"Sure."

Jarvis opened the door and in limped Dell.

The sheriff tossed his cane to the floor then backed Lynch against the wall, his forearm to the biker's throat. "You fucked my sister?"

Jarvis seized Dell's arm. "What the hell are you doing? Let him go."

Dell pressed on Lynch's windpipe, his face twisted with rage. "You fucked her like one of your skank bitches?"

Stars clouded Lynch's vision, but he had no leverage to propelled Dell off him.

Jarvis wrenched harder. "Sheriff Albright...*let...him...go.*"

Abruptly, Dell released the pressure.

Lynch bent forward, coughing and gasping, massaging his throat. Once he'd caught his breath, he straightened.

The sheriff thrust his finger at him. "Stay away from my sister or I will fucking kill you."

Lynch couldn't blame a brother for defending his sister. If the situation were reversed, he'd feel the exact same way.

Jarvis positioned herself between the two men. "Settle down."

A loud knock turned everyone's attention. Newman stood in the doorway, a cell in his hand. "Um...sorry to interrupt." He cast a nervous glance to everyone in the room then looked at Jarvis. "But the Portland office is on the phone for you." He handed the phone to Jarvis and left, closing the office door quietly behind him.

"This is Special Agent Emma Jarvis," she said into the phone. "Yes...what can you tell me, Agent Romanski?" As she listened, her hand reached out and clutched the chair back with whitening fingers. "All of them?"

Her high-pitched voice shriveled Lynch's stomach. The news must not be good.

She pivoted, her wide-eyed gaze holding his. "I understand. Yes...thank you for calling...good-bye." She disconnected the call, and the normally stoic Agent Jarvis looked to be fighting tears.

"What happened?" Lynch asked.

She cleared her throat. "Um...well...the tip on Junkyard Taylor's half-sister paid off. Turned out her father's family owned a small industrial park that had been vacant for years. That's where the girls were found. Twenty-three of them." Her shoulders lifted on a big inhale. "All safe."

His mouth dropped open. "Seriously?"

She nodded. "Seriously. Of the four men guarding the girls, two were killed at the scene, but the other two are alive, at the local hospital and, most importantly, talking. This could be the break we've been hoping for against Blackwell." She smiled the first genuine smile Lynch ever remembered her having. "And it's thanks to you, Callan. You're a hero."

"Good God," Dell grunted as he bent over and reclaimed his cane.

Jarvis's smile became an instant scowl. "Problem, Sheriff?"

Dell scowled back. "Yeah." He pointed to the squad room.

Lynch watched Graham Dupree veer around the desks on his way to the front entrance. Minus Shasta. Remorse knotted his chest,

"Callan a hero?" the sheriff scoffed. "The bastard took advantage of my sister."

Jarvis planted her hands her hips. "If that's true, why isn't she pressing charges?"

Not answering, Dell shambled behind his desk and flopped into his chair.

Jarvis picked up her briefcase and opened the door. "Let's go, Callan." Outside the office, she gripped his arm as they walked to the entrance. "I don't give a shit what Albright says...to those girls and their families, you and the Streeters *are* heroes."

He shrugged off her compliment. "Not heroes, counselor. Just criminals. With, as you put it, criminal minds. So what's next?"

"Well, there's paperwork–"

"What's next for me?"

She pursed her lips. "I'm not exactly sure..."

"While you figure that out, I'll be at the clubhouse."

"That's not a good idea. Not with Blackwell still at large."

"We got rid of the surveillance shit so no place is safer than the clubhouse, counselor, believe me." He held the front door for her.

"Really?" Jarvis walked through then turned, her head tilted. "You'll be safe surrounded by people you were informing on to the FBI?"

"Gonna hafta face the music sometime." He donned his cut. "Might as well be when I've got good news to share. 'Sides, they're family. After everything that's happened, I need to be around them...no matter the outcome."

Jarvis hesitated, then sighed. "Fine. At least I'll know where you're at. And you're to call me the instant anything happens, understand?"

A small, ironic grin torqued his mouth. "Whatever you say, counselor."

But he wouldn't do anything of the kind.

~*~

Shasta stared numbly at the paper in her hand, but didn't read the words.

After Graham left, she stayed in the interrogation room asking God to strike her dead. When no divine intervention happened, she shuffled out to her desk, ignoring all the pointed stares, where she'd stayed for the past four hours.

Self-loathing burned in her throat and eyes. Not only had she shamed herself, she also embarrassed the hell out of Dell. But the worst part was hurting Graham. The only person to have done more for her than her father.

And she trampled his feelings.

She prayed the truth about her being with Lynch would remain a secret. Graham definitely didn't deserve that to be fodder for the gossips in Stardust. Dell plopping into the chair next to her desk interrupted her thoughts.

"Hey."

"Hey yourself," she answered. "You need something?"

"Yeah. My office."

She glanced across the squad room to see Jarvis and several other agents congregated behind the closed door. "What's going on in your office?"

He picked up the Mother's Day pencil holder Wyatt made out of a soup can. "Dunno. Some conference call with the FBI bigwigs in Washington."

She plucked the memento from his fingers and set it back down. "And you weren't invited?"

"Bingo." He folded his hands in his lap. "You talk to Graham?"

Tears gathered in her eyes. She sat taller. "Not since he left. He took Wyatt to the cabin and there's no cell service there. Can you give me a ride home?"

Dell sighed. "I can't help but think if I hadn't asked him to sit in on Callan's interrogation..."

Her brother's remorse surprised her. "What happened isn't your fault."

He grunted. "I know. It's Callan's."

Confusion knitted her brow. "Lynch's? How you figure?"

"Because he took advantage of you."

"Took advantage of me? What do you think happened? That he threw me over his shoulder and forced me to his trailer?"

He arched an eyebrow. "So long as you brought it up, how *did* you end up there?"

She held her brother's gaze. "Ever consider maybe I went there of my own volition?"

Dell's complexion flushed red.

"Of course you didn't," Shasta quipped. "Because that wouldn't fit your opinion of me still being a teenager in need of protection or of Lynch being a low-life gangbanger." She canted forward and narrowed her eyes. "Contrary to your belief, I'm a grown woman, able to make my own decisions. And mistakes. Besides, if Lynch is such a bad guy, how come – when charged with *murder* – he didn't say I was with him last night?"

Her brother's nostrils flared, his mouth pulled into a harsh frown.

"If I hadn't outted myself, you'd be none the wiser, would you?"

He glanced away with a noisy inhale. The muscle twitched in his cheek. "That doesn't change who Callan is."

"You're right. It just proves he was never as terrible as you made him out to be. As you *wanted* him to be." She noticed Jarvis opening the office door. "Looks like the FBI party is over." She picked up her pen. "I've got work."

She'd never spoken to him like that. So...dismissive. Rude even. But she didn't care. The time had come for her dear brother to stop holding onto past grudges and misconceptions. He needed to realize the truth about Lynch, and her.

Jarvis walked up. "Thanks for the use of your office, Sheriff."

Dell smirked as he struggled from his chair. "Anything for the cause, right? Now if there's nothing else..."

The agent blocked his exit. "Actually, there is something else." She rested her hands on her hips. "I've been instructed to place you in protective custody."

"Protective custody?" Dell railed. "What the hell for?"

"For your protection. Obviously," she replied dryly.

"That's ridiculous. I don't need protecting."

Jarvis shook her head. "It's been my experience when a crime syndicate is threatened, anyone associated with the case can be in danger."

"What about your star witness? Lynch Callan? Is he in protective custody?"

"As a matter of fact, yes. He and the rest of the Streeters are in lockdown at the Streeter clubhouse, and I've just sent two teams of agents who'll be posted outside."

Dell leaned on his cane. "You don't have the authority to place me in anything, Agent Jarvis."

"You're right. I don't. But the U.S. Attorney General's office does."

Jarvis inclined her head. "And this order comes directly Washington, D.C."

"Is my brother really in danger?" Shasta asked.

The agent looked at her. "It's more a precaution, Mrs. Dupree, but a necessary one. And to that point, the AG wants you and your husband and son in protective custody as well."

Shasta's insides went cold. "Us?" She looked at Dell then back to Jarvis. "But why? We're not associated with anything."

"It's another safeguard," Jarvis soothed, "to include all of Sheriff Albright's family in the protective order. You know the old saying...better to be safe than sorry." She glanced over her shoulder and signaled another agent. "Special Agent Newman will take you, your husband and son to a safe house in Reno."

Newman nodded to Shasta. "Ma'am." He held the back of her chair. "If you'll come with me."

Shasta stood on rickety legs. "This is happening right now?" She fumbled with a folder in her desk. "But I can't go now...I've got work to finish."

Jarvis took the file from her. "It'll have to wait, Mrs. Dupree. Agent Newman will take you home so you can pack a bag for the next day or two. Is that where your husband and son are?"

"Um...no." Shasta's pulse skyrocketed. "Oh my God. They're at Graham's cabin. In the woods. In the middle of nowhere." She groped at the bottom drawer of her desk for her purse. "And we have to get to them...*right now*."

Jarvis gripped Shasta's arms in a firm hold. "Mrs. Dupree...I need you to remain calm. Agent Newman will take you home first and then to the cabin. He's one of the FBI's finest. He'll take very good care of you and your family, I assure you. All right?"

Shasta nodded, feeling like she was one of those bobblehead dolls.

Jarvis's smile took the slimmest edge off Shasta's panic. "Good."

Newman took Shasta's elbow. She pulled back. "But what about my brother? Who's going to look after him?"

Jarvis slid her gaze to Dell. "That'll be my job, Mrs. Dupree. I need to brief him on some new information, so we're not quite done here. But he'll see you in Reno later tonight."

"Okay." Shasta stared at Dell as Newman directed her to the

stationhouse entrance. "Bye."

Her brother raised his hand in farewell and a hand closed around her throat. She couldn't remember him ever looking so...worried.

~*~

After making sure the Streeter clubhouse was cleared of all surveillance gear – of which there was a shit-ton – Lynch sat at the bar watching a tennis match on ESPN. He didn't see the action on the screen, though. The image of Shasta bursting into the interrogation room refused to leave his head. Why in the hell had she done that? Yeah, she saved his ass, but at a price. A very high price.

He tipped the beer bottle to his lips and took a small sip. He wondered how Shasta's brother reacted with her. Lynch remembered how the good sheriff had reacted with him...shit...it still hurt to swallow. But he felt confident Dell wouldn't do anything to Shasta. Maybe ground her for eternity. He scoffed a quiet laugh. Like that was even possible.

"What's so funny?" Grunge hitched his butt onto the next stool.

"Nuthin'." Lynch set his beer down, glanced over his shoulder then gave the treasurer a sidelong look. "Meeting over?" Talk about needing his ass saved. That meeting would determine his fate.

"Yup." Grunge grabbed a fistful of peanuts and motioned to the bartender. "Gimme a beer, Josie my darling."

Lynch kept his impatience in check while Grunge took a long swig from the frosty bottle. "And?"

Grunge set his beer down with a satisfied groan and wiped his mouth with the back of his hand. He looked at Lynch. "And...we're not gonna kill you."

Suspicion narrowed Lynch's eyes. "I feel there's a but coming."

"Nope." Grunge wagged his head. "No buts. Not gonna kill you. Not gonna disown you. Nuthin'. You're in the clear, brother." He gulped more beer.

Lynch bit the inside of his cheek. This seemed too good to be true. "What was the vote?"

"Unanimous."

He jolted upright. "No way."

Grunge nodded and leaned his elbows on the bar. "Everybody agreed if it weren't for you, we'd still be part of that slave trade." He grunted. "Disgusting business. Under the circumstances, we figured your betrayal was justified."

"You're shitting me...no retribution? At all?"

Grunge gave an exasperated sigh. "Would it make you feel better if we'd decided to kill you?"

"It'd make a helluva lot more sense. Betrayal, no matter the reason, is still betrayal."

"True, and for what it's worth, Picket wanted to barbeque your nuts. But what you did..." The treasurer paused to clear his throat as tears brightened his eyes. "...what Flyer died trying to do, made us think maybe betrayal can be justified."

Emotions constricted Lynch's chest and he bowed his head.

Grunge gripped him by the back of his neck with a toothy, albeit watery, grin. "Just don't fucking do anything like that again, understand brother?"

Lynch choked a strangled laugh and wiped the tear slipping down his cheek. "Understood."

Grunge winked and got to his feet. "Good."

Lynch stood as well and pivoted...to see the rest of the Streeter crew standing in a semicircle a respectable distance away. Each brother came up and embraced him, even Picket.

Grunge slapped the bar. "Patrón all around, Josie my darling."

She smiled. "Coming up."

Once the tequila was poured, Grunge lifted his glass, his expression grave. "To Flyer, Rolo and Hez...three of the best goddamn brothers a man could ever have."

Glasses clinked together to a solemn, "Hear. Hear."

Lynch downed the shot, the burn in his throat quickly matching the burn in his eyes.

As more shots were poured and drunk, the atmosphere turned reverent as each Streeter recounted a story or two about their fallen comrades. Soon hearty laughter shook the liquor bottles behind the bar.

Lynch splashed more alcohol into his glass as his cell phone chimed with an incoming call. The ID read Jarvis. He walked to the quieter side of the room and before answering. "Everything okay, counselor?"

"Shouldn't I be asking you that? What happened between you and the Streeters?"

He glanced at his brothers smiling and joking. "Things are fine on this end."

"Glad to hear that...I think. Wanted to let you know two teams have been assigned to watch your clubhouse for the next forty-eight to seventy-two hours."

His blood pressure spiked. "What the hell for? Are we under house arrest?"

"No. Everyone's free to come and go as they please. But if anyone does leave, they should expect...company."

"Then I ask again, what the hell is this for?"

"Protection."

Lynch laughed. "You're kidding right?"

Jarvis sighed. "I'm not trying to offend your male pride, but I've got an icky sensation things are about to get very real very soon."

"Yeah?"

"Yeah. And the last time I felt this, we lost Olson."

Worry squeezed Lynch's body. "What about Shasta? And her husband, son and brother," he added in a rush.

"All taken care of." Amusement tinged the agent's voice. "They're on the way to a Reno safe house as we speak."

His muscles relaxed. "Thank God for that."

"Anyway, promise you'll stay put until I get back."

"Get back? Where you going?"

"I've been requested in Portland to help debrief the girls as well as interrogate the remaining suspects. I leave tonight and should be back in a week. If you need anything, Sam's in charge. And...Callan..." Jarvis's tone turned serious. "...be careful."

"Still worried about me, counselor?"

She snorted. "Asshole."

Lynch laughed. "You got that right." He sobered. "But I promise to be careful."

"Good. I'll contact you when I'm back."

He disconnected the phone and rejoined his brothers. He detested the idea of hiding, especially from a shitbag like Blackwell, but given the situation maybe it *would* be best to let the feds handle Blackwell. Besides, he thought as he tossed back his shot and Josie poured him another with a flirty wink, he had other things to occupy his time.

His phone rang again, this time with a text...from a blocked call. An attachment. With a knot forming in his gut, he opened it.

And his vision zeroed down to nothing.

The picture was of a young boy, sleeping on what appeared to be a tattered sofa.

He instantly recognized the child. Shasta's son.

On the heels of the first text came a second one.

Behind the Grab-n-go on 314. Twenty minutes. Come alone or the kid dies.

Lynch's knees weakened and he had difficulty catching his breath. A cold sweat beaded on his forehead and he feared the tequila he'd just swallowed was about to make a return trip.

"Hey, brother."

Lynch forced his gaze to Grunge's.

"Everything okay? You look like you're about to hurl."

Lynch glanced at the partying Streeters then pulled the treasurer to the end of the bar. "No. Things are not okay." He showed Grunge the picture and subsequent message.

"I know that kid," Grunge said. "Ain't he related to the sheriff?"

"His nephew."

"You gonna go?"

"Do I have a choice?"

Grunge scratched his chin. "You could be walking into a trap."

"What's your point?"

The older man shrugged. "Guess I don't got one. Want me to come with? Someone should have your back."

Lynch shook his head. "I'll be okay, but I do have a favor..." He quickly explained about the FBI agents watching the MC. "How 'bout you and few of the brothers head out...in opposite directions."

"Leaving you clear to skedaddle?"

"Something like that."

Grunge blew out a heavy sigh. "I gotta be honest, I don't like this, not one goddamn bit."

"I won't risk the kid's life. And this is...personal...between me and Blackwell. Ever since he tried to kidnap my mom. I'll need a bike, though. Mine's still at Ma's house."

"All right...if I can't talk you outta this, here." Grunge dug in his jean pocket and extracted a key. "Take my ride. Tiny'll stay here to keep an eye on things while we're gone. I'll take his."

Lynch took the ring. "Thank you, brother." Lynch gave him a quick hug and a thump on the back. "And let's not tell anyone else about this, okay?"

Grunge pursed his lips with a reluctant nod. "Just hope you know what you're doing."

So did Lynch.

~*~

Leaning against the Dumpster at the back of the Grab-n-Go, Lynch checked his watch. Fourteen minutes had passed since he'd gotten the texts at the clubhouse. Six to go...

He resisted the impulse to look around because he knew he couldn't see anything. Given the sun had set, the lengthening shadows of the Ponderosa pines and thick underbrush blocked his view.

He crossed his arms and ankles, his right palm resting on the grip of the nine mil Grunge insisted he take. The relaxed stance belied the ratcheting tension in his muscles. Ready to spring into action.

Anticipation quivered through his blood. He always felt this way right before a fight. And he couldn't wait to get his hands on Blackwell.

But he reminded himself, the kid came first. Then Blackwell.

A rustling sound snapped his head to the left. He eased from the building, peering into the dense foliage, his senses on high alert. He didn't see any movement.

After a slow count to fifty, Lynch inhaled a breath, his muscles relaxing a notch – then pain splintered through his skull.

And everything went black.

Chapter Twenty-Seven

OUTSIDE THE STATIONHOUSE, dread crawled over Shasta's skin like fire ants. The sun had set behind the western mountains as Newman marched her to a black sedan, its lights blinking in the process. The agent held the passenger door for her then jogged to the driver's side. In less than three minutes, he pulled to a stop in her driveway.

"Wait," Agent Newman commanded when she pulled the door handle.

He came around, helped her out and walked beside her up the porch steps, his gaze combing the area. She fought her shaking hands to unlock the door. All this paranoia only amped up her panic.

Newman followed her into Graham's room then up the stairs to hers and Wyatt's rooms. In a trance, she tossed random articles of clothing into a suitcase. After adding a few toiletries and Wyatt's Game Boy, Newman escorted her back to the car.

He handed over his cell. "Maybe you should call your husband and tell him we're coming."

She shook her head and slipped into the passenger seat. "There's no service out that far."

With a sigh, the agent re-pocketed his phone, got behind the wheel and turned the key. Shasta gave him directions to the county road which led to the single-lane, paved road which then led to the sixty acres of Dupree land, and Graham's cabin. Not that it in any way resembled the rustic version of a log domicile. Quite the contrary. The circa 1940s one bedroom, one-bathroom bungalow had been enlarged and modernized to include three bedrooms, two baths, along with lovely hardwood floors and a state-of-the-art kitchen. Add that the cabin sat on the shore of a small lake stocked with trout and it was, in a word, idyllic.

Shasta loved the pastoral setting, but only went when invited...a number she could count on one hand. The cabin was Graham's retreat...his sanctuary away from everything. And she respected his need for solitude. Thankfully, as the only structure on the road, it was impossible to miss, even with her fuzzy memory and the dusky evening sky.

The car headlights streaked across the single-story house and icy foreboding settled at the base of Shasta's spine.

Gnarled branches from the nearby oaks swept across the exterior on a gust of wind. All the windows were dark, save for the single light coming from the small hurricane lamp in the front one. The normally welcoming home looked like the set from a bad horror film.

She shivered. The sooner her family got out of here and to the safe house in Reno, the better.

Newman halted the car and scrutinized the vicinity. "You should stay in the car."

She opened her door. "I'm going."

The agent grunted a response as he too climbed out. He left the headlights on because the quarter moon did nothing to enhance visibility. Shasta hurried to the house, the gravel crunching under her shoes. Newman grabbed her before she reached the wraparound veranda.

She jerked away. "Let go of me."

The agent tightened his grip. "You smell that?"

She took a deep inhale, and her brows knitted. "Gasoline?"

He nodded and kept one hand secured on her arm, while extracting his gun with the other.

Her jaw dropped. "A gun? My husband and son are inside."

"I know that, ma'am."

"Then what are you doing?" she hissed.

"Being careful," he answered.

Newman warily ascended the stairs, Shasta in tow, and walked her across the wooden planks. He situated her to one side of the door with a stern look then released her arm. He gripped the knob, turned it and slowly opened the door.

Frustration and fear clawed at her throat. She wanted to burst into the house. Shout for Graham and Wyatt. Make sure they were all right.

As the interior crawled into the view, the first thing she saw was the outline of the roughcast mantle over the fireplace on the far wall, and the Dupree family portrait that hung over it. Two sets of adults and two boys. Graham and his parents as well as his father's sister, her husband and their son, Graham's cousin, Ian. All of whom were deceased.

Like frozen molasses, Newman advanced into the room, his weapon at the ready. He swerved sharply to his left to check behind the door. Shasta crowded him, unable to get past his massive body, frantically trying to see beyond his hulky frame.

Finally Newman allowed her access. With air scraping her throat, she dashed inside, barely noticing the increased stench of gas.

Shadows dominated most of what she saw, but Shasta recognized the various pieces of antique furniture. The solid walnut hutch with the curved glass that stood on one side of the hallway leading to the bedrooms, opposite the fireplace. The 18th century sideboard buffet next to the archway at the back of the living room. Through the portal, she discerned the small dining room table and three chairs. And the knockoff Louis XVI sofa still resided in the middle of the floor rug...with a small body on it.

Wyatt.

She rushed to her son, falling to her knees beside him. "Wyatt?" She stroked his hair. "Wyatt, honey, wake up." Terror seized her chest. "Oh, God...why isn't he waking up?"

Newman lightly placed two fingers to her son's neck for a moment then lifted one of Wyatt's eyelids. "I think he's been drugged."

"Drugged? Who would do such a thing?"

"I don't know, but I don't like this." Newman holstered his weapon. "We need to get out of here. Now."

She stood. "What about Graham?"

A groan from behind zoomed her heart into her throat. The agent instantly had his firearm back in hand.

Newman motioned for her to stay with Wyatt as he prowled into a murky corner. She sank to the floor, her arm wrapped protectively around her son's head.

Tense seconds ticked by. Her pulse thrashed in her ears. Finally the floor boards creaked, and Newman pushed a wheelchair into the faint pool of lamp light.

Graham.

Had she not already been kneeling, Shasta would've crumbled into a puddle or relief. But...why was there a bag over her husband's bowed head? And even more disturbing, why were his wrists tied to his chair?

The answers came when Newman removed the bag...not Graham.

Lynch.

But what was he doing here?

The agent checked the Streeter like he had Wyatt.

"Is he all right?" Her voice sounded tinny.

"Seems to be," Newman answered. "He's got a nasty bump on the back of his head, though." He extracted a knife and cut the ropes binding Lynch's wrists to the armrests. He then peered at something on the floor behind the couch. "What the hell...?" He moved closer.

Shasta stood and peeked over the sofa. "What is it?"

Newman knelt beside an unmoving body. "Adam Murphy. And he's dead."

She plopped onto the cushion next to Wyatt. "Oh...my...God..."

Bile burned her throat. What in the world was going on? Adam dead? Why was Lynch here? How did he even know about the cabin? And where was Graham?

Newman pulled out his phone and swiped the screen. The device chirped once. "Shit." He stuffed the cell back into his pocket then came around the sofa and none-too-gently elbowed Shasta into standing. He scooped Wyatt into his arms.

"What are you doing?" she demanded.

"Getting you and your son out of here." The agent turned to the door. "I'll come back for Callan."

Panic swelled in Shasta's chest. "We can't go. What about Graham? He doesn't have his wheelchair. He could in one of the bedrooms, unconscious and hurt."

Newman flattened his mouth. "You smell the gas. This place could catch fire any second. I won't risk your safety." He jerked his chin to the door. "Now let's go."

She headed for the hallway. "Take Wyatt outside. I'll just be a minute checking the rooms."

"Goddamn it...wait."

She stopped and looked over her shoulder. Newman carefully deposited her son back on the couch and came up beside her. He flipped on the hallway light switch, but nothing happened.

After another colorful expletive, the agent propped his foot on the wall and unstrapped a handgun from its ankle holster. He held it out to Shasta. "You know how to shoot?"

She shrank back slightly. "Why do I need a gun?"

"Is that a yes or no?"

"Yes, I can shoot."

"Good." He chambered a round and pressed the weapon into her hand. "The safety's off. Stay here and try not to shoot me when I come back."

Shasta watched him move stealthily down the dark corridor until blackness enveloped him. Lynch moaned and she dashed to his side. "Hey..."

His eyelids fluttered as he lifted his head. "Shaly?" It sounded like the word hurt his throat.

She gripped his hand. "Yes...it's me."

He blinked, his focus unclear. "Go. Get outta here...now."

"We will once Agent Newman finds Graham."

Lynch shook his head then groaned. "You...don't understand. Danger...you're in..." His eyes rolled back. "...dan...ger..." His head sagged down to his chest.

Shasta carefully jostled his shoulder. "Lynch?"

A loud thump from the bedrooms jolted her heart. She hastened to her feet. Adjusting her sweaty hold on Newman's gun, she tiptoed toward the unlit hallway. Slow, steady footsteps approached.

"Agent Newman?"

No answer. But the footfalls grew nearer.

She retreated as an indistinguishable figure gradually walked forward. She knew it was a man, but she also realized it wasn't Agent Newman. This man was taller and not as broad in the shoulders.

The first thing she saw were his shoes. Even in the weak illumination, she could tell they were expensive, with a polished shine. Next came slacks with crisp, tight creases. Newman wore an unkempt suit.

"Agent...Newman?" She hated that her voice quaked.

"No, sweetheart. Not Agent Newman."

Shasta recoiled at the familiar baritone voice. "Gr...Graham?"

He stepped fully into the living room. "Not Graham either."

Shasta stumbled into the sofa, the gun dropping from her limp hold next to Wyatt's feet.

This wasn't possible. Simply. Wasn't. Possible.

Her husband...*walking*?

Yet he was, strolling like it was an afternoon in the park. Dressed in dark pants and a black turtleneck that emphasized his trim waist, he looked as athletic as he did before his accident.

The accident...

Her body temperature spiked and perspiration beaded on her upper lip. Her muscles weakened. "How..." She shook her head. "How is it that you're...walking?"

Graham beamed a grin. "Been doing it for years now, sweetheart."

His cavalier dismissal of something so radical and unbelievable obliterated her shock. She straightened. "Just what the hell is going on, Graham?"

A fierce scowl replaced his smile. "I said I'm *not* Graham."

"Then...who are you?"

His expression instantly became buoyant again. "Ian Blackwell." He clicked his heels and bowed slightly. "At your service."

She shook her head. "Ian's your cousin and he died–"

"No." His sharp tone hurt her ears. "*I'm* Ian."

"But Graham–"

He grasped her upper arm in a vice-like grip, hauling her against his hard chest. "I told you I'm *not* Graham. I'm not that insipid weakling, understand?" He flung her away and she fell against the couch arm.

She whipped her head up to stare at him. Talons of fear sank into her heart. Graham believed he was Ian? How? Why? What the hell was wrong with her husband?

She licked her dry lips and stood. She cast a nervous look down the hallway. "Where's Agent Newman?"

Graham waved his hand. "Back there." He brushed imaginary lint from his sweater. "He'll have quite the headache when he wakes. That is if he wakes up."

Shasta inched backward, but tripped and glanced down. Her stomach heaved. Adam Murphy. She scuttled from the inert DA. "What...what happened to Adam?" she stammered.

Graham swiped his finger along the sideboard then flicked off the dust. "He was getting close. Too close."

"Close to what?"

"To discovering my secret. I had no choice, sweetheart."

"So...you...killed him?"

He scrunched his features with a scoff. "No. *I* didn't kill him." His smile reminded her of a crocodile. "I have people for that kind of thing."

People for that kind of thing?

Shasta now knew, without a doubt, what was wrong with her husband...

He was mad. Insane. Totally and completely. There could be no other explanation.

Thoughts whirled through her head. What was she going to do? How was she going to save him? *Could* she save him? And what about Wyatt, and Lynch, and Agent Newman? She edged her way around to the front of the sofa, hoping to use the furniture as a barricade.

Graham closed the distanced in measured steps. "I hadn't wanted it to be like this."

"Hadn't wanted what to be like this?" she repeated. Maybe if she kept him talking, he'd snap out of whatever delusion had gripped his mind.

"This." He threw his arms in an emphatic arc. "It was supposed to be uncomplicated. Simple. Without all this...god-awful drama." He wagged his head. "It's been tough, all these years, watching you from afar. Not being able to tell you the truth. Not being with you." He swept his gaze over her, and bile rose in her throat. "The worst part was having you think that..." He visibly shuddered. "...invalid was your husband. But all will be well very shortly."

"It will?" Shasta kept her voice as composed as possible. "How's that?" She swallowed. "Ian?"

Joy lit up his face and he caressed her cheek. She struggled not to pull back. "Because we'll finally be together. It's our destiny, you know. To be together." He frowned. "Despite what your father said."

She inhaled a small gasp. "My dad? What about him?"

"He didn't believe me when I said you were fated to be mine." Graham pressed his lips into a thin line. "He called me a sick bastard.

Said hell would freeze before he allowed his daughter to be with someone my age. After years of being his friend, for him to turn on me was unforgiveable."

Shasta wrapped her arms around her middle and locked her knees to keep standing. "What did you do?"

His eyebrows rose. "I eliminated him, of course."

"Eliminated him?" Her blood chilled. "You mean you killed him. You *killed* my father."

Graham narrowed his eyes. "Do not raise your voice to me. But, yes. One of the few times I took care of business myself." He reached for her, but she angled from his touch. He crossed his arms with a sigh. "Surely you realize it had to be done. Your father stood in my way. In *our* way. Just like your brother, and..." He cast a hateful look to the wheelchair beside her which held the unconscious Lynch. "...him."

"My brother and Lynch?"

"Yes...it was the perfect plan. Kill your brother and frame Callan for the crime. One obstacle would be dead, the other on death row." Graham sighed. "Unfortunately, things didn't turn out like I'd hoped. And while I'm loath to allow your brother to continue breathing, it's a small price to ensure others are out of the way to our happiness."

"Others?"

Graham pinched the bridge of his nose with a noisy exhale. "Really, sweetheart...must you repeat everything I say? Yes...others, as in Callan."

Comprehension cleared her mind.

The gasoline. Lynch out cold and tied to the wheelchair. "You're going to burn down the cabin, with Lynch inside?"

"He's been between us for far too long. Just like your father. Once Callan's gone, it'll just be you and me."

Stars outlined her vision. She glanced down at her son. He looked so small. So vulnerable. "And Wyatt?"

"It needs to look like the invalid died in the fire." Graham's expression seemed almost...sympathetic. "And lots of people know he brought the boy here."

Her stomach roiled. "So you're just going to...leave him?"

"I can't have anything, or anyone, sully our future. But don't worry, sweetheart. He won't suffer. I promise. He's been sedated and will die from smoke inhalation long before he burns. He won't feel a thing."

"Won't feel a thing," she mimicked, her voice a shrill shriek. "You're talking about killing your son. *About burning him alive.*"

"He is *not* my son."

"Of course he's your son, Graham. You're the only father–"

She never saw his hand. Pain roared across her cheek. Blood flooded her mouth. She staggered backwards, landing on the couch, next to Wyatt's motionless body.

"Call me that cripple's name again," Graham bit out, "and I'm going to get upset."

Cool metal pressed against Shasta's knuckles. She wrapped her fingers around the forgotten gun and rose to her feet, the weapon hidden behind her right leg. "I won't let you do this."

Graham gave her a patronizing smile. "And just how do you plan to stop me?"

She leveled the gun at his chest.

He laughed. "Oh, please. You won't shoot me."

She stiffened her arm. "Yes I will. I'll do whatever is necessary to protect my son. And you."

"Protect me? From what?"

"From yourself. This isn't you, Graham. Something's happened to you. You *love* Wyatt. He's *your* son. You wouldn't hurt him. You wouldn't hurt anyone."

His nostrils flared. "I warned you not to call me that." He took a menacing step forward.

"Don't come near me."

When he didn't heed her warning, she switched her aim and fired a round just over his right shoulder. He jumped as the bullet imbedded in the fireplace mantel. She immediately trained the gun on her husband again.

Shock blanketed Graham's face, then his complexion turned an ugly, mottled red. "How dare you... You think this makes a difference? It doesn't. You can't prevent any of this." He tipped his nose in the air. "It's already started."

Shasta inhaled a breath...and cold fingers seized her heart.

Smoke.

She moved toward the hall and the pungent smell grew stronger. "What have you done?"

"What was necessary to ensure our future."

Too late she realized Graham had lunged forward and snagged the gun barrel. Agony scorched up her arm as he twisted the weapon from her grasp.

"See?" He smiled a triumphant grin, the gun in his hand. "I said you wouldn't shoot me." He moved to the side and waved her toward the front door. "Now, come. I soaked the bed linens with lighter fluid. It's just a matter of minutes before the gasoline I poured on the floor catches."

Shaking her head, she backed away.

Graham pinched his lips together. "Enough foolishness, Shasta. We need to go."

"I'm not going anywhere, Graham. That's right, *Graham*," she taunted at his angry glower. "Your name is Graham, not Ian. And if you think, for one nanosecond, I'm leaving with you, you're not simply crazy, you're fucking deranged."

The tendons in his neck bulged. He jumped forward, locked his hand on her arm and dragged her toward the door. "I've had it with your childishness. You're coming with me."

She torqued from his grip, clawing at his knuckles. "Let me go."

"Ow!" He released her and looked at the blood trickling down his fingers. "Why you ungrateful bitch." He backhanded her and the force hurled her into Lynch, almost toppling over the wheelchair. "I'm offering you a future, goddamn it. A life. The best fucking life you can ever imagine. Why can't you accept that?"

She straightened. "Accept that you murdered my father? That you tried to murder my brother and now you want to murder my son? Accept that?" Her loud scoff bounced around the room. "Never. There will never be a future for us because I will *never* accept you."

Graham's eyes widened, showing the whites. He pointed the gun at her head. "So you'd prefer to die?"

She upped her chin. "Yes."

His lethal gaze tapered. "As you wish."

Shasta held his stare. She had no doubt Graham would shoot her – would kill her – but she'd rather die than be with him.

She looked over at the peaceful face of her son. Undaunted by the threat of death, she sat beside him and stroked hair from his forehead. She gathered him into her arms. She kissed his soft cheek. Graham moved to the side, out of her peripheral vision. She began to rock, humming Wyatt's favorite lullaby.

She felt the cold, hard edge of steel against the back of her head. Absently she wondered how a bullet in her brain would be explained in the aftermath of the fire. Not that it really mattered...

Tears stung her eyes, but she wasn't crying because she feared dying. She didn't. She'd be with Wyatt, and Lynch. Guilt pinched her heart Lynch never knew his son, at least not in this life. But he would in the next.

She also regretted having to leave Dell all alone. She could only hope her brother would be all right.

Shasta ceased her humming as the gun barrel pressed closer. She tightened her embrace around Wyatt and buried her face in his neck. His scent reminded her of when he was an infant. All warm and cuddly. She envisioned his green and white nursery with the musical mobile hanging over the crib and the morning sunlight streaming through the curtains...

The faint sound of wood creaking intruded on her thoughts. She shoved it away. She wanted to stay where she was...with Wyatt and the multitude of his stuffed animals surrounded by the fragrance of baby powder.

She heard a muffled grunt. A deafening blast resounded in her ear. Fiery heat tore through her head.

Then nothing...

Chapter Twenty-Eight

SHASTA DIDN'T KNOW what hurt worse, the pain erupting through her skull or the shaking that intensified said pain.

She always figured dying would encompass a bright light then deceased loved ones, namely her mom and dad, would take her hand and lead her through Heaven's gates. Maybe there'd even be a chorus of angels singing.

She never imagined it would have this level of horrific pain.

Great. More shaking. And a voice. From very far away...calling her name, but it wasn't either of her parents...

"Shaly...c'mon, Shaly, baby. Open your eyes."

With supreme effort she cracked one lid, but saw nothing. Probably due to a warm liquid which coated her eye. She licked her lips. "Lynch?"

"Oh thank God." Relief steeped his voice. Strong yet tender hands gripped her upper arms, encouraging her sit up.

Dizziness assaulted her while agony stabbed her brain. She placed her palm to her head.

Lynch stayed her action. "Easy. The bullet grazed you."

She blinked to clear her vision, and Lynch's worried face came into slow focus as he squatted in front of her. "What are you doing here?"

He yanked his shirt over his head. "Got a text with a picture of your son threatening his life if I didn't show up at the Grab-n-Go. When I did, someone knocked me out. I woke up here."

"So you're here because of Wyatt?"

He paused in dabbing her face. "I wasn't going to let anything happen to your son, Shaly."

The pain in her head dwarfed the agony which battered her heart. Lynch was here, and in danger, to save Wyatt...a kid he didn't even know. But should. Because Wyatt was his son...

Lynch stuffed the bloodied shirt into his waistband. "Can you stand?"

"I...I think so." She grasped his shoulders as he helped her to her feet. She teetered then found some semblance of balance. "I need to tell you something."

"Tell me later." He again pressed his shirt to her head. "Hold this to your wound. Right now we need to get outta here. When soaked, lighter fluid burns slow, but once it reaches the gasoline, this place'll go up like a tinderbox. Can you walk?"

She nodded. "How long have you been conscious?"

"Long enough to know your husband is Blackwell. Definitely didn't see that coming." Lynch lifted Wyatt into his arms and led the way outside with her stumbling behind.

"What happened to Graham?"

"I tackled him just as he shot you. God...I thought for sure you were dead."

"Where is he now?"

"Dunno. The chicken shit ran out the door." He laid Wyatt in the sedan's headlight beam. "Whose car?"

Shasta whipped around to stare at the cabin. The quick movement roiled her stomach and jellied her knees, but somehow she remained standing. How could she have forgotten the FBI agent? She looked at Lynch. "Agent Newman is still inside."

"Shit." He shoved to his feet. "Where?"

"Down the hall...in one of the bedrooms I think." She grabbed his arm when he started for the cabin. "You're going inside?"

"Don't have a choice. Stay put. I'll be right back." He bounded up the porch steps and disappeared through the door.

Shasta dropped down beside her son and cradled his head in her lap. Did Lynch have a choice? Of course he didn't.

Stroking Wyatt's hair, she stared at the door and willed Lynch to emerge. Time seemed to stop. How long had he been inside? Was he in trouble? Did he need her help?

She carefully shifted Wyatt off her knees when a crash snapped up her head. A back room window shattered. Thick smoke billowed out. Seconds later, a reddish glow appeared in the front doorway.

She vaulted to her feet. A blast staggered her back.

The cabin exploded into a fiery ball of orange and yellow flames.

Oh dear God – Lynch!

She ran forward, but the intense heat of the fire kept her back. "Lynch! Lynch!"

An ominous laugh pivoted her around.

Graham walked toward her, his teeth gleaming in a triumphant grin. "Callan's dead."

She held her ground as he advanced. "You don't know that."

"Oh, come now, sweetheart." Graham stopped in front of her. Newman's gun dangled from his hand. "The fire must've hit the gas main. Callan's gone, and good riddance." He trailed his fingers along her cheek. She jerked away.

Graham blew out a sigh. "There's no use fighting me. This is destiny. *Our* destiny. From now on, it'll just be you and me." He glanced at Wyatt, and aimed the weapon at his head. "Once I eliminate the last trace of Lynch Callan, that is."

Instinct took over. Shasta sprang, seizing Graham's wrist in both her hands. She drove her knee up and into his forearm. He grunted at the impact then elbowed her hard in the midsection. Pain hemorrhaged through to her spine. She doubled over and nearly lost her grip, but she hung on. She *had* to hang on. She plunged her teeth into the fleshy part of his hand.

He howled and shook her loose. "You fucking cunt. I'll kill you for that." He clenched her hair in a punishing hold, wrenching her head back.

His wild-eyed, maniacal expression loomed before Shasta. With all her strength, she fought to keep Graham from pointing the gun at her face. She kicked his knee in hopes of throwing him off balance. It worked. Unfortunately when he fell, he took her with him. She bashed the weapon into his temple.

She hit the ground with a jarring jolt, but barely noticed the additional pain. She grappled the gun away then scrambled to her feet. Graham scuttled onto his hands and knees and she quickly jumped out of reach.

She leveled the gun at him. "Move and I will fucking kill you."

He chuckled – *he had the audacity to chuckle* - and sat back. "We both know you won't shoot me, let alone kill me, sweetheart."

"I wouldn't be too sure about that."

He fingered where she'd whacked him with the gun then looked up at her with an amused expression. "So now what? What's your grand plan? Wait for the police? The fire department? It'll be hours before anyone gets here and then what?"

"You'll pay for your crimes."

"What crimes? There's no proof I've done anything wrong."

"You confessed to the murder of my dad and the attempted murder of my brother."

"Wives can't be compelled to testify against their husbands, sweetheart."

A satisfied smile lifted her lips. "But as you keep reminding me, you're not my husband. And I won't have to be compelled. I'll testify. Willingly."

Graham barked a laugh. "And you think that'll make a difference? It won't." His expression darkened. "No one and nothing can touch me. I'm invincible. It'll just be a matter of time before I'm free. Free to kill your brother and anyone else who dares get in my way. Because you will be mine, sweetheart. *You. Will. Be. Mine.*"

Icy terror twisted Shasta's heart. If Graham wasn't stopped, she and her family would constantly be in danger. But who *could* put an end to Graham once and for all? No one...except for her...

She gripped the gun in both hands. "Get up."

Confusion flickered across his face. "Why?"

"Because I have enough knowledge of forensics to know when I shoot you, the trajectory of the bullet will show you were on the ground while I was standing. And I don't want to explain that detail to the authorities."

His eye twitched. "Guess I won't be standing then."

"Fine." She squatted. "I'll do it from here."

For the first time, she saw fear in his eyes. "Killing me in cold blood? That's not you, Shasta."

"But it *is* you, isn't it? You were prepared to kill Lynch and my son in cold blood without an ounce of remorse. Christ..." She shook her head. "I thought I knew you. I *cared* about you. But I was wrong." She stiffened her arms. "Good-bye Graham."

"Shaly!"

The shout turned her head. Lynch came around the side of the blazing cabin, helping an injured and staggering Agent Newman.

Joy stole her breath at seeing Lynch alive. But in the next instant, Graham sprang at her and grabbed for the gun. It went off. The recoil landed Shasta on her butt.

Graham's expression was one of surprised disbelief. He looked down at his chest and touched his sweater. His fingers came away dripping with a dark liquid. His eyes rolled back into his head and he collapsed in the dirt like a ragdoll.

Dead.

Chapter Twenty-Nine

SHASTA LOCKED HER car then made her way up the sidewalk to the stationhouse.

Almost two weeks had passed since that horrid night at Graham's cabin. She still couldn't wrap her head around the fact the man she'd married, and whom she'd lived with for almost eight years, had been a monster.

No...monster was too gentle a description for Graham. He'd been an ogre. A fiend.

Tears stung her eyes. How could the man who'd helped raise Wyatt, who changed his diapers and fed him at three a.m., so nonchalantly plan to burn him alive? Alive? Even now, the acrid reek of smoke invaded her senses while her skin pebbled with the memory of the intense heat of the fire. To think of her baby in the midst of that...

She shivered and pulled open the door, but the stabbing pain in her side halted her movement. She'd suffered several severely bruised ribs along with a concussion. But Wyatt, thank God, appeared none the worse for wear. He didn't remember anything past the hot chocolate Graham gave him...hot chocolate that had been laced with a sedative.

She hadn't yet gathered the courage to explain any of the events to her son. She simply told Wyatt his daddy went on another business trip, a plausible excuse. She'd also glossed over the reason why they were staying with Uncle Dell. The thought of sleeping under the same roof she'd once shared with Graham turned her stomach. There'd be time enough later to tell Wyatt the brutal truth about that night.

Another shiver hit her. Graham's shocked expression when he keeled over dead continued to haunt her. She hadn't had a choice...she knew that. It'd been either him or her. But how would she ever be able to tell that to Wyatt? Tell him how she'd killed his father?

Murdered him?

Ignoring those thoughts, she walked inside and paused to look around. Everything seemed the same, yet so very different.

The number of FBI agents had diminished greatly. Now just a few sat at various desks doing paperwork while Agent Jarvis sat in Dell's office talking with her brother. Shasta waved to Joan, who had a surprised look on her face, then headed to her desk. She'd only sat down when a voice said behind her,

"What the hell are you doing here, sis?"

Shasta pivoted around. Her brother stood there, with Jarvis – and neither of them appeared happy. "I work here, remember?"

Dell frowned. "Has the psychologist cleared you?"

She dropped her purse in the bottom drawer. "For heaven's sake...it's not like I operate heavy machinery. I do filing."

"Still–"

With her foot, Shasta closed the drawer with a distinct thunk, cutting off Dell's protest. She faced her brother. "I can't stay at your place all damn day by myself. I'll go crazy."

Realization registered on Dell's face. "Shit...I forgot...Wyatt went back to school today."

More tears pressed at Shasta's eyes, but she held them back as she straightened the neat pile of papers. "Yes, he did, though it went against every one of my maternal instincts." She sighed. "But I suppose I can't keep him encased in bubble wrap for the next thirty or forty years."

Jarvis stepped forward. "Mrs. Dupree–"

Shasta held up her hand. "Please do *not* call me that. I'm changing my name back to Albright as soon as possible. In the meantime, call me Shasta."

The agent gave her a kind smile. "All right, but only if you call me Emma."

"Deal."

Emma's smile waned. "As I was saying...Shasta...you should have clearance before returning to work."

"Really? And do I need clearance before giving my statement? I may not know a lot about police procedure, but I do know waiting two weeks to take someone's statement isn't normal."

Dell rubbed the back of his neck. "Uh...look, sis..." His voice trailed off.

"Perhaps we should talk about this some place more private," Emma suggested.

With a reluctant nod, Dell led the way to his office. Though Shasta wanted to object, she followed behind.

Once everyone had settled in their seats, Emma twined her fingers together and focused her attention on Shasta. "The truth is...we don't need your statement."

Shasta blinked. "Why not? I was there."

"Yes, but Agent Newman said you were unconscious almost the entire time."

Shasta's mouth fell open. "No I wasn't. I mean I was for a little while, but not for almost the entire time."

Jarvis slowly shook her head, her mouth in a thoughtful frown. "Well...that's what the official report says."

Shasta narrowed her eyes. "If it says that, then how did I kill Graham?"

Emma glanced briefly at Dell than back to Shasta.

The hairs on Shasta's neck rose. "What is it?"

Clearing her throat, the agent shifted. "The final report states...Lynch Callan shot and killed the individual known as Ian Blackwell."

"*What?*" Shasta nailed her brother with her deadliest glare. "*What did you do?*"

Dell held his hands up in surrender. "Nothing."

"Bullshit." Shasta swung her gaze to Jarvis. "Lynch didn't kill Graham. *I did.*"

Emma pursed her lips. "The official account will say that–"

"But that official report is *wrong.*" Shasta sprang from her chair and plowed her fingers through her hair. She paced the small office then whirled around to glower at Dell, her fists on her hips. "How could you do this? The only reason Lynch was even at the cabin was to try and save your nephew. *He's innocent.*"

Dell held her gaze. "I told you, I had nothing to do with this."

She scoffed. "Like I believe you? This is just like the time you brought Lynch in for no goddamn reason then put him on display, naked, in the interrogation room."

Emma sat taller. "What's this?"

Disregarding the agent, Shasta planted her hands on Dell's desk and drilled him with her stare. "You'll do anything to hurt Lynch, won't you? Anything to send him back to prison." She straightened. "Well not this time. I. Will. Stop. You."

Shasta stalked from the office, grabbed her purse then marched out of the stationhouse. She didn't have a clue how she'd keep Dell from sending Lynch to prison, she only knew she would. She had to. Lynch had been through enough, because to her family.

He'd go through no more.

~*~

An hour later, Shasta propped her cell between her ear and shoulder so she could use both hands to fold Wyatt's laundry.

After storming from Dell's office, she'd gotten on the phone to the FBI office in Reno with the sole objective of reaching Agent Jarvis's boss. She'd eaten her way up the federal food chain until finally accomplishing her goal of speaking to Special Agent in Charge Landau. However, the man was less than helpful.

"I'm not sure what I can do, Mrs. Dupree. The report filed by Agent Newman plainly states Lynch Callan shot and killed Ian Blackwell."

"You're not listening to me, Agent Landau. That report is wrong."

"You're alleging Agent Newman falsified his report? That's a serious accusation."

Shasta stifled her groan. She didn't want to throw anyone under the bus, but how much loyalty did Newman really deserve? After all, he turned on Lynch...the man who'd saved his life.

A knock landed on the front door. "I'm not saying anyone falsified anything." She walked from the bedroom she'd been sharing with Wyatt and into the living room. "But your agent got the events wrong." She opened the door. "I was there and..."

Cognizant thought fled her brain. Lynch Callan stood on the porch.

Wearing a stone-gray t-shirt and washed out jeans, but no cut, he appeared exceedingly at ease for a man recently accused of killing someone.

She cast worried look down the street, grabbed his arm and towed him inside the house, closing the door with a thud. "What the hell are you doing here?"

A groove appeared between his eyebrows. He nodded to her hand. "You on the phone?"

She glanced down at the cell. "Crap....ummm, Agent Landau...?"

"Is everything all right, Mrs. Dupree?" The agent sounded concerned.

"Everything's fine. I'll, uh, get back to you." She disconnected the call and stared at Lynch. "My brother is looking for you."

"Shaly–"

"He and Agent Jarvis are convinced you killed Graham." She snatched her purse off the end table.

"Shaly...babe...you need to listen–"

She rifled through her wallet, spilling used receipts and various other pieces of paper onto the coffee table. "I don't know how much money I've got...damn...only twenty-seven dollars, but here's my ATM card. The pin is 0517." She extracted a key ring. "And take my car." She pressed the keys, debit card and crumbled bills into Lynch's hands. "You need to go. Dell will stop at nothing to make sure you end up–"

Lynch tossed the money and keys onto the end table then gripped her shoulders with a solid shake. "Calm down, Shaly."

He wanted her to calm down? How? He faced murder charges because of her.

He tugged her to the couch. "You need to sit down."

She pulled away. "No. *You* need to get in my car and drive. Get as far away from Stardust as you can before they arrest you."

He hauled down on the sofa cushion next to him. "No one's getting arrested."

"How can you say that? The FBI report says you killed Graham. I won't let you take the blame for what I did."

She stood, but Lynch tightened his hold on her hand. "Shaly, the report says what it does because I admitted to the killing."

"You *what*?"

"I confessed."

Her posture wilted. She was like a boomerang, going from one emotional extreme to another. Tears gathered then spilled down her cheeks. "But...why? To somehow protect me? It was self-defense. You and Agent Newman both saw that."

He held her gaze. "What have you told your son about that night?"

Her eyebrows rose. "What's that got to do with this?"

"Just answer the question."

She looked away. "Wyatt's too young to understand."

"What about when he gets older?"

Guilt clogged her throat. "What about it?"

"He could find out the truth, including the fact you shot his dad."

"There's no guarantee he'll find out anything."

"There's no guarantee he won't either. Jesus, Shaly...this is biggest news to hit this area since the silver rush. Reporters are swarming the area. An FBI investigation into human trafficking. The murder of a deputy sheriff and the local DA. The fire. Shit...the gossip mill will be chewing on this for years."

She stared at her clasped hands in her lap. "So?"

"So...it could lead to questions." Lynch covered her hands with his. "And if your kid's anything like you, he's gonna want answers."

She looked at him. "That's why you confessed? To spare Wyatt learning the truth?"

"No son deserves to learn that kind of truth about his parents."

"And you think I'll allow this?" She shook her head. "You went to prison once because of me...I *refuse* to let you do that a second time."

"No one's going to prison, Shaly."

"What makes you so sure?"

One side of Lynch's mouth ticked up. "For one, I've got a kickass lawyer. For another, I've got the backing of several noted FBI agents, as well as the sheriff of Grant County."

"Wait...Dell's supporting you?"

"Yeah. It was his suggestion I come talk to you. So you see, I'm in no danger of going back to the joint." He traced a finger along her jaw line. "But even if that wasn't the case, I still wouldn't let you take the fall for killing Blackwell."

Tears again blurred her vision. "Why?" Her voice hitched.

He cradled her face with his palms. "Because I love you. I'd do whatever was necessary to protect you. And your son."

A sob caught in her throat. Lynch enclosed her in a loose hug and rocked her gently as her tears dampened his shirt.

He loved her so much, he'd sacrifice himself not just for her, but for Wyatt. Without hesitation. Without question. Without any regard for his own safety. And how did she repay that unconditional love? By keeping his son a secret.

Did she dare tell him now? The words tickled her tongue. But how would he react? Would his love for her turn to hate? Could she chance that? A part of her died the day he went to prison. She'd never survive if he rejected her outright.

Lynch eased her away. "What the hell...?"

Her heart froze in mid-beat. Too late she realized what had fallen from her wallet. Seemed Fate had decided for her.

He picked the frayed photo off the coffee table. "This is me right after I was born. Why did my mom give it to you?" He turned the picture over, and his body went rigid. "Wyatt Albright...Dupree?"

Shasta didn't know how long they sat there with her hands clasped tightly together in her lap not looking at Lynch. But she felt his gaze boring a hole in her head.

"You want to explain this, Shaly?"

She closed her eyes at the severity in his voice. The anger. Inhaling a breath, she prayed for the strength to endure what the next few minutes would bring.

She met Lynch's glare. "What's to explain? You read the name. That's a picture of Wyatt."

His stare sharpened. "You're not going to even try denying it?"

"I can't deny the obvious. You're Wyatt's father."

Hurt flicked across his expression. He flopped against the sofa cushion and gazed at the photo. "When–" He coughed. "When'd you find out?"

"Just before Labor Day that summer. I wasn't sure how you'd react so I waited to tell you."

He didn't look up.

She swallowed the sour taste in her mouth. "A few days later, Dell got shot and you were arrested. I went to see you in the county jail, but was told you didn't want any visitors except your lawyer."

No reaction.

She willed away more tears. "I know I should've written to you, explaining about Wyatt, but didn't. I told myself you probably wouldn't have accepted the letter. Truth was, I was afraid. Afraid of how people would treat Wyatt, and me, if they learned you were his biological dad. The only person who knew about my pregnancy was Graham, and he never asked who the father was. He suggested we marry to give Wyatt a name. So we did. And for seven years, I kept quiet. I lived a lie. I know there's nothing that'll ever make up for what I've done. Just please know how sorry I am for–"

Lynch snapped up his head. The contempt in his eyes shriveled her heart. "The last thing I want to hear, is how sorry you are."

Pain, the likes of which she'd never experienced, lanced her chest. Yet she'd earned Lynch's wrath. Earned it and more. No way could he forgive her. Nor should he.

She collected the discarded items from her wallet, stood and headed for the kitchen.

"I don't know what your plans are..."

His rusty voice turned her.

Lynch stared at Wyatt's picture, tracing his thumb along the edge. "But I want to help...you know..." He looked at her with overly bright eyes. "...provide for him. Any way I can."

Shasta's brain screeched to a halt. "You do?"

"Of course. He's–" Lynch coughed and sat forward. "He's my kid."

She sank onto the sofa. "Aren't you angry?"

He barked a harsh laugh. "I'm way past angry. I'm fucking livid."

"At...me?"

His gaze rifled to hers. "At you? God no. At myself." He shook his head. "I wasn't there when you needed me."

Lynch's fury at himself floored her. "Ummm you got arrested, remember?"

"No excuse." He reverently placed the photo on the table. "Let me know the details about the money, okay?"

"I will. That's very generous. I don't what will happen with Graham's estate. The government might confiscate everything because of the federal charges." She touched his arm. "Thank you."

He nodded,

She cleared her throat. "I'm not sure if I should ask this, but does offering to help with Wyatt mean, someday...maybe...you might consider forgiving me?"

"Forgive you for what? For making the best out of a fucked-up situation? Christ...I can't imagine what you went through. How confused you must've been. How scared. Knocked up by the guy accused of shooting your brother. If anyone needs forgiving, it's me."

Shasta's heart melted into a puddle in her chest. She twined her fingers with his and smiled. "Tell you what, I will if you will."

One side of his mouth quirked up. "Deal."

His eyes darkened to the color of storm-tossed waters and his grin slowly faded. Her pulse sped up. She licked her lips and his gaze dropped to her mouth. A groan rumbled in his chest. She leaned forward as her eyelids coasted closed...

Lynch stood, jumping her backwards.

He wiped his hands on his jeans. "I should go." He beelined to the front door.

Shasta leaped to her feet. "Go? Why?"

"Because if I stay, something's gonna happen between us."

"And that's a bad thing?"

He gripped the knob. "You know it is, Shaly."

He opened the door, but her hand shoved it shut. She situated herself with her back against the wood, her arms crossed. He shifted away, wariness in his eyes.

She glared. "Why is it a bad idea?"

"Look, Shaly–"

"Don't 'Shaly' me." She heaved from her spot and moved forward. "You just forgave me the world's biggest sin *and* you said you loved me. I said I loved you too, in your trailer, in case you forgot."

He stepped back. "I remember."

"And knowing that, you're gonna leave? Just walk out?"

"Ummm...no?"

She poked him in the chest with her finger. "Damn right no. After everything we've been through, don't we deserve the chance to be together? A chance to be happy? I sure as hell think we do."

Lynch slanted away from her. "That's a mistake."

"Really?" She recrossed her arms. "Give me one reason why"

"I'll give you two. One, your brother won't approve."

"Oh, pffft." She waved her hand in the air. "Dell has no say over my life."

"And what about your son? What'll happen if Wyatt finds out I killed his dad–"

"Graham wasn't his dad. You are."

Moisture brightened Lynch's eyes. He ducked his head.

She relaxed her stance and tangled her fingers with his. "And you didn't kill Graham. I did." She tightened her hold. "When Wyatt's old enough, he should know everything that happened. He needs to understand the lengths his dad took in order to protect him – and his mom."

A tear eked from the corner of his eye. "I...I don't know what to say."

She tripped her fingers up to his shoulders. "Say you love me."

He wound his arms around her waist, pulling her close. "I love you, Shaly."

She cupped his face and stared deep into his eyes. "And I love you. Now kiss me like you mean it."

So he did.

Chapter Thirty
(Epilogue)

Two months later...

"DISSOCIATIVE IDENTITY DISORDER?" Shasta looked up from the file in her hands and met Emma's gaze. The agent and her brother sat across the table in the sheriff department's conference room. Lynch stood behind Shasta's chair, reading over her shoulder. "I don't know what that means."

Emma laced her fingers together on the table. "You might know it as Multiple Personality Disorder."

Shasta gaped. "You're saying Graham had a split personality? Is that a joke?"

Emma shook her head. "I'm afraid not."

"I was his wife...how did I not know?"

"Because chances are Graham Dupree didn't know himself."

Lynch scoffed. "What a crock." He slouched in the seat next to Shasta, his thigh press against hers. "Dupree didn't know what he was doing? Yeah, right. Imagine me, or any Streeter, using that excuse."

"It's not an excuse," Emma countered. "D.I.D. is a real disorder where one personality dominates...in this case Ian Blackwell and is aware of everything. While the other personality...Graham Dupree knows only his world."

Lynch grunted again.

Shasta swatted his arm. "Be nice." She looked back at Emma. "So that's why Graham kept saying he was Ian at the cabin? Because of this disorder?"

"Yes."

"What causes this...dissociative thing?"

Emma sighed. "Any number of factors...a genetic predisposition for mental illness, a severe trauma." She paused. "Prolonged abuse."

"Abuse? Graham never said he was abused."

The agent glanced at Dell.

Shasta's stomach squeezed. "Am I missing something?"

Her brother sat forward. "What do you know about the steamer trunk in Graham's office?"

"Nothing. I rarely went in his office. Even to clean."

Emma cleared her throat. "In that trunk we found journals and a few audio cassette tapes."

Shasta shivered, suddenly cold. "O...kay."

"I'll spare you the gruesome details, but at the cabin and from the time he was less than a year old, Graham Dupree was systematically mental, physical and..." The agent swallowed. "...sexually abused."

Shasta gasped. "Dear God – by whom?"

"His cousin, Ian."

"What? No. Graham always said he and Ian were like brothers."

"Our forensic psychiatrist says that's how predators typically work. They become an essential part of their victim's life, making their victims dependent on them."

"How was that possible? Ian was just a little boy when Graham was born..."

"There's no age requirement for being a psychopath."

Closing her eyes, Shasta pressed shaky fingers to her temples.

"That's not all, sis," Dell said.

She peeked up. "There's more?"

Her brother's expression was grim. "Unfortunately. Remember the story about the African safari Graham was supposed to go on with his family in the sixth grade?"

Shasta nodded. "But he didn't go because he got mono. He ended up staying with Dad and Grandma and Grandpa." Another chill hit her. "Graham's family died in a small plane crash."

"Turns out no one went to Africa. We found a shallow grave at the cabin with the remains of five bodies. All shot in the head."

Shasta's hands flew up to cover her mouth. Lynch wrapped his arm around her shoulders.

Emma pulled a file out from her open briefcase. "Dental records confirm those bodies were Maxwell and Irene Dupree, along with

Charles, Margret and Ian Blackwell."

Shasta slowly lowered her hands. "And you think Graham, at age eleven or twelve, *killed* them?"

"Not Graham, Ian. And yes, the evidence is indisputable."

"Evidence like DNA and fingerprints?"

"No, nothing like that–"

"Then what?" Shasta demanded.

Lynch's arm tightened. "Take it easy, Shaly."

"You take it easy. You weren't married to a man who might've killed his entire family. You didn't have Wyatt around him." Shasta gave the agent a hard look. "I ask again, what evidence?"

Emma blew out another sigh. "Our handwriting expert concluded one of the journals was written by a younger Graham Dupree. In it, he referred to himself as Ian and detailed how he drugged everyone, then shot them."

Shasta's stomach heaved. "Jesus...this is so unbelievable."

"You need to remember it was Ian, not–"

"Not who?" Shasta snapped. "Graham? Ian? Ian? Graham? God only knows who I was married to."

Emma's gaze drilled into her. "Listen to me. You were married to Graham Dupree. A good man and a loyal public servant."

"Who lied about everything. His family. Being paralyzed."

"Dupree didn't lie because he *didn't know*. As far as his paralysis went, that was very real for him."

With a groan, Shasta buried her face in her hands. "I don't know what to believe anymore."

Lynch massaged her neck muscles. "What would cause this guy to jump back and forth from being Dupree to Blackwell?"

"A trigger of some kind," Emma answered. "We've surmised the reason he killed his family in the first place was because Ian had joined the army and planned to leave Stardust."

Shasta looked up. "But if Ian abused him, wouldn't Graham be happy he left?"

"Not necessarily. It's like I said, abusers make themselves indispensable to their victims. Ian's leaving could have been perceived as an abandonment by Graham, causing a psychotic break. And since abusers are seen as having all the power and control, that could be why Graham took the persona of Ian Blackwell...to emulate that power and control."

Shasta threaded her fingers through her hair. "I want to forget any of this ever happened."

"Sorry, I can't do that," Emma said, "but I can change the subject. To a happier one, I suspect." She extracted a large manila envelope and slid it across the table.

"What's this?" Shasta asked.

"Deeds to the Dupree home as well as the lake property."

Shasta's eyes popped wide. She looked inside the packet. "Thought the federal government was seizing everything."

"It was pointed out the illicit activity was in fact that of Ian Blackwell, and not Graham Dupree. And given how instrumental you were in bringing down Blackwell, it seemed fair to allow you some compensation."

"Hardly instrumental." Shasta closed the envelope. "But...thank you."

The agent dipped her head in acknowledgement.

"Whatcha gonna do with the real estate, sis?" Dell asked.

"Sell, and put the money into a college fund for Wyatt."

"Bet you'd get a nice nickel if you sold the sixty acres to a developer."

Shasta shook her head. "No developer, but maybe a conservation group will buy the land. I like the idea of all that ugliness being taken over by nature. Kinda purifying in a way." She stood, as did Lynch. "In the meantime, brother dear, you're stuck having me and Wyatt live with you. That okay?"

"Better than okay. House is too damn big for one person anyway."

"Good." Shasta grabbed her purse and Lynch ushered her to the door.

"Speaking of your son," Emma said, "how's he doing?"

"Better, though he misses Graham terribly, but knowing the official report said Graham died trying to save him has helped. Thank you again."

"No need to thank me for that. I honestly believe if your husband had had a choice, he would've stopped Blackwell."

Shasta sighed. "I still worry the truth might come out some day, though."

Emma gave her head a firm shake. "It won't. The only people who know exactly what happened that night are in this room, plus Sam. As far as the good people of Stardust are concerned, Graham Dupree, along with the entire Streeter MC are heroes for helping foil a human trafficking ring."

Dell snorted. "Good God. The Streeters were *part* of that damn ring."

The agent scowled. "We've been over this. You know it's in everyone's best interest to stick to the story."

"Yeah...yeah," Dell muttered.

Lynch gripped the doorknob then paused. "What's gonna happen to the Fuentes's case, counselor?"

Emma's frown darkened. "It'll stay active, though the bastard has probably gone farther underground than a gopher. But we'll get him. Eventually."

Dell slid his gaze to Lynch. "Same could be said for...other criminals."

Lynch feigned shock, his hand over his heart. "Criminal? I'm not a criminal. As the new owner in the Stardust Bowling Alley, I'm an upstanding member of the community."

"Who's trying to become a licensed cannabis grower in Nevada," Dell grumbled.

Lynch shrugged. "If you can't beat the system, game it." He slung his arm over Shasta's shoulders with a toothy grin. "'Sides, your sister doesn't think I'm so bad."

Shasta elbowed him in the ribs.

"Ow, Shaly."

"What did I say about being nice?" She met her brother's angry glower. "We're going to pick up Wyatt and Aiden and take them to Tahoe for the afternoon. Wanna join? You could take a vacation day."

Dell sat straighter. "Can't. Emma and I still have some reports to write."

Shasta did a double take at Dell's use of the agent's first name then bit the inside of her cheek to keep from smiling. She hadn't noticed how...close he sat to Emma. She cleared her throat. "See you later then."

Dell scooted in tighter to Emma, reading the file she'd laid out. "Yeah...later."

Outside the conference room, Shasta turned to Lynch. "Why do you have to antagonize Dell like that? You know he's having a hard time with us."

Lynch grabbed his cut off her desk and headed toward the entrance with her beside him. "If he's having trouble with what happened in there, how the hell is he gonna deal with us getting married?"

Shasta's brain stuttered then stopped completely. As did her feet.

After a few steps, he pivoted. "Something wrong?"

"You think we're gonna get married?"

His forehead creased. "Well...yeah."

"You never mentioned it."

He crossed his arms, his expression suddenly guarded. "I'm mentioning it now."

Her insides tingled. "You seriously want to marry me?"

"Yes. Why so surprised?"

"I don't know. Guess I never thought it'd ever happen."

He dropped his arms. "But you want it to happen, right?"

His uncertainty warmed her heart. She placed her hands on his chest and smiled. "More than anything. But you know we have to wait a while."

He nodded. "Already figured on a spring wedding. May 17th."

"May 17th?"

He cocked his head. "Don't you remember? That's the day we met."

Her smile grew. "I remember."

"And my life hasn't been the same since."

She looped her hands around his neck. "Mine neither."

He glanced behind her. "Your brother's staring at us, and he doesn't look happy."

She brushed her mouth to his. "Tough."

"Thought you didn't want to antagonize him."

"Thought he had to get used to us being together."

A grin played at Lynch's lips. He drew her closer and kissed her, hard. She speared her fingers through his hair as his sexy, musky scent filled her senses. He angled his head, driving his tongue deep into her mouth.

A loud crash echoed.

"Shas-Ta!" Dell bellowed.

Giggling, she broke from Lynch, grabbed his free hand then raced out the door.

And toward their future.

The End

A note from Lynda

Thank you for purchasing *On a Knife's Edge*. I hope you enjoyed reading about Shasta and Lynch as much as I enjoyed writing about them. Please remember the three Rs: Rate, Review, Recommend. I'd be grateful if you helped spread the word.

You can drop me at line at Lynda.r.bailey@gmail.com. Or check out my website www.authorlyndabailey.com.

Happy Reading!
L.

About Lynda

I have no doubt I was born a storyteller.

I remember telling my first "story" in kindergarten. I informed my teacher, Mrs. Downing, my mom had just had a baby boy. She hadn't, of course, and while I got thoroughly admonished for my "storytelling," I wasn't deterred from what would become a lifelong passion.

From making up tales as a kid which centered around my favorite TV shows to today, I love telling stories! Stories with handsome guys and spunky gals, that always...*always* end with a happily-ever-after.

My romances are full of passion, with heat levels ranging from hot to sizzling! I've been a finalist in numerous writing contests, including RWA's® prestigious Golden Heart® in 2010. Please join me for laughter, love and that all important HEA.

Now please enjoy the following excerpt from my BDSM romance, *Shattered Trust...*

Start of Chapter Five

ON WEDNESDAY AFTERNOON, Liam pulled the final load of lunchtime dishes from the dishwasher when the creak of the door announced someone had entered the kitchen.

"I need you to tap a new keg of Bud Light," Kate said from behind.

"No problem," he replied over his shoulder, to no one as the door swung closed. He sighed.

That's how it had been between since Sunday. Kate would give him an order then leave before he could respond. He didn't fault her for acting this way. She'd owned up to a ton of shit, a reality that had to be eating her alive.

He dried his hands and headed out the swinging kitchen doors. A part of him was grateful for the distance Kate put between them, but another part zinged with hurt at her coldness, considering what they'd shared. Well, what she'd shared.

Shit, St. James...get it together. You don't want any of her drama.

He needed to keep his head down, his mouth shut and do his job, until he got his truck fixed. Once that happened, he'd be gone from Trustworthy.

In the keg room, he disconnected the used line for the Bud Light and placed the drained barrel off to the side then attached a new line to the fresh cask. Finished, he grabbed the old keg and turned.

Kate stood in the doorway, her arms crossed. As usual.

The sight of her slender body jolted him, and he nearly dropped the keg on his foot. "Hey...you surprised me."

She didn't look at him, but rather her gaze wandered the space. "You never put things back."

He shifted. "No, I was gonna wait until after we got the next delivery."

She stepped into the tiny room, and the room got even tinier. "This setup is more logical, isn't it? Having the domestic beers in front does make it easier because they're more popular, huh?"

He shrugged. "But the other way worked for a long time. I'll put it back if you want."

"No. Keep it this way. It's better." A small smile whispered over her lips. "In case you hadn't noticed, change can be a hard thing for me."

He tried to ignore how her modest smile snagged his breathing. Another shrug. "I'll do whatever you want."

Her gaze held his for a long heartbeat.

He looked away first. "I need to start the dinner prep."

She blocked his exit. "I took your advice. I called a counselor. Several in fact."

He wanted to jockey around her, but with the keg in his hands he couldn't. Not without knocking her over. "That's good."

"I've got a problem, though. I don't have insurance and they all charge over a hundred dollars an hour. I can't afford that." She looked down and scuffed her shoe along a floorboard. "So I was kinda hoping I could...pay you."

"Pay me to do what?"

She lifted her head, her lips pressed together.

Realization punched him in the solar plexus. "You mean pay me instead of a counselor?"

Her shoulders boosted up a fraction. "Yes."

The keg thudded to the floor. "But I'm *not* a counselor."

"But you know...things, right?"

Oh, he knew a great many things, none of which she was prepared to learn. He perched a hip on the cask and rubbed the tightening muscles in his neck. "You're not serious."

She upped her chin. "I *am* serious. And this was your idea."

Liam's inner sadist perked up at her blatant defiance. He shoved it down. Now was not the time to unleash his sinister side because she didn't mean *that*. She couldn't. "My idea was for you to get professional help. Not ask me to play therapist so you can lie on the couch and talk about your problems."

"Why not?"

Why not?

He stared at her. Was she honestly suggesting they talk? No way did he want to *talk* to her. Spank and whip her – make her shout his name...yes. On a couch, a bed. In the keg room right now...fuck yes. But talk? No way in hell.

She was his boss for crissakes, and he wasn't some psychoanalyzing analyst. If anything went awry, the least that would happen is he'd get fired, again. The worst, she'd end up more fucked up than she already was. A possibility that had a cold sweat breaking out on his forehead.

The word "no" perched on his tongue, but refused to come out.

He'd be lying if he said he wasn't attracted to Kate. With her shoulder-length hair so perfect for yanking and her pert ass so perfect for spanking and her lips so perfect for sucking his cock, she possessed all the physical attributes he enjoyed in a bottom.

But more than her desirability, she prodded the softer side of his dominant personality. The part which wanted to ease the hurt he inflicted. Yes, it was his nature to dominate in the bedroom, to taunt and torture, but he also took immense pleasure in the aftercare. The assurance everything was all right, for everyone.

With startling clarity, Liam realized that's what he wanted to do with – and for – Kate. Comfort her. Show her a different kind of a Top-bottom relationship. Demonstrate how wonderful and healthy such a bond could be.

He'd wanted that ever since her tormented utterance of her safe word.

What the fuck? Was he insane?

Kate's pain and mistrust ran deep. Too deep to be remedied by someone like him. She needed an honest-to-God therapist and not him. Because he sure as shit didn't want to "talk" with her.

So if he couldn't say yes and he couldn't say no, that left getting her to change her mind about him...helping her. And the best way to do that would be to explain to her exactly what his *help* would involve.

He abruptly stood. She flinched. He prowled toward her. She backed away.

"You should know," he said in the silky voice he used when playing out a scene, "that I do most of my talking with my hands."

A gasp puffed from her mouth. "What does that mean?"

"It means our...conversations will be physical. Not verbal."

He pinned her to the wall, crowding her space, but not touching her. Her warm scent filled his senses, and his dick with blood. "You will submit to me." He employed his best Dom voice, low and husky, with a hard edge that tolerated no denial.

She angled her face away from his. "N...no. That's not what I'm paying you for."

"You will pay me with your submission." He tucked his index finger under her chin and brought her gaze back to his. "Whenever, wherever and however it pleases me."

She closed her eyes and two twin teardrops leaked out. Her jaw trembled so hard, her teeth clicked. His Dom fairly danced with glee as his cock continued to swell.

She licked her lips, leaving a shiny path he longed to follow. "What if I can't...submit?"

He dropped his hand and took a big step back. "Then nothing. We go back to the way things are right now."

She huddled tight to the wall, her body shaking and her breathing ragged. He worried she might hyperventilate again.

After a slow, silent count to twenty, and she still hadn't moved, Liam hoisted the empty keg and turned to leave.

"I don't want to feel this way anymore."

Her hushed words stumbled his feet to a halt. *Fuck.*

"Can you fix me?"

He slammed his eyes shut. God*damn* it! He didn't want to look at her. He wanted to keep walking, out of the room and out of the Bluebird. Permanently. But that wasn't going to happen. He glanced over his shoulder.

She still hugged the wall with her arms wound so tightly around her middle it was a wonder she could draw a breath. Her wide-eyed gaze snared him. Kept him rooted to the spot. She looked helpless, so fucking helpless, yet determination etched her mouth. She might be scared, terrified even, but she had grit. By God, she was beautiful.

He fortified his resolve. He wouldn't allow himself to be wooed by her enticing vulnerability or her quiet courage. This dangerous plan needed to die, for both their sakes. He graced her with a sinful grin. "When I'm done with you, you'll be either fixed or broken completely."

Her eyes ballooned as her mouth formed a perfect "o."

Liam again pivoted toward the door. He had to get out of there before succumbing to her magnetism and agreeing to anything she wanted.

"All right."

Goddamn it...no!

He kept his gaze on the doorjamb, not daring to look at her. "All right...what?"

She moved into his peripheral vision. "All right, I accept your conditions."

He briefly closed his eyes then gave her a hard stare. "You need to be sure about this, Kate. Very sure."

"I am."

He shook his head. "You're too emotional right now to be sure of anything." He shifted the keg in his hands. "We'll talk later, once you've thought long and hard about what you're proposing. Then you can give me your answer."

Not waiting for a response, he walked out.

Made in the USA
Middletown, DE
12 February 2025

71151095R00167